DEFENDERS

LAURY FALTER

CONTENTS

1 VISITOR

The night before humans learned they weren't alone on this earth, the city of New Orleans was thriving.

Beneath expansive balconies lined with sophisticated wrought-iron balustrades, lived a constant hum of eager bartering merchants and lazy conversations drifting from open restaurant windows. Tourists and residents fanned away the humidity of an approaching thunderstorm as they waited for tables and observed the kaleidoscope of bright, rich colorful artwork of southern life that seemed to constantly be within arm's reach no matter where you stood throughout the French Quarter. Horns honked along the narrow, cobblestoned streets, mingling with thumping rock music that seeped from clubs along Bourbon Street; and on the quieter, tree-lined avenues, musicians huddled in doorways below flickering gas lamps and consumed by eerie shadows, playing slow, melancholic Jazz melodies while street performers played out their skits on crates to those who paused to watch. Everyone's tills spilled with cash before the sun had even set, and I wondered for the third time if I'd closed up the small parcel I used for commerce in Jackson Square too soon.

"It's a single night off, Magdalene," observed an English accent to the right of my shoulder. As always, it sent a thrill through me. "And, who knows," he added, "you might even enjoy yourself."

I rotated my head to find Eran's striking blue-green eyes smiling back at me, a motion that forced me to work myself free from their captivity. This was his charm, and I had met no girl unaffected by it. Their color was staggering enough — a beautiful, tranquil hue that felt like you were looking over a wood railing into the shallows off a Caribbean beach — but it was their intensity that told you that as calm as they appeared, he actually missed nothing at all, a result of having spent the majority of his existence fighting. Even being clothed in jeans and a black tee-shirt and projecting the casual appearance of a typical teenager, Eran exuded comfortable ease, as if the world would find him to be a testament of strength and resilience every time it dared to challenge him.

"You've worked hard this summer," he pointed out, "and tomorrow we start another attempt at finishing senior year, along with a guarantee of copious amounts of homework." He was trying to be playful, but it stung no less.

A weak grimace broke the still surface of my stiff face. "Yes, those teachers love to torture us," I muttered.

"Us especially," he added.

"You would think that since we personally know the principal they would ease up."

"Ms. Beedinwigg is too admirable to use her influence in that way," he reminded me.

"But she could put on the pretense that she might," I suggested, and he tipped his head back to laugh into the darkening sky.

"Where are you taking me?" I asked, shifting the slinky black cocktail dress as it twisted around my waist. It had been fighting me the entire fifteen-minute walk from the house that Eran and I shared with our three housemates.

"A place where you will not be suitably dressed," Eran replied bluntly.

"*Not be?*" I repeated, instantly slowing my pace.

Eran held back a grin as he avoided my stare.

"Do you know I've already tripped twice?" I demanded.

Without waiting for a response, I veered off our path and through a tourist shop's open door. Under the bright, halogen lights, tee-shirts hung from every available spot on every available wall, silkscreened with phrases designed to shock. I reached for the nearest one before I felt Eran's hand take hold of mine.

"There's no time to change," he insisted and drew me back out into the street without releasing his grip.

We turned a corner quickly, onto a row of brownstone homes shaded by bowing trees and obscured by a distinct lack of street lighting, as he maintained his forward pace. Without ever looking in my direction, he remarked, "Those brown eyes of yours are much more beautiful when they're not glaring at me."

"Flattery," I muttered, twisting my hand toward freedom.

"Um-hmm," he replied, untroubled, ignoring my struggle and maintaining his easy, tender grip.

"I'd like to remind you that I typically wear biker boots and ride a Harley Davidson motorcycle," I warned.

His profile lifted in an arrogant grin. "A five-foot girl with hair down to her waist and eyes the size of hubcaps does not intimidate me, Magdalene, no matter what she wears or rides."

"How about one who can maneuver a sword better than most men?" I challenged.

"Now that," he agreed with a nod, "earns my interest. Lucky for me that you don't have one."

I snorted in agreement and turned my glare to the side, toward inanimate objects.

A saxophone's long, expressive notes stirred the night, making us pause to listen, and humbled by the lure of the moment, Eran came to a halt. Turning swiftly toward me, he took my other hand and stared down at me with genuine sincerity. "This is a date, Magdalene, our first one I'd like to remind you, and for that reason you are appropriately dressed. And forgive me for saying this but ... I'm attracted to the way you look."

Despite my irritation at the tight, all-too-revealing clothes and awkward angle of my heels, I was flattered. Undeniably.

"Thank you," I replied, and surveyed him quickly. He looked different in the shadows here than he had at the base of the stairs where he'd waited for me before leaving on our date, but he was no less intoxicating. His clothing easily revealed the well-established muscles along his arms, back and chest, and being of average height and lean build, and with a stunning face framed by seductive, wavy brown hair, Eran was entirely breathtaking.

His eyes relaxed and humor grew in them. "You're welcome," he said and paused as the entertainment he felt broke through into a smile. "You really do look good. I like you in your usual clothes too, but ..." He stepped back for a sweeping view of me. "Wow..." Closing the gap between us again brought a waft of heat and the earthy, sun-drenched scent of his body, and in the warm, damp air it was almost palpable as it hit me, stealing my breath instantly. "Do I have Felix to thank for it?"

Shifting my ankle to alleviate the heels' pinching, I muttered, "You do."

Eran smiled understanding. "Living with a gregarious chef who has a flare for both fashion and swamp meat cuisine can pose challenges."

"Yes, it does."

"I'm thankful that our other two housemates didn't interfere with his efforts."

"They tried. He was undeterred."

Eran chuckled quietly, momentarily closing his eyes to imagine the arguments that must have ensued. "Against a temperamental Irish man painted in tattoos and a mild-mannered African woman who has a gift for stabilizing the craziness? Felix prevailed over Rufus and Ezra both? I'm impressed."

I shrugged, acquiescing slightly to the humor of the situation, and admitted, "I was too."

Eran's laughter deepened briefly before quieting to a sincere gaze.

"I'll tell him of my appreciation when we get home. Until then..." He bent forward and settled his sweltering, soft lips on mine before pulling back just enough for our noses to brush. The unexpected gesture instantly made my heart leap in my chest, nullifying all discomfort my outfit was causing and instinctively making me lean into him.

With his whisper hoarse and tinged with unashamed temptation, he murmured, "Until then I'd like to enjoy it. Would you mind remaining as you are for a few hours more?"

Slowly, I nodded, breathing him in, openly seduced by him, and he whispered, "Thank you."

He hesitated then, his breath thick with an urge that I shared, but a subtle, disappointed groan ended it as he turned unexpectedly and led me up a set of forest green concrete steps toward a mustard yellow and olive green-trimmed home where we had stopped. I had ignored it entirely even though we'd been outside it for the last few minutes.

Narrow in size and tucked between two other homes of the same dimensions, the house was unassuming. A window to our left was draped with shutters the color of an avocado and a thick satin gold-colored curtain, but a soft yellow light flickered behind it and a sign hung around an iron fleur-de-lis doorknocker giving me a hint as to the type of people we might find inside. It read:

We aren't much for visitors,
but hoodlums are warmly welcomed
at the end of our constantly sharpened blades.
We are serious.

"This is a restaurant?" I asked, my eyebrows arching together.

"It is," he said, casually, and made no attempt to let our host know that we'd arrived.

"Do we need to knock?"

"They already know we're here."

A few restrained seconds passed and the door opened to a stocky man dressed in a crisp, black tuxedo with a forehead that curved into the shape of a mushroom and a bulbous nose that seemed to consume the rest of his face. Small eyes scrutinized us beyond the folds of his flushed cheeks as the side of his thin lips turned down into a frown.

"Word," the man commanded.

"Blatherskite," Eran replied, and I glanced at him curiously.

"Of which we don't allow any within," our 'pleasant, welcoming' host warned briskly.

Eran tipped his head in acknowledgement, which seemed to be the criteria for entry, and the man swiveled on the heel of his polished leather shoe to march down the short hallway.

"It means –" Eran began, but I interrupted.

"Don't talk at length about nonsensical topics."

Impressed, he gestured for me to enter. I fell in behind him and we followed the bristly man as he waddled down the floral runner into the back of the traditional but stately house.

We were led past the parlor, study, and library, all of which were impeccably decorated in the rich colors and polished antiques of a Southern highborn home, and out the back door. The view from the top step leading down into the yard stunned me to a halt. Built in a patchwork of private dining areas with a single stepping stone path winding between them and separated by thick flourishing green shrubs, sat intimate candlelit tables for two and a small patio where a jazz band played slinky music. We were the last of twenty guests to arrive and younger than the rest by forty years, which warranted their curious looks.

"I thought ..." I said and fell silent.

"That you would be over-dressed?" Eran concluded for me.

"Yes."

"Miss Elowen breaks from the southern tradition and demands her guests dress opposite their natural appearance. To minimize pretentiousness."

I thought of my wardrobe back at the house comprised of tee-shirts, jeans, hooded sweatshirts, and a dismissed floral dress shoved into the back of my closet bought for me by Felix in hopes I would break down and wear it by choice. No, in my sultry cocktail dress, I was out of form as much as if I'd worn Felix's dress. The only consolation was the fact that most of the other guests presented henna tattoos and fake piercings, leather and head scarves, making me realize these people were on display themselves. I could easily envision the women in the same black dress and heels as I wore and the men in classic business suits.

"But you …?" I said, turning to Eran. As I did, our griping host caught my eye at the base of the stairs, where he held a dinner jacket open for Eran.

"I made arrangements," Eran said plainly, offering his hand to me for a safe trip in my unsteady heels down the steps.

When he slipped on the extra layer, it was obvious how difficult it would be to find anything Eran didn't wear with casual sophistication. Even a miscellaneous piece of clothing laid over his shoulders looked as if it were cut specifically for his lithe, muscular frame. I had to stop myself from staring as we were seated in the far corner.

Our table for two nested beneath a tree bough draped with small lanterns suspended from the branches, where a specialty drink and glass of water were already on the table for us. Our griping host gave no pleasantries, no announcement of nightly specials, and no menus, but instead swiveled again on his heel and marched off as Eran smiled, amused. He was spellbinding in the jacket, offhandedly refined, and he didn't meet Miss Elowen's dinner guest requirement in the least.

"How did you hear about this place?" I asked, as our host began delivering small, immaculate, artful plates to each table.

"Some here in the city have come to me for help. Miss Elowen is one of them."

I tilted my head curiously. "What kind of help?"

"The kind that prevents them from using the local law enforcement."

"Hmm," I mused, "that kind."

He grinned subtly as Miss Elowen's host entered our quiet domain and placed a single plate on the table piled delicately with fruits and vegetables and drizzled with three sauces and announced, "The Storm," before retreating in a huff again.

Observing it, I realized something wasn't quite clear to me. "How did Miss Elowen know to find you?"

"She's heard of us."

I lowered my voice so that it wouldn't carry. "Is she human?"

"No," he replied simply, and I nodded thoughtfully before turning my attention to our food.

The Storm was a colorful mess, like a blast of chaotic colors.

"Felix would be jealous," I murmured, scooping up a portion closest to me with my fork. On the first bite, The Storm's flavors became a blend of earth, heady ionization, and sweet grass before they gave way to the aftertaste, a peaceful, cleansing balance of fresh confection and crisp coolness. After chewing and swallowing, I corrected myself, wide-eyed at the taste, "No, he'd be *covetous*." Eran laughed out loud as I declared in awe, "Miss Elowen's a culinary master."

"Just a bit different than frog leg oatmeal," he agreed, and I giggled.

"Just a bit."

We finished the plate rapidly, and just in time for our host to swipe it out from under us and replace it with a pot steaming purple mist and swirling with gold flakes. "Dragon's Breath," he snapped and disappeared around the hedges again.

"So do you think we'll have time to be teens this year?" I asked, evaluating the soup.

"You mean will you spend an inordinate amount of time on your phone, shop for clothes every spare moment, and sneak out in the middle of the night to meet boys?"

I chuckled through my nose and muttered under my breath, "I can guarantee you that won't happen."

Responding to my statement with a knowing grin, he went on, "Or do you mean will I consume large quantities of pizza, stay up late, and play video games?" he asked, navigating his spoon around the shared pot before us. "I'm not sure I'll be allowed the time, me being your requisite guardian and all..." He glanced up from beneath his lashes to catch my reaction, which came in the form of a sneer to confirm I still abhorred him bringing up his compulsory responsibility over me.

"Careful," I warned, "you're treading very close to the level of becoming a blatherskite."

Eran let out a hearty laugh which fell away as our host approached our table, empty-handed this time.

"Miss Elowen wants to thank you in person. She's in the kitchen," he said through his permanent scowl. He then turned and left abruptly, leaving Eran to find the path there himself.

"I'll be quick," Eran promised, stood, and disappeared around the hedge.

Without his company to preoccupy myself, I passed the time evaluating the only visible sliver of the house, the left corner of it where a small, curtained window was opened only a few inches and the delicious aromas of Miss Elowen's cooking seemed to escape. While surveying it, I brought my hand up to shield against a small but luminescent light disturbing my view and my fingers accidentally brushed the thick, fake lashes Felix insisted I wear. The awkward weight of their glued contact to my skin along the base of my eyelid shifted and the lash suddenly tumbled down my cheek to the table. There it lay, black wisps against the white linen tablecloth, like a centipede rolled over in death.

Instinctively, I pinched the end of the remaining fake accessory that still trapped my other lid and meant to pull it off too, and be free from the uncomfortable deception altogether, when I noticed our host scowling at me from across the yard. Hands folded properly at his waist, eyes slits, and lips turned down, he silently shook his head in warning.

I wanted to insist he wear them for a night and see how he felt.

Instead, I rolled my eyes, stood, and picked up the centipede. Our host interpreted my actions to mean I would need a bathroom for a reattachment procedure, raised a hand and pointed to an arched wooden door against the back wall.

Apparently one of Miss Elowen's many quirks included excluding guests from using her personal bathroom.

I skirted past two tables where the women appeared entirely more comfortable than me, and left the property in search of a mirror. Beyond the garden yard's wall, sat a small concrete courtyard surrounded by brick buildings and decorative torches, and a long, narrow alley leading to the back door of a bar where conversations and dim light drifted from its opening.

Inside, I worked my way through the packed, small, round tables and curious patrons, cradling the centipede in my palm. The bathroom was small and dingy and the mirror's foil had started to erode at the corners, but the reattachment was successful and I was heading back to the restaurant in under a minute.

Only when I reached the interim courtyard between the properties did I learn that there would be a delay.

Three men leaned lazily against one wall, eyeing me with the same concentration as when I'd entered the bar where they had been drinking. This time, however, they didn't let me pass.

"Where you going?" a pot-bellied man with a toothpick protruding from his lips asked, sliding backward to block my path.

The other two – one tall with a pitted face and another squat with a receding hairline – also shifted their stances to form an obvious but intentionally discreet wall.

At this point, I sighed.

"Yeah, where you goin' in such a hurry?" Pitted Face slurred.

I wanted to ask if the would-be-assaulters had any unique questions of their own or were they all given the same taunts to ask their would-be-victims. Instead, I was reminded of the time and made an effort to deescalate the situation.

"Gentlemen, I –"

"Gentlemen?" Pot-Belly sniggered. "No one's called me that before."

"Sure hasn't," agreed his friend with the receding hairline.

"You're a nice girl," Pot-Belly said, leering. "Want to be nice to me?"

"I'm actually trying to be, but my –"

"Don't say 'boyfriend'," Pitted Face contested. "No boyfriend here as I can see."

Seeing no progress, I sighed, my shoulders sinking with the exhale. "Look, I'm on a date that I don't want to have disrupted."

"Oh, a date?" cooed Pot-Belly. "I got a date for you."

"Listen," I said, my eyes narrowing as my anger rose. "I –"

"I'm listening," Receding Hairline mocked.

"I don't have time for you three. Not tonight."

"Well, tonight's all we got, pretty girl," leered Pot-Belly, taking a step toward me.

His advance brought us too close for my comfort, and easily in striking distance, so without thought, I rotated to the side and sent a heeled foot into the man's stomach. The sides of it rolled up around my shoe as it sank into the spongy resistance until the man tripped and fell backwards, ending up on the ground, his weight jiggling with the impact.

When he'd gained his breath again, he spat, "You bi-"

"You're welcome," I said, already having lowered my leg and repositioned myself defensively.

"For what?" Receding Hairline asked, not sure whether to laugh, although his eyes glowed from his friend's defeat.

"I landed my foot so that my heel would leave the least impact," I said. "Next time, you'll get the full blow."

"You think that, huh?" Pot-Belly asked, struggling to stand.

"Everything all right here?"

Eran's voice startled me as he came through the arched wooden door from Miss Elowen's yard.

Pot-Belly finally got to his feet as the other two shuffled nervously as if they were waiting for directions from their ringleader. Pot-Belly gave Eran a quick survey as I replied.

"I gave them fair warning," I said with a shrug.

"And clearly, they didn't listen," he muttered, standing opposite me, with the three men between us. He tipped his head at me in a gesture that asked if I needed assistance and I shook my head in rejection.

"Boyfriend's come to help, eh?" Pot-Belly jeered, breaking into a smile. Apparently, he had decided that two teenagers in evening wear shouldn't be concerning, despite my earlier hint toward it.

"Oh no." Eran chuckled and folded his arms across

his chest. "I came to watch."

As he settled back with a smirk on his face, looking a lot like an expectant ticket-paying customer waiting for the entertainment to begin, the men hesitated.

"Make sure he don't move," Pot-Belly commanded, pointing a finger at Eran as he turned back toward me.

"I'm the least of your worries," Eran mumbled with a pitying shake of his head.

Pot-Belly didn't listen and took two angry, hulking steps at me. As he did, the rank smell of body odor hit me, and this time, I sent my foot across his face in a roundhouse kick. He stumbled back, dazed and blinking to regain his sight.

"Help me," he commanded Receding Hairline.

Both came at me.

A quick assessment told me that they were equal in height, so I sent another side kick into Receding Hairline, who tipped backwards flailing to catch himself before sprawling onto his back, and then into Pot-Belly, this time with the full length of my shoe connected to him, as promised. He seemed surprised when my heel broke skin and a small pool of blood formed on his filthy white tee-shirt, gawking at me from the ground where he'd landed.

Before Pitted Face could assist his friends, I used my momentum to spin toward the wall, race up it, and take hold of a metal torch holder mounted there. As I dropped back to my feet, my body weight brought the torch holder with me, and as I turned it over in my hands, evaluating my adversaries, it's long shaft and thick circumference gave me just the baton I needed.

My series of strikes that pummeled their jaws and arms felt smooth, easy, and almost pleasurable to execute. The air seemed to part for my motions and the ground felt like it was rising up to steady my footholds as I swept my weapon down on them in rapid sequence.

"Enough," Pot-Belly called out from behind an elbow he was using to block my retaliation. "Enough, please, enough."

"Call her off, man. Call her off," Receding Hairline moaned, evidently pleading with Eran.

"Don't address me," Eran replied coolly. "She's the one who you insulted."

"I'm sorry," squealed Pitted Face. "I'm so damn sorry! Please stop!"

"Me too, I'm sorry," Receding Hairline blurted.

It took another lengthy second, but Pot-Belly eventually conceded. "I'm sorry. I'm sorry," he said in a near whisper.

At that, I stepped back, appraising them. They were curled into fetal positions, elbows still raised in defense, too scared to look me in the eye. Blood splattered each of them.

Tossing the torch holder aside, I bent down toward them as it clanged into a corner and rolled still. "The next time you have a desire to attack a lone female, remember what happened here, because she might be the one who *doesn't* stop."

When I stood, something in the trees, that hadn't been there before, made me pause, and as I looked up, Eran joined me. A woman no taller than four feet, soft around the waist and down her limbs, clothed in a floral dress and spotless apron, wasn't in the trees at all. She stood on the wall, as if she were a sentinel, observing what had taken place. A pattern of dim lights filtered through the leaves from the foliage in her yard to display her wide nose, full downturned lips, and the dense, polished sword held in her right hand.

"I warned you three not to mess with my customers," she said plainly in a nondescript accent and then turned, leapt off, and disappeared into the other side.

"Miss Elowen?" I asked Eran quietly, which he confirmed with a nod.

I stepped through the men and met Eran on the other side, who opened the arched door for me.

"Remember this night, gentlemen," I advised, and passed through.

Inside Miss Elowen's yard, three facts stood out to me immediately. First, the jazz band in the corner had stopped playing and were sitting vigilant in their seats. Second, every guest was standing at the ready, their food forgotten, their faces welcoming but alert. Third, a hushed but diminishing sound came from them, a faint whisper that seemed to emanate from their backs; and as Eran and I passed through the garden on the way to our table, I noticed something I hadn't before. All of Miss Elowen's guests had two oblong slivers in the fabric between their shoulder blades and the tips of white feathers were contracting back into each one of them.

* * *

Four delicious courses later, our sourly host handed Eran a check that showed a zero balance, and we thanked him for the complimentary meal. He huffed that it was for our inconvenience and stomped his way to the next table. Miss Elowen remained as elusive as she had been before the incident so Eran suggested we head home. School started tomorrow.

We passed through the narrow, cobbled streets of old New Orleans, across commercialized Canal Street and onto Magazine Street, where the bustling traffic gave way to a quieter pace along a row of quaint residential homes. After we turned down a slender driveway bordered by an overgrown hedge and into a rustic, overgrown backyard, warm and welcoming light cascaded from the windows of the two-story Victorian home we shared. And entering through the back door into a small, modest kitchen, the ever-present smell of sweet, tangy coffee greeted us, before the noise of Rufus and Felix arguing overtook it.

"Why kin't ya make somethin' normal fer a change?" Rufus griped through his thick Irish accent from his standing position against the counter as he evaluated his latest tattoo trailing along his massive forearm. As a caricature artist by trade, he was a walking billboard, adding new drawings to his broad seven-foot body regularly.

"Because normal is boring," Felix huffed, his wiry frame shaking violently as he clung to a bowl tucked into his curved gaunt arm, whisking a bright orange liquid nearly the shade of his rust-colored hair. It appeared as though the momentum controlled him rather than the other way around. Resembling a broomstick in length and width, he had chosen a physically non-laborious profession of performing palm readings, leaving him plenty of energy to cook up strange concoctions in the evening. He gasped when seeing us, nearly spilling the contents of the bowl in his rush to set it down, and beamed. "Tell me *all* about it!" He clapped and ran in place for a few seconds to release his excitement, which brought out a dramatic eye roll from Rufus.

"Yes," said Ezra calmly entering the kitchen with a smile, her large, round frame covered in a patterned dress and a medley of colorful bracelets and hair beads. "Do tell." She made her way to the coffeemaker, swept back the dreadlocks dangling over her shoulder, and poured the aromatic black liquid into the mug she held until it nearly breached the brim. "Any longer a delay and Rufus may need to perform CPR on Felix."

Rufus made a revolted sound. "If that day ever

comes, yer as good as dead," he remarked, which turned Felix's pale, thin face into a brief scowl.

Theatrically breaking his slit eyes from Rufus by jerking his head in my direction, Felix insisted, "Go on, Mags."

Eran and I had already taken a seat at the small, round kitchen table, so we settled in to explain all that Miss Elowen had served. Felix demanded elaborate details, hurling questions at us, until he was satiated, leaning back against the refrigerator and sinking into deep contemplation.

"And that's not all we encountered at Miss Elowen's," Eran remarked, his eyes gleaming mischievously.

"Oh?" Felix replied intensely, slinking into a seat at the table and leaning forward with apt interest.

"Magdalene," Eran said, "made a few friends tonight."

"Or rather enemies," I muttered, shaking my head at the memory.

Ezra raised her eyebrows at me, set down her coffee and gave Eran a patient, steady look.

"Three men chose to be victims to Magdalene's skill with a torch handle," Eran said.

Felix feigned shock as he exhaled, "Mags", while Rufus moved in for a high-five approval.

I met Rufus's mammoth, chapped hand as Eran went on to describe the incident. When he was done, Ezra confirmed for peace of mind, "So these men were obviously human."

"Very much," he confirmed; and she settled back into her seat, raising her mug for a lengthy sip.

"Unlike the rest of Miss Elowen's guests," I suggested, earning their interest. "Our kind were there too."

"Ahh," Felix moaned curiously, a slight, awestruck

grin pulling his taut face. It transitioned into apprehension as he took the sugar spoon and began twirling it through the bowl of white granules. "No fear of, say, the other kind coming back?"

Eran watched him sympathetically. "You would be one of the first to know."

"You have … lookouts," Felix pressed. "Right?"

"I'm kept well-informed, Felix," Eran reassured.

With that assertion, both Rufus and Felix moved again, taking deep breaths. Ezra, however, eyed her coffee as she asked, "And how are your friends, Eran? And by friends I mean –"

"I know what you mean," he assured, his tone heavy, and I felt the weight of unease sweep through him. "They've been trained to fight. That is their skill, their identities as a whole. Without enemies, there is no place for them, so they have dispersed and found positions in civilian security services."

His eyes glossed over, growing distant, so I put my hand on his fingers laying across his thigh below the table, intending to administer comfort. Feeling it, he came back to me, gave me an appreciative smile and rejoined the conversation as Ezra wisely led us onto a different subject.

"Talking about dispersing," she said, sliding a postcard, postmarked from Scotland and signed by 'Hermina and Hoffstedler' across the table at us. Being my official parents, and Ezra's long-standing friends, they kept Ezra updated on their worldwide travels out of courtesy as I remained rooted in her home trying to finish my final semester of senior year. For the next hour, we discussed their route through Europe, with Eran, Ezra, Rufus, and Felix commenting on each stop, each being widely traveled themselves.

When yawning became too frequent, we retreated to our rooms where Eran and I closed our doors and waited until the house was silent before reopening them – a tradition that kept us together while forced into separate living spaces by Ezra's house rules.

The storm that had been pushing the warm air through the city finally arrived and a torrent of water began cascading over the edge of my balcony's roof as his body moved through the shadows toward my bed. The thick drops hitting the pavement outside with a thundering roar made his movements undetectable by sound, but streetlight filtering through my windows left streaming shadows down his broad chest. Breathing in the aroma of ozone and earth filtering in from the cracks in the house, I curled into the covers and pleaded, "Stay with me."

He reached my bed and settled onto the edge of it, the weight of him making a deep enough indent that I rolled around his hip. That touch sent a current of electricity through me, and given the pause in his movements, I figured he felt the same. "Ezra would have my head for violating her rules of conduct," he said tenuously.

Even obscured through the shadows and rain streaks he was undeniably handsome. Accented in the silver of the night, his muscles bulged and his skin was flawless; he looked more like a silver god than a teenage boy. At the moment, I couldn't care less about Ezra's rules.

"She's allowing us to live here despite knowing the risks," I argued softly.

A slight smile teased his lips. "She's counting on us having the integrity to reject those risks," he countered.

"Hmmm, well," I mumbled thoughtfully. "I'm sorry to say that I failed her in that pursuit." And he bent over in stifled laughter.

"Come lay with me," I moaned.

He sat back again and warned teasingly, "Satisfying that impulse will lead to great danger."

"I beckon danger," I replied, and he chuckled.

"Yes, you do."

He stood and turned swiftly to face the bed, and I threw back the covers, but he shook his head and lifted them back in place before laying on top.

I protested with a dejected moan but he placed a hand on my hip to settle me. Through the thin layers of fabric between our skin, his heat was both comforting and intoxicating, but when I looked down at the source, Eran's fingers were lifting away too quickly.

"Don't move." My reaction was immediate and nearly inaudible, and it made Eran pause. His lips turned up in a cautious smirk – a motion that stole my breath and left me swathed in a world that held just the two of us. His touch returned, settling down tenderly, and I exhaled, stimulated, before briefly closing my eyes. When I reopened them, there was an unrestrained fire behind his translucent blue-green irises.

His hand shifted and his palm's warm weight wandered down the outside of my thigh, flattening to broaden his touch. "All these years, all this time, and you still take my breath away, Magdalene."

My weak attempt to control my urges ended and I carried my hand over the space between our bodies, to his stout shoulder, and rested my fingertips on its highest point. We were no longer breathing easily, taking short inhales when our bodies needed but otherwise forgetting this function altogether. My fingers traveled along his muscle's crest before dropping to the solid line of his waist, where I found the billowy comforter in my way. Irritated, I crawled my fingers over it, brushing his rigid stomach in their progress; and he drew in a sharp breath and swallowed, never shifting his eyes from mine. Flattening my hand, I intentionally, just barely grazed his torso, taking in the crests and valleys at a leisurely, intoxicating pace.

He swallowed again and, through a low growl, he grumbled, "Magdalene, I –" But he exhaled deeply, closed his eyes to regain himself, and then abandoned the effort entirely. Without warning, I found him rolling up and over my body, pressing me into the bedsheets, his heat quickly enveloping me, removing all thoughts from my mind so that I was solely conscious of him.

His lips lowered to mine, bringing with them greater warmth and Eran's rousing smell, which had evolved through the night to sun-drenched wood and earth. We met tenderly, slowly, before our kiss deepened with greater need; and my head tilted, arching into him; and I moaned, lifting my hands to the quivering muscles across his back; and suddenly he was off me, his body twisting around to face the French doors leading to the balcony outside.

The doors, previously locked in place, now moved in the wind before slamming with fury against the walls, rattling the glass. The slanted rain shed droplets across my hardwood floors inside and left my balcony glistening in the lights from the street as Eran abruptly stepped onto it. Sturdy and strong, his shoulders rolled back in defiance, his face carved into alert temperance. I raced for the doors' threshold, determined to stabilize them, one hand already on a door handle and my second reaching for the other when I came to a stop, slipping my fingers over the back of my neck to subdue the tickle there.

My gaze snapped to the distance beyond my balcony railing and darted across the night sky. Eran did the same, vigilantly, scanning all that was visible from the balcony – rooftops, tree peaks, and street lights – before moving to the railing and surveying the street.

"It's the storm," I reasoned. "The electrical charge."

"There's no lightning, Magdalene." He didn't turn around when answering.

"Then let's find out with certainty," I muttered.

Surprisingly, my voice carried above the pounding rain and Eran's body, soaked through his flannel pants and lighting his chest iridescently, spun around to step inside. He met me at the French doors, preventing my exit.

"Eran," I said in frustration.

"No, Magdalene," he warned.

My eyebrows shot up in offense.

"No," he replied emphatically.

"I'm not one of your –" I mumbled attempting to make my way around him. He stepped to the side and blocked me. "I –" Sighing, with an irritated glare at him, I acknowledged, "It's – It's gone."

"I know," he said, his focus remaining locked on my face.

He was evaluating me, determining my level of dedication at getting by him to conduct surveillance of the area for any sign of life. A few seconds passed before he spun quickly, closed the doors, and rotated back to me, turning the locks into place without physically touching them.

"Go to sleep, Magdalene."

"Good idea," I asserted and walked to my bed easily – too easily.

I listened for his footsteps heading for the door but the old springs of my wing-backed chair in the corner groaned and when I looked up Eran had dropped into it.

I slid into bed and fumbled with my bedcovers before irritably acknowledging, "You're going to watch me until I fall asleep, aren't you?"

"Yes," he replied unsympathetically, resting his head back, watching me down the length of his nose.

"So I can't leave."

"That's correct."

His admission lit me up. He knew this, both in sensing it and by the downturn of my lips, but he showed no reaction, continuing to stare over his cheeks. The rain shadows dripped down his face, contorting it – and still he was handsome. Damn it.

"Sleep," he insisted, turning to watch the door contemplatively, because I was no longer a threat, having relegated me to more of a nuisance. There was someone else who now captured his attention.

Despite my best effort, I did eventually fall into a comatose state, and on waking, I found a sun-drenched room and Eran's slumped figure, still in the chair, still guarding the door.

2 NEST

Eran didn't react as the stack of 'highly nutritious worm flour' crepes were placed in front of him, which vexed Felix, who perpetually demanded respect for his culinary skills and waved a hand in front of Eran's nose to get it. That motion disrupted Eran's intent stare out the kitchen window and his reactionary instinct took over, clasping his fingers around Felix's wrist and forcing it to the table's surface, his muscles flexed and ready for further deflections as needed. Felix ended up bent to the side, angling to alleviate the pressure, breathing harshly through his nose as Eran immediately withdrew his hand.

"Felix, I'm sorry."

Felix stood up quickly, rubbing his feeble wrist, and gave a quick nod of placation as he briskly stepped back to the counter and out of Eran's reach. There, he muttered something about making a nourishing, delicious breakfast for our first day of school only to be assaulted, before Rufus snapped at him to stop his olagoning, which was Irish slang for complaining.

"All right, what happened?" Ezra demanded,

surveying us from her chair at the kitchen table where she lowered the newspaper. Her new array of colorful jewelry, ones that matched her vibrant caftan dress, clinked on the table's surface.

"Nothing," I replied, too quickly, and she narrowed her gaze at me. To appease her, I shrugged and she shifted her demand to Eran.

"Something," she asserted. "Eran looks ten years older today."

Felix turned from the counter and nodded, his face speculative. "His shoulders *are* two inches higher."

Rufus grumbled something unintelligible under his breath but agreed with a jerk of his arm.

They were correct. While Eran's youth didn't allow for bags under his eyes or sallow skin brought on by a long stretch of waking hours, there was still the unmistakable distant stare of deep contemplation and a release of his usually impassive face while being consumed by wary thoughts.

Eran discreetly glanced at me before addressing them. "It's important that you all know, so you can be cautious. I'll need the added eyes on Magdalene. She felt the hair on her neck stand up last night."

I expected the sharp inhales and sudden shift of their heads; it was the common reaction among them.

"We can't be certain it was anything of importance," I countered.

"Why?" Ezra asked, and I turned cool eyes on Eran.

"Because someone refused to let me go," I replied accusingly.

She noted the battle of wills between Eran and me, and decided to ignore it. "When did it happen?"

"Around midnight," Eran replied, observing me for any retaliatory reactions.

"I believe I heard a commotion right about then," Ezra reflected.

"From Mag's room," Felix elaborated.

"Humph," Rufus mumbled, because his deep-sleep snoring prohibiting him from waking to any distractions.

An extended silence told me that they were waiting for me to explain it, but I remained silent, not wanting to fan the flames of unwarranted drama.

Eran explained for me, instead. "The doors to her balcony flew open."

"Inexplicably?" Felix exhaled, wide-eyed.

Eran's face stiffened at Felix's melodrama, the very scenario I was trying to avoid, and confirmed, "Yes."

I waited for a hail of concern to shower over me and the mandate for a schedule of protection to be set, but they went still, like statues positioned toward the only breathing person in the room.

"But you have –" Ezra began.

"Protocols in place to alert me of any new arrivals," Eran confirmed.

"Then it would have to be someone already here," she deliberated.

"Or it could be nothing at all," I pointed out before taking a worm crepe from the top of Eran's stack, folding it in half, and taking a bite. Surprisingly, the worms were blended into obscurity and the thin pancake tasted like one made from wheat. "These are excellent," I said to Felix, hoping to turn the conversation onto a different course.

"Thanks," he muttered, his offhanded reply confirming that he was with the others on the seriousness of the topic at hand.

"We should get to school," I suggested, standing and grabbing hold of the bookbag I'd previously slung over the chair. "Felix, great breakfast."

He nodded, face remaining ashen, pan still in hand, the newest creations inside it having unrolled without him noticing.

Through the thick silence that had fallen over the kitchen, Eran followed me out the door and into the shed where my treasured Harley Davidson motorcycle sat undisturbed. I had bought it with my own money – an 883 Sportster built with a stunning blend of silver chrome and black metal – which I had cherished ever since.

If anyone had visited my bedroom last night, at least they left my most prized possession alone.

Standing on the opposite side of it, Eran advocated, "Downplaying this is not the wisest approach, Magdalene."

I handed him the spare helmet and slipped mine over my head.

"You know I can feel your fears, and last night was – "

With the key already in the ignition and me seated, I turned the engine over drowning out his argument. For good measure, I revved the gas a few times, which he knew was gesturing but it convinced him to slide his leg over the seat and settle in for the ride.

After I backed down the driveway and into the street, we found that the city was awake, but just barely. Through the hazy, damp air, we saw men spraying down the debris left on the cobblestone streets in the French Quarter and business suits filtering in and out of coffee shop doorways.

We stopped at our favorite bakery, where its owner, Mr. LeFrau, had already bagged our lunches. The short man beamed at us from behind his thickly-greased, pinched moustache as Eran exchanged the bag with our money. Inside, was my beloved muffuletta sandwich, a tradition in New Orleans, made of salty olive salad, thin-cut deli meats, provolone cheese, and crusty, soft Sicilian sesame bread to hold it all together. Mr. LeFrau had also wrapped Eran's preferred roast beef po' boy sandwich, a French bread roll of meat, iceburg lettuce, tomatoes, and pickles whose name humbly began during a New Orleans streetcar strike when the Martin Brothers Coffee Stand and Restaurant in the French Market gave the strikers sandwiches free of charge and called out to the staff as they came in "Here comes another poor boy." Eran likes tradition.

It took another five minutes to reach our school – a small, private campus of vine-covered, red brick buildings known as the Academy of the Immaculate Heart. The parking lot was already swarming with students, people streaming between the cars, over the lawns, and through the glass, double-door entrance.

"We should say hello to Ms. Beedinwigg," Eran suggested, tipping his head at the black Conquest Knight XV vehicle, an ultra-upscale armored SUV, parked in the Principal-designated spot.

I frowned, because I knew he was insisting on it as a ploy to keep me in his sights while he relayed the news to her that he'd delivered to our housemates.

"She'll want to see you," he asserted.

Together, we walked through the throng of students, past a huddle of teachers who eyed Eran and me with uninhibited contempt – based on an unwarranted reputation we had gained after several unfortunate incidents arose at school – and into the noisy, echoing white corridors lined with light green lockers. Eran and I knew only a handful of people at the Academy, despite the impressive number of attempts at finishing our senior year, so we made our way to the principal's office without hindrance.

The anteroom was buzzing with activity, so no one noticed when we approached Ms. Beedinwigg's door and knocked. While we couldn't see movement beyond the textured glass there was the distinct sound of a blade slicing the air and, after our knock, metal grating smoothly into a small sheath. Eran glanced at me and we laughed quietly before the door opened.

Ms. Beedinwigg's blade was again hidden and her slender hands were hanging freely down her slim body. Any loose strands of her auburn hair had also been tucked away, into the constant bun piled loosely on her head. The only hint that something might be a little off about her were the combat boots extended below the hem of her grey floral ankle-length dress.

"An educator educating herself, hmm?" Eran asked, adroitly hinting at her delay to the door.

"Always," Ms. Beedinwigg replied, grinning smugly.

As we entered, she stepped aside, lifting an eyebrow curiously when Eran closed the door behind him.

"How are Ezra and Hermina?" she asked casually entering into conversation, and I was reminded that she knew them both.

"Well," Eran said as we took our seats at Ms. Beedinwigg's desk. "Hermina will be returning from Scotland soon and Ezra is counseling two new teens. Ezra would like to see you when you're available."

"We have lunch planned this week," Ms. Beedinwigg informed. "Any progress on the college front?" she questioned, glancing at me.

"Why do you always look at me when you ask?"

"Because I already know toward what career Eran is leaning," she said simply.

"Oh?" I said, suspicious. "Which would that be?"

"An educator."

Eran chuckled through his nose, impressed.

"You, however, are struggling," she said, her eyes sharpening on me.

I drew in a heavy breath, shifted my legs and turned with disinterest to look out the window.

"Combativeness is not a career, Magdalene."

"In some fields it is," I retorted, and she smiled with strained annoyance.

"Mr. Hamilton has bought a nice private university in the northeast should you opt for it," she hinted.

"Being that Mr. Hamilton is our financial benefactor and long-serving, loyal confidante, I'm not surprised."

"That's not an answer," she groused.

"No, it's not."

After sighing in defeat, she openly conceded, "Which we can discuss later. Instead, why don't you tell me what you've really come to discuss."

Eran accepted the solicitation without delay and replied bluntly, "I need to review the school's most recent security protocols."

Ms. Beedinwigg stared emotionless at Eran while processing his request. Her eyes flickered to me and back to Eran before replying tightly, "What's happened?"

"Magdalene's alarm went off last night."

Her eyes were back on me before I could finish turning my head toward her. Great concern clouded them briefly before they cleared and lucid thought returned. "You have –"

"Yes, my own safety measures are in place," Eran assured. "But there are public areas, such as your school, where we are at a disadvantage."

"And the other sites. You've secured the Alps?" she asked.

"Yes," Eran replied.

"And London?" she pressed.

"Yes," he said firmly, growing impatient. "What we need, Ms. Beedinwigg, are your security protocols."

Her lips pinched in nervous distress and she stood. Distracted, she edged around her desk and headed for a row of grey filing cabinets painted with the words "Authorized Personnel Only". Eran and I watched as she asked crossly over her shoulder, "Who got out? And how? Or are they new?"

"No, not new," Eran said, "I would have been alerted. And if it was one of our enemies who has somehow found their way to freedom, then we have a much bigger problem."

Ms. Beedinwigg halted and looked up, her back muscles tensing visibly through the thin fabric. "Because others might follow," she inferred.

"Yes," Eran replied in a hard voice.

"It could be no one. It could be that everyone is overreacting. We simply don't know," I reiterated for the third time in Eran's presence, and again Ms. Beedinwigg stopped as Eran sighed.

Swiveling her face toward us, her eyebrows dipped as she evaluated me before shifting them to Eran. "She's not taking this seriously."

"No," Eran grumbled. "She's not."

Shaking her head, she returned to finger-walking the files before pulling one free. After lifting a packet from inside, she handed it to Eran and leaned against the desk, giving him time to evaluate it. The document read across the front in bold letters "Readiness and Emergency Plan – The Academy of the Immaculate Heart".

"Updated two months back," said Ms. Beedinwigg. "I'll alert my guards, conspicuously, and you'll keep me in the loop?"

"Of course," Eran replied, head ducked, already flipping through.

"Page thirty-six," Ms. Beedinwigg advised. "You'll be looking for the terror threats section and the material before that is on fire and earthquake safety."

Eran nodded, still thumbing through the document.

"So you have no idea who it was?" she asked, head ducked, arms crossed, expression vexed.

"No, there's no distinguishing between them," Eran replied for me. "There's only the alarm."

"Alarm," she murmured. "It is a good word for it, isn't it?" She was discreetly implying that I shouldn't be so unmoved by the experience, by the indication that one of our enemies was on the loose and had apparently stopped by our house for a brief visit.

The bell chimed, informing us that we had five minutes to get to our first class, and Eran slipped the protocols into his bookbag. "I'll return them," he assured.

"No need. I'll get a copy from Leroy, the lead guard. I need to brush up on them myself." Ms. Beedinwigg sighed heavily. "Here we go again, it seems."

"We'll see." Eran turned to me. "I'll escort you," he stated in a manner that could not be mistaken as a question, but it was all right. I already knew he would insist.

We left Ms. Beedinwigg's office with the two of them entirely business-focused, she heading directly for the head guard's office, as Eran and I went in the opposite direction.

"Mr. Morow's, European History, right?" Eran confirmed. Without waiting for an answer, he remarked, "Your favorite teacher." His sarcasm actually made me smile.

The walk was short, allowing only a few of the incoming freshman students to gape at Eran as he walked down the hall, but I was certain there would be more at lunch. Wearing a black tee-shirt fitted to his muscular torso and jeans that hugged his well-built thighs, his body caught their eyes; but it was his strikingly handsome face and translucent blue-green eyes that kept them there. I walked with stern dedication in ignoring them as we reached my classroom door. People were taking their seats as Mr. Morow studied

Eran and me with a cold stare from his desk at the front of the room. Ignoring it, Eran swung to face me, his signature smirk lifting one side of his lips.

"I thought we'd gotten past all that," he teased, nudging his chin at the hall from where we'd just come.

I frowned and rolled my eyes, flatly refusing to admit I was irked by the parade of gawking girls.

"Try to enjoy the class," he said, his voice husky and just low enough for my ears alone before he leaned down and placed his lips leisurely on mine. It sent a bolt of excitement through me, temporarily paralyzing my thoughts beyond anything that wasn't Eran's touch.

Mr. Morow abruptly cleared his throat but was drowned out by the final bell. When it ended, he called out sharply, "We will begin now," although everyone but me was already seated.

Eran stood back, his voice drifting away from me as he did. "Play nice."

I lifted an eyebrow cagily and watched him step around me to head back in the opposite direction. There, the sight of his muscles shifting below his shirt as he adjusted his bookbag's strap, made me pause, and fighting my urge to remain there, watching him, I patiently stepped toward the door, preparing myself for Mr. Morow's accosting glare.

"Magdalene," Eran said suddenly, and I turned to find him stopped in the center of the vacant hallway.

"Hmm?"

His expression was solemn, which concerned me until he spoke. "You know you're the only one I want. No one else exists to me."

Exhilaration sparked, spanned outward, and tickled the inside of my belly. I nodded and he returned to striding down the hall.

"Ms. Tanner!" Mr. Morow's irritable voice barked.

My scowl matched his as I entered and found the

only available seat midway up the farthest aisle. I evaded the number of eyes on me, walking at a hurried pace out of the sole reason to 'play nice'. Once seated, Mr. Morow deepened his glare as his eyes drifted down my body. Dressed in a black shirt, loose jeans, and biker boots, I certainly stood out in the sea of pastel cardigans and polo shirts, but it was the history between us that made him irrevocably hostile.

"There are a few ground rules you'll need to follow while in my class," he said standing and walking around the desk to face the room. He continued his languid stroll to the front of my row, hunching slightly like a stalking animal. "There will be no explosions in my classroom ..." he announced, entering my aisle. "No destruction of school property ..." he added, continuing up the aisle, narrowing the space between us. "And no elongated number of absences regardless of the excuse. There will, in fact, be no disruptions and no drama whatsoever. If drama does occur, you will not be sent to the principal's office, where you likely would be given preferential treatment." He stopped suddenly at my desk, standing over me, staring down. Up close and with unrestricted view, I noticed his straw-like white hair was thinning and that his belly had expanded two inches outward. "I will simply fail you." I raised my head to look him in the eye. They were narrowed, so not much was visible. "This is my domain. I own these four walls and everything between them for the span of time that you are here. Nothing will interrupt me. Nothing will distract me. Of these points, I am not certain how much more articulate I need to be in order to be understood." Hands clasped behind his back, leaning into my personal space, he waited for me to respond. I peered past him where all heads were turned in my direction, knowing that if it were in any doubt, Mr. Morow's beeline for my desk and his overbearing speech, had made it abundantly obvious that his threats were targeted entirely at me.

My first instinct was to hold up my thumb and forefinger and say, "Maybe just a smidgeon more clarity would help" but Eran had asked me to be nice, which really meant to not provoke my teacher on the first day; so instead, and against my better impulses, I nodded at him, slowly. But I did add a look of unambiguous disdain for my benefit.

Settling for my response, Mr. Morow spun around and marched back to his desk where he distributed the syllabus and launched into homework expectations, which were excessive. He then announced a pop quiz to "assess our current skill level" even though it would apply to our overall grade. That lasted until the end of the hour.

By the time I reached the hallway, Eran was waiting in the middle of it, grinning.

"Pleasant class?" he asked, smirking as we met.

"You felt my anger rise up, didn't you?" I asked, falling into step with him.

"I sure did."

"No," I replied flatly. "It was not pleasant."

Eran grinned. "May I offer what I feel is sage advice?"

"No."

Chuckling, he acquiesced and fell silent, taking my hand as a physical gesture of support instead. It helped. Instantly. His natural warmth never failed to seep through my skin into my core, calming me no matter where I was or who might have picked a fight with me.

Sensing it, he murmured, "That's better," and squeezed.

For the remainder of the walk, neither of us spoke, our touch, the soft brush of our skin between our fingers and across our palms, became my only thought, and when I glanced at him, it was apparent he was absorbed by it too. There was only the stiff tension that falls over one another when thoughts become too indecent to mention in public.

When we reached my classroom door, he quietly groaned in disappointment before mumbling, "We're going to have to find the janitor's closet."

I giggled and he leaned forward to kiss me on the lips, before promising in a louder voice, "I'll be close."

"I know." And as much as I knew it was out of incumbent responsibility over me, I liked it.

He heaved his bookbag strap up his shoulder, turned, and walked back through the thinning crowd. Again, I watched him go, realizing that we'd spent every waking moment together throughout summer and that these classes were testing our patience in being forced apart.

Sitting through the next fifty-five minutes of Advanced French was mind-numbing, and not because of the repetitive nouns Ms. Gantry had us recite toward the final leg of the hour. I already spoke French – along with German and Latin – fluently and had only selected the elective course out of an intent to balance it with the grueling weight of more challenging required curriculum. Around the mid-hour, I was wishing I had taken Ezra's advice and chosen a new language for the experience. The time did, however, provide an opportunity to let my mind wander, which it did by summoning images of Eran's body moving beneath the thin fabric of his tee-shirt, the glint in his light eyes as he smirked, and the way he smelled of an arousing blend of earth and sun.

"Mademoiselle Tanner," Ms. Gantry snapped, forcing me to realize the class's recital of French nouns had ended. "Since you evidently think you are too worthy to join your classmates in our exercise and consider your language skills to be superior, why don't you read the phrase on the board?" She folded her arms across her chest and tipped her head to the side, challenging me. "I was intending on leaving it as bonus homework, but why do that when we have you to do the work for us?"

"Sorry Ms. Gan —"

"In French," she commanded.

A few snickers slithered out from a brunette in the front row and a blonde next to the windows.

"Oui," I said. "Je suis désolé, Madame Gantry." Her eyes sharpened to cold stone as I apologized with faultless pronunciation.

"Now the phrase on the board."

Feigning ignorance this time by slowing my delivery and acting out a painstaking dissection of the words, I read, "Petit a petit, l'oiseau fait son nid, which —"

"Means?" Ms. Gantry demanded.

Her tone and manner were curt enough to make me abandon my attempt to appear inept and I rattled off the translation effortlessly. "Little by little, the bird makes its nest."

The bell rang, noting that the hour was up and Ms. Gantry's thin lips disappeared as they pinched into a sneer. "All right," she said stiffly. "That will be all for today, class. Ms. Tanner, stay behind."

I sighed and noticed a few sympathetic glances in my direction as I slid the class syllabus into my bookbag and remained seated. The rest of the students streamed out and into the hallway as Ms. Gantry finished shuffling the papers on her desk. Not bothering to look my way, she strolled around its front edge and leaned against it, again crossing her arms over her chest.

"That phrase, Ms. Tanner, you read so eloquently from the board was meant to impart my students with a valuable lesson, a reminder of what they can gain from my class. Do you know what I'm referring to?"

"Yes," I replied flatly, noticing the number of students entering the hallway and the growing noise coming through the open door.

She gestured impatiently for me to explain.

"It's a motivational phrase that says by patience and perseverance anything can be accomplished. You were telling them to work hard and over time they will see the results."

She dipped her head in a half-nod, trying to hide the irritated frown that confirmed I was correct. "And to you, in particular, it is a —"

"Warning," I interrupted.

She raised her head, both stunned and agitated.

"You are telling me that right now I am building my own nest."

"An unstable one," Ms. Gantry reinforced. She sighed and shook her head. "You do have a mouth on you, Ms. Tanner. I encourage you to use it in the education of the French language and for nothing else. I am well aware of your reputation. Let's see if we can make it through this last semester and finally send you off into the world ... in one piece."

I stared her down, intentionally, before pointing out, "I should get to my next class."

"Yes," she grumbled. "You should."

I stood, swung my bookbag over my shoulder and walked out the door with her heated eyes on my back. Immediately outside, Eran came into my peripheral vision, holding back a grin.

"Well," he said under his breath, "when Ezra asks what kind of first day you've had, it won't be a dull recitation."

I growled quietly in the back of my throat in unwilling agreement. "I've handled far greater assaults than what these pitiable teachers throw at me, and yet

...”

"I know," he replied tolerantly. "I've personally witnessed them."

"And yet, they irritate me."

"And you don't know why," he hinted.

"No, I don't," I groaned.

"Because you can't hit back," he said simply, making my head jerk up. "You act fairly, impartially, Magdalene, and you expect others to demonstrate the same integrity. But these teachers have the upper hand, an unfair advantage, and they employ it –"

"Maliciously," I interjected.

"Injudiciously," Eran clarified, "is the word I was about to use."

"I like my word better."

He chuckled. "I know you do. Your nature is to contest those who take advantage of others and your preference is to do it aggressively, oftentimes with weapons or fists. Case in point, last night outside the restaurant."

I laughed quietly through my nose before concluding his argument. "And I can't apply them here."

"Exactly."

A few quiet, reflective steps later, I nodded. "Yes, that's the source of my anger."

"I know."

"Thank you," I said, smiling slightly at him. "That helps."

"Good," he remarked. "So, I realize you don't care but it's a useful change of topic … It looks like Ms. Beedinwigg's emergency plans are fairly well thought out. Worst-case scenarios are covered, designated actions and participants are delineated, current resources are included – of which these are unfortunately limited, but an addendum mentions a time schedule in which resources are being acquired and they seem to be keeping pace with it. In short, I can work with what we have here."

"Excellent," I said, trying to sound enthusiastic, strictly for his benefit, and failing.

We turned a corner and the next hallway was equally as busy, but it was three teachers huddling outside a classroom door who we nearly bumped. Being so focused on the video one of them was showing, they didn't notice us at all, which was atypical. Teachers at the Academy were instructed to be observant, and seemed to relish the opportunity to catch those misbehaving – Eran and myself in particular. The fact they didn't even look up was odd. They gasped as we passed, heads down, consumed by something else entirely.

"Are those ..." Mrs. Terlich said under her breath, "wings?"

My legs stiffened at that point and I stumbled, but Eran caught my elbow and hauled me up.

"Thank you."

"You're welcome."

I waited two more steps before asking, "You heard that, didn't you?"

"Yes," Eran replied rigidly.

Another two girls to our right, on the opposite side of the hallway, had their heads ducked and were watching a video. And a group of three boys were doing the same a few feet down, their mouths ajar. This is when Eran stopped.

"Mind if I take a look?" he asked.

One of them shrugged, tapped the screen, and extended his hand toward Eran. I wedged myself in between them and watched as the grainy, unfocused image of a man hovering in the air shook and then settled in the center of the screen as rising, panicked screams rose up through the small speaker. Appendages that extended from the man flapped slow and deliberate as he seemed to be surveying those watching him on the ground from what appeared to be a distance of twenty or thirty yards. The picture sharpened and blurred again, but before the camera operator could steady his or her hand, the man spun around – allowing an uninhibited view of the connection between his wings and their attachment to his skin – and propelled himself upward. At this moment, Eran and I both leaned in for a better view. The lighting was cast against a grey cloudy sky, distorting the wings colors, which was of particular concern to us. If the wings were white, our tension would ease slightly because this was the color of our allies – the Alterums – and would be an indication that the man had simply made a mistake, flown into a populated area and been identified before he could flee. If they were grey, we would be struck with the same shock equal to turning a corner and coming face to face with a nemesis in a vacant hallway because that hue would indicate we were again facing an enemy – a Fallen One – who should be dead, buried deep underground, where we had left them. But the color scale was misleading, obscured by the overcast sky. The camera jostled again as the operator tried to follow him, but the man only swept back across the screen once, shrunk to half his original size by the effects of distance, before disappearing entirely in the cumulus clouds.

"It's a hoax," one of the boys claimed.

"A good one," insisted the one showing the video.

Without a single indication of concern, Eran clapped one of the boy's shoulders lightly. "Thanks for showing us."

"I'm telling you..." the third boy began but didn't bother finishing.

Eran and I left the three of them to debate the video's validity while we did the same on our own.

"No one we know would do that," I said.

"No," Eran agreed. "That entire act was meant to provoke."

"But our enemies," I said, keeping my voice low even though I was using a non-descript term to refer to them, "were always elusive to humans, too. They wouldn't reveal themselves even if one has escaped; especially not now, after centuries of living in secret."

"Unless one had something to gain from it."

That notion led me right back to the belief that the video was a ruse and that the sensation on the back of my neck was nothing more than an unexplained phenomenon. If he were a Fallen One, there was nothing to gain by revealing himself to the humans. He would be alone in this world, and he wouldn't want to squander the advantage of obscurity before he could extort, murder, or otherwise ruin the humans he came in contact with – which was the key reason the Fallen Ones remained hidden at all. He was far more likely to be an Alterum, one of our kind, having been caught unexpectedly in the air and who fled after realizing he was noticeable.

By the time we reached my next class, the strain was visible on Eran's face. "I can see your thoughts," I said.

"And what is it I am thinking?"

"You lack information and you're beating yourself up over allowing your confidantes, friends, and fighters to disperse around the world when you need them at your side to apprise you of what is happening."

Eran smiled slightly. "You're underestimating me, Magdalene."

"I am?"

"What better way to learn all that is occurring than to blanket the earth with my informants."

Stunned, I leaned back, briefly speechless. "I didn't – didn't foresee that approach."

"Good, then it's possible our enemy doesn't either."

I nodded, humbled, but I still wasn't diverted from the thought that was marring his stately, normally stoic expression. "Why then do I see dread in your eyes?"

"Because," he said, his lips pressing downward with worry. "Not a single informant of mine saw this coming."

3 PROVOCATION

Eran grew steadily quieter throughout the day, drawing into his reclusive cave to deliberate, comprehend, and plan. He said two sentences at lunch: "Water or soda?" and a flat, unconvincing, "Yes, my classes are stimulating."

I didn't blame him, considering I have the same unrelenting trait. Once we find a problem, neither of us drop it, step back, or let it go until it is solved. We are like a dog with a bone – a rabid dog. In this case, I knew Eran would be secluded in his cave at least until we got home, because he didn't have enough information to finalize a course of action and wouldn't get it until he spoke with his informants.

Regardless, I kept to myself, slowly eating my sandwich on the outside lawn next to Eran who had forgotten about his own lunch, watching the people around me squint dubiously at their phones and tablets and debate about the legitimacy of the video that seemed to have captured everyone's attention. Afterwards, he walked me to my subsequent classes, reviving just long enough to kiss me before falling back into reflection.

After the last class and a reticent ride home, we walked into our kitchen tired and emotionally-drained, ready for blistered black beetle stew or whatever new culinary concoction Felix had invented. I was somewhat relieved to find hamburgers and a salad on the table. The fact that the hamburgers were made of alligator meat and the salad had charred ants – tossed in "for texture" as Felix put it – wasn't even an issue.

"Stop actin' the maggot," Rufus was complaining as we opened the door.

Eran gave me a curious look and I whispered the translation, "Stop fooling around", and he nodded understanding.

"I'm telling you," Felix demanded, pulling freshly baked hamburger buns from the oven, "other Alterums have done it, too!" The rolls smelled strange, making me wonder if the rest of Felix's worm meal had found its way into the dough.

"You're wrong," Rufus countered.

"Done what?" I asked taking a green chip from the ceramic bowl set on the small, round kitchen table, but setting it back after it smelled of algae.

Felix swung around, jaw dropped and wide-eyed. "Revealed themselves to the humans."

Eran fell into his designated chair at the table, brows raised at the dramatics, eyes drained from the day's inner debate.

"We're discussing the Alterum," Felix announced.

"Assumedly an Alterum," Rufus mumbled.

"Who is seeking fame," Felix declared.

"Assumedly seekin' fame," Rufus added under his breath.

"Stop that!" Felix snapped at Rufus, who ignored him in favor of slicing a tomato with a fresh grin pulling at his cheeks.

Eran and I attempted to subdue the grins breaking free across our faces as Ezra entered the kitchen.

"Alterums have been known to seek notoriety before," she demurred as she poured herself a cup of coffee.

"David Gaffney," Felix suggested pointedly.

"Yes," Ezra replied, smiling to herself, leaning back against the counter in reflection. "Who would have known that crop circles would catch on like they did? And all over a simple wager."

"And Cheryl Cornwall," Rufus remarked, rejoining the conversation from the counter.

Ezra laughed. "Indeed, planting mysterious objects from earth on Mars for our space program to find has become a bizarre pastime for her."

Eran smiled tolerantly, but it was clear to me that he wasn't convinced.

"Aye, but none o' them have allowed themselves to be caught on camera," Rufus alluded, to which Eran replied, "Exactly."

"Do you have the sense whether it could be an Alterum converting into one of our enemies?" Ezra asked, tense at what his answer might be.

"A Converter?" Eran leaned back in his chair. "The thought has crossed my mind. I am told when a soul has been cast out from the afterlife I'm allowed fair warning, but there is no way to know when one of our kind is going to commit a crime against humanity. We do not know the future or any one person's destiny, and the efforts made to establish criteria that might lead us to believe they will commit a crime in the future have all been proven failures. The idea to commit a crime lives only in those individuals and until they execute it, we have no way of knowing."

Felix stood warily holding a silver salad bowl. "I've never seen an Alterum turn."

"Well, you might be now," Ezra warned.

After a thoughtful pause, Rufus brought the tomatoes to the table. Chairs were pulled out, our housemates sat, and we stacked our alligator hamburgers with accoutrements. After a few tense seconds, Felix dared a glance at Eran.

"You think he's doing this for a reason, don't you?"

Eran kept his head down, preoccupied with his burger, in part because he didn't want to further excite anyone. "I don't have enough information to determine that yet, Felix."

"A sinister reason," Felix insinuated.

Rufus groaned and snapped, "Let the man eat!"

Felix pinched his mouth shut into a scowl before opening it briefly enough to risk a retort. "Well I am only asking…"

As the conversation devolved, it turned to where Felix bought the alligator meat and Rufus's disgust at Felix's answer. Their bickering took us into the night, long after Eran and I washed the dishes and Ezra abandoned her attempt to mediate a truce, but eventually their minds grew more tired than their mouths and everyone headed for their respective bedrooms.

Our nightly ritual resumed, which felt soothing and placating given that the nervous unknowns about the winged man had latched onto the backs of our minds. Following a schedule always seems to have a restorative affect, so the house went quiet before I even finished brushing my teeth.

When Rufus's snoring began, I reopened my bedroom door before pulling out my textbook on human anatomy. The first day of school and already Mr. Cantor had assigned a chapter to read on the skeletal system. Seemed unjustly torturous. Lucky for me, this one actually piqued my interest. The chapter was a good reminder of vital information on where to land an effective strike – an advantage if any other man attempted to assault me in a bar's courtyard.

I was reviewing the eight cranial bones of the human head – rehearsing quietly what was not listed in the book such as their maximum threshold to breaking point – when Eran's bedroom door gradually squeaked open and an electrical pulse of excitement ran across my skin. He was still awake.

I rolled off my bed and onto my feet, landing with a soft thud to cross the floor in a hurry. My footsteps sounded heavy, making me grimace at their reverberation, but I yanked open my door anyway and Eran's calm, handsome face stared back at me, illuminated by the light on my nightstand. The soft, buttery glow tinged his wavy brown hair a rust-color and drew out the contrast of his clear blue-green eyes – ones that were sweeping a gaze down my body.

My immediate thought was that he had exhausted his patience in living across the hall from me and had come to break Ezra's household rules. He raised a straight index finger to his lips and gestured for quiet while pointing at my feet; and my heart did an anxious flip. But then he walked past me, and my shoulders dropped, alongside my deflated ego.

With striking furtiveness, he moved to my closet and pulled out a black hooded sweatshirt, one with horizontal slits across the back, and my darkest jeans, handing them to me before closing my bedroom door. My job was clear: change. Which I did with celerity as Eran strolled to the French doors leading to my balcony.

Realizing he was dressed entirely in black also, with twin cuts in the fabric of his hooded sweatshirt, I whispered, "Where are we going?"

"Washington, D.C.," he replied, somberly, ending his

surveillance of the night beyond my balcony and swinging around to check my progress.

I was just pulling the sweatshirt over my head, a motion that briefly left my belly exposed. I knew Eran noted it when he went still, his eyes momentarily locked on my torso with unmistakable yearning. He didn't blink for several seconds, finally forcing himself to look away and step back into the room before his face loosened again.

"Umm, ready?" he mumbled as the warm night air swept into my room.

I stepped up to him, not bothering to restrain my satisfied grin, which he responded to with a frustrated press of his lips. Clearly, he was forcing back both a clear desire over what he had seen and my satisfaction over his reception to it, but all temptation was immediately erased as we walked to the balcony railing. There, Eran turned the lock without approaching it, creating a grating sound that seemed disconcertingly loud across the peaceful night. After listening for any sign of our housemates, and on hearing none, we rotated our shoulders forward, pressed the muscles across our backs to the surface, and released the continual tension from between our shoulder blades. The hushed whisper of our emancipated appendages, the rustle of our clothing as they emerged through the slits in our sweatshirts, and their subsequent snap outward in preparation for flight was subtle, just enough to stir the night. Their expansion was the only sign needed for us to leap across the balcony railing and over the edge. We plummeted a few feet before our appendages could pump once and propel us upward. Another few thrusts and we were over the treetops.

The lights from the streets, homes, and businesses faded quickly and we were soon enveloped in darkness with the wind consuming the quietness as it rushed past our ears. We passed through a dense cloud, its dampness leaving us dewy, and into an air current that aided our propulsion.

I followed Eran across the southern states, avoiding air traffic as best we could, and began our descent an hour before dawn in the eastern time zone. The swath of white speckled lights across the eastern seaboard city quickly grew larger and sparser as we settled into Georgetown, onto a narrow residential street a few blocks from the Potomac River. The brick homes around us stood within a few feet of one another and offered no front yard, just a short path to the doorways under square arches. Vines draped a grey building on the opposite side of the street from where we stood and narrow trees rose up like giraffe necks from the slender alleys between the homes. Despite first impressions, the street boasted an upscale impression, with welcoming potted plants at the doorways and luxury cars lining the curb.

After our feet touched the ground it was clear, given the humid heat, that our sweatshirts weren't for comfort but concealment; and noting this, we each pulled the hood over our heads as our appendages sank back below the skin between our shoulder blades.

Eran turned to face the home beside us, and I did the same, scrutinizing it for any sign of life. But it was Eran who identified it first.

"You don't want to do that," he warned in his thick English accent.

"Do what?" I asked, leaning forward beyond my hood's edge, at a loss over what he might be referring to. I was just standing there.

A slight tip to the right of Eran's head led me to a tall, dense potted palm plant at the side of the house, where a handgun's barrel was aimed at us. He wasn't speaking to me, but to the person holding it.

The simple scuff of a foot sounded unusually loud on the otherwise hushed street as its owner stepped forward, dressed in black body armor, hunched forward, arms outstretched, finger on the trigger. As he moved with stealth determination, another one just like him appeared at the opposite corner of the house, moving in the same manner – directly toward us.

Eran sighed tiredly through a frown. "We are here to see –"

"Shut up," the squat one to our left interrupted. "Check them for weapons."

"If you touch her in any way," Eran said, his voice tightening, "I'll be required to use force."

An air of resolve surrounded us then, and it was clearly coming from Eran.

"So will I," I added, and again the eight cranial bones of the human head along with their maximum threshold to breaking point ran through my mind.

They tore their eyes from Eran and snickered at me, making me hope they made an attempt.

Continuing to narrow their distance between us, they kept their heads bowed and eyes aimed at us from behind their weapons.

"Campion," Eran stated firmly, "will identify us to – "

"I said shut up," commanded the squat one.

When they were within a few feet, Eran cautioned, "You've been warned."

Keeping his firearm steadily aimed at me, the squat one reached a careful hand toward my waist, coming within an inch before Eran leaned toward it, seized it, and yanked the man off balance. As the man flailed, the other one sped up his pace, but Eran sent a booted foot into his stomach before he could reach us.

The benign click-click-click of their firearms, the skidding of feet across the pavement, and exerted exhales filled the night as Eran single-handedly took them on. I desperately searched for an opportunity in between Eran's strikes but within seconds he had swept the feet out from beneath the squat one and, as that one fell with a splat, twisted around the oncoming body of the other to flip him onto his back.

Eran confiscated both firearms and stepped back, deftly removing both the cartridges and cocked bullet inside the barrels before another voice entered the fray.

Deep and unconcerned, it called out with quiet calm, "Colonel."

I turned as the obsidian man emerged from the shadows. In the dark, only the whites of his eyes and patch of short, frizzy, starkly white hair stood out.

"Campion," Eran greeted without looking up as he finished his rapid disarmament of the men's guns.

"Stand down, men," Campion commanded with natural ease.

The two of them, weighty around the middle and through the joints, struggled to get to their feet.

"They were standing outside the ambassador's home," said the one who had done all the talking to this point, more rolling to his feet than pushing upward. "They were staring at it, at three o'clock in the morning."

"I'll take care of them from here," Campion said simply.

He creased his eyebrows in confusion. "They're calling you by a different name."

"A nickname," Campion assured. "Good job, Rich. Back to your post."

Rich jerked his head in a nod, took the firearm and magazine from Eran, gave us a suspicious glance, and marched back around the side alley of the house.

"You too, Mitch," Campion said. "Good job, but I've got this one."

Mitch remained hunched and avoiding our eyes as he accepted his weapon and left for his post on the other side of the house, an indication he had just been reproved.

"Magdalene," Campion nodded with restrained courtesy toward me.

"Campion," I said using the same gesture.

Readdressing Eran, he said, "I've been expecting you, sir."

With Campion being Eran's first lieutenant, that shouldn't have concerned me. It did. Because it meant a true and perilous reason existed for the two of them to re-connect.

"Do you have a place where we can speak privately?" Eran asked, moving directly to our reason for coming.

"Yes, sir. All rooms in the house are vulnerable, but only I have access to the recording equipment."

"You've bugged your employer's house?" I asked, taken aback.

"Yes," Campion replied flatly, without shame.

"And the ambassador?" Eran pressed.

"A heavy sleeper who won't awake for another three hours," Campion assured as he led us inside.

The rooms were warmly decorated in dark wood and accent lights illuminating painted artwork, with the greeting room where we stopped being comfortably decorated with plump, luxurious leather chairs. We each sat down as I critiqued the room for hidden devices. I saw none.

Launching to the heart of the conversation, Eran asked, "Who is he?"

"I'm working on it, sir."

"And the humans don't know?"

"No, sir. The ambassador has been quietly making phone calls."

"I'm surprised they're paying any attention at all," I

interjected. "There are so many videos of hoaxes and spoofs these days."

"The humans ordinarily don't," Campion said, "but before being caught on camera by a bystander the target was tracked on radar, flying over all top-secret military installations in the Western hemisphere, consecutively, making a beeline for each one."

Eran remained stoic as he processed this information. "Evidently, he had access to the knowledge of their locations."

"Yes, that's where I started my inquiries," Campion confirmed.

Eran nodded thoughtfully, as I began to better understand Campion's purpose at the ambassador's home.

"How long have you been employed here?" I asked.

"Two years, three months, thirteen days, five hours, seven —"

"I get it," I interrupted. "The fact you called the winged being a 'target', already earned a leadership rank on the ambassador's security team, and have bugged the ambassador's home tells me that you didn't take this job out of coincidence."

Campion waited for Eran's approval, which came in the form of a nod, before confirming, "It was strategic."

"Did you two expect this to happen?" I asked, nearly demanding.

They were silent before Campion declared stoically, "The more you prepare for the unexpected the less the unexpected will be prepared for you." As I caught Eran's nearly undetectable but proud smile, I realized I'd just heard a mantra Eran likely drilled into his fighters over time.

When Eran's smile faded, he asked, "Any idea where the target originated? Or when he was first detected?"

"Radar picked him up directly over the first military

installation." Campion paused and pinched his lips closed in a weak frown. "He nosedived from above until he was within radar's range."

"All right," Eran replied, without showing any of the nervousness I was now feeling. "And where did he disappear?"

Campion turned cagey, which was unusual for him. "Sir, the target traveled across the Atlantic to the United Kingdom, angling sharply upward and out of radar's range directly over the passageway." On this assertion, I understood Campion's reticence.

"The passageway?" I repeated as Eran sat very still.

Campion glanced at me before settling his stare back on Eran. "It was as if he were leading the humans to it. The ambassador – and others – were wondering what two men were doing standing next to a deep hole in the middle of an unpopulated field outside London on a large parcel of land owned by one Mr. Johnathon Hamilton."

"Obviously you haven't told them that the men are employed as guards by our financier, Mr. Hamilton, who purchased the property in order to protect the hole?"

"No, sir," Campion replied, subduing a grin at Eran's sarcasm. Growing serious, he continued, "But they are investigating it and they may just reach that conclusion on their own."

"Yes, I expect that will be the case," Eran replied tightly, his gaze falling to the floor where I could see him working through the limited time we might have before that happened.

Campion shifted his eyes to me momentarily. "Have you considered enacting Measure 103 and reuniting the guardians with their messengers, sir?"

I groaned and opened my mouth to protest.

"Yes, I have," Eran said. "Alert the guardians to

await further instructions."

"I'll put them on notice, sir."

I balked, a half-groan, half-squeak, and then made another attempt to object, remarking to deaf ears, "We messengers can take care of ourselves."

"Yes, you can," Eran admitted. It did no good to point it out, however, because he followed it up with a commanding decision. "As for reestablishing full safety protocols, it may be safest to keep everyone where they are for now."

"You mean hidden," Campion clarified.

"Exactly."

"Yes, sir."

Eran stood abruptly, causing Campion and me to do the same. "Keep me informed."

"Yes, sir, I will."

Eran paused, making no effort to turn toward the door. "Are you doing well, Campion? Are you taking care of yourself?"

Campion's genuine appreciation was obvious but what struck me was Eran's concern. I had seen him defend Campion and others under his command with ferocious resolve, enough to send a chill through the most determined opponent, but I had never seen this softer side. While there had never been any question, if one needed a visible example of Eran's dedication to his people, it came through plainly now.

"Yes, sir, thank you for asking," Campion said with a tip of his head.

"Good, if you need anything," Eran insisted.

"I know to ask. Thank you, sir."

After a firm nod, Eran made his way toward the door, with Campion and me following, but before leaving the house, he offered his hand to Campion, a brief clutch of each other's muscular forearm, in a time-honored guardian exchange.

Outside, the three of us surveyed our surroundings for any prying eyes, and seeing none, Eran and I rolled our shoulders forward and set our appendages free. Eran tipped his head once more at Campion and we lifted off the ground, pumping our wings rhythmically until we were well over the city and out of view.

Eran's speed could have carried him back to Ezra's house in minutes. No one could match it. Including me. But again, he slowed his stride, remaining beside me for the length of the trip, and we set down as the sun was lighting the horizon.

As I stepped up to open the French doors to my bedroom, I stopped and turned back to him, deciding to comment on something that had bothered me during the flight. "You didn't tell Campion about the doors flying open, or about what I felt."

Eran's head tipped forward curiously. "You're not warming to the belief that we face a true threat, are you?"

"No," I replied flatly.

"No," he muttered, "of course not..."

"But if I did I'd pursue it," I stated.

He turned serious. "I know you would."

"I just figured you would inform Campion because you *do* believe."

Eran paused to consider his explanation before delivering it simply. "Sometimes too much information can be misleading. I don't want him going down one path until he's evaluated all the others."

"Ahh," I replied and took a step toward my bedroom when he shifted suddenly to my side and took hold of my waist to rotate me to face him.

Raising his hands to tenderly cradle my face, he waited until my curious gaze locked onto his concerned one. But he didn't speak. His eyes took me in, absorbing every detail of my eyes, nose, mouth, slowly, methodically, as was Eran's way.

I felt my eyebrows furrow as confusion settled over me. "What is it, Eran? What are you not saying?"

His reply was simple but delivered with desperate need. "I know you disagree with my assessment and a strong part of you is doing so because I didn't give you the chance to confirm it one way or another during the rainstorm, but I'm asking you to please stay alert."

I nodded in his hands, his desire to touch me restricting the movement.

Only then did he exhale with slight relief and drop his arms.

I, however, wasn't placated. "Can I ask you something, something I have never understood?"

"Yes," he whispered, emotion working its way into his face, a mixture of desire and worry.

"You are my guardian. I understand and do my best to accept it. But beyond professional obligation, what drives you to protect me?"

"You have never been an obligation to me, Magdalene."

I blinked, taken aback, and continued my press for an answer. "Thank you, I'm just – I'm surrounded by friends who I would call family, who are trained to fight. I've survived on my own. I'm more equipped than most to handle a deviant Alterum; and despite it all, you worry."

"Because you can still be wounded," he said, emphasizing it, another effort in his eternal quest to convince me of it.

My bewilderment only deepened then. "How? I am capable of defying death, eternal death. This is proven, you know it. What more can hurt me?"

He considered his answer and drew a heavy breath before he spoke. "Magdalene, I've seen warriors in battle with eyes gouged, limbs torn, their scalp hanging from their skull as they attacked with impenetrable will against their opponents. And I've seen others who were physically untouched, kneeling on the ground, weeping uncontrollably, the world lost to them, their mind split and devoid of thought. Dangers do exist beyond the flesh, emotions can change you to your core, alter your belief in who you are, manipulate your identity, and as we both well know, emotional pain can be greater than the physical. It can kill you even while you remain alive and breathing."

He was reflecting on the hardest time of our existence, when we were separated and it nearly consumed our will to live, and I was humbled into silence by the memory of it and his pointed use of it in his explanation. Then I found a whisper of my voice. "Yes," I murmured, "we do know that."

"Yes, we do," he said, his voice heavy.

A moment passed between us, difficult enough to steal our breath, wrapping us in emotions, before he found a way to break free from it. Leaning forward, he kissed me, gently, light as a breeze, and far too quickly.

"I smell berries," he said, lifting his head to stare curiously at me.

"Rufus committed to making blueberry pancakes this morning," I said through a smile.

"Ahh."

"With traditional wheat flour," I added.

"That'll be a nice reprieve," he replied, genuinely relieved. I chuckled and he added, "Don't tell Felix I said that."

My laughter grew louder as he opened the French doors and ushered me inside.

"Downstairs in twenty?" he asked, eyebrows raised as he passed me.

"Twenty," I confirmed, watching him go.

After a race to shower and slip into my traditional

attire of tee-shirt, jeans, and biker boots, I reached the kitchen to find Eran calmly sitting at the table in a fresh pair of jeans and fitted tee-shirt. The morning sun streamed light across his chest, deepening the shadows beneath his muscles and defining their strong contours. From below his naturally wavy hair, his translucent eyes locked on me with unashamed interest as I entered; remaining in place as I walked to the stove and peeked over Rufus's thick, heavily-tattooed arm at the steaming griddle.

"Smells good," I commented and received a pleased grunt.

Not to be outdone, Felix was hastily whipping up a pitcher of syrup, his frail body wobbling as he stirred furiously in competition. "Huckleberries," he announced, his voice warbling with his efforts. "Excellent source of A, B, and C vitamins."

"Mmmmm, thank you."

He beamed with pride briefly before his face fell flat. "So, any more indications on the back of your neck?"

"No," I replied simply and walked to the kitchen table as Eran and I exchanged a look.

Neither of us volunteered the information that Campion had passed on to us during the night; both of us knowing it would only unnerve them without due reason. Until we knew whether Eran and Campion's 'target' was conclusively nefarious, there was no sense in upsetting anyone.

As the pancakes and syrup were brought to the table, Ezra entered and sat with us until we'd finished our plates, polishing them completely. Conversation rolled through dinner options with lots of rejections by Rufus over Felix's suggestions. We eventually settled on pasta, which even Rufus agreed on until Felix mumbled something about knowing a fantastic squid sauce he could add to the dish. As the two of them argued, Ezra noticed our red-rimmed and sunken eyes, stared deliberately at Eran and I for a few seconds, but didn't acknowledge it. We took that as our optimal time to leave, said goodbye, promised to do the dinner dishes, and headed to school.

After a quick stop for our sandwiches at Mr. LeFrau's, we made it to the door of my first class with less than a minute before the second and final bell rang. Mr. Morow was already glaring from his seat through the open door when I came into view; his exasperation deepened when he recognized he was looking at me.

Eran's eyes danced as he deliberately ignored my teacher. "Try to stay awake."

I groaned and whispered, "That'll be a struggle."

He chuckled quietly and swept downward to kiss me. It was slow and deep, tenderly parting my lips. His aroma of sun and earth surrounded me; and as his kiss lingered I inhaled him deeply and leaned into him. When he pulled away, our lips remained in place so that the growing space between us tore us apart.

He drew in a deep breath, his chest expanding to nearly touch mine, and exhaled slowly. At the end of his exhale, he whispered, "I love you, Magdalene."

"And I love you."

The bell belted a shrill ringing overhead and Eran stepped back. "Must tell Ms. Beedinwigg to replace those damn antiquated ... " He let his voice fade. "I'll see you after class."

"MS. TANNER!" Mr. Morow barked.

Disregarding him, I nodded to Eran and he tipped his head to urge me into class.

I rolled my eyes, that gesture turning me toward the door where I saw Mr. Morow standing, fire blazing in his eyes. Hurrying to my seat gave Mr. Morow enough time to stomp to the door and slam it shut, even though Eran was already gone.

As I settled into my seat, I avoided the shaking heads and grimaced expressions from others in my class by pulling out our mandatory textbook.

"Now," Mr. Morow demanded, spinning to face the class, his voice hollow and nearly echoing off the walls. "You will answer this question today ... How can the – Write it down! It comes in several parts! How can the interaction between Europe and the World be characterized, how can poverty versus prosperity most aptly be described and explained, how do objective facts and subjective interpretations differ, how do states and government institutions of power affect and are affected by, how do the identities between European nations diverge and remain the same over the course of the years 1450 and 1556, during the Renaissance period throughout Europe?" His mouth pinched closed as he surveyed us scribbling onto paper or typing into our laptops the ridiculously protracted question. "If anyone read the required chapters last night, you'll have no problem answering it. *Did* anyone read the assignment?"

No, I was in Washington D.C. trying to determine if the world is at risk, I mused cynically.

"None of you checked your syllabus for the assignment?" he badgered, shocked at our ducked heads and silent cowering. He snorted in offense. "Well, then, geniuses, we'll need to walk through it together, won't we?"

The next thirty minutes were a twisted mess of barked questions from Mr. Morow and humbled answers by the students. I was called on once, to describe the societal existence of peasants. Having lived during a portion of that time in question on earth and therefore having first-hand knowledge, I answered correctly and appropriately. "Different from us and yet similar to us in many ways," I said. "While they dealt with famine and disease and had to defend against marauding armies, they still lived with their families under one roof homes made of expert carpentry, played dice and cards, used herbs to season food and keep their houses clean, drank wine and ale – because clean water was hard to find – and had to deal with overbearing bosses." On this last point, I tipped my head insinuatingly toward Mr. Morow.

"Wrong," he snapped and went on to describe them living in hovels – dirty, poor, and depressed.

While it was frustrating knowing that history was being contorted by a depressed, poor, dirty man, something far more important caught my attention.

One row over and two seats up, a girl had her cell phone extended in front of her, hiding it just below the head of the boy in front. She had muted it but was playing a video that moved rapidly and drew me in. After replaying the fifteen second clip several times, I grasped why she was risking Mr. Morow's wrath to watch it. The scene showed Eran and Campion's target flying effortlessly alongside planes on an airport tarmac, directly next to the passenger windows. He passed three planes waiting for take-off before angling upward, into the sky, toward a plane that was already climbing in the air. He easily caught up with it, surpassed it, flew ahead, moved into the path of the oncoming plane, and stopped, keeping himself aloft with slight pumps of his appendages hidden behind him. The plane kept its course for only a few seconds before making an abrupt right turn. He followed it, seeking its new direction, intent on disrupting its path again, but the plane had lost its velocity. Smoke began to stream from one engine and then the second as it began its descent, tilting in the right angle where it had sought to avoid a collision.

While Mr. Morow harangued a boy on the other side of the class for not knowing the answer to his question, a girl in front of me whispered, "It threw something.

Into the engines. Replay it. Watch his shoulders."

By the third replay, I caught the slight jerk and despite the distance and blurred shot, I grasped one factor clearly: His intentions *were* malevolent. And I stood.

"Ms. Tanner! Sit down!" Mr. Morow commanded.

Head straight forward, leaving my bookbag behind, I marched down my row and toward the door. Mr. Morow, who was in its vicinity, stepped sharply to the left, blocking me.

"You will sit –" he began to say, but I darted to the right in an attempt around him. He moved quickly for an unwieldy individual and succeeded in obstructing the door.

A slow, malicious smile crept up across his pale face.

I closed my eyes against the irritation and calmed my fury before leaning forward to tell him quietly, "Mr. Morow, Eran is coming for me. This very minute. And when he gets here he will defend me at any cost." My subliminal hint to Mr. Morow that he would not want to face Eran's fury was met first with cynicism and then with second-guesses, and eventually, the smile from Mr. Morow's face began to fade. "And I do mean at any cost, sir."

I stepped around him without impediment and left the room.

The hallway was quiet, given that everyone was in their respective classes, as only my feet slapped the buffed, shiny tiles. I made it around the corner before Eran came into view at the other end. His face was chiseled into determination and he moved more like a charging bull than a teenager escaping class.

"You saw?" I asked when we were just a few feet apart.

"I did."

"His appendages moved too quickly for me to

65

distinguish their color."

He nodded sharply in agreement and replied in a rush, "We have company."

"Ms. Tanner, Mr. Talor," Mr. Morow's mocking voice came up behind me.

I turned to find him with Leroy, the lead guard at the Academy, a man who towered over everyone, including Eran.

"You are out of class, in violation of school directives," Mr. Morow declared. "Isn't that correct, Leroy?"

Leroy appeared less enthusiastic, as if this weren't the first time Mr. Morow had sought him out to turn in delinquent students. "You two will need to get back to class," he said tiredly.

"Leroy, I've been meaning to tell you how impressed I am with your Readiness and Emergency Plan," Eran said politely.

Both Mr. Morow and Leroy jerked their heads in surprise.

"It's clear you spent time to evaluate all possibilities."

"You've seen it?" Leroy asked, cocking his head.

"Briefly," Eran replied slyly. "I'm not trying to placate you with artificial adulation but it's good. I've had some experience with that sort of thing and your rigorous planning was impressive." Leroy's eyebrows crossed in dubious suspicion at the teenager before him and Eran added, "Experience through my family. We're in protective services."

"Ahh," Leroy replied.

"Mr. Marsh," Mr. Morow huffed, and Leroy turned his head to him, finding an impatient frown.

"Yes, ummm, you two should probably get back to class now," Leroy said.

Mediation had failed.

"With all respect," Eran replied coolly, "Magdalene

and I will be leaving school grounds."

Mr. Morow's mouth fell open.

Eran tipped his head toward me. "Are you ready?"

"Yes," I said with an affirmative nod.

Mr. Morow's face quickly turned a strange reddish-purple. "Leroy?"

But Leroy was shrugging at Mr. Morow.

Eran and I were already walking away, toward the main doors when Mr. Morow stressed from behind us, "*Leroy?*"

"What do you want me to do?" Leroy asked. There was a nonchalance in his tone that felt somewhat rewarding.

"Stop them!"

"You heard the same speech I did."

"But –"

"Those two students have the right to leave school grounds at their will."

"But –" Mr. Morow pled, although his voice was weaker now.

"Those were the principal's instructions."

And it became evident that they were no longer a threat.

Thank you, Ms. Beedinwigg.

Seeing the light spilling in from the glass front doors of the main hall up ahead and without slowing my pace, I asked Eran, "Where are we going?"

"Shopping."

4 SUPPLIES

Ten minutes after we left our school's parking lot, Eran directed me to a quiet lane in the residential area just beyond the heart of the French Quarter. Bar music spilling out into the streets was muted from our distance, as if it were being swallowed by the serenity that engulfed this part of the city. Surrounding us stood unmarked, weathered buildings of various colors erected directly next to each other without the space of a fist between them. They lined the rutted, battered sidewalk with nothing but a single narrow cement step up to the door, and no element of welcome was instituted outside them. No potted plants, no signs, no trees to shield visitors from the sun. Regardless of all this, Eran stepped off my bike, walked with easy assurance to the nearest door, opened it, and entered without hesitation.

Awestruck, and slightly unnerved, I followed him.

When the door closed behind me, my eyes needed to acclimate to the darkness. I braced myself for any impact; even with Eran nearby there was no telling what we stepped into. No natural light made it inside, with only small lanterns across the ceiling and sconces every few feet along the wall offering any assistance. Their flickering cast a dim, rippling glow across the wooden shelves in the center of the room and their odd curiosities stored there, in no particular order. A sweeping view of just one shelf showed a human skull, a bowl of white pouches, small embroidered dolls, and a human foot preserved in a glass jar. On the next shelf down sat a wrinkled black hat – in the style of a witch – dusty and suspiciously sprayed with caked mud, a collection of green glass jars, a dagger, a cauldron small enough to hold in the palm of my hand, stacks of tarot cards and bowls of assorted stones polished to a high sheen.

Motion through the shadows ahead made me instinctively brace, but the natural tenor of Eran's body got my shoulders to fall and my hands to unclench. Eran's fingers slipped through mine and he led me down the aisle to its end where a long, vacant counter sat with a single antique cash register set off to one side.

"Hello?" Eran called out as I surveyed the candles hanging from their connected wicks over nails along every available space of the opposite wall.

An elderly woman with wavy, silver hair down her back shuffled through a small archway and inched a cautious path to the counter before looking up at us from below puffy eyelids. "Eran," she said with pleasant surprise, her voice strained from years of use.

I glanced curiously at him, but he didn't notice.

"It's time, Madame Benoit," he said simply.

And she tipped her head in a manner that conveyed she understood.

"I brought her to you so that you may have a visual representation."

Again, she made the same gesture and knowing expression, and in unison, they turned to survey me.

"Time for what?" I asked suspiciously.

"Something I commissioned a while back," he said to me before addressing her. "You still have the material?"

She nodded again, her eyes traveling slowly from my head to my boots. "Petite, just as you said, yes," the woman noted out loud, "but holds her shoulders back with confidence and her neck is a tad elongated attributable to proper posture. You are correct. She does not hold herself like a respective teenager."

I accepted the compliments, but it didn't alleviate my curiosity. "What exactly is she making?" I asked Eran.

"I'll explain in a moment," he said. "The measurements remain the same," he confirmed to her.

I leaned toward Eran and asked quietly, "You have my measurements?"

He smiled in response.

"Due date?" she asked, finally shifting her eyes to him.

"Hour, actually," he explained. "We need it by end of day."

She stared back, stunned by the turnaround request.

"There's no way to avoid it," Eran replied.

Her stoicism lingered just a breath longer and then she nodded. "It can be done."

"Excellent, we'll be back," Eran said, taking my hand and guiding me back to the door.

Outside, shielding ourselves from the now blinding sunlight, I stopped abruptly and he turned slowly to face me, a grin across his lips.

"It's a gift. For you," he explained. "And I wouldn't want to ruin the surprise."

"It isn't clothing, is it?"

"Really?" he asked, offended that I suggested he wouldn't know any better.

"Just checking."

He turned back to the street and strode to my bike.

"You'll be pleasantly surprised," he assured. "She's well respected."

"Is that how you found her?" I asked, meeting him on the opposite side of my bike.

"She came to me for help."

"Help like Ms. Elowen needed?" I clarified, slipping on my helmet.

"Yes," he said, strapping his helmet in place.

I stepped over my bike and settled onto the seat. "We've been together every waking minute," I remarked, although it sounded like the hint that it was.

"Exactly," he replied casually.

"You help them while I sleep," I deduced. "At night."

"Most of what I do requires concealment." And I understood this to mean in more ways than one.

I nodded slowly and turned the key in the ignition, letting the engine warm before shifting into gear. "You keep yourself immersed in our world," I remarked.

"It's a world that still needs us, Magdalene."

I kicked the gears into reverse, backed up, and shifted them again before turning the gas – all without responding.

I knew what he said was true, and yet I kept my relationships with Alterums, with our kind, to a minimum, as I'd always done. I'm a recluse – in effect, I think someone coined the term to describe me – so spending time with others who weren't in my immediate vicinity was a departure from my natural habits. Eran was the only exception. I would search the depths of hell to be with him – and in fact, I already have.

Eran directed me onto Royal Street, where we passed elegant four-star hotels with hanging ferns adorning their balconies and luxury shops with storefront windows showcasing exclusive artwork and sophisticated home furnishings. It was at the block that began boasting antique stores that Eran indicated I should stop. We parked outside a fine art gallery where two men in shabby clothes were passing a bottle of liquor between themselves as a man with a tilted toupee and glossy black suit shooed them off.

"Mr. Leroux," Eran called out, stepping onto the curb and entering the man's peripheral vision.

The man snapped his head twice at Eran in a double-take glance, seemed to realize his time had run out to evict his street side tenants, kicked one of the drunken men at the side of his rear, and strode to Eran. By the time he reached us, his attitude had evolved remarkably fast to amicable, even complimentary.

"Eran, it ezz always a pleasure," he pronounced through a thick French intonation while extending his hand in greeting.

"Thank you, Mr. Leroux," Eran said, accepting the handshake with a single, firm pump as the two drunkards evaluated him with obvious curiosity.

"Hey," one said, slurring the word amazingly well, "how come you don't act like that to us?"

"Yeah," the other one said in support. "How come you don't – " he repeated but stopped short, apparently forgetting the rest of the sentence.

Mr. Leroux's thin lips dissolved into a strained white line. "Come in," he urged Eran and me, "a-vay from zee sewer smell."

We followed him inside, detouring around Mr. Leroux's second kick to one of the drunkard's hips. The drunkard squealed, leaned into his partner to avoid the assault, and tumbled over the man's lap.

Mr. Leroux was huffing and muttering under his breath as he closed the door behind us. His short frame then marched directly to me where he bowed, flattening one hand on his toupee as it attempted to slide off his head and whipping the other out to the side in a grand gesture.

"Madame Magdalene," he said reverently, "I am most humbled by your vee-sit. I apologize greatly for zee errant display outside."

"Mr. Leroux," I said, "I've seen worse."

He chuckled, stood, and broke into deeper, belly-fueled laughs.

Eran interrupted with a slight throat clearing and the man snapped his mouth shut, stood straight, and inflated his chest outward, as if he were standing on-guard.

"We would like entry," Eran said, in yet another coded request.

Mr. Leroux's eyes widened briefly before his shoulders lifted into a hunch, he rubbed his hands briskly together in anticipation, grinned mischievously, giggled, and indicated gleefully, "Follow me."

Mr. Leroux's art gallery was dimly lit with small, bright lights beaming down directly onto the richly colored canvases and light marble statues. As we moved along the path of a wide shadow between the commanding displays, I murmured to myself, "It's like a dream."

Mr. Leroux stopped and tipped his head to the side. "But you do not dream, yes?"

"No, I..." I said, "I don't."

"No, how could you?" he asked. "When you visit zee afterlife during zee night?"

It was a rhetorical question, prompted by him because, apparently, he knew my skill and that as a messenger I did not fall asleep like others but instead worked to deliver messages taken during the day from the living to the deceased in the afterlife during the night.

"Ahh," he said suddenly, snapping his fingers as if an idea came to him. "But zis is what you imagine dreaming to be, yes? You are concentrating on zee work while zee shadows lead you down zee path." He nodded thoughtfully to himself as he surveyed this gallery with new appreciation. "Gud ... gud ..."

We reached the back of the short building and entered his office, consecutively, given it was no bigger than a private bathroom. He stopped at the back wall and opened the thin interior door to reveal a closet, hooked his fingers around one of the three hangers dangling from a metal bar, and yanked. The trigger opened the opposing wall, grinding it quietly inward to reveal a small chamber. The light spilling from it was dim and warm, making the red and gold hues from inside seem to glimmer.

Mr. Leroux stepped back, nearly into Eran, who nimbly shifted to the side, and ushered us in as he attempted to continue his retreat back to the gallery.

Eran ducked and stepped in first before offering me a hand, which I didn't need but took anyway. As I stood to my full height on the opposite side of the hidden threshold, Eran watched for my reaction as the room came fully into view. I gasped.

The chamber could have fit just five slender people, tightly, but it was breathtaking nonetheless. Filled with precious memorabilia of the Alterum's time on earth, all fifteen centuries of it, every spare space on the wall was taken with only a few inches separating each item and its accompanying placard describing the item's significance.

"It's ... It's ..." I abandoned my effort to characterize it further and simply laughed.

"Awe-inspiring," Eran inferred correctly.

"Yes," I breathed.

Releasing my hand, he urged, "Look around."

I immediately moved toward a delicately embroidered dress of purple and gold satin pinned to the wall. Beside it was a white placard chiseled with its origin: Éléonore, Messenger & Educator, worn during her murder by Isabelle, Fallen One, which led to eternal death, 1535 Paris.

"I remember this," I said, my voice only a whisper. "This was the day Abaddon turned his daughter into a Fallen One." Leaning in, I inspected the fabric closer. "It still has Éléonore's blood and the cuts made to her fabric where the blade landed," I said, almost inaudibly, pointing to the brown stains across it.

Next to the dress, a piece of rock sat erect on a pedestal, grey and jagged, it could have come from anywhere, but the placard next to it identified its significance. Reading it out loud to myself, I drew in a breath when I recognized it. "Fragment of the Fallen Ones' prison, Undated, The Alps."

"Mr. Leroux ... he-he knows about the prison."

"Many do. Although its exact location remains a mystery."

"By your doing?"

Eran smiled in confirmation.

"But it's vacant now," I pointed out, given that all prisoners escaped in one massive breach to join in a final battle between our kind and our enemies, the Fallen Ones, in the middle of a London field a few years back. They were now incarcerated below that field in a massive cavern, a place with its own evil that left all prisoners hunched into themselves, mumbling mindlessly, and for all purposes, in a state of complete incapacity. This alone was the reason for Mr. Hamilton's purchase of the London field and the two guards permanently stationed outside the hole – a hole that led directly into that cavern.

"The prison could still be of some use," Eran muttered, his comment striking me, because of its intended meaning: If this deviant terrorizing the humans turns out to be an enemy, the prison would need to be reopened, at least as a temporary stop to hold the deviant.

I didn't have the nerve to contemplate that possibility further, or to react to Eran's evident remark about it. Instead, I moved to the right where a white armband with a swirl of color the hue of a clear, sunlit sky was pinned. Next to it, the placard read: Unifying cuff worn during The Great Battle, 2011, London.

"The battle in the London field has been named The Great Battle?"

One of Eran's eyebrows rose questioningly. "Was it not one?"

I turned back to the cuff, evaluating it, noting the speck of dirt, one tinted red, on its edge, and the memories of the assault flooded back to me.

A massive presence on both opposing sides had met in a clash that shook the ground and deafened the ears. Swords clashed, shards of ice flew, fire – its temperature so intense I could still remember its heat singeing my cheeks from yards away.

"Yes," I whispered, humbled. "It was."

I rotated my head back, viewing the wall and the staggering number of pieces attached to it.

"This is ..." I said and exhaled, only able to shake my head in amazement.

"A museum," Eran spoke the words for me. "Of our world."

Nodding lightly, still speechless, I leaned toward a piece of paper torn from a book and marked with black chalk, its placard signaling it came from the Book of Dossiers, a compilation of profiles of our enemies and a few of our own kind. The piece of parchment tacked to the wall had become scrap when it was torn free and its artist began a new rendering. It still had the outline of a face, a man with large teeth, a flat nose, and a long forehead, alongside the standard descriptions that had not been filled in. The sections for name, abilities, weaknesses, known accomplices, and past residences were blank.

As I reached to touch it, Eran's hand came up to stop me. "Just a second, Mr. Leroux takes a certain amount of pride in his collection … which you'll want to keep in mind as you see what's behind us."

Those words steered me in that direction, where the elements hanging from the wall caused me to draw a sharp breath and immediately step forward to close the gap.

The two simple pieces of wood, nailed into a cross, weathered into a splintering, bleached gnarl, was as beautiful as it had been when I last saw it, planted over my grave. Still readable were the letters down the center stake that formed my name: Magdalene.

"My cross," I whispered through an exhale.

"Removed so that your grave would remain safe."

"I can't believe it …"

"Mr. Leroux found its historical nature to be of inherent worth and asked to maintain ownership over it. I hope you don't mind."

"No, not at all," I said adamantly. "I'm glad I'm not the only one who values it."

Unable to tear my eyes from the wood, I remembered back to the first time I'd seen it and what happened immediately after it.

"You're trembling," Eran commented and wrapped his powerful arms around me.

It felt surreal to be held by him while remembering his death over my gravesite, even now, after so many other deaths and so many years between that moment and the one where we now found ourselves. As an Alterum, I sometimes struggled to accept there were both positives and negatives to our seamless eternal existence and the continuous, detailed memory of our past lives; but undeniably, I sometimes wished for blissful ignorance about what had happened to us and those we love – a state I had been able to experience for a brief time when I first arrived in New Orleans. The humans, I sometimes felt, were lucky.

"You're all right," I whispered, pressing my face to his body, needing the palpable feel of him.

"Yes, I am," he replied. "Maybe this is as good a time as any to get to why we're here."

I blinked, realizing that, yes, there was a purpose for our trip, other than to drudge up old memories. "And what is that? Another gift?" My joke fell flat, but he smiled out of courtesy anyway.

"In a manner of speaking," he said before coaxing my body to the left, toward the corner of the chamber we passed on our way in.

The sword hung straight, its sharpest point toward the earth, cleaned to a high sheen and glinting off the light dedicated to illuminating it.

"No," I exhaled, momentarily questioning my sight.

"Yes."

I stepped forward and, ignoring the rule about no-touching, swept it off the wall. In my hand, the gold and silver grip felt natural, an extension of my wrist, and as I carved the nearly four-foot sword through the air, it made a whisper, as if it were speaking to me, telling me "Hello, old friend, it's been a while."

"Far too long," I whispered.

"Yes, it has been. I thought you might be needing it … although I hope I'm wrong."

"How did it get here?" I asked, swinging around toward Eran, feeling my eyes burning with pleasure.

"Mr. Leroux found it, a few months back. I allowed him to have it for safekeeping."

"But you never told me," I said, sounding accusatory, which was legitimately how I felt.

"No, I didn't."

"Why?" I pressed.

He ducked his head and ran his fingers through his hair. The strands sprang back into place, shining in the golden light. I was distracted by them until I saw his concerned expression. "You won't like my answer."

"Tell me anyway."

"All right," he said after a brief pause, resigning himself to it. Given his demeanor, I braced myself. "Magdalene, you defend this world and those in it vehemently. You've given your life for them, you've inspired them, led them, trained them, acted as an example to which they try to meet. Both among the Alterums and the humans."

His voice trailed off, so I pressed, "But?"

"But you've always been independent of them. And maybe that's part of your allure. You walk among them, but you are not one of them. And they sense that. Maybe if you were inconsequential, someone on the periphery, someone who left no mark in their evolution, they probably wouldn't pay as much attention to you. But you showed them what was possible, what was possible in them, what they could be together. And that makes them want to be a part of you. This way," he motioned toward my sword hanging at my side, "they can be."

Taken aback, my chest tightening from nerves, I tried to speak in an audible voice, and failed. "You always make me sound more important than I am."

Eran smiled gently. "You don't see what we see."

A sudden inhale came from the door where Mr. Leroux was now standing, mouth ajar, as he stared at the sword in my hand. His shocked eyes rose to mine, where he saw no contrition.

Eran's warning ran through my mind: *Mr. Leroux takes a certain amount of pride in his collection.*

"Mr. Leroux," Eran began to explain but I interrupted.

"This sword has been mine for six centuries –" Then Mr. Leroux cut me off.

"Shhhh," he whispered. "Shhhh…"

Then he reached his hand out to place it on mine, the one holding the sword we both claimed ownership of. Lightly, his fingers settled on mine before being pulled back to his side.

"You are here because of zee Fallen One, yes?" he asked.

"We don't know if it's a Fallen –"

Mr. Leroux waved impatiently to quiet me, having already made up his mind on the winged target's motives and then halted to look up at me through his thick eyelashes, awaiting my answer.

"Yes, we are here to engage with him."

"Gud," he affirmed with a declarative nod. "Zen, may I wrap it for you?"

He held out his hands and nodded again, at his palms, encouraging me to release my sword. Hesitantly, I did and he whipped around to the chamber's interior door.

Eran exhaled audibly then and tipped his head, impressed at Mr. Leroux's leniency.

We followed the man to his desk where he began boxing my sword, which was a good idea, I realized. Carrying a visible sword around New Orleans could cause us some trouble.

"I vas in France before," Mr. Leroux reminisced as he worked on concealing my merchandise. "Paris. A beautiful city. Simply beautiful. It is why I chose zis accent," he pointed out, enunciating intentionally. "It was zen that I saw what a Fallen One could do. Just one of zem." He shivered despite the office being temperate. "I heard zee whispers of zat one making agreements and deals with zee royalty. Persuading zem to do zis and zat and I thought, eh," he said with a casual shrug. "What could one of zem do? He eez just one. Not much. Not much… And zen peepel are fighting in zee streets, peepel are dying, peepel are storming zee Bastille. And I know then what just one of zem can do." He finished by slowly shaking his head in pitying reflection.

"You were present during the Storming of the Bastille?" I asked.

He nodded, head remaining down, as he tied packing string around the long, narrow, wrapped box. "I vas. I lost a wife during zat revolution, but I saw a very lovely young woman who delivered a message to her for me."

My breath stopped as he continued.

"At her estate, weeth two dogs at her feet and Eran by her side."

I refilled my lungs quickly to clarify, "You're talking about me."

He nodded again, looked up, and lifted the box toward me.

"I've delivered a message for you?" I whispered, overcome.

"Oui, and now I deliver zis back to you," he said, holding the box higher, insisting I take it. "So zat you may prevent yet anozer battle, anozer needless round of bloodshed."

He fell quiet but remained pointed and deliberate in his stare.

"I'll try, Mr. Leroux," I whispered.

"Do not try," he replied. "Do."

I tipped my head at him and slipped my hands around the box. Eran smiled lightly at me as I turned with him toward the door. Mr. Leroux didn't say another word to us as he walked us back to the front but once there he took hold of one of my hands and kissed the top of my palm.

81

"Thank you, Mr. Leroux."

He nodded firmly and ushered Eran and me out the door. "Now go," he urged, "and take gud care of my sword."

"You bought a sword?" one of the drunks asked to the right of our feet, gawking up at the package I carried.

"Thought he only sold pieces of paper with paint on them," the other commented.

This offended Mr. Leroux enough for him to scream at them in French, words that were clearly obscenities, which only escalated as we walked back to my bike. Their screaming match only grew from there so that even the roar of my engine didn't drown them out. Only when we moved out into traffic did their voices fall away.

Eran, who was chuckling against me, from behind, directed me back through the French Quarter. While holding on to my sword, he directed me onto the interstate and we took the I-40 west before exiting and driving deeper into the bayou. The road turned bumpy and then the broken asphalt gave way entirely to rutted dirt. Trees, thick enough to blot out the sun, grew to become the dominant foliage on both sides of the road and when we stopped, the pungent fragrance of swamp water and moist earth surrounded us.

There were no parking spots outside the weathered, derelict building Eran had directed me to. In fact, there was no parking lot at all, so I pulled my bike to the shortest level of weeds lining the front and killed the motor. When I stood up, the weeds reached my shins.

The rain a few days earlier still saturated the area, enough to make steering my bike a challenge, so when my boots hit the ground they sank into their own footmark. Each trudge toward the door resulted in a slurping sound until we reached the dry cement block serving as a porch. We stomped the clumps from our feet, spraying the weeds living along its side and the discarded tire propped against the building's wall, and entered.

"What exactly are you shopping fo– ?" I asked as the door closed behind us, falling silent as the interior came into view. "Here?" I finished under my breath.

The single room was evidently a residence – housing a stove, bed, and refrigerator, which rattled and wobbled in a constant attempt to survive against its dilapidated state. But the room was also a store front, holding twenty or so glass display cases lined up in two rows with a main aisle down the center between them. None showed a speck of dust and each was lined with soft, pliant red silk where various forms of blades nested in no particular order or organization.

A woman sat in the back corner, overwhelmingly larger than and seemingly ready to consume the decrepit desk where she was hunched. But on standing, to a towering height that brought the crown of her head within an inch of the ceiling, I got a full view of her. Stocked with muscles larger than most men, a head twice the size of ours, and a massive nose flattened over her pinched lips, she seemed more of a living mountain than a human being. She tipped her head back for a better look at us, even though the thick, wiry blonde hair cut just above her shoulders was no actual obstruction to her sight.

"Finally…" she grumbled under her breath, a phrase that could have meant she was intolerantly waiting for her next customers and the wait had been long, but it carried a hint of impertinence that made it feel more personal to me.

She sauntered her hulking body down the side aisle and met us at the front.

"Miss Ingrine," Eran said, extending a hand to her.

She took it and pumped it once hard enough to rattle Eran's shoulder. "I'm –"

"I know who you are," she replied, waving him off. "And I know why you are here."

Eran's eyebrows rose. "You do?"

She frowned, perturbed by the insinuation she hadn't. "You want only the best."

Eran chuckled at himself. "Yes, yes, of course I do."

Miss Ingrine spun on her heels and led us between the cases. "Do you have honor, Eran?" she asked abruptly, her back to us.

While I would have bristled if the question had been sent at me, and likely followed it with a curt snap, Eran remained calm, replying simply, affirmatively, and with his own verbal blow. "I thought you said you knew of me."

Miss Ingrine snickered, although she seemed to respect him a bit more for it. She stopped at a case. "While my scimitars, katanas, rapiers, and falchions are all excellent, you strike me as a Viking kind of man."

"Yes." Eran nodded. "I would agree."

She carefully slid the glass door aside and painstakingly withdrew a gold handled blade adorned with crisscrossing gold ribbons wound around the handle and ending with a striking ornate knob at the top. It was lavish, robust, and made of detail that indicated it had been constructed for someone of importance.

"Joyeuse," she announced and extended it carefully to Eran.

Eran's head tipped downward, although he remained locked on Miss Ingrine, his mouth slightly ajar. "Are you certain?"

Again, her lips pressed into a frown at being questioned. "Quite. He gave it to me himself." As Eran continued his dubious stare, she sighed impatiently.

"Being its designer, he asked me to preserve it. After his death, I secured it in a safe, confidential site and on returning here resurrected it."

Sensing the tension, I leaned into Eran, who caught on to my confusion.

"Joyeuse is Charlemagne's personal sword," he explained.

My mouth fell open. "The man known as the father of Europe?"

"The very one," Eran said, his tone shifting subtly to quiet reverence. "So, the ones on display at the Louvre and in Vienna?" Eran hinted to Miss Ingrine.

"Counterfeits," she replied tersely.

Only then did Eran take hold of it, his palm sliding around the handle with easy confidence. He deftly maneuvered it to test its comradery with his own body, composing whistles through the air around us, before smiling lightly and handing it back to Miss Ingrine.

"Yes," he replied with an affirmed nod.

She tipped her head and withdrew the gold scabbard, one studded with antique stones, to slide the sword into its home. She laid it on the glass and turned to me.

"I see you have brought another's," she said, her eyes falling to the box Eran had handed to me before entering the store. "May I?"

I hesitated, but she made no abrupt aggressive gesture, despite this apparently being her natural tendency, and her patient stare won me over.

She delicately freed the paper at one end and slid the box onto the glass case. On opening it, she paused, evaluating it with a critical eye. Then her hands, large and seemingly clumsy, carefully lifted it with caring admiration. Her fingertips began to tenderly caress the blade's length, as it if were a living entity, who she deeply loved. She became lost in its sight, mesmerized until it was clear she has stepped into a private world that Eran and I were only privy to a peek. "Metal is an especially potent bit of nature," she murmured. "Versatile in form – of liquid, of solid – which can be shaped into various tools for humans. And those tools often oppose one another. It can provide shelter and it can be formed into devices that obliterate that shelter. It can defend and it can kill. In many ways, it is like nature itself, always seeking balance from the opposing poles within which it exists but has no control." She sighed reverently at the blade. "Like nature, it can be light or dark ... thoughtful in its approach to molding and impulsive ... forgiving and stubborn." With each word she shifted her bowed head between Eran and me, with me being on the undesirable end of her descriptions. I thought I was being sensitive until she finished. "It can create peace," she said and lifted her gaze to glare squarely on me. "And it can inspire war."

I reached out to take hold of my sword and pull it back to me, but she resisted.

"Metal in the wrong hands can be catastrophic," she warned briskly.

I felt the familiar feeling of anger wash over me and the coldness enter my eyes. "Anything in the wrong hands can be."

She blinked and her face took on a new expression, of disgruntled agreement. Her fingers unfolded from my sword and she stepped back.

Eran observed this odd exchange with reserved readiness, moving again only when Miss Ingrine had stepped back.

"Would you mind wrapping my purchase?" he asked, his tone steady.

"Of course," Miss Ingrine replied before picking up Eran's sword and scabbard, cradling it to her chest, spinning on her heel and marching to the desk in the corner.

Eran and I stayed rooted in place and quiet until she returned, but a silent exchange drifted between our eyes in which we determined that Miss Ingrine had chosen her profession wisely. Crafting blades was an admirable, and solitary, pursuit.

"It'll be no charge," she said on handing Eran his sword, now wrapped in the same coarse, brown paper as my box.

"I appreciate it, Miss Ingrine. And if we learn of anyone looking for a new blade, we'll send them your way."

She nodded cordially, although without a smile, and we left the store. Only then did my muscles release.

"Tense," I muttered, stepping onto my bike.

"I was ready," Eran replied, insinuating he had been alert to the woman's critical approach to me.

"Any ideas what that was all about?"

Eran shrugged.

"She mentioned war," I mused, staring into the trees.

"Maybe she thinks you'll prevent one."

"No." I shook my head, slowly, in contemplation. "She thinks I'll start one." My voice fell to a mumble as the realization came over me. "That's why she held onto my sword."

"Magdalene," Eran said, waiting for me to turn my head in attention before continuing. "Anyone who knows you knows that wouldn't be the case."

I hesitated.

"Now, back to the first store," Eran prompted. "Your gift awaits."

I started the motor, backed up into the soggy weeds, and headed for the Interstate, trying to shake the undeniable feeling that Miss Ingrine saw something in me that no one else had. Not yet.

Only the rush-hour traffic jarred my uneasiness, which required greater attention to negotiate than an open road; so we reached the vacant street east of the French Quarter just as the sun was setting. Shadows cast a darkness over the surrounding buildings, giving this quiet area of the city an eerie presence. Even our footsteps seemed particularly loud as we entered the store. Then it was silent again, absorbed in solitude, despite the destruction now surrounding us.

Every shelving unit had collapsed, product scattered the floor. The sconces along the wall were broken, oddly giving off more illumination now that the glass was no longer a hindrance. Pieces of shattered skulls, broken candles, and shards of glass lay everywhere. Tarot cards were strewn across the heaps as if someone had flicked them into the air. Across the demolition, the counter and cash register stood, the only objects untouched.

This time, Eran didn't call out.

For confirmation, I pointed to the back of my neck and shook my head in the negative.

He nodded but stealthily opened the box under his arm and gripped Joyeuse ready at the handle. I did the same with my sword.

Leaving the boxes at the door, we walked with vigilance to the front, careful not to stir anything made of metal or glass or risk giving anyone left in the store forewarning that we were approaching.

We stopped at the archway to the backroom and listened. My worst fear was that it would be quiet. Sobs would be a good sign. Because it meant that Madame Benoit who owned the shop had survived its destruction. When nothing stirred, I gripped my sword tighter to calm the fury swelling in me. Sensing it, Eran glanced back at me, saw my enraged eyes, and gave me a look that conveyed I needed to contain it. I brushed his suggestion aside with a sharp jerk of my head to the backroom. He appeared frustrated, but only until he stepped into the opening.

Instantly, a dagger flew through the arch, causing him to twist to the side in avoidance. I stepped forward, but his hand flattened and rose to stop me. When another two daggers came at him, he diverted them with an easy flick of his other wrist. Silence followed and then a surprised, hesitant voice called out.

"Eran?"

"Jameson? What the ... are you doing?" Eran shouted back. "Magdalene is with me. We're coming in. Don't throw anything at her."

"Funny," Jameson muttered.

Eran didn't lower his sword, Joyeuse, until he had surveyed the interior area, and neither did I. Once inside, we found Jameson, tall and slender with a tawny tan, standing on the opposite side of a small room lined with cardboard boxes. He brushed aside the straight blonde hair falling into his eyes and observed us closely as we entered. Next to him stood his girlfriend, Jocelyn. With traits directly opposite him, her pale skin and long, wavy, inky black hair, always reminded me of the old adage that opposites attract. She was keeping an eye on Madame Benoit, who weakly held onto the back of a chair.

"Is she all right?" I asked, and Madame Benoit nodded.

"Were you involved in that?" Eran motioned to the front of the store.

"No, unfortunately," Jameson replied flatly. "We may have been some defense."

"No one was hurt," Madame Benoit replied, weary but resolute.

"Can you tell us what happened?" I asked, stepping forward.

"We were just getting to that part," Jocelyn mentioned.

Madame Benoit finally dropped into the chair she'd been holding for leverage and closed her eyes. I thought she might cry but when they reopened there was only anger in them.

"He came in alone, hooded so I could not see his face. Walked to the register and then paced the counter. Back and forth. Back and forth. Slowly. Like a caged tiger. I asked him if he was seeking any particular item. He said, "Yes. Knowledge." And then he started asking about the four of you."

"Us?" Jocelyn blurted, although we were all equally struck by that news.

"About what you had bought recently. Weapons? Defensive measures? If any of you had bought anything in bulk."

"What did you tell him?" Jameson asked.

"The truth, that you had not. He then said something about a demonstration on declining if you should. He then simply went … went insane. And … And you see what he left behind."

"Do you recall any distinguishing characteristics about the man?" Eran asked, his eyes lit and expression filled with suspicion.

"You mean to ask if he was one of us," Madame Benoit stated. She shook her head but answered, "No, I cannot tell for certain. His only distinction was that he had an accent, a blend, which told me that he had traveled extensively."

During the brief pause that followed we watched Madame Benoit's head fall to her chest and one hand cup her forehead.

"Rest," she muttered to herself, as if coaxing her body to do as she was telling it.

"Yes, we'll have our people handle the cleanup, Madame Benoit, don't you worry," Jameson promised and received an appreciative squeeze by her hand for it.

Madame Benoit's head snapped up then and she hobbled across the room, opened a random cardboard box, and hauled out a large patch of black leather. "One merchandise remains," she said proudly to herself. Holding it as high as her hunched frame could, she carried it to me, placing it unsteadily against my shoulders so that the leather hung down the length of my body. Surprisingly, after what she'd been through, the satisfied smile of artisan pride eased her distraught face. "Yes, it fits."

With my fingers already helping to keep the fabric up, she turned away before I could thank her and shuffled up a concealed staircase near the back door. During that time, I realized what it was I now held. My suit. My black suit. The kind I wore each time I went to war with our enemies. Eran had another one made for me, complete with flexible leather, secured latches at my waist for additional weapons. Except that this newest version had an insignia embossed on the upper left arm, one that resembled the white and blue band hanging in Mr. Leroux's hidden museum closet, but with a pair of wings lifting that band and two words printed across the horizontal stretches: Defensor Piorum.

Glancing at Eran, I smiled, sending my thanks through the glow in my eyes. He tipped his head and a subdued, pleased grin crept up.

I nodded to the insignia, questioningly, and he tilted his head to the side for a better look before shaking it, confirming it had not been part of his request.

And I realized that Madame Benoit had just given us a name.

Jocelyn noticed our silent exchange and leaned to the side for a better view of what it was we were discussing.

"Defensor Piorum," she read. "Latin."

Jameson, who had been watching to make sure Madame Benoit reached the second floor safely, remarked, "Means Defender of the Righteous. Why? Where do you see it?"

Jocelyn motioned to me. "It's on the side of her suit."

Jameson's eyebrows rose curiously. "Well then, I'd say that's how the woman sees you."

Eran stiffened at his statement, something only I caught sight of as I was in the act of correcting Jameson.

"Us," I said. "That is how she sees us."

Eran nodded, his expression turning warmly, I knew he'd picked up on the fact that I had remembered what he'd told me in Mr. Leroux's museum and the fact that I had now acted on it.

"So now that you know why we're here…" Eran hinted.

"You saw the video at school, right?" Jameson asked. "I know you did because rumor has it you walked off school grounds."

"You heard about that?" I asked, stopping the folding of my new suit and looking up in surprise.

"We were in Forensic Science class when we saw you walk past," Jocelyn confirmed.

"And we heard about it at lunch," Jameson added.

"Of course," I muttered. School gossip was one of my peeves, especially because Eran and I had been the focus of it more than once.

"You know how they are," Jocelyn remarked, distinguishing themselves from the rest of the student body. And they *were* different.

Jameson and Jocelyn considered themselves witches, and had proven their skills of levitation and mind-reading several months back when we worked together to end the lives of seven Fallen Ones holding their world hostage. So, with certainty, they were verifiably different than those sitting in our high school classrooms.

"Anyways," Jameson went on to explain, "we knew why you left after seeing the video and determined we needed to prepare our defenses too. It's convenient you're here. We were going to stop by Ezra's house later to talk to you."

"To formulate a plan," Eran concluded.

"Or at least to discuss the beginnings of one. I'm not sure we have the knowledge we need to formulate one yet," Jameson said.

"Agreed. I'm working on that," Eran replied.

"Good." Jameson seemed relieved.

"There's something you should know," I ventured, and the three of them turned curiously to me. "About who he might be and about who you are."

Immediately catching on to the direction of my thoughts, Eran warned, "Magdalene."

"It's time," I said, concretely.

Still, he disagreed. "Magdalene, by telling them of their true background, you'll be –"

"Stunting their learning in this life. Yes, I'm aware. But they need to know who and what they are or there might be no world left in which to live that life."

Eran nodded. "Duly noted and on further thought … agreed."

I returned to Jameson and Jocelyn, who had been watching our debate openly entertained, but their humorous expressions fell when I spoke directly to them. "Your power doesn't come from the elements."

"You're right," Jameson concurred easily. "It comes from our ability to *manipulate* those elements."

Drawing out my reply, I countered slowly, cautiously. "Nooo."

"No?" Jameson said, offended that I might know more about his own kind than him.

Eran sent me a look to tread carefully, which I heeded. Educating someone about their own origins can be just as dangerous as leaving them to think they had no origin at all. "Your power was given to you before you were born, and you have likely used it each time you have visited here."

"Visited here?" Jocelyn mumbled. "As in earth?"

"Each time?" Jameson added.

"Most of us have fallen or been born into this world many times. Some of us are born without those recollections –"

"Reborns," Jocelyn noted.

I paused, impressed. "Yes. And there are others who enter this life knowing who and what we are, with memories of past lives."

"Alterums, such as yourselves," Jameson concluded. "Yes, we are well aware of them."

And I knew they were. Several months back, Alterums had been instrumental in the fight to free their world.

"And then there are others such as yourselves," I continued.

"Such as ourselves?" Jameson said, singling out the most disturbing insinuation.

So I drew a deep breath and laid it out before them. "Those who are Alterums but do not know it."

As Eran and I braced ourselves for their reaction, Jameson and Jocelyn traded dubious expressions torn between thinking I'd gone crazy or whether there was any validity to my declaration. They were remarkably methodical in everything they did, and related well to Eran for that reason.

"So by that logic," he said, remaining pensive, "you must believe that Jocelyn and I have wings."

"Appendages," I corrected him. "And, yes, I figure you do, but have never willfully extended them."

"For reasons of pure curtailment, so we can get back to more important matters, I'll play along."

"Jameson," Jocelyn scolded him for patronizing us and he turned humble.

"Sorry," he said. "I have this feeling we are on limited time."

"Yes, I get that feeling too," Eran said.

Jameson's arms briefly extended to the sides in a shrug. "All right, what do I do?"

"Roll your shoulders forward, elongating the area between your shoulder blades and, I imagine, you'll need to concentrate."

"On what exactly?" Jocelyn asked, already doing as Eran instructed.

"Pressing out what is flattened between your skin and muscles."

She stopped and tipped her head to the side. "Why does that sound gross to me?"

"Because nothing should actually *be* between your skin and muscles," I proposed.

She nodded and pointed with certainty at me, and resumed her practicing.

Jameson, who was by then hunched over, almost to the waist, and straining enough to make the veins in his neck bulge looked like a bodybuilder. He only needed to lift one knee and twist at the waist for the perfect stance.

Unable to help myself, I began to giggle. The three of them looked at me and I waved for them to continue. "Sorry, I'm sorry."

Then Jocelyn gasped, jabbing a finger toward Jameson's back.

There, two small mounds rose under his shirt, just between his shoulder blades.

"You're ... You're doing it, Jameson!" Jocelyn was standing now, eyes wide, mouth open.

"It's..." he gasped, "It's..." Exhaling, he collapsed forward, catching himself on his knees. "I can't ... I can't go any further."

"Well if it's any consolation, the hardest part is over," Eran assured.

Jameson gave him a look of disbelief from his bent position, still panting.

"You two," Eran said to Jocelyn, whose face was fixed into a shocked expression, "practice. Spread the word to your people. I'll work on information gathering."

She nodded, speechless now.

I did the same, contemplating my method of contribution. "And I will – "

"And you," Eran said, turning toward me. "I need *you* to fall asleep."

5   IMPROMPTU MEETING

Eran and I entered the house our usual way, through the kitchen, which was now dark and strangely absent of the aroma of brewed coffee and the fervor of argument between Felix and Rufus.

"They're not back from the Square yet," I mumbled, my nickname for Jackson Square which had been built in the French Quarter to herald one of the country's presidents but had evolved into a four-sided plot of lush green grass surrounded by a moot of pavement and an outside ring of active shops and lively, open-windowed restaurants. It was also where my housemates and I conducted our business – Rufus selling caricatures, Felix performing palm readings, and me delivering messages between the living and the dead.

"Ezra must be reporting in to her supervisor," Eran added.

I nodded and we headed into the living room and up the staircase to my bedroom door. To my surprise, he trailed me in, and to my disappointment, he headed directly for the wing-back chair. With my orders clear, I marched to my bed, kicked off my boots, and slid out of my jeans before laying down and noting the distance of ten feet or more between us. It felt like an empty gulch.

He was staying within eyesight range for my security, I realized, but he had no intention of taking advantage of the empty house – not when I should be unconscious in the next few minutes.

"I fall asleep better with you beside me," I remarked nonchalantly before laying down and waiting for his next move.

"That wasn't subtle," he replied.

"It wasn't meant to be."

He chuckled and it took him a few seconds of tense internal debate, but then he stood and moved to the bed. He propped the pillows and sat up against them, as I slipped into the bend at his waist to rest my head against his taut stomach. There was a brief pause in his breathing when we touched and then a slow, measured inhale. My head rose with it, and sank with his exhale, and rose again, where the paced, comforting series of waves began lolling me to sleep.

"You tensed up," I whispered.

"Can you blame me, considering where your head is located?"

I laughed softly. "Not now, back in Madame Benoit's store." I slid my head up to rest again his shoulder.

"Thank you," he said, commenting on my adjustment.

"You're welcome." Musing on how both of us had experienced life inside older, aged bodies once before, I mumbled against his chest, "I imagine living in a younger body comes with certain challenges."

He laughed under his breath. "Magdalene, it doesn't matter what age I am, I still respond to you that way."

A slow smile crept across my face. "Do you notice how much easier it is to move in our bodies when they are younger?"

"I do."

"And how, even at the age we are now, skin feels heavy, like canvas blankets drenched in water, weighing us down?"

"Yes."

"I feel that distinction every time I wake up."

His head shifted for a better look at me, but I wasn't sure if he was successful. "You never mentioned that."

"Sometimes it takes me a few minutes to calibrate myself here. I have to shove aside and ignore the way this body feels oppressed. It's easier on the other side."

"It's been a while," Eran murmured, "but I remember."

"Even with our appendages, gravity makes it all cumbersome."

Ordinarily, Eran would laugh at the paradox but not today. He sensed a seriousness in me, shifting slightly to try and catch my expression.

I drew in a substantial breath and tried to exhale the concern I felt. It didn't work. "They think of us as heroes, Eran, as Defensor Piorum."

He hesitated, his breath pausing for a few beats.

"There you go again," I pointed out. "You're tensing up."

"Humph," he muttered in an attempt to deflect it.

"That's twice, when the phrase Defensor Piorum has been brought up. You don't think it suits me, do you?"

He laughed cynically under his breath. "I've never known anyone *better* suited."

"Then why the hesitancy?" When he didn't reply, I reinforced, "If I see an enemy, I'm going after him. I'm not one to sit on the sidelines."

"No, you're not. When it comes to danger you're like a moth to flame. You'd fly through a Category 5 hurricane if someone were in trouble."

"And you wouldn't?"

"You know I would."

"Yes, you would. So I don't understand your reluctance over the phrase Defensor Piorum."

I felt his body stretch and his head knock lightly against the headboard where he laid it. "Magdalene," he said, sounding more tired than I felt. "It isn't the phrase, it's the meaning."

"Defender of the Righteous?" I translated, confused.

"What do defenders do?" he asked.

"Defend."

"Against what?"

"An enemy."

"And what is an enemy bent on doing?"

"Destroying its opposition."

"And what happens if that opposition, that defender is you?" he concluded.

It came together for me then. "You're still worried about me."

"Always," he said, his emotions strained. "Magdalene, always. I am in love with you. It goes with the territory."

"Eran," I sighed. "I can't be harmed."

"Anyone can be harmed," he replied flatly, reminding me of our conversation on my balcony in the early morning.

It was hard to argue with someone who for nearly his entire existence had lived in the realm of hurting others. A certain amount of knowledge is always picked up when evaluating enemies, and universal truths are often discovered through the combining of that knowledge.

"And I've had enough of seeing you harmed." His emotions were raw in his voice – a deep blend of desperation, anger, and resolution.

I tightened my arm, which rested across his chest,

increasing my hold on him, and his tense muscles eased. "I love you too," I whispered.

He drew in a deep breath, exhaled, and kissed the top of my head, a tender pressure that sent a wave of heat through me.

Knowing where my mind and body were leaning, he charmed me with a gentle command. "Sleep."

I groaned, moved deeper against him and drew in his scent, of fresh wind and wood, until it no longer filled my nose and the sounds of breathing were replaced with subdued, whispered conversations.

Again, I groaned, although this time it was because I felt the cool, hard bench against my head instead of Eran, confirming that I had accomplished part of what he had wished – fallen asleep and awakened in the afterlife.

"Magdalene," someone implored urgently and the stench of stale tobacco and fresh alcohol hit my face.

I brushed my hand through the air, trying to stir it away. "Really, Alban? Couldn't you opt for a more pleasant personal aroma? You have the choice on this side," I reminded him.

"Why would I do that?" he asked, genuinely bewildered.

I opened my eyes to his overgrown, shaggy beard and two small eyes peering over it. Beside him and a step back stood Ariela, his close friend. Both were squat with Alban rotund and her slender, and while he had masses of hair covering his body, she did the same with jewelry. Her neck and arm cuffs sparkled with multi-colored jewels as she chastised him. Both were messengers, but didn't seem to have any sense for urgent deliveries.

"Alban, stop. Give her room to stand, at least." To me, she explained briefly, "He has a bet going with Caius and wants you to weigh in."

"Another one?" I waved him aside. "Don't you two ever get tired of wagers?"

"Never," he growled loudly, from behind a smug smile. "Now, Caius thinks the United States government would pull up and study the Fallen Ones from that hole you sent them into if they knew –"

"Alban," I interrupted, already sitting up and preparing to stand.

"Find someone else?" he surmised.

"I'd appreciate it."

He shrugged and lobed off to find another victim, his feet never actually reaching the ground as he hovered several inches over it.

He had plenty of choices. The Hall of Records, where I awoke in the afterlife every time I slept on earth, was filled today. Small groups and busy individuals floated down the arched hallway, the hems of their togas, dresses, and cloaks fluttering at their airborne feet, some pulling scrolls of places where people had died from the countless pockets lining the three-story walls while others were bent over observing the scrolls they had already found and unraveled. No one sat on the white concrete benches lining the hall, as these were reserved for those returning from earth for the evening, and because rest of any kind wasn't actually required in the afterlife.

The Hall of Records was a cooperative meeting place where – when messengers weren't pulling scrolls from the pockets embedded along every square inch of the walls and delivering messages to those named on those scrolls – laughter and conversation were the common sounds. So it was not surprising to me when Ariela sighed as she watched Alban move in on an unsuspecting visiting educator. "We'll be pulled back to St. Petersburgh soon, and he'll start up there with the humans."

St. Petersburgh was where she and Alban were residing, working on carrying messages between the living and the dead for the people on that side of the world. In fact, nearly every messenger had scattered across the globe from Sydney, Australia to Seattle, Washington, setting up their message delivery services in the cities in which they settled. I was the only one working the New Orleans area.

The mention of a deadline prompted me to roll my shoulders forward and release my appendages. I was in the air before they had even fully uncurled.

"I need everyone's attention," I said loudly, instantly earning it.

Out of courtesy, no one spoke above a delicate whisper in the Hall of Records and as I broke the serenity, I realized no one had ever done so in my presence. In fact, all heads turned toward me were showing expressions of curt irritation or curious surprise.

"I imagine some of you have heard of the one with appendages parading in front of the humans on earth. Some of you may have even seen the videos." More than a few heads nodded while those from the farthest distance raced forward – the force of their movement causing a slight uplift in the subtle breeze that continually drifted through the hall. Their urgency made me realize that Eran, our housemates, and I weren't the only ones with a keen interest in the man's disruptions. "Out of caution, Eran has declared that Measure 103 should be enacted." Immediately, murmurs filtered through the crowd. Only Alban seemed confused.

"What's Measure 103 again?" he called out.

Having found Jerod and Dante in the crowd to question about his wager, they stood beside him, and their faces – which were normally turned down in disgust at others – only deepened at Alban.

"All messengers are to immediately reunite with their original guardian and to remain under their protection until further notice."

"What's this about? Is this more than just a rogue Alterum?" someone called out.

"Yes, what do you know?" another added.

As an explosion of questions came my way, the group closed in toward me in their eagerness for answers. Again, I waved them down and spent the next few minutes explaining the little that Eran and I had learned. They seemed unsatisfied – with both Jerod and Dante pinching their lips and rolling their eyes – and as they dispersed to wait for the strange pull of their souls back to their bodies on earth, a few hung back in groups to discuss it all further with disgruntled frowns. Searching the crowd, I found only two messengers weren't present, one being my most ardent supporter. They would need to know about Eran's decree, too, so I searched for a scroll marking one of their names and moved my finger across the curved print. Instantly, the Hall of Records fell away like grains of sand blown in the wind and I found myself moving at the speed of a jet plane over provinces of the afterlife that had been populated by other souls.

I caught sight of a carnival swarming with ancient dinosaurs, illuminated rides, and souls painted in body paint and brightly colored feathers. Their clamor rose high enough that I could hear them from overhead. A few territories away, a tropical island with a small shoreside town was engulfed in flames. Surrounded by tall-mast ships, it looked like the Golden Age of Piracy was being relived, with one significant exception. In this place, anyone impaled with a blade would stand again, heal, and return to their role-playing. They were in my path, causing me to soar directly through them, where I noted the smell of burning wood and felt the breeze of a blade as it passed by my ear. When I came to a sudden stop, it was in a province entirely different, this one made solely on a broad white canvas of nothingness. Only one structure existed here. A coliseum. My path ended inside an observer's box as souls filled the theater before me with several hovering overhead in groups awaiting the performance's start.

"Magdalene?" Hoffstedler said to my right, his voice tainted with confusion. His careful, patient almond-colored eyes evaluated me curiously from below a head of chestnut hair. I had seen him in his older years on earth in past lives in which his head was covered in chalk-white hair and his skin creased with wisdom lines, but he was still youthful on earth as a middle-aged man and here in the afterlife he kept himself to a boyish twenty-something. His eyes gleamed back at me, waiting for an explanation on my arrival into a province I would never venture to without reason.

"Magdalene," Hermina's strong, controlled voice encircled me as her arms wrapped warmly around my shoulders before releasing me. Standing back, she surveyed me with hazel eyes and tipped her head in a quizzical gesture, letting her thick, straight mane of auburn hair fall off her slender shoulder. Here, where bodies were formed from thought, there was no need to adjust ourselves for comfort, but habits were hard to break and more than once I'd caught souls making minor corrections which would only be needed on earth. Keeping with Hoffstedler, the love of her existence, she too was younger here, and her hair much longer. "We've been missing you in the Hall recently," she said in a way that led me to believe she was leading in to a far more important topic.

"Yes, different timetables, but we're getting your postcards back in New Orleans."

"Excellent, we'll be pulled back soon yet again, so

you have limited time to tell us what you've come to tell us." The last half of her statement was drowned out by the roar of the crowd even as she pitched her voice to overcome it. Hermina frowned and turned to her host.

The weathered, heavily-tattooed woman was sitting with her feet propped on the railing, a cigar in her mouth, grinning widely enough that her gold-capped incisor glinted. "Earth Atmosphere Modulation," she shouted. "Like you've done with your province." She tipped her head to me. "Doesn't allow for minimizing voice decibels."

I didn't know anyone else was using my trick to mimic earth's physical limitations – gravity, volume, etcetera. I applied it to better train against our enemies, who resided in that environment, but couldn't understand why this woman thought it was any value. Until she stood up and the crowd quieted.

"I would like to extend our thanks to this match's competitors. Known as historic leaders in their own right, each has proven their worth on the battlefield. Fierce, terrifying, and notorious, they have developed legendary status on earth. But which shall be worthy of victory now? Without their troops? Facing their competitor alone? They have agreed to compete in an earth-simulated environment and have opted for hand-to-hand combat as their style of fight. Please welcome to my arena the very man who sacked Rome, who came to be known as the 'master of soldiers', and was nicknamed Alaric the Barbarian. Please welcome … Alaric the Visigoth king!" A portion of the crowd roared in what seemed to be enthusiasm –" and the man who founded the Mongol Empire – the largest contiguous empire in history stretching across what is now known as Central Asia and China. But you will know him by his earth name … Genghis Khan!" The other half of those present made the same level of praise for their competitor and I leaned toward Hermina, slightly shocked.

"You've come to watch this?"

In answer, she turned to Hoffstedler and nudged him.

"Hmm? Oh, yes." He'd been dragged into the glamour of it all too. He paused to watch the competitors enter the arena, each making their own ritzy spectacle.

"Hoffstedler!" Hermina sighed.

"Of course, yes. Jaqueline —"

Their host jerked her head over her shoulder and demanded a correction. "Jack."

"Right, Jack," Hoffstedler started again, addled. "I have a message from your ..."

Again, the crowd suffocated all words from the air.

"That old coot?" Jack shouted and rolled her tongue over her gold tooth. Swinging her hand into the air, the gesture ignited the crowd and turned the two opponents in the arena into clashing bodies. "What's he want?" Jack called out to Hoffstedler.

Hoffstedler leaned in and delivered the message he'd come from earth to pass on. When his lips stopped moving, Jack tossed her head back and bellowed laughter.

By this point, Alaric had a gash streaming blood on his right forearm and Genghis Khan was limping. As all good warriors do, each was using their weaknesses to their advantage. Alaric's height allowed him great leverage across the ground while Genghis Khan's towering frame helped him own the field of attack from above. The sight of a fight brought another wave of urgency over me.

"Hermina," I said, growing impatient just as Hoffstedler stood back.

With his message delivered, they gave me their

undivided attention.

"Eran has called for Measure 103, hasn't he?" Hermina asked.

"Yes," I said, surprised she had deduced my message.

"The one terrorizing the humans isn't an Alterum," she declared, which even in this place sent a jolt through me. Hermina moved among the Alterums, developed relationships with them, knew them. If anyone could make that determination, it was her.

"How do you know?"

Her answer was blunt, and slightly stung. "You are the only recluse here, Magdalene. Everyone else's business is widely discussed. If an Alterum was disgruntled enough to contrive this, we'd have an inkling of an idea who."

"And there isn't one," I concluded.

"Not even the most remote," she replied and settled back to evaluate me. "Do you need us? We can be there within hours."

"No, it's safer if we remain separated for now."

She nodded, once, sharply. "We'll locate our guardians as asked."

"Magdalene, you know this is just the start. His desperation in seeking the humans' attention reveals he has a far greater objective in mind."

"You're not alone in that belief." I didn't add that it was Eran who shared it with her.

Then they were gone, their presence in the afterlife having been swept back to earth where they would inhabit their palpable bodies for another day.

I sighed loudly and Jack twisted in her chair. "I know," she yelled over the din, a frown on her face but enthusiasm in her eyes. "I'm wanting the other to win too!"

I couldn't care less about the competition. We could

be facing a far greater battle. I forced a smile, extended my appendages and flew toward the Hall of Records. Halfway there I made a detour and angled for my province until I could see the jungle and the New York street where my combat skills were tested and the half-moon beach of golden sand and soft, warm, aqua water where I recuperated. This scene had greeted me on every death, had nurtured me when I was tired and lonely. It had been my sanctuary. And now, as I surveyed the world I'd built, entirely designed around an enemy who may or may not be loose, it was inadequate. It did not reflect the world we live in today, and therein was the problem.

I held up my hand, preparing to gesture away all that lay before me. It wasn't necessary, given that thought built my world and it was all that was required to destroy it. But the gesture allowed me time and that split-second was something I needed.

If I did this, if I wiped clean the details of what lay before me, down to a blank slate, I would be agreeing with Eran, that we are facing not just an Alterum inconsiderately acting out a wicked streak but an entirely new enemy.

Eran leaned on the side of caution, which meant he worked at being ready if and when a situation arose. It was one of the reasons he'd gained trust from so many others. Because of this, he was tasked with protecting the lives of those in his legion, my life, and the lives of Reborns who were as naïve as babies to dangers that had surrounded them on earth for so long. He would err on the side of caution now. And the fact was, I trusted him also, a trust that had been built across lifetimes over the course of surviving impossible odds. But I refuse to be a mindless sycophant or damsel in need, so I needed to answer the question that remained:

Did I believe he calculated this risk correctly?

My hand lowered.

Yes, yes I did. I believed it.

I knew this because I agreed with Eran implementing Measure 103 – it was the only reason I carried his message to the messengers. Until this moment, I never before conceded to the idea that messengers required guardians. I was repelled by the idea. But it was more than my acquiescence on an issue I had never acquiesced to before. It was that I had a terrible, but undeniably concrete feeling that something tragic was about to happen.

I raised my hand again, swept it across the jungle and dark city street, stopping at the edge of my beach. That held too many memories. And then I lowered it to my side. I would rebuild – once I knew what kind of an enemy we were dealing with.

I then made my way to Eran's province, landing on the porch to his log cabin built as a replica of the one he'd constructed for us in the Appalachians on earth. Its musky, wooden smell filled the air, mingling with the pine needles from the towering trees that surrounded the area and the fresh, pungent moist dirt, dampened by a storm that is never seen but always perfectly timed to have just passed. The hushed pouring of water over rocks, where a stream sprang from the distant, jagged mountain tops cloaked in misty, white clouds, ran down to the small, tranquil lake where the cabin sat.

Two Adirondack chairs were placed, as usual, near a small campfire on the shore, but I chose to sit on the cabin steps, petting Annie and Charlie – our two Dogue de Bordeauxes – as they laid on either side of my legs, their noses almost touching, and listening to the lap of the lake before me and the squeal of the hawks coming down from the mountains to soar over the water.

At some point, I lowered my eyelids and when I felt the familiar pull drawing me back to my body on earth –

like an outstretched rubber band attached to my back – and the peaceful smell of pine and fresh dirt was gone with one inhale and replaced with the smell of rain clouds and the streets of New Orleans, I reopened my eyes. Eran sat on the edge of my bed, watching me with steady, unwavering attention, as if the world would wait for him as he waited for me.

"Pleasant night?" he asked with a faint smile, one eye remarkably translucent, as a ribbon of morning light laid across his face.

"For the most part."

His forehead creased as he turned curious. "The messengers didn't harass you about my Measure 103?"

"Oh, no, they did."

He gave me a sympathetic smile.

I shrugged. "I'm used to dealing with difficult messages. I once had a woman attack me while I conveyed a message from her husband on earth who told her that she was his least favorite wife."

Eran grinned. "I'm figuring she learned that you had adept defensive skills."

I nodded. "Very quickly."

He chuckled. "I enjoy hearing about situations in which you defend yourself," he murmured, gazing at me.

"Alleviates your fears for me?"

"Some fears … Some of the time."

"Maybe a day will come when you will no longer worry about me or my safety."

"No," he replied simply. "It won't."

I smiled back at him, having expected that answer.

He had turned skeptical eyes toward my French doors, intently surveying the sky beyond them, as I noted, "You have bags under your eyes. Did you get any sleep?"

His lips shifted into a smile, but it was strained. "Not

much. Lots of messages on this side as well," he explained.

"You had visitors last night?"

"A few."

That news made me push myself to a sitting position, where I leaned against the headboard for a better view of him.

"What did they know?"

Eran thought briefly and I realized he was trying to condense the information to a digestible amount before speaking. "He appeared first over Germany, did nothing more than hover. That incident wasn't caught on video. His next appearance wasn't either. The following day, same location, same time, he stayed there until Germany's Luftwaffe –" He paused. "Which means –"

"Air force," I said. "Go on."

He smiled with a light sense of pride and continued. "They scrambled their jets, he took off, they followed him to the edge of their airspace, they turned back and he kept going. The next day, same thing, although that time the Americans tracked him. And the rest you know." He exhaled and leaned forward to rub his hands roughly down his face. Speaking through his palms, his voice turned angry. "If only I could find the damn moron. Tell him to stop this nonsense. Before someone really gets hurt."

"You think he might be an Alterum?"

He sat up again and shook his head uncertainly while it remained tipped toward the floor. "No, no actually I don't."

"I know you don't," I whispered.

"You don't either," he said, raising his eyes to meet mine.

"No," I acknowledged quietly. "But you knew that about me before I did."

He agreed with a nod. "I did."

"Will you kill him or imprison him?"

Eran's lips pinched tight with tension. "A strong part of me wants to send him back to the grave we left him in, but capture it will have to be."

"Would make it easier for you to learn how he escaped," I agreed.

Eran swung an impressed gaze at me.

"Yes, Eran," I sighed, "I've spent how many centuries with you? I was bound to pick up a few strategies."

Standing to avoid his amused stare, I started across my room for the closet.

"I'm glad you did," he replied, humor in his tone.

By the time I pulled out an 80's rock band tee-shirt, jeans, and my biker boots, the squeal of the bed springs had not come. I thought of my new black leather suit hidden under my mattress and how much I'd rather wear it than cotton. Emerging from the closet, I found Eran continuing to observe me, his expression subdued again. His somber eyes drifted from my face down the length of my body, covered only in a long tee-shirt.

"You really do take my breath away, Magdalene."

I stopped, suddenly self-conscious as to how I looked. From the full-length mirror propped to my right, I could tell my chocolate-colored curls were a twisted nest and my naturally pale face had red blotches across my cheeks.

"Sometimes," he said, sighing loudly as he stood, "I dislike that you leave your body during the night."

As he headed for the door, I asked seductively, "What would you do if I didn't?"

He stopped and angled his solemn face to me. "That is a question more serious to me than you know."

I tipped my head toward him. "Enlighten me."

He hesitated before strolling directly for me, halting within inches. Staring down, his heat and scent

113

surrounded me, bringing with it familiar peace followed by a wave of excitement. When he spoke it was calmly, quietly, contradicting the burning in his eyes.

"There are times when I watch you sleep. You don't breathe. There is no rise and fall of your chest, no pulse in your neck. When I first noticed it, not in this lifetime but several lives back, it made me grip your arms, which of course you didn't feel, and call out your name, which you didn't hear. You were cold to the touch and your skin was firm, congealed. In the dark, it took on a different shade. No one warned me, any of us guardians, no one thought to, on what happens to messengers when you visit the afterlife, so I stayed at your side, my eyes never leaving your face, waiting for the sun to rise, for you to return, terrified that you wouldn't. It was the first time I felt completely and unequivocally helpless. I wasn't me in that span of time, not until I saw you stir, and then I stood back and regained my composure."

"I remember," I whispered, the words slipping from me unintentionally. "You were standing, away from me, but watching, with a nervous grin."

His grave, handsome face moved into that subtle countenance and then he confessed, "I didn't want you to know how much I cared." That revelation warmed me inside, then he blinked and his expression fell away to sobriety again. "The hours before that first inhale, that first flare of your nostrils, that lift of your collarbone were the longest hours of my existence, Magdalene, and in that time, I thought about what I would do if you were gone, having passed to the other side. Would I carve out a life of my own? Would I await my own death, living a senseless life in this hollow world? That internal debate was concluded within the length of a breath. I knew right away I would cease to exist in any constructive manner without you with me. And I acted on that decision the first time we were separated on this earth."

"I remember that too," I said, barely audible as the memories of that time swept through me.

"From then on, from that first breath on that first morning I watched you wake, all I've ever wanted to do was drag my fingertips across your skin and coax back its color and movement, leave a trail of kisses across your forehead as you draw life back into your lungs and whisper into your ear how much I love you until your eyelids flutter open. So, my answer to what would I do if you never left your body? Feel overwhelming gratitude to the fate that allowed it. But that's not the question you're truly asking, is it?"

"No," I said honestly.

"What you're asking is what would I do if I had the power to wake you?"

I nodded. "Yes, that's what I'm asking."

He grinned suddenly, mischievously, brightening the moment. "Everything in my power, Magdalene, damn well everything within my power."

He spun on his heels and marched from the room as I clutched my clothes, wrinkling them with my fingers that had curled tightly into my palms.

My first deep breath came a few minutes later and by that time I heard the resistant squeal of the floorboards outside my room. I dressed quickly and, coincidentally, met Eran in the hallway. He held back a grin – knowing the physical tension he'd left me under – and took the stairs down as if nothing had passed between us at all. I followed his squared, powerful shoulders in through the kitchen door where it was surprisingly empty. The lights were out, the stove was cold, even the coffee pot was turned off.

Eran and I paused at the threshold.

"Eerie," I muttered.

"Hmmm," he mumbled. "Yes."

"Wonder where they —" I interrupted myself as my eyes drifted to a note on the kitchen table. Picking it up, I informed Eran, "Ms. Beedinwigg and Mr. Hamilton asked to meet with them. We weren't home or they would have had us join. There are pancakes in the refrigerator. Chocolate chip by Rufus and rhubarb and skunk meat by Felix, who would like to add that they don't smell."

"Hmmm," Eran replied again as he gradually moved to peer through the window over the sink. The day was overcast, draping the trees outside in darkness and stealing the color from their leaves.

"Wait." My head snapped up to look at Eran. "We weren't home?"

"No," Eran replied, moving to check the backyard, pulling aside the curtains at the door leading to it.

"Where did we go?"

"Our cabin in the Appalachians."

Concluding what he'd told me earlier, I added, "So you could speak with your informants privately."

"Yes."

"And how did I get there and back?"

"I carried you."

His answer was entirely feasible. With my soul leaving my body when I sleep, I could have been flown to the moon and back and wouldn't have had a clue about it. It was one of the reasons Eran remained awake during the night when he felt I was at risk.

"Eran, stop surveilling through the windows. I'll tell you if I feel any danger."

His shoulders relaxed slightly as he finally rotated to face me. "Do you want the pancakes?"

"No."

"We should go then."

"What are you not telling me?" I demanded, and when he didn't answer, I concluded it myself. "You knew our housemates were gone, didn't you? You saw Felix's neon green car was missing from the driveway."

He nodded.

"And you know to be cautious because Ms. Beedinwigg and Mr. Hamilton wouldn't call a meeting with our housemates unless it was absolutely necessary, which is why you're checking the windows."

He nodded again.

I'd exhausted my interrogation and stood awkwardly silent in the center of the kitchen. "All right," I said, more to myself than to him, pushing back an uneasy feeling. "All right."

He extended his hand to me and I took it, and we walked alert out to the shed. Eran handed me a helmet and picked up his own, and we latched them to our heads, as he and I glanced at the workbench to our left. Obscured behind decades of cobwebs, dust, and a slight covering of mold, littered with empty paint cans and miscellaneous tools that had now rusted over, it appeared benign. That was the reason Eran chose to hide our swords below it, where he tucked them into the far-left corner underneath, concealed by the shadows. It was odd to see such prized possessions – coveted around the world – leaning against a rickety wall, surrounded by filth. It felt even more odd to leave them behind, both of us knowing we couldn't carry them where we were headed.

We straddled my bike, I turned the engine, and we drove out to the street. Refraining from our traditional stop at Mr. LeFrau's bakery, with each of us too anxious to reach Ms. Beedinwigg, we drove directly to our destination. She would be at school this time of day, performing her rituals and following her schedule in case anyone was watching; so, after we pulled to a stop in the parking lot next to Felix's car – it's bright lime color and the fuzzy dice hanging from the rearview mirror too notable to miss – we headed directly for Ms. Beedinwigg's office.

It was quiet as usual, a small Italian woman in her sixties filing paperwork at the line of grey cabinets against the wall. She tipped her head at Ms. Beedinwigg's door and Eran knocked politely. A second later, it opened to Rufus towering just inside, his heavy, tattooed arms and massive chest filling most of the doorway.

He leaned in quickly and whispered, "Careful treadin'. Blimey, she's mad."

Ms. Beedinwigg appeared behind him, curtly motioned for us to step inside, and swept the door closed. Dressed in one of her traditional drab dresses, with her auburn hair loosely piled on her head and glasses hanging from a delicate chain around her neck, it was clear she was in disguise. Only her military boots peeking out from below the hem of her dress gave any indication that she wore a black leather combat suit beneath her loose fabric.

"It's about time," she scolded.

"What's this about, Ms. Beedinwigg?" Eran asked, remaining calm, even as my temper flared at her attitude.

She had moved back to her desk, where she spun around and evaluated him. "You didn't bring them with you," she replied cryptically. "Good."

"No," Eran said, continuing his polite demeanor, "we wouldn't think of breaching your security protocols."

"Bring what?" Felix asked, shuffling his gaze between Ms. Beedinwigg and Eran.

Rufus, who stood beside him, sighed loudly and rolled his eyes. "She just got done explainin' they went on a shoppin' spree yesterday!"

Felix smiled smugly and retorted, "So ... you don't

know either."

Rufus scowled at him and fell silent.

Taking pity on them both, Ezra, who had been standing silently in the corner, explained, "Ms. Beedinwigg is referring to the swords and suit you two purchased yesterday."

"How did you know?" I asked, pivoting toward Ms. Beedinwigg, "where we've been?"

She adjusted her glare to pin it on Eran. "You think you're the only one with scouts?" She huffed. And just in case he answered in the affirmative, she snapped, "You're not."

Eran, whose body had fallen into stoic resilience since we entered Ms. Beedinwigg's office, asked quietly, "Where is Mr. Hamilton, Ms. Beedinwigg?"

"He said he would be running late." She exhaled through her frustration and sank slowly into her desk chair, while she clearly tried to reign in her emotions and return to the reserved, parental demeanor we knew her by. "He doesn't need to be here to begin. I'll fill him in later. And I'd really like to know," she said, her voice tightening, "exactly what you all know and aren't sharing. Because I can guarantee that a purchase of the Joyeuse sword and retrieval of Magdalene's sword means we're dealing with something significant." She paused and shook her head. "You should have come to me, Eran. I have a right to know when people I care about are in danger."

Eran wasn't paying attention to her any longer, and neither was I. His behavior had turned stiff and impassive, and I only saw this in him when he was assessing a threat. With his focus having shifted to be less in the room to whatever was above it, I drew my head back toward the ceiling and listened. Beside me, our housemates did the same, with only Ms. Beedinwigg diverting. She swiveled in her chair to look out the window.

The compression pulse began in my head; rhythmic and powerful, it traveled down to my chest while growing louder and drawing closer. By the time it came into view, everyone was staring through Ms. Beedinwigg's office window where the school grounds stretched across a field to a wall at the property's edge. Between it and us, the source of the sound lowered into view, steadily and with commanding authority.

"Ms. Beedinwigg," I called out over the rotors' loud pulsations, "why is a United States Army Chinook helicopter landing on our school lawn?"

"Weapons, Ms. Beedinwigg," Eran stated tersely as if he were insinuating she might have them.

She stood warily as the wheels touched down and the wide door opened across the tan fuselage. When twenty men dressed suspiciously in Army Ranger combat gear streamed out, rifles in hand, she reached below her desk and withdrew two sai blades, her preferred weapon of choice.

"Eran, Magdalene," she said, handing each of us the pointed, three-pronged metal blades before revealing that she had two more for herself under the desk. She rotated the weapons effortlessly in her hands, positioning them for striking, and then the glass window shattered behind her.

6 SIEF

"For the twelfth time, I'm just a high school senior."

The water glass set before me looked quenching but I wasn't about to place it against my parched lips – not after seeing what they used to subdue Eran and my friends. After breaking through Ms. Beedinwigg's office window, they sent weaponized darts into the chests and shoulders of everyone in the room. I was the sole exception, getting a front row seat at seeing the people I love crumple to the ground like ragdolls. Eran was stepping in front of me when the dart hit him above the collarbone. He didn't even have time to pull the needle from himself before dropping to the tiled floor. I screamed and ran for Eran when something tripped me. I fell forward, the weight of various ropes suddenly straddling my back. I reached for them and my fingers found freedom through the holes only to be held back by the webbing. It was an old-fashioned net they'd thrown over me and, in my thrashing, I'd managed to entangle every one of my limbs against it. Screaming, I was lifted onto someone's shoulder, where I attempted to strike our kidnappers. The net effectively kept that from happening and I was tossed into the Chinook helicopter where my head was bagged and I was given just the rotor blades' pulsating sounds and the lift and lurch of flight to calculate where they were relocating me. No one spoke the entire duration, which I estimated was just over an hour. Only me. I spent the time warning them – repeatedly – to release me before they endangered themselves. I'm sure that got a few genuine grins. Then I was hauled out of the chopper – again over someone's beefy shoulder – and carried inside, where they dropped me into a chair, zip-tied my hands behind me, pinching off my appendages and restraining me from attacking them when the hood was pulled free of my head.

I expected to see a grungy, vacant room with blood-stained floors below flickering halogen lights – only the fact that the chair they set me in was made of plump leather kept me guessing. When they pulled the hood off, I found they had carried me into a bright, modern conference room with a series of flat-screen televisions across the upper part of the walls. The twenty-person table was made of polished, solid wood, and the water in my glass was crystal clear and cool enough to form condensation. When the Paper-Pusher came in, dressed in military fatigues and introducing himself as Captain Benson, he offered me a warm meal, which I declined. He then tried to get on my good side, which didn't work, and had failed impressively at even getting me to provide my name.

"Once again," I said, sighing from tedium, "you need to explain to the one in charge ... before my boyfriend revives –"

"I'm the one in charge."

"No, you're a paper-pusher, and you're going to get the other men in this facility hurt if you don't listen to me. When my boyfriend wakes up –"

"If you're nothing more than high school seniors, as you say you are, I will have nothing to worry about with your boyfriend. He's secure." The man appeared to be about thirty and wore a moustache to make himself look older and more authoritative. It didn't work. He'd been trying to impress on me his superiority since he'd entered the room several hours earlier. That didn't work either.

"Listen –"

"*NO*," he barked, his patience finally wearing down, "you listen to *me*. This will move a lot faster if you drop the act and admit the truth about who you really are."

"Like. I. Said." I leaned over the table to shorten the distance between my glare and him. "I. Am. A. High. School. Senior."

The Paper-Pusher exhaled irritably and opened his mouth, his eyes chilling into anger. But his rebuttal was cut short by the door opening and another armed man walking in. Wearing a green military dress uniform with a green-beige button-down shirt and matching tie – and being decorated with four stars down his shoulders and six rows of military-designated ribbons across the left side of his chest – he was clearly of a higher rank. But it was his demeanor – grave but earnest – the kind Eran would take a second look at, that told me the man led others and protected those others with profound duty.

Paper-Pusher met the man a few steps into the room and muttered, "I don't know why we kept her conscious."

"So she couldn't inform her friends in the afterlife," the man said, intentionally loud enough for me to overhear.

He caught my slight bristle at his reply and I silently cursed myself. Those words would have no meaning to an ordinary high school senior, but he knew they would with me, and therefore he knew about me.

My immediate instinct was to retort that now I knew why they hadn't knocked me insentient with a poisoned dart, with only a potent dose of willpower to hold me back. I remained silent and a thought traveled through my head: Eran would have been awestruck.

"Benson," the man said, clapping a weathered hand on Paper-Pusher's shoulder, "take a break."

"Yes, sir." Paper-Pusher saluted the man but stopped at the door, on guard.

"Benson, there's some pretty good donuts in the commissary."

It was a hint and we all knew it.

"But, sir, you-you want to be left alone?"

"Yes."

"With one of *them*?"

I didn't like his tone and narrowed my eyes to show it.

"She's not the one I'm concerned about."

My thoughts skidded to a stop at Eran and the commander knew it. "Benson," he warned and the man left the room promptly.

"He's still not conscious," the commander informed, "but he will be shortly."

"If you hurt him…" I seethed, anger swallowing me whole.

"We haven't." The man took a seat just one chair down from me. "I heard you two were close." I wanted to tell him that was an understatement but the less I said the better.

He stopped to appraise me further, as I did the same with him, feeling like each of us were sizing the other up. He was maybe sixty years old, but the wrinkles adorning his mouth, forehead and chin could just as easily have been the results of experience in battle. I'd seen it before, soldiers returning home with lifeless expressions. Over time, the life returned but it was a veiled light through hardened expressions. This man seemed to have found some peace after all he'd seen, given that just above a stern set of lips sat battered, sympathetic eyes.

"My name is John."

"What rank do you hold, John?"

"Chairman of the Joint Chiefs of Staff. The rankings used for your kind are still unclear to us, but –"

"I'm familiar with your title." In fact, I was sitting before the most senior and highest-ranking officer in all of the United States Armed Forces. "You work for the President ... and the Secretary of Defense."

"I counsel them."

His reply impressed me. Whether by principle or out of pure honesty, he made no effort to grandstand, and because of it he had done what Paper-Pusher had failed to do – disarm me a notch. Then he almost entirely defused me. Leaning forward until his elbows were on his knees, he took on the persona of an old friend in a private conversation as he delivered a frank and passionate plea.

"We need your help, Magdalene."

I blinked back my shock but made no effort to respond.

"The world faces a threat that we, humans, are not yet prepared to handle. We've known this for some time, which is why we have been watching you for some time –"

"You've been watching me?" My next thought was *'How did Eran not know?'*

Without pausing to explain, he continued, "We have some understanding of you and your kind, but our knowledge of what you call the Fallen Ones is limited, at best. We have been aware of this hidden, elusive threat but they have been evasive and therefore difficult to study. Now one has emerged from obscurity. That is why we need your help. To subdue the threat. We want to work with you."

"You have an interesting way of asking," I snapped.

"Granted, you may be less willing to provide it after the way your friends –"

"My loved ones," I corrected.

He nodded, duly chastised. "Have been treated."

"Treated?" I demanded. "They were assaulted. With poisoned weapons. And are now being held against their will."

"A measure I personally apologize for, taken strictly for our safety."

"A simple invitation would have been fine," I retorted. "You wouldn't have had to fear us then."

His face tightened at my last word, which accurately conveyed the uncertainty of his future. Restrained in tone and manner, he asserted, "We couldn't be certain how you might unleash your abilities when we approached you."

"That doesn't address my concern," I remarked coldly.

"Right," he said, sitting back in his chair, one arm leisurely lifted to rest on the table. "Your loved ones will be released."

"When?"

"When they regain consciousness."

"All of them?" I demanded. *Or maybe you expect to keep a few of us hostage until the rest of us do your bidding*, I thought.

His eyes, that had conveyed kindness earlier, now belied him. "Of course."

"I want to see Eran."

"That can be arranged."

"Now."

The emotion fled from his soft eyes, leaving only coldness.

Realizing he could just as easily leave my loved ones locked away, I conceded slightly. "Please."

"I'll see what I can —"

"You're the Chairman of the Joint Chiefs of Staff," I retorted. "You're telling me that someone has power over you and your interests?"

I was playing a delicate game, I knew, testing the line with a man's ego, a man who had already proven that self-image wasn't as important as getting the job done.

"Power fluctuates, Maggie," he said, using my informal name. "Sometimes you hold all the cards and sometimes you don't."

It was both a veiled threat and meant to send clarity on my situation. He could not be swayed through ego. There was too much at stake. His own people's lives, in fact. He was also pointing out that I was currently in the latter position, the one without the power.

"From what I've been told," he said steadily, eyeing me like a snake, "and keep in mind that I have yet to see it myself, you and Eran attempt to protect the human race. It's the only reason I'm spending any time with you at all. Now that we've both made requests, I'll actively try to fulfill yours, then we'll see if you're as benevolent as you've portrayed yourselves."

He stood quickly, his lean, muscular body effortlessly sending him into a towering posture. He paused to stare down at me, making me begin to contemplate defensive maneuvers, which somehow he could see happening.

"We have more to fear from you than you do from us," he stated plainly, pivoted on his heel and marched out the door.

Paper-Pusher re-entered the room, standing at ease beside the door, a smug grin on his face as he watched me. That expression faltered and then fell away completely when the building shook around us a few minutes later. The chair I sat on rolled slightly on its wheels as Paper-Pusher lowered his head and curiously stared at the ground. The next vibration rattled the walls, upsetting the television screens mounted there, creaking in protest. A series of tremors followed, oscillating the floor and sending compression blasts through the air. As I stared at the door, Paper-Pusher mounted his rifle to his shoulder.

"That won't help," I advised.

"Do you know what it is?" he asked, noticeably panicking.

"This is supposed to be a secure building, correct?" I asked, nailing down the source of his fears.

"Yes."

I simply smiled back.

"What is that? WHAT IS THAT?" he screamed.

Then the door exploded open, crumpling like a tin can and flying free from its hinges, slamming against the adjacent wall. There in the broken archway stood Eran, fists clenched, nostrils flared, shoulders heaved forward. He had not extended his appendages just yet, not feeling the need for them, evidently, but that made him no less intimidating. He entered with the ferocity of an enraged bear, marching directly past Paper-Pusher.

"Are you all right?" he asked, his eyes already scanning my body for injuries.

"Behind you," I warned.

Eran continued his pace as Paper-Pusher aimed the rifle at his back, but before Paper-Pusher could fire his weapon, it was yanked from his hands by Eran's invisible force over metal and hit the wall with enough energy to bend the barrel and leave a puncture where it hit clear through the plaster to the building's interior piping.

Eran broke the plastic at my wrists and then his arms were around me, warm and safe, like a blanket on a cold night. I breathed him in, closing my eyes, melting against him, my hands finding the muscles along his back and reminding me that strength was securing me now. I could have stayed that way for hours but he adjusted slightly. I moaned and he kissed me on the crown of my head before rotating to stand in front of me, facing the door, his anger subsiding now.

As he did, John walked in, casually, a man who had seen enough combat to no longer fear it, or at least no longer show that fear. Paper-Pusher had already fled but a flood of troops in black tactical gear swarmed through the door, weapons pointed at Eran the moment he came into their view. Their rustling, the jarring of their equipment and gear, fell silent almost at once as they found their positions encircling that half of the room. John stood calmly a few feet in, with the same demeanor as Eran – each gauging the other as John and I had done earlier.

"His name is John," I announced, sliding around past Eran's shoulder.

Eran nodded once and shifted to block me again.

I sighed.

"Eran," John said, his deep voice remaining level, "you beat me to it. I was about to release you."

"I'm sure you were," Eran replied, without any hint of doubt while never moving or taking his eyes off John.

"Stand down," John ordered, and for a second I thought he was rudely demanding it of Eran. Then the weapons in the room lowered.

"Leave us."

John's command was followed promptly and silently and he took a seat again at the table. Motioning toward the other chairs, he suggested, "Please."

Eran pulled a chair out for me, behind him, and then another for himself, again blocking me. I angled it so that I could see around his shoulder.

Watching us, John opened the conversation with an observation about Eran. "You do move like you've been alive for centuries."

Eran showed no reaction to John's reference on how in depth he or his team had researched us. Instead, he asked steadily, "What do you want with us, Mr. Chairman?"

The corner of John's eyebrow twitched, the only sign that he was surprised at how much Eran knew about him.

"Well, Colonel," John said, pausing again to observe Eran's reaction at knowing his title too. When he saw nothing, he continued. "I have a few people who are interested in meeting you two. Our leaders from around the world."

"What kind of help were you referring to when you asked for it a few minutes back?" I questioned, bringing Eran up to speed while moving John to provide more details to us.

"The kind that requires your skill set. The elimination of a mutual enemy."

Eran's tone turned cool then. "Where are my people, Mr. Chairman?"

"All here. All safe."

"I'll need to see that for myself."

John spoke louder, with a commanding tone, to someone else listening. "Bring in the others." He immediately returned to an amiable manner and tipped his head at Eran. "You'll find no lasting effects from the tranquilizers. I know personally," he added, turning his head halfway to listen as Paper-Pusher entered the room, rifle at the ready.

Ezra, Ms. Beedinwigg, Felix and Rufus filed in, heading straight for our end of the table. I could see that their hands were unbound and no visible skin was bruised or cut, but Eran's ability to locate internal injuries was what I was relying on. He evaluated each of them closely and when he said nothing I relaxed slightly. They walked deliberately with reasonable speed and stood beside and behind us. Paper-Pusher's unit followed them in, dressed in the same camouflage as their insecure lead and took positions in the far corners, where John allowed them to remain.

"Where are we?" Felix asked, using the deep, somber tone I'd only heard on occasion – when we and others were in danger.

"S-I-E-F," Eran replied, drawing surprised stares. "The confidential Strategic Intervention Enforcement Facility. Logistics division."

"Apparently not so confidential," John muttered under his breath, casting a cold eye at Paper-Pusher. "Can we get any of you a glass of water?" John offered.

Felix opened his mouth and drew in a breath but was stopped short by a slap to his shoulder by Rufus.

Noting the exchange and Felix's restraint, John said, "All right, shall we begin?"

"Yes, Mr. Chairman, that's a good idea." The voice came from the door, spoken by a swift-moving man as he entered the room, the business suit he wore seeming out of place in the middle of camouflage and military dress uniforms. Despite his speed, I would have recognized him anywhere. Anyone on my side of the room would have, proven by the sharp inhales and shuffling of bodies among them.

The man who we knew to be our benefactor, our confidante, who had financed several of our efforts against our enemies, who had assisted us through countless hazards, took a seat at the table, opposite John, on the military-side of the room. As he turned on the tablet he had carried in under his arm, Ezra broke the silence, her tone quiet and demoralized.

"Mr. Hamilton …"

Ms. Beedinwigg, however, had more choice words for him. "You son-of-a-"

"Bronte," he said, cutting off her curse, tipping his head properly at her.

"You will address me formally until I get an explanation, and very likely thereafter. *Mister* Hamilton," she spat as an afterthought.

"Very well," he replied flatly. Remaining seated, he gave her his full attention, speaking with the same blueblood articulation we knew him to use but now with an official air to it. "I am employed by a covert agency within the United States government where I was retained under the explicit directive to gain access and knowledge of the beings that have fallen from the afterlife and that now populate this earth under the presumption that one of them … at some point in time … will pose a threat to our existence. We now face that threat."

"How long have you been employed by them?" Ms. Beedinwigg demanded.

His focus returned to the tablet where he rapidly moved between screens, forcing him to divide his attention between it and Ms. Beedinwigg. Muttering, he answered, "Three months, five days, two hours and …" he briefly checked his watch "ten seconds prior to meeting you."

"The entire time," she exhaled softly. In a clearer, commanding voice, she pressed, "You used me. You found me and used me to get close to them."

"Yes," he replied evenly.

"You've been feeding the government information about us."

"Yes," he said, in the same brisk manner.

"And you told them where to find us."

"Yes."

Quietly, with unyielding intent, she whispered, "I'm going to kill you."

He continued swiping his screen. "Fine, but please do wait until the human race is out of danger. Mr. Chairman, we are ready."

John, who had been stoic during their exchange, nodded without expression and the screens around the room blinked to life. "Feel free to sit. This may take a while," he impressed.

Ezra was the first to pull out a chair, directly beside me, and the others followed, all keeping to our side of the table.

Each flat screen panel snapped to life around the room, broadcasting faces of varying nationalities. They were noted only by country and name. Only one did not have any notation. Positioned near the hole in the wall that Eran had made earlier from Paper Pusher's firearm, its screen reflected the room where we now sat.

"You referenced them as the leaders of the world," Eran pointed out, surveying the screens, hinting that the images weren't what he expected.

"Presidents are figureheads," John explained. "Those who truly pull the strings are the ones working behind the scenes. These are the top String Pullers. Mr. Hamilton, please proceed."

Mr. Hamilton nodded. "Thank you all for joining us. While you know the Chairman and myself, I'd like to introduce our guests. They are present at our request." I opened my mouth to retort but Eran calmly placed a hand on mine, sedating me. "You may recognize them from my report titled Relatives and Associations numbered 425FBNUO," Mr. Hamilton remarked, which jolted me, considering he was referring to us as having been identified to others without our knowledge. And I wasn't the only one. Ms. Beedinwigg's hands curled into fists and Rufus grunted. Mr. Hamilton didn't seem to notice as he proceeded to name those on our side of the table. "They will be present for questions after my briefing. For the record, this is emergency meeting BN201 and we are here to discuss the airborne threat mentioned in this meeting's notice. Now, what we are dealing with is a Class Two foe –"

"Oy!" a man with a bulbous nose hidden in a portly, round face interrupted in a thick accent. The country below his image on the screen noted 'Russia'. "Foe? What is a Foe? Speak English."

John and Mr. Hamilton exchanged a glance, as if expecting this reaction and John openly suggested, "Why don't you give them a brief crash course."

Mr. Hamilton nodded. "F-Os, Admiral Ivanov. Short for Fallen Ones."

Admiral Ivanov appeared perturbed, an indication that the explanation was unsatisfactory.

Containing his frustration with a deep breath, Mr. Hamilton went on. "For you who did not have time to read the reports, there are those who walk among us who are not human."

"Zee clairvoyants," the woman representing France interrupted. "Ezz zat what we are dealing – ezz zat who is taunting us?"

Mr. Hamilton quickly interjected before the discussion went sideways. "I'll answer that question in a moment, Madame Martin. And they are more than clairvoyant, more than what that simple term suggests." He tapped his tablet and the screen that mirrored the room where we sat flashed to a new, static image of a human skeleton laid across a wide table. The only distinction was that bones that formed wings were extending from the anterior rib cage. Apparently, the screens visible to the broadcasted leaders were modified to also show the image because all expressed interest, some even leaning toward their screen, squinting curiously.

A gaunt man two screens to our right, with a neck twice the length of his head and a sharply pointed chin, interrupted. The country noted below his face was Denmark. "You mean to tell me they – they actually ..." His eyebrows dipped. "Exist?"

Mr. Hamilton paused, attempting to withhold a disgusted glower. "Yes," he said flatly.

"To further clarify for Mr. Christensen," said Madame Martin, who hesitated before summing up the overall question, "you mean to say that there really is life after death?"

"Yes," Mr. Hamilton said, his tone punctuated before continuing despite the number of jaws dropping across the screens. "Now, as shown in my Report 312FBNUO, they have the capability of flight. Their bones are like birds, strong yet hollow. But unlike birds, their wings are embedded and hidden beneath their skin, emerging only on command. There are two types with this ability – Alterums, of whom you see seated with us here," he said motioning to our side of the table as those on the screens visibly scrutinized us. "They reincarnate with the ability to remember their past lives, and can average hundreds of years of life on earth."

"How long have you lived?" The Admiral nudged his chin at Eran and me.

When we remained silent, Mr. Hamilton answered, "They've been coming here since the 1400s."

Several eyebrows rose but no one replied, allowing Mr. Hamilton to move back on track. "Now, the other type visiting us are called Fallen Ones, whom we call 'FOs' for short. Both types of groups move among us quietly. You may pass them on the street without any indication, even while each one comes with an exceptional ability. Some may breathe fire, some are telekinetic, some can detect coming geological disasters

– earthquakes, volcanic eruptions, etcetera – but again they keep these traits concealed using them when they feel threatened or wish to overpower a human. Really, for all intents and purposes, the only true distinction between the two groups is that Alterums opt to come here by their own free will, live out their lives here, grow old here, die, reincarnate, and return here when the desire arises. The FO's, however, have been cast here from the afterlife and are thus forced to remain here. Because of this, they seem to slow the degradation of their organic bodies if not halting their aging process entirely such that they can live in their current bodies indefinitely."

"You consider that the *only* distinction?" Ms. Beedinwigg interrupted, seething, her fury almost palpable.

Mr. Hamilton shriveled slightly below her stare and conceded, "Other than the Alterums assumedly holding an allegiance toward us humans while the Fallen Ones do not."

"Assumedly?" she pressed.

On this point, Mr. Hamilton pushed back, leveling his eyes at her. "Yes, Ms. Beedinwigg. We do not hold a treaty with them and until we do we cannot consider them allies just yet."

The addition of the words *just yet* seemed to quell the rage in Ms. Beedinwigg, for now, but it enlightened us to two facts. First, Mr. Hamilton, despite the longevity of our relations with him, had always seen us not as friends but as potential foes, keeping himself at arm's length to us at all times. Second, Mr. Hamilton's allegiance was undoubtedly to the service of his country, within which we were not citizens in his eyes but unwelcomed visitors.

The lack of loyalty he finally revealed to us cut deep and I scoffed loud enough for Eran and John to turn their heads to me while Mr. Hamilton continued.

"Most importantly and of particular interest to us during our research is a subgroup within the Alterums called messengers. Messengers demonstrate a unique skill whereby when falling unconscious, their souls leave their bodies and travel into the afterlife, where they remain until they awake or their bodies die off completely here on earth. Those are the clairvoyants you mentioned, Madame Martin. They are uncommon, about a few dozen exist, and just about the only way to distinguish them is when they opt to use their skill to pass messages between the humans and the deceased. They are a mirror image of us, so you won't have a clue you're even looking at one. Given their unique ability and their vulnerability when visiting the afterlife, each messenger is assigned a protector called a guardian, whose entire objective is to keep their ward alive, going so far as to give up their own life for the sake of that task. They maintain close ties, if not living in the same household or nearby, then certainly they are in perpetual contact. We have a messenger and her guardian at this table, in fact, whom live together, Magdalene Tanner and Eran Talor." He gestured to each of us, making a sideline remark, "They hold high ranks within their kind."

"Now Fallen Ones, or FOs, are classified into three categories. Classification One represents Alterums who have not yet posed a threat. Their wings are white." This made me bristle because we were automatically being grouped with our enemies and viewed as a potential menace. I began to speak but Ms. Beedinwigg beat me to it.

"Just a minute now," she demanded. "Alterums are not Fallen Ones and they pose no threat at all."

"*Yet*," Mr. Hamilton enunciated. Ms. Beedinwigg started to counter but he cut her off. "Bronte —"

"I told you not to call me that," she fumed.

Showing no emotion other than a brief pucker of his lips, he corrected, "Ms. Beedinwigg, was there ever an Alterum who became a Fallen One?"

She refused to answer, knowing he was correct.

He tipped his head at her, attempting a conciliatory gesture but receiving a scoff and roll of her eyes in return. He chose to ignore her response and returned to his original topic, as an elderly man from Portugal whose name on the screen was Mr. Silva, cleared his throat, intentionally stopping him.

"I'd like to know the answer," he declared.

"It is quite simply yes," Mr. Hamilton stated, glancing at Ms. Beedinwigg for her reaction. With her glare set in place, he frowned and returned to his explanations. "The other two categories of FOs are clearer in their distinctions. Classification Two represents those who have chosen the malevolent path. Their wings are grey. They are demonstrably dangerous to humans taking advantage in any way possible – monetarily, physically, mentally – but they also present a greater risk to messengers. Messengers dying by their hands do not travel back to the afterlife upon death – which is considered by many to be heaven, nirvana, the afterworld, the rest of eternity. You get the idea. Messengers are instead sent to what they call an *eternal* death, which is understood to be what we, humans, would consider hell, purgatory, the underworld, a place of torment. Again, you get the idea. Luckily, there are fewer Class Twos, we believe, and it helps that both messengers and FOs can sense each other through electrical stimulation, thereby avoiding contact or altercation if needed."

"Just a minute," the representative from China interrupted, his name indicated as Mr. Wang. He held up a plumb finger, wagging it as he iterated his question.

"What do you mean by electrical stimulation?"

"Neural stimulation through low-intensity electromagnetic fields," Mr. Hamilton explained, as if that might be sufficient. After scanning their confused gazes, he added impatiently, "Electrical devices plugged into a wall socket and turned on are surrounded by electromagnetic fields. The messengers and FOs are the same, surrounded by an electromagnetic field of energy that, when they get close enough to each other, can trigger a charge."

It was ironic that Mr. Hamilton downplayed the point as only a single charge. For me, and many other messengers, and judging by the faces of some Fallen Ones, the charge was not a simple pulse but an extended current and it was not low-energy but, in fact, was intense enough to make some grit their teeth or grip their knees.

Returning to the intended topic, Mr. Hamilton leaned back over his tablet. "Now, the Class Twos we know about are listed here." He tapped his screen a few times and projected a spreadsheet listing names, abilities, past residences, among other details. In short, what he had compiled was a modern-day, computerized version of the Book of Dossiers, a book of sketches and profiles on each of our known enemies which was destroyed by a defiant Alterum before she understood its value. The fact they had reassembled the information was remarkable and slightly unnerving. Eran remained rigid at the sight of it, an indication to me that he was just as unsettled by it, while staring guardedly at Mr. Hamilton who continued talking mindlessly to us. "The third classification is the greatest threat. They have even been given their own name by the Alterums. *Elsics* have black wings, a reaction from being imprisoned alongside their own kind for what is the equivalent of lifetimes on earth, and they have metamorphosed because of this incarceration into more animal than human. They are extremely long-lived and fear nothing, and if anyone – messenger, guardian, human – is killed by one, we too end up in eternal death. But whichever direction your metaphysical beliefs may lean, I imagine you don't wish to test this theory."

Admiral Ivanov interjected to ask, "Which one are we dealing with now?"

"We don't know. There are conflicting reports about the wing color on this FO and all videos acquired show varying color hues."

The admiral seemed unimpressed by this setback.

"And you say there is no way to locate him or identify him in a crowd?" asked the representative from Iceland, by the name of Mr. Lindholm, his face set in a continual frown.

"In truth, he shouldn't even be here."

Mr. Hamilton's point drew inquisitive stares.

"Meaning?" Madame Martin said.

"All FOs should be confined to eternal death. In the place that exists below the hole that Magdalene created in the field outside London."

Again, I tensed. They knew more about us than I ever expected and knowledge could sometimes pose a danger even in the most elementary hands.

On seeing blank expressions from those on the screens, Eran saw an opportunity to redirect the conversation and made an attempt at it. "Mr. Hamilton –"

"We mentioned this hole to you in Report 109FBNUO," Mr. Hamilton explained, gesturing to Eran, amid the transfixed, expressionless stares across the screens. "Eran created the place of eternal death – hell, purgatory, underworld, whatever term you wish to give it – long before any of us were alive as a means to restrain the dangerous souls on this plane. And

Magdalene opened a passageway to it during the Great Battle in the London field where the hole now exists."

"Mr. Hamilton," Eran said, louder, "I'm more than happy to answer —"

But Mr. Hamilton was already elucidating, determined to remind his audience on what they should already have known, exasperated they didn't. "The Alterums and FOs went to battle in that field a few years back. While the Alterums prevailed, there was a moment when many were killed by Elsics in the conflict and, as I mentioned earlier, a death by an Elsic results in perpetual death. Magdalene was herself killed by a FO and was thus sent down into eternal death where she created the hole to help herself and the other Alterums escape. The Alterums prevailed in that battle and in the interest of keeping up pretenses, we maintained satellite surveillance of the hole and allowed the two ever-present guards to keep watch over it."

I didn't appreciate the term "allowed" and, on seeing it, Mr. Hamilton amended his choice of words. "Left. Left the guards undistracted by us."

The Admiral cleared this throat, sat back, and folded his hands together over his round belly. "All right, Mr. Hamilton, so how do *we* kill them?" he asked bluntly, unashamed that he wasn't distinguishing between which group he'd like to annihilate, even while we sat in his presence.

"That's a bit tricky, sir," Mr. Hamilton explained and sighed while trying to determine how best to clarify why. "You see, sir, because each one, whether Alterum or FO, has their own unique strengths, which protects them, thus, one needs to determine their opponent's individual strength, maneuver around it, and then strike."

The Admiral sat very still as he processed that information. "Difficult to do when they don't hang a sign around their necks telling us what strength they hold."

"That's correct. My spreadsheet is helpful in identifying individual capabilities, although it is unfortunately incomplete, so if this FO or Alterum we are dealing with –"

"FO," Ms. Beedinwigg shot back.

Mr. Hamilton appeared perturbed but skipped ahead without opening a debate. "Is not listed on my spreadsheet or we haven't determined his or her strength –"

"It'll be of little use. Only way to figure out that strength is in the midst of battle," the Admiral concluded.

Trying to hold back shame, Mr. Hamilton nodded.

"Well," the Admiral grumbled, "I don't know about the rest of you but I am interested in hearing from the Alterums themselves."

Nervous shuffling by Felix drew my attention before Eran asked, "What is it you'd like to know, Admiral?"

"What reassurance do we have that you are a reliable source?" he asked.

"None," Eran replied.

"Well then how do we know you aren't working with this … this FO?"

"Because we are in a worse position than you. FOs use humans for their enjoyment while FOs want *us* eliminated. You see, messengers have the ability to send their souls into eternal death and guardians, such as myself and those who work with me, have dedicated ourselves to protecting humanity."

"So you get in their way," the Admiral summarized.

"We get in their way," Eran agreed.

"And what about you?" the Admiral nudged his chin at the screen. "Magdalene. Can she be trusted?"

"Magdalene has the most to lose," Eran answered.

"She has a ... *special* ... relationship with the FOs, having been a particular thorn in their side since she first came here. She was the first to determine their weakness – in that messengers can dispel the FOs to eternal death – and for it, she has been hunted by them every time she's come. Killing a guardian wins FOs honor among their kind. Killing a messenger wins them feared notoriety. But killing Magdalene, well, that would make them a genuine hero."

"I take it she has never been killed by one then?" asked the Admiral.

Eran, prickled by the answer, fell silent. He took it as a personal failure that I had been.

"At least once," Mr. Hamilton interjected. "By the FO in the London field."

"All other times I've died by age or Eran's hands," I added, and nearly every set of eyebrows rose at my comment. Realizing my mistake, I clarified, "Eran and I, as all messengers and their guardians do, have a pre-arranged agreement whereby if the messenger risks losing their life at the hands of a Fallen One, I mean a FO, then the guardian is to take the messenger's life instead so that he or she may end up in the afterlife, circumventing eternal death."

Uncomfortable silence followed my account, making me think I'd made another misleading claim. Then the Admiral shook his head solemnly.

"I imagine you have some stories to tell. We shall share a vodka sometime."

Eran nodded respectfully. "I'd enjoy that, Admiral."

"Mr. Hamilton described you as having powers," Mr. Silva from Portugal remarked.

"Yes, that is correct," Eran replied.

"What powers do you own and how do you get these powers?"

Intentionally excluding the first half of the question,

Eran replied, "Our strengths are born from conquering our greatest struggles. Thereafter they become our power and leverage over others. For example, a girl named Sarai was disfigured as a human and shunned because of it but on becoming a FO she gained beauty and the ability to make any man fall in love with her when speaking to them."

"That is difficult to believe," he countered.

"You have the luxury of doubt. I know others who did not."

"So who is zee most dangerous FO?" Madame Martin asked.

"Lotharius," Eran and I answered quickly, earning glances.

"One of the Sevens?" John asked, and yet again I was disturbed by how much our government secretly knew about us. Eran felt the same, I knew, as he swung his gaze to John and then to me. The Sevens were the last of the Fallen Ones to be eradicated, in the Louisiana swamps, just outside New Orleans.

It didn't occur to me until after I saw the concern in Eran's eyes that he was equally as worried about Jameson and Jocelyn and the others like them who fought alongside us in that conflict and who attempted to remain clandestine, rooted in the private world they had created within themselves. But if John knew about The Sevens, then it was highly probable he knew about the others too.

"No," Eran said simply. "Lotharius is more dangerous than any of The Sevens were, or any FO throughout time, for that matter."

A noticeable discomfort swept over those on the screens.

"And why ezz that?" Madame Martin asked. "How did he earn that reputation?"

"Lotharius led the defense against FOs before he

became one of them. What he did to them made them fear him. What he can do to us is significantly worse."

"How ezz that?" she pressed.

"Lotharius's strength comes from being able to identify Alterum and FO abilities, often before even they have learned about it themselves. He then manipulates them, using their abilities to satisfy his own ends."

Mr. Christensen from Denmark sighed and grumbled under his breath, "Does anyone else feel like this is beyond us?"

"He is your most feared adversary and yet I've never heard that name," John said, swiveling accusing eyes at Mr. Hamilton.

"It's improbable that you would. He isn't controlled by ego. Progress drives him, and with his ability, he is inclined to remain hidden while those around him – disciples as he calls them – propel that progress."

"He's done this before?" the Admiral asked.

"The battle that Mr. Hamilton mentioned earlier, that took place in the London field, was led by a FO named Abaddon. He is one of Lotharius's disciples."

I drew in a sharp breath, my eyes widening.

"You didn't know?" Ms. Beedinwigg whispered to me, to which I shook my head. "Neither did we."

"Could this Lotharius be the one we are dealing with now?" Mr. Silva asked, turning rigid as he awaited a response.

"No," I replied immediately, and all eyes turned to me. While everyone in the room was curious, Eran was visibly unhappy. He didn't like me close to FOs, anywhere near them, and especially not without him present. And if I knew that Lotharius wasn't a threat now it was because I had checked on him to make sure of it.

"I snuck past your guards," I admitted to Eran.

"I know," he replied, through a frown.

Avoiding Eran's accusing stare, I declared to the room, "Lotharius is incapacitated."

"How do you know?" Madame Martin asked.

"Magdalene," Eran said, sternly, twisting in his seat to face me, clearly insisting I not answer.

"Because I've seen him."

"Magdalene," Eran warned again.

"Below ground? Through the hole?" John pressed.

"Magdalene, enough!"

"Yes," I replied flatly. "I saw him below ground. I'm the only one who can."

John and Mr. Hamilton's faces hardened as they stared closely at me, although I was more preoccupied with Eran. He was furious, with nostrils flared, until John spoke with tense restraint.

"We sent four men down that hole," John admitted slowly, choosing his words carefully. "Their hearts stopped a few feet in. When we sent in drones every one of them froze before dropping out of GPS detection. But before they did," he added, resting back in his chair and folding his hands across his trim belly, "we got a fairly clear picture of what's below. Bodies. Live bodies. Thousands of them. In catatonic states. Seemingly in great distress." He observed us critically before adding, "And you're saying Lotharius is one of them."

"Yes."

"That's enough, Magdalene," Eran said quietly, disheartened now.

"So," John stated, as if he was coming to a conclusion, "anyone or anything who enters is consumed like the others you found there. The only one unaffected is the one who created the hole. You." He quickly turned his head to Mr. Hamilton. "Did you know this?"

"No, Mr. Chairman. I believed that she'd only been down once … and escaped."

The tension in the room soared then, as Eran turned to face them and shifted slightly in front of me, a defensive maneuver. Confused, I swept my gaze across the room at those staring back at me. Only when I saw the abject fear in their eyes did I understand.

Eran had been cautious not to give away any personal information about us, even going so far as to use Fallen Ones as examples to explain abilities. He'd also tried to deter me, stop me from disclosing what I just had – that I was the only one capable of entering and leaving the most feared place known to humankind. Eran did this because he knew the only logical outcome. They now dreaded me, and John succinctly put into words why.

"If what you said earlier is true, if you gain your strengths – or differentiate yourself from the others of your kind – by overcoming a particular challenge, then I would gamble that your exclusive ability to venture into that hole is not because you created it but because you overcame the effects of its destination."

Eran was as still as a rock next to me as his sense of dread seeped into me, like cold water streaming into my veins. I turned to him, confused.

"I don't understand," I whispered, although in the dead silence it was audible to the farthest person in the room.

Eran's shoulders sank as he released the breath he'd been holding, looking like a man who had fought a long battle and was now witnessing its dire conclusion. Softly he explained what John had already realized and what Eran had known for far longer than he let on. "At some point in time, Magdalene, you conquered hell."

I blinked but otherwise found my muscles unable to move, my mind entirely focused on trying to reason through the implications of what I'd just heard. Even as I processed it, my subconscious took over.

"No," I muttered, my mind in disarray.

If I conquered that place, where the Fallen Ones, the FOs, now exist hunched over, rigid, in desperation, clutching themselves, mumbling in mindless trances, then I could never have been like them. I would have needed mobility to free myself and if that were the case, I blocked it out. And understandably. Those souls were tormented, plagued with never-ending nightmares in an awakened state. And yet, even as every fiber of the idea repulsed me ... it all made sense. And Eran knew it. He might have actually known it since the battle in the London field when I'd freed him, his guardians, and the Alterums through that hole I'd created. He'd gone so far as to hint it in Mr. Leroux's museum. And he was correct. I *have* always been independent of the other Alterums. Because I was different. My first instinct is to fight – always. I'm more comfortable alone than with others, in the shadows than in the light, living in discomfort than in luxury. I fear nothing but the Fallen Ones. And now I had to ask, could that be because I'm one of them?

Eran watched me with grave concern as my hand came to my mouth. Somehow, his handsome face found its way through the haze distorting my thoughts, and his expression told me that later tonight, when we'd left this place and laid in the privacy of my room, he intended to talk through what I'd just learned. For now, he pivoted slowly to John.

"Mr. Chairman, you brought us here to help you," he said. "Let us. My guardians and I are trained to handle FOs. We have interacted with them for centuries and therefore have gained comprehensive knowledge about them far beyond what is compiled in Mr. Hamilton's spreadsheet. No insult intended, Mr. Hamilton," Eran added to which Mr. Hamilton accepted with a nod.

John's lips turned down in discontent. "What are you suggesting?"

"Release us, all of us, and then stand down."

The Admiral, and several others, had a physical reaction to this suggestion. As voices began to rise up and argue, overlapping each other in their condemnation, Eran stood, a gesture that appeared more threatening than Eran intended yet had the anticipated affect. They shut up.

"You are not equipped to handle this threat. I judge you've already determined that for yourselves or we wouldn't be here. You've made attempts to detain and deter him and you've failed. Allow those of us who *are* equipped to do the job for you." When no one answered, Eran insisted, "What do you risk by letting us try?"

"Losing control over the situation," John replied bluntly.

"With all due respect, John," Eran said with cool resolve, "you never had control."

John's eyes did not turn cold with offense. There was no ill intent in them. He truly had no ego in this dispute. Instead, his amber hues transformed into steady determination as he lifted a hand in a slow, slight gesture that meant nothing to us until a dart launched from the barrel of a rifle by one of the armed men still standing against the walls. It explained to me why John allowed them to stay in the room during the confidential discussion, not only for safety, but for one final maneuver against us.

"You're correct, Eran," John said evenly, watching as Eran took a step forward, the arrow still protruding from his neck as he fell, face-first, to the ground. "But I do now."

As thumps hit the floor around me, and the bodies

of those I love once again were incapacitated, I understood we were under attack.

Rolling my shoulders forward, I thrust myself from the seat, intent on releasing my appendages and launching myself at John. He watched me serenely, even with full awareness that any physical contact between us would end in him being injured, or worse. Yet, he made no visible effort to evade me, because he was more prepared than I gave him credit.

My first indication something was wrong came when my legs registered as uncooperative, laying like limp noodles off the seat's edge with my feet dangling to the floor, and my attempt to stand resulted in a face-plant. On impact with the unforgiving ground, something pushed the skin aside at my shoulder and then snapped off completely. I rotated my head to find a cylindrical cartridge with a needle protruding from its stem lying next to me. I commanded my arms to slide forward and under me, to propel me into a squat, but they didn't respond; instead they remained carpeting the floor like dead branches.

"Clear," a man's imposing voice snapped from the far-right corner of the room.

"Clear," another one shouted, from somewhere near the door.

"Clear."

"Clear."

"Clear."

The series of confirmations ended and no sound was left in the room. I could no longer control my head, or look up at my adversaries, but with my eyes still functioning I could see the tips of black boots positioned in a modified shooting Weaver stance. Then the squeak of a chair told me someone was moving.

Weighty, unhurried footsteps closed in on me and the rustling of clothing brushing against skin became louder as someone knelt beside me with a heavy exhale. Then John's voice began to speak over me.

"Now, you have two options, Magdalene."

I squirmed, moaning in my effort to get at him.

"We don't have much time," he chastised. "There was less toxin in your dart but it will quickly catch up, and I need you to hear me. You have two choices. You can enter an altercation with us, and we will consider anything *but* compliance an altercation. Or you can help us eliminate the threat. Your housemates and school principal will be returned to you, but we will keep Eran as collateral. You have my word, Magdalene, that he will not be harmed during your mission. I cannot speak to what will happen to him if you fail."

Again, I did my best to writhe but the numbness was creeping up my neck now and I could only exhale loudly.

"Eliminate the threat, Magdalene, and you get your husband back."

7 SUBSTITUTE TEACHER

I woke up with a scream clawing for release from my throat and, when I expelled it, the Hall of Records shook. A handful of scrolls rattled from their pockets and fell to the ground where they disappeared, reappearing seconds later back in their specified pocket locations.

The words *you get your husband back* swept through my mind as I snapped upward, sensing those in the hall flocking to me.

John knew intimate details about our past, that Eran was more than a guardian to me, that we had exchanged vows as husband and wife in our previous lives on earth, and that those vows still held true today.

He had detained the one person who could motivate me to get the job done, a strategically powerful move for him – and an egregiously dangerous one too. Incensed, my hands balled into fists, pressing indents in my thighs, as I fought through the blindness that came with rage.

"What happened?" Hermina bent over beside me, her apprehensive eyes nearly filling my sight. Behind her and on both sides of us, were the other messengers, just as triggered with worry.

"He's got Eran —" was all I had time to say before I felt the pull back to my body on earth.

With time moving differently in the afterlife, slower, I opened my eyes to a familiar sight – the ceiling of my bedroom in New Orleans. I sat up and pushed my legs off the bed, searching the room before my feet ever landed on the floor. Seeing no one, no armed men, no Chairman of the Joint Chiefs of Staff, I ran for my bedroom door, swung it open, and crossed the hallway into Eran's room. The bedcovers were thrown over his pillows, the television screen he used to monitor news around the world was black, he was nowhere in sight.

Swinging around, I raced to Rufus's room at the end of the hall and found him spread across his bed, his tattoos blending into a colorful bedspread stitched together by Felix during one conciliatory Christmas.

"Rufus!" I shouted, and he jerked upward as if his body were scissors snapping together, arms and legs flying outward, disrupting a stack of books piled three feet high next to the bed and sending the tower crumbling to the floor.

"Hub...Hum...Huh..." he rattled off, blinking to clear his head.

"You're home. Are you hurt?"

He went still, swung his head toward me and gave me an offended glare.

"Good."

I ran out the door and down the hall to Felix's room, swinging his door wide. He was still unconscious. I sprang over the miscellaneous items dropped irrelevantly across his bedroom floor and stood over him.

He was breathing.

When he shot upward, sucking in a loud, hoarse

breath, wide-eyed and panicked, I jerked backwards.

"You're home. Are you hurt?"

He swung crazed eyes at me and I braced myself, not knowing the individual effects of the chemicals they had pumped into our bodies. Mouth ajar, drool glistening in a stream down his chin, he nodded. "They have Eran," he muttered.

"I know." I turned and raced out his door, down the stairs, and into Ezra's room. She was already awake, standing unsteadily, groggy and trying to regain her bearings.

"I'm fine," she confirmed before I even asked.

"I'm calling Ms. Beedinwigg."

But before my sentence was even finished, the old rotary phone mounted to the kitchen wall began to ring. I caught it on the third rattle.

"Magdalene?" Ms. Beedinwigg demanded through the staticky line.

"It's me," I affirmed and she breathed a sigh of relief.

"I'll be there in five." And the phone went dead.

I looked outside, noticing it was still dark.

"Four o'clock," Ezra said, shuffling into the kitchen, still fighting the drug's after-effects. "Just before dawn." She stopped at the counter, one hand on it to brace herself. "How do we get him back?"

"I'm working on that," I said, and she nodded, her head still down.

"We're going to need caffeine," she muttered. "*I* need caffeine." Her hands went to work, preparing a pot, which I noticed was extra strong.

Felix and Rufus came through the door as the coffee drip began to gurgle.

"Ms. Beedinwigg?" Felix asked.

"On her way."

She came through the front door then, slamming it

aside in a hurry. Apparently, she had driven even quicker because she'd made it in three minutes. I appreciated that.

"All right, who can help us?" I asked as Ms. Beedinwigg entered and took the steaming coffee mug Ezra had extended to her.

"Should we enact Measure 104?" Ezra offered. "It's about time the messengers and guardians congregated."

"Bring them all here?" Felix reiterated with an affirming nod. "Makes sense. They can help us."

"Can they?" I asked pointedly, a little terser than I expected. "Sorry, I'm …"

"I know," Felix replied, presenting a sympathetic smile.

Rufus reached out a massive hand and laid it on my shoulder. "They won't go hurtin' the only insurance policy they have."

I nodded, feeling a rush of anger swell in me before uttering, "You knew … what they were doing?"

"From the second that wanker opened fire on Eran. Aye…"

"Opened fire," I muttered to myself, the words sparking a memory.

"Aye, when that bast –"

"Opened fire," I blurted again. It was the words Eran had used when threatening the guards outside the ambassador's home, the ambassador who Campion worked for.

"Aye …" Rufus looked at me curiously.

My eyes wide, I rushed for the phone. "Campion … knows an ambassador who might know where the SIEF facility –"

"Hang up the phone," Ms. Beedinwigg instructed.

I ignored her.

"Because he resigned," she announced.

I set the phone back in its cradle and rotated slowly

toward her. "How do you know?"

"It was the first phone call I made," she said.

"No," I said, slowly, "how did you know to call him?"

"Eran and I thought it would be a good idea to place Campion strategically in line with an informed government official, in case we ended up needing the ambassador or the information." She scowled then. "It was Mr. Hamilton's suggestion." Her face hardened then. "Well speak of the devil himself."

A soft tap drew everyone's attention to the back door, where the kitchen light spilled out onto Mr. Hamilton's rigid, narrow features. Ezra was the only one courteous enough to open the door for him, and he stepped inside sheepishly. The second he did, I had him up against the wall and my hand around his neck.

"WHERE IS HE?" I screamed.

And then hands were pulling at me, away from my victim.

"If you kill him, you certainly won't find out," Ezra said into my ear.

Huffing, I glared back and waited.

"I thought you might need help," Mr. Hamilton admitted, straightening his suit jacket before correcting his askew tie.

Several scoffed, myself included. Ms. Beedinwigg didn't simply stare but seemed to emanate hatred for the man.

"You can help by telling us where you have Eran," I spat.

"I *don't* have him," Mr. Hamilton replied earnestly. "They do. And they've relocated him. Probably because they knew I'd return here to help you."

We viewed him critically, deciding on whether he was telling the truth.

"I-I just don't know," Felix exhaled, voicing the

thoughts of the rest of us.

"He's a trained liar," Ms. Beedinwigg stated, eyes narrowed at Mr. Hamilton.

"But I've never lied to you," he replied and Ms. Beedinwigg flared up, her chest expanding as she took a step toward him. Adjusting to deflect any strike, he added steadily, "You just never asked if I were working for the government. If you had, I would have told you."

"Omission is lying," she hissed.

"A lie is a false statement. I've never lied," he said, holding his ground.

As they traded barbed stares, he added carefully, "I-I also wanted to explain myself further to you, Bronte."

"*Stop*," she snapped, "calling me by my first name."

"In truth," Felix mumbled, "it does sound a bit odd for a man to call you by your last name when he's known you personally for decades."

Ms. Beedinwigg shifted her glare to him and he shrunk back into the kitchen chair where he'd been sitting.

"I imagine you are developing a strategy," Mr. Hamilton remarked. Without waiting for confirmation, he suggested, "Might we try Gershom? Magdalene's best friend at school?"

"He's no longer at school," I replied, trying my best to hold back my own anger. "And he couldn't help us anyway."

"Doesn't he have the ability to locate FOs?" Mr. Hamilton pressed.

Of course, I thought to myself. *He wouldn't be thinking of ways to get Eran back. He was thinking about how best to accomplish his mission.*

"D'you get that information off your list?" I retorted and Mr. Hamilton looked slightly taken aback.

Rufus strolled his hulking frame to stand over Mr. Hamilton. "How 'bout we jost exchange you fer Eran right now?"

"Yes, I considered you might think to do so," Mr. Hamilton responded.

"So you took precautions to ensure it couldn't happen," Ms. Beedinwigg accused.

"I did. Any harm to me will result in harm to Eran." Mr. Hamilton sighed and dropped his shoulders. "Look, I want to help. The more minds thrown at this fight the better our odds at winning it."

An exchange of uncertain expressions filtered through the room.

"Can you two even work together?" Felix blurted, angling his question at Ms. Beedinwigg.

"To get Eran back, I can do anything," she replied plainly before hardening her voice at Mr. Hamilton. "I'll kill you later."

He nodded like a formal waiter after being given a command by his employer.

"But going through Gershom won't help," Ms. Beedinwigg mentioned, her tone turning back to her formal, business-like manner. "He disappeared with Campion." I blinked back surprise, which she noted. "Because he was working undercover with Campion."

"He was?" I asked, slightly taken aback before sensing that reminder that I keep everyone, all Alterums, at a distance suddenly stab me in the stomach. When Ms. Beedinwigg nodded at me for confirmation, I exhaled and looked past Mr. Hamilton, out the door's window to the backyard. The sun was rising. I could see the back wall of the yard now. "We can't utilize the ambassador or Gershom, so I suppose it's business as usual. I go to school. You all go to work," I said, noticing that I was rubbing the area where their needle had penetrated my body. "We'll draw in the target best that way."

Ezra blinked, her jaw falling open. "Tell me that

you're not setting yourself up as bait."

"You're not setting yourself up as bait," Ms. Beedinwigg remarked flatly.

"He can't harm me," I reminded them.

"No, he can't kill you," Ms. Beedinwigg corrected. "He can still subject you to a lot of pain before taking your life if you're caught."

"Well, I can't think of a better idea."

They again glanced at one another, this time with guilty expressions.

"And I'm not asking for one."

Without waiting for their responses, I walked back to my room, mentioning to Ms. Beedinwigg that I'd see her at school. She tipped her head at me, a faint proud light in her eyes.

I showered quickly, and although I said that everyone should behave normally, I did pull the black leather suit from beneath my mattress and slid it on.

It felt loose in the knees and elbows, with just enough give to allow for striking maneuvers, and somehow the oval holes in the back, between my shoulder blades, were less drafty than my tee-shirts. Otherwise, it was tight, fitting perfectly to the contours of my body. Eran and Madame Benoit had done a nice job with my measurements.

Eran.

Given that he could feel my emotions from a distance, I wondered if he could feel me now, could sense the gnawing worry about his well-being. I stopped in the middle of my room, my eyes on my closet and its rows of tee-shirts waiting to be picked, without actually seeing any of them. Closing my eyes, I felt the air around me, so distinct from the afterlife, heavy, weighty, almost tangible here, and then I concentrated on sending Eran a message through it, hoping it was thick enough to serve as a transmitter.

We have a plan and we're executing it. Just a little while longer now.

I paused but didn't reopen my eyes or move. That message wasn't good enough, I realized, and started again.

You'd think as a messenger I'd have learned a few things about drafting messages while I relayed them. The ones that have always touched me the most are the heartfelt ones. It didn't matter if they were articulate or spoken with brevity. The tears in my client's eyes, the swallowing as they cleared the lumps in their throats, the shudder of their shoulders as they held back their emotions, the tremble of their mouths as they tried to steady themselves. Those actions are all more impactful to me than the words. But you can't see me, so words will have to do.

I understand what you mean by it only taking a second, the span of a thought, to decide your future when a loved one's security is at stake. There is no roadmap, no sage advice that can help subdue the fears. I stand here desperate for you, hollow without you, because you are my roadmap, my sage advice. You always have been. Even as I shoved you away, refusing your guardianship, you are a necessity to me. You are my life, Eran, my existence. Without you nothing survives. And because of it, nothing will keep me from you. Nothing.

I then felt a wave of thoughtful tenacity wash over me. When I stepped into my closet, clothes were of even less importance to me than a few seconds earlier. I grabbed the first shirt, it was green, I think, and slipped it over my head. Once I had my jeans and boots on, I strode down to the kitchen were Felix and Rufus were making breakfast and Ezra sat at the table. Ms. Beedinwigg and Mr. Hamilton were gone. The only distinction between this morning and the others was that no light banter was being thrown between the two men.

I forced a grin. "No time for breakfast, I'll see you for dinner." If Eran wasn't paroled by then. If I wasn't trying to find him.

They did their best to smile back.

When the door closed, I tried not to look at the trees. My built-in radar would tell me if a FO was close, I reminded myself. Still, it was irritating. One of my enemies was out there, and I wanted to see him first.

In the shed, as I pulled my helmet over my head, my eyes drifted to the swords beneath the workbench. I wanted mine at my side, but there was no way I could carry a sword onto school grounds. It would be confiscated and locked in a secure location where I couldn't get to it anyway. Not to mention, its presence at my hip would definitely be out of the ordinary. I might as well carry a sign that says, "We know you're watching. Beware."

So I climbed onto my bike, rode it to Mr. LeFrau's bakery, picked up my lunchtime sandwich, and avoided any pestering questions by the man by saying Eran was sick today. It didn't matter that I'd never seen Eran, or any guardian for that matter, suffer any illness or ailment, ever. Eran had told me once that it was a criterion to become one.

I continued to school, parking my bike in an empty spot and noting that Ms. Beedinwigg's heavily-armored vehicle was in her reserved space. I imagined she had already put her security guards on alert today, without providing much detail as to why. She was probably also watching the school grounds with binoculars, knowing her.

I strolled in through the glass doors of the Main Hall, navigating around groups bent in gossip, feeling with potent awareness the emptiness beside me where Eran would normally be. I barely noticed the talk about how the school had gone into lock-down when the military had come in through Ms. Beedinwigg's office window, nor did I care. In the hallway, I made my way to my first class, thankful the teacher was someone other than Mr. Morow and Ms. Gantry. Today would be Mr. Task, American Literature, a portly man with a deep love for his career that transcended the grimaces and groans by his students when he danced around the room quoting Shakespeare. And, unlike the other educators at the school, he had never bothered me or Eran about our reputation.

The sound of locker doors slamming shut and the temporary up-pitch in volume by other students filtering inside told me that class would be starting. Apparently, I'd already missed the first warning bell. I was so focused on making it to my seat that I didn't even notice the prick to the back of my neck until I'd entered the room. I came to a halt just inside the door, my eyes darting across the room in search of its cause.

"Well hello, Magdalene." The voice came directly in front of me. It was familiar, although not immediately recognizable until my eyes stopped on him.

Having been first my private security guard before his conversion to a FO and then a security guard at our school before the Great Battle in the London field, I knew him well. He still had a mop of curly brown hair and his skin remained translucent, like all FOs, but his eyes were tired, as if he had single-handedly waged a war against a massive opponent.

"Marco?" It was all I could say.

While he flicked his wrists to discharge the energy that our proximity created between us, my internal alarm was shockingly intense, and it was everything but the low-energy electrical current that Mr. Hamilton had described. My teeth snapped closed, clenching until I tapped the skill I'd developed throughout centuries to bring the charge under control. Then the world came alive around me. I heard the taps and felt the vibration climbing my calves of the multitude of passing students' footsteps. I smelled the fresh air drifting in from the outside mixed with the distinct, pungent aroma of deodorant coming from the guy in the first row. I tasted the metallic smell of Marco's breath in the room and nearly gagged.

Control, I told myself. *Control*.

Eran was undoubtedly feeling the sensation of fear in him, and was probably working to pummel through whatever doors stood between me and him. The two-inch crumpled metal door to the conference room at the SIEF facility, left mangled against the wall, told me that they wouldn't risk the same mistake. Eran's doors this time were likely made of concrete.

"Still, no welcoming greeting?" Marco mocked. "You never allow me that," he added, genuinely disappointed. "Even after all the time we've known each other, after all we have shared. I must say, you've grown older, more mature, more *attractive*, Magdalene." He paused and with all sincerity dipped his head to add under his breath, "I've missed you." Then his face tilted back and the brown lock that draped over his eyes fell aside, and I could see the glint of trouble in them. "Missed speaking to you, that is. It was lonely watching you all this time."

I was so stunned – to find him alive, not underground, not with the rest of the FOs, having survived, somehow, against all odds, having lived quietly without us knowing, while he remained fully aware of us, for such a long time, before revealing himself, by standing here, in my first period classroom – that I didn't move, even as he turned away.

"Good morning, class," he said, grinning with amusement, pleased with himself for catching me off-guard. "I'm substituting for your teacher today. He is tied up."

Maybe it was instinct, or the darkness in me that

came from the place where I originated below ground, but my next steps were without thought and directed at him. I crossed the three paces, barely touching the tile with my feet in my rush to get to him. Then I had my hand around his neck and had forced him up against the wall, slamming him against the whiteboard and rattling it enough that my senses detected the loosening of its bolts in the corners. My free hand went for my hip only to find bone and fabric there. My sword, damnit, I left it at the house.

A commotion ignited behind me. Curse words, metal chairs scraping across the floor, unintelligible screams followed. Then hands came around my arms, many of them, pulling my arm down, dragging me back.

As I lost my grip, Marco feigned surprise at my behavior, bringing a hand to his throat and coughing lightly.

"There she goes," someone warned.

"At it again," another mumbled.

"Always, just a matter of time."

"Get Ms. Beedinwigg," I demanded, throwing a pointed finger at the door.

Shannon, a girl from the third row who always seemed to know the answers to hard questions, ran for the hallway but Marco stopped her.

"Wait!" he called out and she skidded to a standstill just inside the classroom. He straightened his posture, which had been slumped in defense, and strolled toward her with commendable composure, having made a sudden recovery.

"Shannon!" I barked. "Ms. Beedinwigg!"

Marco leaned over and closed the door with calm authority. He waved off the teacher from the class next to us, reassuring her through the window, even as I screamed for her to get Ms. Beedinwigg. She paused, recognized it was me, scowled, and marched back in the direction of her class.

Turley, a brawny guy who could have played offensive football if our school had a team, still gripped my forearms. As I considered my next move to free myself, Marco clapped his hands and made an announcement.

"Magdalene and I will need a moment in the hallway. Please take your seat. We'll be back in shortly." Still at the door, he reached over and swung it open before gesturing genteelly for me to go through.

"You first, Marco."

His leer deepened and he seemed to hold back a mocking laugh but he did step out.

Turley loosened his hold and I snapped my arms free the rest of the way while following Marco into the hallway. The movement behind me affirmed that the rest of the class was doing as they were told and once I closed the door, there were no peering eyes or listening ears disrupting Marco and me.

"What did you do with Mr. Task?"

"Is that his name?" Marco asked offhandedly.

"Where is he?" I demanded.

"In the janitor's closet," Marco said with a shrug before his eyes turned cold. "Almost did away with him all together. He was as surly as that elderly storeowner. Both are lucky I didn't find the time to do with them what I wanted."

"Storeowner?" I said in thought before the image of Madame Benoit's demolished storefront came back to me.

"That was you? You did that to Madame Benoit?" I took a step forward, my anger momentarily cloaking my physical reaction to him.

He sighed impatiently. "Don't we have more important topics to discuss, you and me?"

"Marco," I said, impressed at my success in keeping

my voice steady, "you're going to accompany me to Mr. Hamilton's residence –"

He immediately broke into laughter. "Well, you certainly haven't lost your sense of humor."

"Where you will be transported –"

"You're too late, Magdalene."

"To the United States government –"

"My job is done," he said simply. "My kind will be freed soon."

I fell temporarily silent. "That's not possible."

He chuckled under his breath. "Anything is possible, given enough time."

I blinked and a chill ran through me. "Time ...," I whispered. "What have you done, Marco?"

"I told you, Magdalene. I've never once lied to you and I'll not start now. I've freed them."

My next thought was of the hole in the London field, a place I found myself now desperate to reach.

"Which brings us to a more important discussion. I've waited, patiently, *so* patiently, and I am *tired*," he emphasized, his shoulders slumping forward, "of *waiting* ... for you, Magdalene."

"I've told you before, I love Eran."

"Ah, but the government has him now," Marco mocked, and I froze.

"How did you –"

"Know?" He smiled impishly. "Who do you think set him up? I told you, anything can be accomplished with enough time. I have to say, that dirty, dusty prison of yours is not at all welcoming and certainly not a home I would have made by choice, but it did serve its purpose."

"You've been –"

"In hiding there, this *whole* time," he said dramatically.

"Since the battle?" I clarified.

"Yes, the one you all now call the *Great Battle*," he mocked and ridiculed the name with a roll of his eyes. "But don't fret, it will be nothing compared to the coming *Great War*."

Ignoring his taunting, I stayed on course. "Because there were no prisoners at the prison any longer."

"And therefore, no reason for you to return."

I paused, trying to understand. "So you've been in hiding all this time."

He bowed playfully, even while I knew it was to demonstrate applause for his own success.

Then I smirked, unable to hold it back. "Why did you hide, Marco? Too scared to join your brethren on the field of battle?"

He tilted his head in spirited offense before leaning forward, causing me to lean back, and whispering his secret with gleeful enthusiasm. "Lotharius."

The name had the opposite effect to me, striking fear and reigniting my senses so that the smell of stale beer emitting from Marco's skin filled my nose. I had to tame it to concentrate on his words.

"He was there, you know. During the *Great Battle*, on the sidelines, observing. Abaddon executed Lotharius's plans flawlessly. I told him not to concern himself with such a petty enterprise, that there were far greater battles to come, but he was correct. Abaddon *did* fail, in one area, and one area only. You. He did not know your strength, that you could lift others from that underground penitentiary. But Lotharius did. I understood later that he insisted on being there, present, to witness your ability. In fact, he synchronized all of it – from the very beginning, Magdalene. He knew of your ability, and he knew you would need to learn of it because Eran would certainly never tell you. That's one courtesy you can always expect of me, Magdalene –"

"Yes," I said impatiently, "the truth. I know."

He seemed content that I'd voiced it. "So Lotharius set in motion events that would lead you to that understanding. And he used Eran to do it. Your feelings for that boy I will never understand, but Lotharius, he saw them as an opportunity, knowing you would follow your precious Eran anywhere, even there. So he found someone who had a vendetta against Eran. Now many do, let's be fair, but Abaddon had all the panache needed to get the job done. Yes, he played with you both for a while, time is one element on our side and we do get bored here, but once Lotharius had apprehended you, in your cabin, in the Appalachians? And he offered you the chance to join him, and you failed him by failing to do so, he warned you that coercion would follow. And follow it did. He was the one who set it all in motion, right up to the battle in the field."

"But why?" I pleaded, flashes of misery and despair on all sides coming back to me. "What did any of that accomplish?"

"Isn't it obvious? Lotharius needed you to create the hole. He needed you down there, so you would create the hole."

Blinking, shaking my head, I asked in confusion. "For what purpose?"

"To free them. His disciples."

"His disciples?" I whispered, ignoring Marco's enjoyment over my shock.

"All of them, Magdalene. They are all there. It's where Eran sent them long before he ever met you."

I exhaled, not realizing I had been holding my breath, because it all came together for me. Eran had been Lotharius's disciple, before he had become my guardian, but he had gone up against Lotharius, defeating him with a group of misfit loners, loners who had ironically the skills to become Eran's guardians, and they imprisoned Lotharius's disciples underground, as

Lotharius fled into hiding. Of course, Lotharius would want them freed.

"Lotharius kept me behind during that *Great Battle*, unseen in that *horrid* prison, as a failsafe. I was to do as I have already done, free them, if he did not return. And he did not." Marco's lips pinched downward. "I suspect Campion found him, being the shiftiest of your kind."

Marco sighed. "If it weren't for The Sevens and that petty conflict in the swamps, this all would have been executed sooner. But as it were …"

He fell into remiss posturing, which I ignored as I felt a wave of desperation sweep over me. The memory of Ms. Gantry's Advanced French class rushed back to me, specifically the phrase that she had written on the board the first day. Petit a petit, l'oiseau fait son nid. Little by little, the bird makes its nest. Marco had executed Lotharius's plan perfectly. Little by little. He revealed himself to the humans. He led them to the hole in the London field. He gave them a reason to investigate it. And he knew that once they saw what was inside, it would provoke them to raise the bodies for further examination. He couldn't do it himself. And he knew I wouldn't do it for him. So, he used the humans. The nest.

My mind spinning, I struggled with three competing priorities. Free Mr. Task from the janitor's closet, stop the hole I'd made from being breached, and detain Marco to get Eran back. But, I reasoned, if Marco was telling me the truth, and there was no purpose for him to make such an elaborate lie, then he's only doing it because all cogs of his plan have been set in motion and stopping them would be improbable. That left me to save either Mr. Task or Eran. Eran won.

My head snapped up, a motion that made Marco immediately suspicious. He had been in the middle of speaking but stopped short. Then, for the third time that morning, my hand found a neck.

For a moment, he grinned above my solid hold and then his voice, hoarse from my grip, warned, "If you kill me, and I go underground, I'll simply be freed alongside them."

"Not if your goal has been met. You said so yourself, no one ever revisits an empty prison."

And Marco's eyes grew wide.

I leaned into him, using my arm as a brace, pivoting my weight, tipping him backwards off-balance. He stepped back, but I kept coming, so he stepped back again, and I advanced further. Suddenly, I was running on the balls of my feet as he tried to steady himself, our feet slapping the tiled hallway, echoing off the lockers, disturbing the quiet.

When I saw something expand from behind him, on both sides of his body, large swathes of thick grey, I knew he was desperate. The grey feathered appendages flapped once, brushing a waft of cool air toward me, and lifting us off the ground. Another pump and our feet were off the ground. But I held on, as he carried us backwards down the hallway.

My senses still ignited, I heard footsteps approaching classroom doorways and I knew Marco and I wouldn't be alone for long. There was no inclination then for me to open my appendages, so I squeezed my fingers, indenting them around his neck, the folds of his translucent skin curling up around my tips, as we reached the end of the hallway. He was heading for a slam against the wall, and I wanted to be ready.

It never came.

I was reminded just how well he knew this school after having been a security guard here as he pirouetted and my body swung to the side, around the corner, away from Ms. Beedinwigg's office. His eyes sharpened in hopes it would dislodge me, but I smiled in confirmation.

"I'm not letting go, Marco."

"As much as I enjoy your touch, Magdalene, I gladly await the day when it is tender."

"You'll be waiting a long time."

"Time is all I have, Magdalene. Now do forgive me for this …"

He jerked viciously to the side, and still I held on, until my shoulders and hips came in violent contact with the lockers against the wall. Burning pain seared through my skin and into my bones as my teeth rattled in my head, and I felt the sickening slip of my fingers from his slack skin. Suddenly, they were gripping only air as I fell flat to the tile below me. My head made another jarring impact as my chin cracked on the hard surface.

Frantic that my objective was loose, I looked up to find him slipping backwards, his long grey appendages carrying him, legs dangling, toward the main hall's exit. He was watching me, his eyes lit up, chin jutted out, waving fingers at me in mock disappointment.

Just before he reached the doors, footsteps came around the corner, drawn by the slam of my body against the metal lockers. A sharp inhale of air behind me said they had breached the hallway.

I sprang to my feet as someone exhaled, "Ms. Tanner …"

Ignoring Ms. Gantry, I briskly stepped to my left, keeping my eyes on Marco, who was disappearing through the exit now, and yanked open the door at my side. I knew this door and its location well, had marked it in my memory, after Eran had suggested we use it between classes. The letters painted across it read: Janitor's Closet

In my speed, the knob slammed into the wall and Ms. Gantry gasped. "Ms. Tanner! What in the name is your prob –"

"She's *always* doing something," a girl's voice muttered from the huddle of students who'd followed Ms. Gantry.

The doors down the hallway squeaked closed. I didn't have time for this.

"Free him," I commanded, never looking at Ms. Gantry or the others, never turning my head from my objective who was escaping.

"Who?" Ms. Gantry demanded, but Mr. Task's muffled panic from behind the tape rose above the noise we created. Ms. Gantry peered in to find him curled into a fetal position, wound in duct tape, writhing against his constraints.

Another draw of shocked air and Ms. Gantry demanded more firmly, "Ms. Tanner, *what* is going on here?"

But I was already sprinting down the tiled floor, away from the humans.

By the time I felt the sun on my face and saw the blue sky unobstructed overhead, Marco was a few hundred yards away and could easily pass for a bird if anyone were watching.

With the entry into the main building nothing more than brick, ivy-covered walls, and no classroom windows peering out over me, I released my appendages in a running leap and jumped into the air. Pumping hard, I looked over my shoulder to make sure no one witnessed it, and saw only one man stepping out of a black SUV in the parking lot, one hand to his ear, talking with calm resolve into a cell phone he held, while watching me with a keen eye.

Mr. Hamilton.

Who evidently had been trailing me.

And was now alerting the military as to the exact location of Marco and me.

I scowled, snapped my head forward, and committed

myself to catching up with Marco. My clothing, however impeded me.

Unable to slip my tee-shirt over my head without slowing my appendages, I simply looped my fingers around its weakest fabric and tore. The arm cuff ripped easily enough, giving me leverage over the rest of the shirt, and soon it fell in tatters through the air behind me. My boots were easier, just a tuck of my toes into each heel with a fixed thrust and they tumbled off my feet and downward. A snap of the buttons and brief shimmy later, my jeans slipped from my hips, down my legs and toward the earth. Then the wind quieted significantly in my ears, coursing over the skin-tight black leather suit, compliments of Eran and Madame Benoit.

Marco's trajectory through the sky appeared leisurely, but efficient, until he casually glanced over his shoulder. On seeing me and the distance that had narrowed between us to just a hundred yards, he did a double-take and then propelled himself faster, physically thrusting his entire body into the effort.

I drew a deep breath and did the same.

He took me over the city in a zigzag, passing downtown, and made a sharp turn at the I-10 Freeway to head back for the Mississippi River. He was faster than me, but I was nimble and shortened the space between us by half when he made his turns. I had nearly caught him above the park stretching along the lakeshore in the French Quarter when something flew past me, its exhaust trail hurling me into a spin, burning my face and sending my limbs flailing against the draft. By the time I steadied myself, Marco had gained distance and the fighter pilot in the F-22 had missed his target.

The pilot circled around and I thought might be coming back for a second pass when heated flames soared by me on all sides. I realized then Marco was getting out of the line of fire launched by the second fighter jet. He dodged the bullets whizzing past me by dipping and falling in elevation, straight down for twenty yards, before returning to increasing his speed. I, however, darted a glare at the jet as he blew by me, hoping the pilot would see it and consider me the next time he opened fire.

The first pilot completed his turn and lobed bullets at Marco from a flanking position, which I appreciated because I was too far right to be in range. Marco deftly swerved down and under again before turning back toward the city. As he did, the fighter jets volleyed for position, revolving back and forth, sideswiping Marco, and tracing his path as he sank lower and lower. I was again caught in the firing line, and the pilots made it clear that they would forgo my life to accomplish their mission. I silently thanked them with sarcasm and fell back, realizing as we gained on the shoreline again that Marco's course was intentional. By the time we reached the city, he would be just over the rooftops and far too low for the jets to fly.

Infuriated at the pilots for forcing Marco into this position while never backing off, I gave up any hope they might do some good and focused on any opportunities ahead to take on Marco directly. The business center towered above the slanted roofs with just St. Louis Cathedral's spire standing as a solitary witness, and none of what I saw helped me formulate a plan.

The jets peeled aside, going vertical, as Marco reached the park, this time low enough that people along the cement pathway pointed at him in the sky. Some ran for cover, ducking and covering their heads in their panic.

Taking advantage of Marco's distraction over the jets

and where they might be going, I gained ground, closing in enough that I could see his hands clenched into fists. He was nervous, and that was good.

I was excited now. He was within my means to catch and the military couldn't interfere. Eran could be back in New Orleans by end of day.

Then Marco dropped to the ground, running to a stop in the middle of Jackson Square. Those gathered there, most of them tourists wolfing down beignets and carrying tourist shop bags, hadn't seen him coming and only a few stepped aside with just two reacting with screams. Still, he drew attention and that attention shifted to me as I landed. By then, Marco was quickly strolling down the crowded street, his appendages having slipped into his back, camouflaging himself as just another human, and all eyes were on me.

While Marco stirred the crowd, I sent it into full-scale panic.

Shouting filled the air, a stampede shook the concrete, people escaped into the doorways of the shops surrounding The Square, a few yelled that there were *two* of us, and none of it mattered to me. I retracted my appendages and kept my eyes on Marco. People darted between us as they fled for safety but we each had a clear line of sight of the other; he peered over his shoulder and weaved through the fleeing humans and I advanced on him, until he slipped into a doorway and disappeared.

I landed as close as I could to him, given the thickness of the crowd, but that didn't seem to help. By the time I reached the entryway, he was gone.

The people inside were cowering against the walls and beneath the tables, half-eaten food dishes of jambalaya and boiled crawfish still sat on the table, their aromas filling the air. I walked through to the back, pushing open the swinging door into the kitchen to find the hard-working cooks still bent over grills and sauté pans. When one of them saw me, he broke his concentration to coolly point at the backdoor. I smiled, nodded appreciation, and followed where his finger pointed.

The rear of the restaurant opened to a small alley encircled by crumbling, vine and moss-covered brick, but no sign of Marco. Overhead, a hundred yards into the air, three Blackhawk military helicopters hovered, their blades sending pulsating vibrations down and spoiling any chance of at least hearing Marco's movement. Irritated and throwing a scowl their way, I released my appendages, flapped once, and my feet left the ground. I angled my leap so that I landed on the back wall, allowing me some visibility. On the opposite side, a vacant apartment building courtyard made of broken, uneven brick and overgrown by unmaintained palms stood in the shadows. The stench of old, placid water and damp earth encompassed it. The brick stretched into a pathway down a tunnel below the building ending at a wrought-iron gate onto the street. A dim light filtered down it, obstructed only by Marco as he opened the gate and stepped through.

I jumped forward, pumping my appendages once, hard enough to carry me through the tunnel. Once inside, they were too wide to do any good and I retracted them, but kept my speed on the balls of my feet.

Shoving open the gate's cool, rough rails, I sprinted across the street, hearing a long, irritated honk from a car to my right and the grating pulsation of helicopter blades overhead, but paying neither one any attention. Because Marco had crossed the opposite sidewalk into an antique furniture store.

I barreled inside it where a woman with white hair coifed into a beehive bun was trying to make sense of the helicopters outside and the two people who had just ran into her store.

"Where is he?"

Her eyes snapped back to me, she swallowed, realizing whatever was happening was now taking place in her store, and unable to speak just looked in the direction of the backroom.

I went that way and found the rear door open. Another back patio, holding only a few dented metal trashcans and one lonely folding chair for breaks. But no Marco. Again, I expanded my appendages and leapt, finding him re-entering the rear of another store on the other side of the wall.

We continued this pace across several French Quarter streets through residences and businesses until he entered a small, abandoned warehouse. I raced inside and at first noticed only the muted beams of sunlight through softly drifting dust particles and the disturbance of birds in the rafters, until I felt Marco's cold fingers around my neck, dampening the spark of his presence across my skin.

I was pulled backwards, toward the door, but I slammed into the wall beside it before hearing Marco's panted mumble and seeing his face drift across my sight. "Once more, I apologize for this."

Then his fist smashed into my jaw.

My head flew to the side, ramming into one of the warehouse's thick, wooden support beams, and the area surrounding me sank away into darkness.

8   HUBRIS

There was no bright light, no tunnel, no greetings by old departed friends, which was ironically advantageous to me. It meant I was still alive. For now.

Only the gentle warm breeze of the Hall of Records brushed my cheeks, and it lasted just long enough for me to question whether I felt it at all. Then I slammed back into my body on earth, opened my eyes, and sucked in a long, hoarse breath, replacing the stale air in my lungs with the fresh, open air that rarely seemed to settle over New Orleans streets from the higher elevations.

"'Bout time," Marco yelled into my ear, through the wind that whipped around us.

We were aloft, the pads of my feet without any pressure against them and only Marco's arm looped across my torso, pinning me against him, and his hand at my neck. Feeling his body solidly against me, my first instinct was a sweeping, unimpeded disgust. Then my senses returned, at a heightened level, giving me a strong understanding of exactly where I was being held.

Stretched out below us was Congo Square, a park

where Marie Laveau, the Creole voodoo practitioner once performed her rituals. It sat just above the northwest corner of the French Quarter. A dozen people were peering up through its trees, some with cell phones raised at us.

We were several hundred yards up, well out of identity range, but in front of us, in a solid line, hovered the three Blackhawk helicopters, their blades cutting the air sharply and irritating my ear drums. I saw the drooping mouth of one pilot as he listened to commands that were muffled to me through his earpiece. He spoke just two words – "Copy that" – and then a gun barrel began shifting in our direction.

Marco had been shouting into my ear the entire time and then stopped to mutter something about me being poor insurance against their assault.

"You moron!" I shouted at him. "I'm a hindrance to them!"

I pitched my head backwards, feeling the crush of soft tissue as his nose shifted aside and then the thick pressure of our skulls connecting. It felt worse than I expected, a dense resounding ringing inside my head exploded, causing me to blink back the pain.

But too much time had passed.

The hail of gunfire was launched at us, the chug-chug-chug of the barrel's automatic fire slowing in my mind, my ear drums detecting each round's velocity and distance as they coursed through the sky. I braced for their impact, expecting the searing heat to shred my delicate organic body, knowing the agony would be breathtaking and leave me speechless as I awaited death.

The ammunition, however, never made it to me. Each round veered in the opposite direction as if hitting and reflecting off an invisible barrier.

The firing helicopter shifted to the side and, strangely, it's gun barrel swiveled in the other copter's direction. The pilots of that craft jerked frantically in their seats, screaming into their linked communication system. The first pilot desperately tried to regain control. Then the rotor blades of both helicopters bent vertical and each fuselage swept to the side, colliding with the other copter beside it. Together, they descended into a level spin, pinned to each other as if the collision had caused their metal protrusions to lock. The remaining helicopter remained hovering until its blades came to a sudden, grinding halt, and it too began to plummet toward the earth.

Marco exhaled relief in my ear.

I dipped my chin and saw the copters settle to a swath of grass in Congo Square, steadily and without damage to the craft or occupants, without use of their rotors or any propulsion system at all. I was still trying to make sense of this when Marco mumbled in the now silent sky, "Of course … Always the hero."

Unlike him, I never saw Eran incoming.

Marco's muscles tensed as he braced for the impact but my body was thrown to the side, a hand gently catching my head in its palm to reduce the sudden lurch.

"Can you fly?" Eran's voice asked, calm but demanding.

I caught only a glimpse of him, the farthest edge of his jostling brown hair, the patch of smooth skin between his eye and his temple, a trace of the color of his sweltering, blue-green iris. And instantly I felt reassured and empowered.

"Yes," I said, my voice stable.

Then all arms, Marco's included, were gone from me, and I felt the soft wind's tender touch engulf my body. It quickly turned harsh as gravity drew me back to earth like a suction. Wind whipped my hair and swiped my skin until I released my appendages and adjusted my trajectory.

Eran expected me to return to the city below, but I did my best to regain ground lost and catch up to assist him. He was vertical now, his hands gripping Marco's collar, propelling him downward as Marco tried to reclaim use in his wings. They curled around Eran and Marco's bodies, trembling uselessly against Eran's aggressive descent.

I didn't think Eran would stop, taking his anger all the way to the ground, but in the last few seconds, he swung their bodies upward and landed solidly on his feet, leaving Marco dumbfounded and wobbly.

By the time I landed a few paces behind them, Marco had his hands restrained in plastic cuffs and was flanked by two of Paper-Pusher's armored men.

Eran spun around and marched to me, meeting me halfway, his hands pressing to my face, his eyes passionate but calming. Breathing heavily, not from exertion but concern, he evaluated me, his eyes sweeping my face with rigid determination.

"A split lip, slight concussion," he muttered to himself, nodded, leaned down and pressed his lips to mine lightly, avoiding my injury. Only when he mentioned it did I notice the swelling and taint of blood in my mouth. He then broke his hold on me, turned on his heel and stomped back to Marco.

I thought he might have a few select words to deliver or begin an interrogation, but no. Simply and with extreme force, he sent his balled fist into Marco's mouth, which I felt was just punishment for Marco, having done the same to me. Marco's head lurched backward, arching painfully over his shoulders and down his back before rolling forward slowly, his eyes closed and his knees giving out. The men detaining him then had to hold him up, opting to begin dragging his body to one of the many black military vehicles now lining the curb of Congo Square. They passed the

Chairman and Paper-Pusher on their way, who were making a beeline for Eran and me.

"Eran," he greeted amiably with a subtle tip of his head.

"John."

"I see we couldn't detain you even in a concrete bunker."

"No, Mr. Chairman."

John observed him and then mumbled to himself, "The rebar."

"Excuse me, sir?" Paper-Pusher acknowledged.

Keeping a respectful eye on Eran, he explained, "Rebar is made of steel, is it not?"

"Yes, sir, it is."

"And steel is a form of metal." John frowned but then laughed with the humiliated deference of a man who has just realized he's been swindled. "Eran's strength."

Paper-Pusher's mouth fell open, and I got the impression he had built Eran's cell without thinking of that fine detail.

"One of many strengths ... John," I mumbled under my breath, which brought his attention to me.

"Maggie, nice job."

"You should thank Eran. He's the one who caught Marco. Something he wouldn't have been able to do if he were still imprisoned."

John watched me steadily, showing no emotion and offering no apology.

"Benson," he uttered in a commanding tone, "continue your confiscation here as your team is doing in Jackson Square. All videos, images destroy. Anything uploaded, remove immediately."

Paper-Pusher promptly turned and began rounding up a few of his men.

"I understand you've raised the bodies," I said,

intentionally not leading into the topic at a gradual pace. And it had the desired effect. John was taken by surprise, moving glowing eyes back to me. Eran did the same before his back straightened and his face fell stiff. "Did you raise all of them? The Elsics, as well?"

"The Elsics are the ones covered in black feathers?"

"Yes," I said briskly.

"Those were left behind."

Eran remained rigid despite this news. "Did anyone you raised have a narrow strip of white hair down the center of his skull with the sides of his head shaved?"

"I believe you mean a mohawk."

"Yes," Eran retorted.

"I don't know, but it may suffice to learn that all but the Elsics have been lifted."

"Why?" I demanded. "Why raise them?"

"The skeleton we exhumed," John said placidly, "was found on a hillside just outside Gettysburg. It wasn't alone."

That struck a chord with me because I had buried friends there. A part of me wondered if John might know it. "Your point being?" I replied sharply.

"Mr. Hamilton has assembled a decent spreadsheet but we recognize there are more of you, how many is still in debate. The greater the number of challengers, the greater the potential threat."

"Clearly, we're the challengers," I muttered.

"Are you?" John retorted coolly.

"The person making an observation is the determiner," I said. "So tell me, John, are we?"

John was unmoved, refusing to take my bait. "We also knew, before you ever entered my conference room, that each of you command impressive areas of competence, unique skills that we cannot possibly match."

"Again, your point?"

"What is the first initiative you take once a potential threat has been recognized?"

Eran's head tipped back as understanding came to him. His voice was controlled but with simmering tension below it, as he already knew the truth to his next statement. "You raised the bodies from the hole to study them."

"Do you blame us?"

"No," Eran said, to my surprise, but his cautionary notice following it led me to understand why. "But you may end up blaming yourselves, John."

"Why?"

"We've never raised them."

"So you don't know what to expect," John surmised.

"More importantly," Eran emphasized, "neither do you."

John bristled, but it was almost imperceptible.

"You should know," I interrupted, "that Marco's plan was for you to bring the others to the surface." For extra measure, I clarified, "He set you up."

John seemed undisturbed by that warning, although it appeared so impressive as to be a façade.

A commotion drew our attention to a corner of the park where Paper-Pusher and his men were suddenly alarmed by a group of people shoving through the perimeter Paper-Pusher had set. Shouts to halt and impede their advance did no good and the group kept on coming.

"Tell your people to stand down, John," Eran warned.

John cast cold eyes at Eran.

"For the sake of your own men," Eran added.

At this point, two of Paper-Pusher's men took physical hold of one man dressed in an impeccable three-piece business suit. The man being assaulted drew in a sharp, offended breath audible over the noise of the city and from our distance of twenty-five yards away. No one in the rest of the group paused, but instead kept a fixed pace advancing toward us. Only one man stood back, observing what happened next, which probably seemed odd to the rest of us watching because he was strikingly opposite the suited-man, being dressed in khakis and a black tee-shirt and covered in scars, some deep enough that they had distorted his nose, one ear, and an elbow.

The man in the suit took hold of the military professional to his left, twisting an arm around his assaulter and flipping him into the air. The man slammed the ground, his body jerking with the force and his rifle tumbling out of his grip.

"John," Eran demanded more forcefully.

But the suited man had already moved on to his second assaulter, looping his arm around the man's muscular bicep and yanking him forward, off-balance, and directly into the suited-man's fist. His opponent didn't retaliate but remained upright for a few seconds longer, and then dropped straight to the ground, unconscious, his rifle hitting the ground vertically and then tipping over.

The group kept coming, despite Paper-Pusher's screaming instructions. A shifting of Paper-Pusher's resources brought his men into a semi-circle between us and the group, military rifles pointed at the incoming entourage.

But the group remained undeterred.

When several of those advancing on us rounded their backs and rolled their shoulders forward, a clear indication they were about to release their appendages, Eran grumbled, "John, you don't want this –"

John stepped forward then, bellowing, "Stand down. STAND DOWN."

Barrels of all rifles immediately sank until they were

pointed at the ground but the men in fatigues kept their stances offensive, even as the group walked directly through them, like sand through extended fingers, without the courtesy of waiting for John to wave them forward.

The first one to reach us stopped directly in front of me and brushed a lock of auburn hair from her eyes. "You said someone has Eran," she explained, glancing at him beside me. "That was the last thing you said to me in the afterlife before you were pulled back. Was that someone Marco?" She looked over her shoulder to the black SUV that had already pulled off the curb and disappeared with two other black SUVs flanking it. "We saw the commotion from the air as we approached."

"I'll explain later. First, I'd like you to meet the Chairman of the Joint Chiefs of Staff." I motioned to John, who for the first time, appeared unsure of the next step. "John, this is –"

"Hermina," he said, stepping forward, extending a hand and reasserting his command over the unexpected circumstances.

She looked stunned that he knew her, took his hand and shook it once, forceful by Hermina's initiative. That took John by surprise, given her motherly appearance and soft-spoken demeanor.

"And this is my husband –" she said, ushering forward a placid, unassuming man.

"Hoffstedler," John deduced, receiving another round of raised eyebrows.

Paper-Pusher then appeared at John's side and was told assertively to stand down, again.

"Did you see that?" someone interrupted, pushing his way willfully to the front. "Did you see those men touch me? And their hands. They were *filthy*." He made a show of brushing the undetectable dirt from his untarnished jacket.

"Jerod," John said, and received a fleeting curious glance from him, followed by a scowl and disinterest as Jerod returned to his clothing. "The one who cares most about his appearance."

"Well, honestly, you'd think slovenliness would be an embarrassment," Jerod defended, "but clearly that isn't an issue with those men."

"Jerod," I interrupted. "This man *leads* those men."

He stopped to evaluate John before announcing, "They require better and more detailed washroom instructions, more stringent clothing detergent, and —"

"Their hygiene is just fine," John replied turning an abrupt shoulder to Jerod.

And Jerod's mouth fell wide open.

"I take it these are messengers," John said to me.

"A few of them."

"And their guardians," John added, intentionally tipping his head at the man who had stayed behind to watch over Jerod sparring with Paper-Pusher's guards. "I recognize you as Gillis."

Gillis, not one of many words, simply tipped his head forward.

John rotated to survey the group, stopping briefly at the stouter faces and ones with stockier frames. "Guardians," he murmured to himself. Eran didn't validate that assumption as John followed his assessment with another comment, this one louder. "Or should I say the reputable Guardian Legion."

And the guardians responded in unison, prompted by the mention of their name. "Huff ... Huff ... Huff."

John was noticeably affected, with the smallest curve of his lips at the ends. "My name is John, and no further introductions are needed on your side."

I understood this to mean that he had read and memorized every dossier Mr. Hamilton had put before him.

"I'd like to invite you back to Mr. Hamilton's house to get to know you all better and for an impromptu celebration. The one who has been terrorizing our people has now been apprehended, thanks to Eran. Which calls for a liquid lunch, wouldn't you say?"

Eran's guardians waited for a nod from him before reacting, and when it came, they joined in with several messengers already grinning and rubbing their hands. Eran disturbed the excitement by offering, "We'll host, at Ezra's house."

John looked back at Eran with knowing respect and tipped his head, even while recognizing that the change of venue gave our side more control over the environment.

"Ezra's!" a few called out, the location not being of all that critical to them.

"I imagine you two will be truant for the rest of the day," John suggested to Eran and me, and I suddenly remembered that we were supposed to be in class.

A quick look around reminded me that despite our true age, we were the only teenagers in the swarm of adults, a realization that regularly amused me.

"No, we won't be heading for school," Eran said.

"We'll see you at Ezra's then," John said amiably.

When Eran smiled plainly in response, I knew he had no intention of joining. And neither did I.

John turned with Paper-Pusher trailing him like the lackey he was and headed for the line of black SUVs.

"Well that's disturbing," Hermina's voice came up beside me, and when Eran and I looked at her, she elaborated. "He didn't ask for directions. Just how much does he know about us and how did he come to find out?"

"Here's someone who can fill you in on all the details," I suggested, motioning to Ms. Beedinwigg crossing the grass from the opposite end of the park.

Mr. Hamilton was keeping pace with her, although remaining a few cautious steps behind.

"Bronte …" Hermina muttered warmly and went to greet her.

As she did, I turned to Eran, who was already nodding in agreement as he voiced the thought running through my mind.

"We need to get to the hole."

"But should we leave …" I motioned to the messengers and guardians as they filtered into smaller groups to find their way to Ezra's home.

"The guardians know what to do."

"Oh," I said, my eyebrows rising. "And what is that?"

Shameless in his approach, Eran pronounced, "To heavily intoxicate John's people and push them for information."

I half-laughed, half-scoffed before realizing the importance of it. "You don't want to be there for it?"

"I'll get reports later," Eran replied surveying the area, already planning which direction he and I should head. "And they'll have better luck without me there."

"Because authority tends to encourage moderation?"

"Exactly."

"Ahh."

"Ready?" He tipped his head toward a neighborhood adjacent to the park, where – it being midday – households were likely to be empty.

"Couldn't be more than," I said, and we began walking inconspicuously in the opposite direction as the others.

I waited for someone to call out to us, but none did, and once we turned a corner I relaxed. Eran apparently did the same because he waited until then to make a confession.

"You look stunning."

My lips curled into a smile. "Better than a slinky black dress?"

Eran chuckled under his breath. "Much… too good not to have bad thoughts."

I made a sound that showed I was pleased by it and he grinned at me before falling serious again.

"I heard you, you know," he remarked offhandedly.

"Heard what?"

"When I was in the cell, I heard – or rather, I felt you talking to me."

Blinking back my surprise, I thought back to what he might mean. When I understood, I tipped my head, smiling slightly. "In my bedroom. I told you that we had a plan to release you …" I could still feel the urgency in my effort to send that message, as if my body was remembering.

"Is that what you were relaying?" he mused. "Words didn't come through, just your feelings."

I laughed in amazement, wondering what elements had ever come together to form our bond to the level that would allow us to sense each other to that depth and distance; but Eran only continued to ruminate over it.

"It reminded me of the first time you interrogated me."

"Um-hmm," I mumbled. "I remember. I called you to my bedroom and you appeared at the foot of my bed."

"Where you tried to seduce me," he said, his tone brimming with amusement.

"And failed miserably."

Eran chuckled. "Oh, you were successful. I just didn't act on it."

A wave of disappointment washed over me, the kind brought on when learning about a missed opportunity.

"The truth is," he continued, "usually, I sense you

190

primarily during periods of intense emotional expenditure, but this time – in the cell – it was different, an impassioned plea."

"Yes, I was desperate."

He nodded.

"I was concerned about you being out here, alone; kept part of my focus on you while another part of me was working a way out of the cell. Then your alarm went off and I was worried about you for a different reason. When I knew the FO was close, and I could not see you, hear you, or touch you, I ..." He inhaled sharply and shook his head.

"You've experienced that before," I reminded him.

"Yes, the feeling was the same, the frantic need to get to you, nothing else mattering, but this time something stood in my way, and it shouldn't have been there. It was the first time I was restrained in all the time I've been your guardian." His attention rose to the sky as his mind returned to the cell. "And I – I was uncontrollable in that scenario."

I observed his profile, but his face remained stoic. "Meaning?"

In a plain, earnest tone, he replied, "There's nothing left of it...Or of the building."

"Paper-Pusher will be unhappy with you."

"I take great pleasure in that," he replied.

We shared a slight laugh and he tipped his head upward. "Shall we?"

After another brief survey of our surroundings and, finding only one of John's SUVs waiting at a distance, but no other prying eyes, we rolled our shoulders forward, and our appendages sprang outward. Eran took the moment to bring my hand, which he still held, to his lips and gently kissed the top of my palm. My heart fluttered and sped up as he did. Somehow he recognized it and glanced up at me from over the tops of my knuckles, his lips sliding to the side in his breathtaking signature smirk, arrogant in that he'd seen a reaction in me, clear blue-green eyes glowing with open enjoyment. I exhaled loudly.

"Sorry," he said, although his smirk remained, telling me that he wasn't entirely.

He released me and chuckled, and his appendages pumped strong enough to draw a draft that stirred my hair. He was overhead and looking down at me then, ignoring the men now stepping out of the SUV.

"Coming?" he teased.

I raised an eyebrow. "Oh, I'll beat you there."

His mouth fell open into a pleased grin. "It's a race then."

I thrust my legs from a squat into a lurch and shoved my appendages downward for an extra kick into the air, and excitedly passed Eran on the way up. I heard him chuckle but didn't wait to ensure he caught up. Using all my strength, I pushed myself through the air, cursing not for the first time at air resistance in this realm that did not exist in the other, and we left the four men standing beside their SUV gawking as we escaped their attempt to surveil us.

The entire time we were in flight Eran easily kept up, but out of gallantry alone, he allowed me to breach the cloud bank that hovered over the London field first. Then we both stopped short as the hole came into view.

"Is this …?" I said, looking around to get my bearings.

"Yes," Eran replied tightly. "It is."

What had once been a dark, hollow, ragged circle a few feet across the earth was now a complex campus of mobile buildings, lit against the night that had settled on this side of the world. Thirty buildings scattered the ground, interconnected by circular, lit passageways where countless people moved like ants with a purpose.

In the center of them, towered a custom crane, with a boom segmented into extensions to allow for reach through curved tunnels. It was currently swiveling from the estimated location of the hole to an opening in one building.

"They haven't finished," I remarked, and a swell of energy struck me again, with the same potency as when Marco informed me of their plans in my school hallway.

The crane's claw re-emerged from the building, loosened and empty.

Without thought or strategy in place, I positioned myself to descend, to stop them from going any further, and Eran reached out, placing his hand on my arm just as a roar rose up from below us.

"Yes, they have."

I cleared my mind and blinked for sharper clarity, and sure enough a swarm of people rushed for the crane, surrounding its base. The crane operator exited the cab and entered the excitement, hands clapping his back just before several sprays of champagne shot into the air.

A single word came to me then. "Hubris."

"What was that?" Eran asked, looking my way.

"It's what Lotharious had warned me about the one time I spoke to him. He warned me about hubris."

Eran didn't reply for several breaths and then a whispered seethe. "Damn him."

"You knew this was his effort, didn't you?"

I hadn't relayed to him yet everything that Marco had told me, but it didn't seem necessary, judging by the steeliness marring his face.

"I realized it while sitting in the cell," Eran muttered, his face stiff and restrained with anger. "The uniting of the FOs, the battle in this field, my death to prompt you to follow me down there. I fed into his plan ..." He shook his head. "So effortlessly."

"So did I," I reminded him, and it seemed to break his glare on the sight below. He turned burning eyes to me and I admitted, "I created that hole down there. I gave the humans a way in." I turned my own gaze back to the dark patch of nothingness below the boom. "And the FOs a way out. Because I've been there. I'm … I'm from … *there*." My eyes locked on the hole as everything else surrounding it fell away. "I lived there. I grew there. I became me there."

"No," Eran said, and suddenly he was in my line of sight and the hole was behind him. Intentionally blocking it, his hands rose to grip my face and direct me back to him. "You became you when you *left* there."

"How do you know?"

"Because we evolve, Magdalene. It's why humans exist, to give them a chance to learn. It's why FOs exist, to give them a chance to redeem themselves. We evolve, and you have too. Do not doubt yourself. You may have been from that place, but you are not of that place, you are not in that place, and that place is not in you." He shook me. "Do you hear me? That place is not in you, Magdalene."

I tried to nod agreement, but my mind fell numb, disoriented.

"Come on," Eran said, although he gave me no chance to respond.

His arms looped below my knees and I felt the lower half of my body lift into his arms and my side roll against his chest. It was warm and solid and so safe that I closed my eyes and breathed him in. Instinctively, my appendages slipped back into my body and quickly after, the wind picked up.

"When was the last time you slept, Magdalene?" he said, his voice accusing.

"We needed a strategy to free you," I murmured.

He sighed in irritation but didn't harangue me any

194

further. No words passed at all as I struggled to stay awake and take in the feeling of Eran holding me. It felt like it had been so long since we'd touched for any period of time longer than a platonic ride to school that my body and mind imbibed on him, drinking him up like a parched tree in the middle of a desert.

The light grew brighter on my eyelids telling me that we'd reached the western hemisphere but when we landed there was no hum of traffic, honking horns, or smell of the city. Instead, I heard gurgling water and breathed in the fresh scent of pine, and when I opened my eyes those trees stood over us, a wispy layer of grey clouds hovering through their tips.

Something delicate and wet fell on my cheek and then another splattered on my forehead, and as Eran carried me up the dirt path to the cabin in the Appalachian Mountains, our cabin, the raindrops grew steadily more persistent. The porch overhang broke their onslaught, but they continued to pummel the grassy hill where the cabin was built and the placid lake beyond it.

Eran dipped, his arm twisted under my back, and the door to our cabin opened. Stepping inside felt like a blanket of darkness fell over us, so he set me on the couch laid in front of the hearth and went about stacking and igniting a fire. Quickly, the living room turned a flickering orange from the glow and warmth cut through the chill. The sound of the rain hammering the roof continued while outside the small windows the world was grey.

Without a word, Eran didn't stop until he'd arranged blankets and pillows across the wood floor in front of the fire, then he turned to me, lifted me again, and set me on them. He made an effort to stand again, but I held onto his neck.

"No," I moaned, and he settled down next to me.

We were now facing each other, only my hand touching the balmy skin above his collarbone, hot from the fire and wet from the storm. His shirt was damp below my palm, so I slid my hand down his chest to the hem resting along his hips. As I did, he grew tense, even as his eyes locked on me and his breathing accelerated.

Through tight lips, as if he were fighting the words from escaping, he insisted, "You should sleep."

"Yes," I agreed softly. "I should."

My fingers found his shirt's edge and I drew it up, my knuckles grazing the swells of muscles traversing his belly. It could go no further than his shoulders and with his arms down, the shirt remained collected there as Eran watched me, determining whether this was the right course of action. Then in one swift movement, he sat upward and pulled the shirt over his head.

The fire cast a glow from behind him, briefly illuminating the bulge of his muscles down his sides as he deftly discarded the fabric. My breath caught in my throat, but I kept my eyes on his torso as he sank back to the covers, again propping his head in his palm, the other arm laying along his ribcage.

Light cascaded across his cheek, highlighting the strong contours of his face, but it was the heat in his eyes that both excited and intimidated me. Still, after all this time.

Your husband.

John's words came back to me. And this was another one of those times when that remarkable title didn't seem possible.

It wasn't simply that we lived our lives as teenagers, and too often I would become consumed by that role, narrowing my choice of words and reactions to fit the part. But so much more impactful was the fact that Eran was a warrior who had experienced more breadth of feelings and a greater duration of both peace and volatility, and still he remained pacified by it all. And in turn it humbled me.

"What are you thinking?" he murmured.

I tried to tell him, to put to words in a way he might understand the indescribable awe I felt for him, and when I failed and I shook my head, he smiled softly, understanding it anyway.

My chest swelled with emotion and a lump formed in my throat. Then his hand rose and gently stopped the tear that carried my reaction down my cheek.

"I love you too, Magdalene."

I drew in a breath, but it caught, rasping, in my throat. And more tears came, and my head grew stuffy.

"Eran ..." I whispered.

"Wife ..."

And our bodies met, leaning into one another, his mouth warm and moist and needing me. His lips pressed to mine until he felt the swelling from my injury there and he pulled away. I seized his shoulders and pulled him back. His kiss was insistently tender then, delicate across my damaged skin, before moving over my jaw and down my neck. When I found myself on my back, his hands under my shoulders, pulling me off the ground, pressing me to his mouth, I arched to meet him. My breath felt thick in my throat and my head woozy as I found my suit sliding down my body; and the heat from his lips following it in a searing wake across my newly freed chest and stomach.

He was patient, taking his time, lingering in areas I didn't know could cause those types of sensations, keeping me awake just long enough to show me how much he missed me in our time apart; and when I awoke the next morning his own skin still had a ruddiness to it that confirmed his effort was equally satisfying.

9 CELEBRITY

"The humans are panicking, and they think you're involved."

Alban announced tipping his head at Eran and me from his seat in the corner of Ezra's living room where we had congregated. He kicked his short, stocky legs out, knocking over a glass bottle, recovered and propped it back up but left the alcohol pooled on the hardwood floor. In fact, nearly every surface remained cluttered with empty bottles from the night before. The only exceptions were when someone needed a seat, and in that case, the bottles were simply pushed aside to make room, along with the plates of possum-meat muffins Felix set out, which went untouched.

I observed the messengers, none of whom had made it to the afterlife the night before, preferring instead to spend the night reveling in my housemates' hospitality. Because of this, they and the guardians were better informed than Eran and I on world affairs at the moment and had spent the last few minutes since Eran and I walked through the door bringing us up to speed. Mr. Hamilton also stood in the crowded room, packing into the corner, shadowed by the curtains, anxious but quiet while Ms. Beedinwigg stationed herself next to the fireplace, arms crossed over her chest, legs astride, frowning. Being the only humans in the room, they appeared weary, awake strictly because of their heightened emotions.

"The government is executing a full media blitz," Ezra went on, "trying to tell everyone that yesterday was the culmination of some failed military experiment, but not everyone is listening –"

"Or they're not buying it," Ms. Beedinwigg interjected from her standing position beside the fireplace.

Ezra agreed with a nod. "Religious leaders are seeing an influx to their churches, synagogues, holy sites; a cult in Montana performed a massive slaying of its followers; some people are even packing up and leaving their homes."

Eran listened thoughtfully, his guardians, the ones who fit into the room, vigilantly watching his reaction. The rest stood in the hallway and kitchen, waiting for their instructions.

"You didn't know," Ezra realized, surprised.

"Magdalene and I spent the night together," Eran replied flatly.

That caused Ezra and Hermina, my surrogate mothers, to exchange a glance.

Indifferent to their reaction, Eran stayed on topic. "And how is it that Magdalene and I are – as you said – involved?"

That struck nearly everyone in the room, evoking a series of shocked expressions, shuffling feet, and nervous twitching.

"Where did you spend the night? On the moon?" Ms. Beedinwigg muttered as she turned on the television.

It didn't seem to matter what station the television was tuned to, the word's 'Breaking News' was heralded across the screen with a picture next to the broadcaster clearly showing Eran and I standing together, with Marco in the background. It was evidently taken from a distance, and therefore was grainy, but we were easily identifiable, as were the grey appendages protruding from Marco's back.

I sighed and let my head fall but Eran showed no reaction. He ruminated a few seconds longer and then spoke with judicious authority. "The governments will handle the hysteria. As for Magdalene and I, our reputations are insignificant in the scope of our situation. Of greater importance is the status of the bodies that have been lifted from the hole." He turned to stare pointedly at Mr. Hamilton, who looked back warily and cleared his throat.

"They are being categorized –"

"Wait," Ms. Beedinwigg said, her arms falling to her side and then lifting to her hips in an offensive stance. "What bodies?"

A few others chimed in with the same question before Mr. Hamilton reluctantly explained what Eran and I had seen the night before. By the end of it, every one of the messengers and guardians in the room was staring in abhorrence at him.

It was Claudius, a guardian known for having a rigid set of principles, who laid it out for the rest of us. "So you mean to tell me that the United States government elevated the Fallen Ones' bodies from the hole, intending on scientifically researching them, but in fact, freed them?"

Mr. Hamilton tipped his head with a blend of caution and embarrassment.

Alban immediately turned to Caius. His voice was low and he looked sickly from behind his thick beard.

"Well, you won."

Caius shook his head in disgust, his charcoal eyes growing a shade darker. "This is one wager I wish I hadn't." With an accusing scowl, he pivoted suddenly to Mr. Hamilton. "Do ya have any idea what you've done?"

"No," Mr. Hamilton said evenly, "and neither do you. If I'm informed well enough, and I am, then none of you has ever raised –"

"Do you know what it took to put them there?" Heath demanded loudly, his typical agreeable disposition nowhere in sight. "We were eradicated, one by one. Our wards, the messengers whose lives you take for granted, were terrorized and then murdered. And you stand there –". Then his true guardian nature came through and his herculean body moved toward Mr. Hamilton, his height and fury combining to make an awesome spectacle.

Eran instantly stood and blocked Heath's path, as Mr. Hamilton actually shrank against the wall.

Out of respect for his superior, Heath stopped at Eran's chest, but the fury reached Mr. Hamilton through his piercing glare.

"No one is to touch this man," Eran commanded. "Am I understood, Guardian Legion?"

"Huff … Huff … Huff …" they called out, filling the cramped room with sound.

Heath stepped back but kept a cold eye on Mr. Hamilton while returning to his spot near the staircase.

"You're awfully friendly with someone who just led you into imprisonment," Ms. Beedinwigg grumbled.

Eran actually chuckled at that statement, realizing the irony. "Mr. Hamilton is a field analyst, am I correct?"

Mr. Hamilton nodded, keeping a wary eye on the rest of us.

"And as an analyst, he recognizes that his trump card

has been freed from imprisonment, thereby terminating all terms of our unwritten agreement toward his safety. Correct?"

Again Mr. Hamilton nodded.

"And yet he is here, at risk to himself, and has offered to help us."

"Help us? Sir —" Stoyan, a genteel but outspoken messenger tried to counter, which Eran didn't allow.

"And because Mr. Hamilton has Q-clearance security level," Eran said, his tone turning forceful, "the highest level possible, he is a great benefit to us. Further, this security clearance and his years of dealings with us have put him in the unique position to witness and attest to the fact that we are inherently more powerful than the humans and that power may be unleashed at any given time."

That was an unveiled threat, which Mr. Hamilton recognized.

"Yes," he whispered, apprehension strangling his voice.

"Now your greatest concern, I suspect, is on the resuscitation of the bodies," Eran went on, intentionally shifting the topic away from Mr. Hamilton. "But that doesn't appear to have happened. Magdalene and I surveilled the site of the hole yesterday and there was no sign of activity that would lead us to believe otherwise. If there had been, I would not have ceased contact for the evening."

"You're right," Ariela, a reserved and observant messenger, called out. "I heard two of the men from the government talking last night. One of them was inebriated and loose-lipped. He said he processed paperwork for his superior, who is located at the site, and all reports have confirmed no effort was made to resuscitate them."

"And we have no plans to revive the bodies," Mr.

Hamilton insisted. "Honestly."

But the faces of those in the room confirmed that statement wasn't good enough.

"If those plans should change, I will inform Eran promptly," he assured.

Rufus grunted from the hallway opening. "Damn right ya will."

"It is likely we'd know before he has time to tell us anyway," Eran asserted.

"Why?" Hermina asked cautiously.

Ms. Beedinwigg exhaled suddenly, drawing a few curious looks. "He's correct," she insisted. "The Fallen Ones would realize their cover was blown the second they looked into the faces of the humans who recovered them. Their shroud of confidentiality would be lifted, their true identities would be revealed and they would have no reason to act within the normal bounds of societal norms."

"And we would know almost immediately because they wouldn't hesitate to infringe," Mr. Hamilton added.

"Infringe. That's putting it mildly," I said under my breath.

"It's the first word that came to mind," he replied quietly through a frown.

"Magdalene is correct," Eran declared. "It would be worse, far worse. But there was no sign of infringing or any other type of rebellion at the hole last night. So it appears, for now, disaster has been averted."

"For now?" Ariela pressed.

"I can't tell the future, Ariela. Given that limitation, I'd like you messengers to remain with your guardians and for the guardians to remain in New Orleans. *For now*," he emphasized.

A chorus of questions about where they would stay rose up, with Dante and Jerod – two messengers who are known for their requirements of luxury and lavish treatments – being resoundingly loud about it.

"I have plenty of rooms," Mr. Hamilton offered.

"And we could use the company," Ms. Beedinwigg elaborated, reminding me that the two lived in the same mansion in the Garden District, despite the awkwardness over Mr. Hamilton's newly-discovered background.

"As for the rest," Eran addressed the room, "I encourage you all to maintain your schedules and routines."

"Speaking of," Ms. Beedinwigg mumbled, checking her wristwatch, "I expect to see you two back in school today."

She pinned her eyes on us until we dutifully conceded with a nod, me in frustration, Eran trying to restrain a grin. He swept his gaze to me where I conveyed through my expression that she, Ezra and Hermina may never break from their maternal oversight, which was such a drag. The idea made me actually *feel* the restricted boundaries of a teenager. He smiled patiently at me and nodded.

"All right," Ezra stood, gesturing with a flap of her hands, "shoo ... shoo. Unless you're prepared to help clean this house, you are all banned from it until I can see my coffee table again."

I stood and headed for the stairs to my bedroom, where I wanted to replace my black leather suit, which I still wore, with something more appropriate for school – a tee-shirt, jeans, and a back-up pair of biker boots – which was appropriate for me, anyway.

"I'll be here," Eran confirmed and then subtly pulled Mr. Hamilton aside.

I showered and dressed quickly and descended a few minutes later to find Ezra, Felix and Rufus united in their effort to deposit the overwhelming number of bottles into the recycling bin. Eran remained in a huddle, talking in low voices, with Mr. Hamilton.

"I'll see what I can find out," Mr. Hamilton promised as Eran noticed me approaching. Then the two stood rigid and adjourned.

"I overheard you," I grumbled after apologizing to our housemates for having to leave and had entered the kitchen. "Any idea where they are?"

"Who?"

"Your first lieutenant, Campion, and my best friend, Gershom."

He looked at me, a proud smile stretching his lips.

"Yes, I noticed they didn't show up with the rest of the guardians and messengers."

"Or overnight," Eran added.

"You're worried that SIEF might be holding them?"

"I don't know what to think," Eran said, opening the back door for me.

While leaving our conversation there, we paused in the shed to find my motorcycle had been returned from the Academy's parking lot – compliments of Felix and Rufus – and to confirm that our swords remained under the workbench. It was obvious to both of us that neither was comfortable with our friends' disappearances, and swords might come in handy if we needed to help free them; but for the same reason I had left mine behind the day before, we drove out of the shed knowing that bringing swords onto school grounds would only cause further problems for us. It was best if we laid low.

In fact, we kept our conversation with Mr. LeFrau short, even though he was less busy than usual. Apparently, many of his 'regulars' hadn't come in that morning. On hearing this, Eran remained cordial but restrained, and I knew he was considering the same explanation as I was … the media's speculation about Marco and the United States military was unnerving the public regardless of John and Mr. Hamilton's attempt to subvert the conversation. Thankfully, Mr. LeFrau didn't acknowledge or pester us about our image being splayed across the media, if he had even seen it yet. That obliviousness was short-lived though.

The second after we parked my bike in the school lot and stepped onto the sidewalk leading to the main entrance, Paul Davies strolled up to us.

"Saw you on the news," he said, making no effort to hide his curiosity.

Eran said something unintelligible in return and took my hand to walk toward the two glass doors I'd fled through yesterday.

"You work for the government or something?" he pressed, following us. "They said it was some kind of government thing that went wrong. But you two were there."

By this point, everyone was watching us as we approached and passed the students collected outside, waiting for the first bell. And while this had happened before, it felt different. Like they had a reason to, whether they knew it as the truth or not. Like Eran and I were exposed. Then Eran replied to Paul.

"You think the government needs a couple of high schoolers?"

Paul shrugged.

"Well, as usual, the media got it wrong. We weren't involved, just happened to be there as bystanders."

"So you – you actually saw the thing? The guy with wings?"

"Briefly."

"Are they really attached?"

"Didn't get a good look," Eran replied.

I was thoroughly impressed with him, despite his years on this earth and his authority over humans and guardians alike, Eran managed to slip effortlessly into the role of a student who was just passing along the rumor, keeping Paul enthralled long enough to dispense misinformation about our involvement.

"So you don't know if they are real?"

"Nah, he was taken away pretty quickly."

"Did you get any pictures?"

"Didn't even think about it. Wish I had, though. Could have sold them to the media. They were all over the place."

Paul chuckled excitedly. "Too bad. Okay, see you later."

We were in the main hall by then and we all knew Paul's statement was an empty promise as he broke from our path toward the science rooms. He was the only one with the initiative to approach us and had done it strictly for the gossip.

"Let's hope that does the trick," Eran muttered to me as we headed for my first class.

The warning bell rang and the students continued their gradual shuffle to their own classes, but every one of them maintained their stare until we met it with our own eyes or we passed them on our route. This left me hoping Eran's effort to downplay our participation in yesterday's drama was successful. While I typically stood out as dissimilar to the rest of the student body, this was different, a little too revealing.

Eran stopped at my classroom door and peered in. Since I'd already described to him on our flight back to New Orleans earlier this morning how Marco had entered school grounds as my substitute teacher – and given his proclivity toward taking nothing for granted – he wanted to see who was running the class today. Mr. Evans, the Spanish teacher, sat at the desk, telling another student that he was filling in for the day, given Mr. Task's assault.

"I haven't gotten a chance," Eran said, turning to

me, his eyes surveying me softly, "to thank you for what you did for me yesterday, for working to free me."

"I didn't *do* anything, Eran," I countered immediately. "You freed yourself."

"Did you make every effort within your power to try and help me?" he asked.

It was a leading question, but I answered anyway. "Yes, of course."

"Then *thank you*."

His lips slowly curved into a smile, which released a swarm of butterflies in my stomach, until his breath-taking face grew serious.

"I really am lucky."

"Yes, you are," I whispered, and he tipped his head back and laughed through the second bell. "But so am I," I added.

Mr. Evans began his stroll toward the door and Eran planted a kiss on my lips, a warm and inviting kiss that left a tingling sensation as we parted.

"All right, Ms. Tanner," Mr. Evans grumbled. "Mr. Talor."

"Sir," Eran said, releasing me and tipping his head cordially at my new substitute teacher.

"Get to class now Eran."

"On my way." He turned for a last look at me. "I'm here. Let me take over now."

I groaned at his secret command for me to let him handle any crisis involving any further FOs, but he only smiled as he strode down the hall.

"Seat, Ms. Talor," Mr. Evans ordered, and realizing he'd switched Eran's last name with my own. "Err, Ms. Tanner."

I walked past him, smiling, holding myself back from telling him that he was more correct than he could possibly know.

After Mr. Evans muddled through the fifth lesson –

and appeared thankful when the bell rang – I found Eran outside my door. He too had gotten sideways glances and a shifting of chairs to angle widely around him during his first class. We shared that experience and the reoccurrence of it during the next two classes. By then, it was evident that either Paul hadn't passed on the rumor Eran started or no one had believed him. I was wondering what we'd encounter at lunch as I took a seat in Mr. Morow's classroom and waited for him to begin.

When the bell rang, he spent no time walking menacingly up the aisle where my desk sat, and with the door closed and me being left inconveniently without any allies, including Eran, it was clear Mr. Morow would take full advantage of the opportunity he had with me.

"Now," he said in a voice loud enough for the entire class, "we faculty were instructed not to discuss the incident of yesterday with you, Ms. Tanner. That you've already spoken to the police. That you've already given all the details you know. But since that demand came from the principal, a-k-a *your friend*, and Mr. Task is a-k-a *my* friend, I think that allows me a little discretion, don't you?"

I didn't speak, but I did narrow my eyes at him. Noting it, his nostrils flared and his pasty skin flushed.

"You think you're a bigwig on campus, don't you, Ms. Tanner? Think you're pretty special, some sort of celebrity. With that phony business of talking to the dead – of which I cannot possibly imagine a single person in their right mind believing – and now this ... this government business you're wrapped up in." He paused to lean toward me, simmering with fury, his words hissing from between his teeth. "I know you were in Ms. Beedinwigg's office when the military advanced on this school – an incident that put this school under lock-down for several hours; I know you and that boyfriend of yours were taken with your principal to ...

to … to who knows where. I don't really care. What I care about is that my dear friend, Mr. Task, was assaulted, kidnapped, bound, and left in a janitor's closet. I care that my school was attacked. I care that since you've started classes here, only destruction has followed in your wake. And then we are given explicit instructions not to question you by the influential friends who protect you?" He scoffed. "You must think we deem ourselves unworthy to be in your presence, little Miss High and Mighty."

I opened my mouth to counter his claim, but he snapped an unintelligible word, carried through a grunt, back at me.

"I've had you in my classes, I've discussed you with other faculty members – of whom share my same feelings – and I've watched you drift through these curricula year after year, wreaking havoc, leaving school grounds when and however you please, returning as and when you wish, without any repercussions.

"Well I'm going to tell you, Ms. Tanner, and I want to make it perfectly clear, so do inform me if it is in any way blurred. Despite your face being splashed across the national media, despite your friendship with the principal and owner of this school, you Ms. Tanner are most certainly *not* special. You are *not* significant to our lives." He swept a hand to motion toward the rest of the students, as his tone turned incredulous. "You hold no value to us. You do not control our very existence. If you were never born, we would keep on living. The world would continue to thrive – likely in a more peaceful manner. You, Ms. Tanner, are important to no one, *no one* but yourself." He drew in a deep breath and settled back, folding his arms commandingly across his chest. "Am I clear?"

"Abundantly."

He stood silent for several seconds, and I could see

him determining whether he wanted to continue his haranguing, and my guess was that he decided against it when he saw no reaction in me.

He unfolded his arms, cocked his mouth in a frown, and marched to the head of the room to pick up his textbook.

Michelle Moller, sitting in the next aisle, leaned over and whispered, "Wow, he really hates you."

"No," I said quietly. "He hates himself."

Mr. Morow, who did not overhear our brief exchange, launched into another tirade, one profusely twisted with inaccurate stories about Medieval Europe. He stood on his pulpit and sermonized, and I didn't bother to correct him once. Twenty minutes until the bell rang, a knock stopped Mr. Morow's huffing and made him approach the door. It was opened before he could reach it, which irritated him judging by the shift of his face into a scowl.

"Mr. Morow," Ms. Beedinwigg stepped inside.

He scoffed and shook his head. "Ms. Beedinwigg, you cannot disrupt my class whenever you feel —"

"May *I* then?" a commanding voice with an offended edge reverberated across the room as Mr. Morow stumbled backwards nearly in a panic while John's robust frame came through the door, stopping in the space Mr. Morow had been filling.

Mr. Morow opened and closed his mouth several times, gave up attempting a verbal retort, and openly assessed John's standard military green dress uniform.

"Professor, my name is John."

"I know — I know who you are," Mr. Morow whispered, wide-eyed. "Mr. Joint Chiefs of Staff, M-Mr. Chairman. And I'm not a professor."

John nodded understanding. "I've come for Magdalene Tanner."

Mr. Morow's head jerked forward and tilted to the

211

side as if he'd misheard.

"Magdalene Tanner," John pressed, his eyes scanning the students until my movement caught his attention.

"She will be missing the remainder of your class, Mr. Morow," Ms. Beedinwigg informed. "Her presence is required elsewhere and John has come to escort her there."

Mr. Morow's head swung back to gawk at me and forward again to perform another sweeping survey of John from head to toe. It was at that point, Mr. Morow straightened his back and harrumphed as if he'd come to some conclusion. At nearly the same time, the classroom began to emit a hum of whispers.

"Is he a soldier?"

"Definitely military."

"So, she *is* involved …"

"Someway, somehow …"

I walked to the door with all eyes shifting between me and John as Eran's attempt to repudiate the media's claims of my involvement with the military and the winged perpetrator exploded around me. John's appearance and request for my presence did that job efficiently.

"Why are you here? And where am I going?" I asked, keeping my voice low.

"Congress has requested you attend a closed session," Ms. Beedinwigg replied.

Mr. Morow made a chocking sound. "Closed – Closed session? With Congress?"

He had gone pasty white again, although this time his skin was beaded with sweat.

"Are you all right?" John asked in concern.

"*Her?*" Mr. Morow demanded, although his voice was barely above a whisper.

"Yes, sir," John said, seeming offended. "Do you

have a problem with that?"

Mr. Morow looked up at John like he'd been scolded. "N-No ... I just –"

John turned a cold shoulder to Mr. Morow and left the room, leaving Mr. Morow paused in mid-sentence, his mouth agape.

As I passed Mr. Morow, I felt the heat of anger rise up, and ignored it. He'd just swallowed his words of earlier, and that was sufficient. However, once in the hallway, I moved to a more imposing demeanor with John. "Eran will be joining us."

"Yes," he replied simply, as if it were a pre-concluded notion.

We marched directly to Eran's classroom where he was already exiting, his Latin teacher, Mr. Trudeau, trailing in obvious agitation behind him.

"If you leave my class, Mr. Talor, I will flunk you. Do you understand? I don't give a damn how well you speak Latin."

Eran turned swiftly to address him. "Well," he shrugged, "Nemo mortalium omnibus horis sapit."

Mr. Trudeau sucked in a sharp breath, and John chuckled beside me as we approached.

"You understood?" I asked, to which he nodded once, definitively.

Ms. Beedinwigg, smiling mischievously, muttered the translation while trying to contain her laughter. "No mortal is wise at all times, not even Mr. Trudeau."

Eran, who kept his focus on his teacher, added, "I have no choice, Dominus Trudeau, Hanniabl ad portas. Hanniabl ad portas."

Mr. Trudeau snapped his head back and furrowed his eyebrows in confusion. "Huh?"

"Hannibal *was* at our gates," John corrected as we reached them. "But no longer."

"Sir." Eran broke his gaze to tip his head at John. "I

heard you were on school grounds."

"Of course you did," John replied, his tone conveying that he'd come to expect Eran's resourcefulness. "We have a car waiting in the parking lot, Eran."

By this point, Mr. Trudeau was giving John the same visual inspection Mr. Morow had, and was left justifiably silent. Even when John tipped his head cordially at him, Mr. Trudeau showed no response other than speechless confusion and reluctance.

Eran reached out, took my hand, squeezed it, and left Mr. Trudeau watching, dumbfounded.

"I imagine someone wants to speak to us," Eran suggested midway down the hall.

"Several do," John admitted.

"And where would they like to meet?"

"Washington, D.C. A plane is standing by at the airport. It's slower than your wings, but I need to get there too and I'd prefer not to be carried."

The image of Eran holding John under his arm as we flew to the east coast made me laugh out loud, which made John gesture a hand in response.

"And that's precisely why."

John led us to a black SUV at the curb just outside the main entrance where the doors were opened for us by two men in military fatigues. As I prepared to step inside, Ms. Beedinwigg stood back.

"You're not coming?" I asked.

"I wasn't invited," she said pointedly before turning sharp eyes on John.

Pivoting toward him, I demanded, "Ms. Beedinwigg will accompany us."

John, who had one foot in the car, placed it back on the ground, his expression instantly turning to a frown. "As I've mentioned before, I don't always hold the power, Mag —"

"That's not good enough," I retaliated.

"And because I did not call this meeting, I have no authority over the list of participants. I am merely your escort. Once we arrive, I'm not certain even I will be allowed to attend."

Eran observed him suspiciously. "Who exactly is requesting this meeting, John? And where will it take place?"

"All sitting members of the House and Senate have requested your presence at a closed-door session held in the House Chamber of the U.S. Capitol. South wing at zero eight hundred hours. You two are the guests of honor, so we shouldn't delay."

He rattled off his response so fluidly that we stood stunned, until Eran recovered.

"We're meeting in private with both houses of Congress?" Eran clarified.

"Yes." John shrugged. "And members of SIEF, televised in, of course."

"Why us?" Eran replied, firmly.

"Eran, if you found a new species walking among you, wouldn't you want to get to know them?"

"Fair question."

John nodded, raising his eyebrows implying he should be given the benefit of the doubt. He then turned to Ms. Beedinwigg. "This isn't meant to be a slight toward you, it's not even personal. If you were an Alterum, you'd be given a seat before I would."

"Understood," she replied, acquiescing but still pinched by it.

"Eran, Maggie," John insisted, motioning to the vehicle. "Time is passing."

Eran didn't move, however.

"Magdalene stays," he declared.

"What?" I twisted to face him. "I will not –"

"I can answer any questions you may have," Eran

continued, stoically.

I gripped his arm and pulled him aside. "I will not –"

"I don't feel comfortable –"

"You feel better about leaving me behind and unprotected?"

"Yes," he replied flatly.

"And what's to stop them from coming for me once you're gone?"

"I've considered that."

I threw my hands up and in the same manner as John had said the words, I retorted, "Of course you have."

"We'll drop you at Mr. Hamilton's house, where you will remain with the guardians until my return."

"I like that idea," Ms. Beedinwigg interjected, nodding.

"It's not your decision," I snapped. "I'm going."

I moved back to John.

"I understand your hesitation," John conceded to Eran. "We have no interest in harming either of you –"

"How about imprisoning us?" I retorted.

"You will be treated with all due respect," John replied.

I lifted my hands again to Eran, gesturing for what other reassurances he needed.

Still, he remained reticent. "What guarantees do we have?"

"You have my word."

"That's all?" Ms. Beedinwigg countered.

A flash of anger crossed his face but by the time he spoke it was gone. "It's the word of the Joint Chiefs of Staff, Ms. Beedinwigg."

"And?" she replied, unimpressed.

John chuckled, dropping his head and shaking it in surrender. "You're right, Ms. Beedinwigg. You are absolutely right. And still, it's the best I have to offer."

We stood in quiet reservation for a few seconds, John openly waiting on Eran.

"We're relying on you, John," Eran said, deliberately.

"That was our expectation, Eran."

Eran again paused but then nodded and guided me into the car.

Ms. Beedinwigg watched us leave, a wary scowl planted on her face. She then spun on her heel and marched to her vehicle. I knew where she was going. Directly to Mr. Hamilton's house and the guardians waiting there.

That awareness sat on my mind the entire drive to the airport, once inside the small private jet, and on landing in Washington, D.C. Casual conversation between Eran and John revolved around military tactics and kept the attitudes between us all complacent, but I was alert to Eran's constant awareness of our environment and the line of questions he led John through to parse out information as best he could. There wasn't much disclosed, unfortunately. On exiting the plane, we crossed the tarmac to another black SUV only a few yards away and it took us through the complex city streets to the Capitol Building. There, we took a private, unmarked entrance where we were scanned for weapons inside the door and where several armed men in military fatigues were added to our entourage, all of whom were familiar enough to John to be called by their first names.

Somewhere down the third hallway, Mr. Hamilton appeared at a corner, as if waiting there for us to arrive, and joined our growing group. Brief, cordial greetings were exchanged as we continued our walk through the unremarkable service hallways and then Eran repositioned himself between John and Mr. Hamilton.

"Has Marco talked?"

Mr. Hamilton glanced at Eran, then frowned. "No,

he appears to be waiting for something."

Eran turned to John and hinted, "You have techniques to counter that, do you not?"

John's eyebrows rose and a curious smile tipped his mouth to the side. "You don't know Marco's strength yet, do you?" His smile fell away and his tone grew irritated. "He doesn't feel pain, and without Magdalene present, he won't fear death, so there's very little we could impress upon him to speak."

Our route ended at a standard grey door, which Mr. Hamilton opened to a warmly-lit carpeted hallway where a handful of people in business suits milled around. Their subtle, hushed voices halted when we came into view and I suddenly knew what it felt like to be a bug captured under a glass jar. In the silence, we crossed the hallway to another door where Mr. Hamilton paused.

"Ready?" he asked, almost gleeful, as if this were about to be the culmination of the hard work he had put in and the visible achievement of the show of respect he sought.

Much less enthusiastic, Eran replied, "For what, exactly?"

"To represent your kind," he said, trying to encourage some fervor.

"I am not a delegate for *my kind*, Mr. Hamilton."

His smile faded and he settled back on his heels. "Of course … Of course …"

Not knowing what else to do, he opened the door. As he did, Eran whispered into my ear.

"Stay beside me at all times."

Then the volume inside the next room engulfed us, actually hitting my chest with a palpable resonation. It was generated by hundreds of people, standing in countless groups, loudly conversing, forming a thunderous buzz that stretched across the auditorium, above to the stacked second-floor seats that filled nearly the entire circumference of the room, and to the brightly lit ceiling above.

The room, while square, had half-moon wooden pews built down the center of it, segmented by aisles. Carpeted in blue with wood panels across every wall and decorated with an ornate marble slab behind a three-tiered podium at the head, where all seats faced, it was stately and imposing.

Mr. Hamilton guided us inside and while we walked along the wall to the podium, and as those in the room gradually learned we had arrived, the sound ebbed away to silence. I adjusted my focus briefly to find everyone present watching Eran and I make our way to our seats, all with curious, apprehensive and unforgiving eyes.

We were directed to sit on the second tier of the podium, facing the auditorium of seats. Our chairs were directly next to one another, each with a microphone embedded in the table and new earbuds in a case beside it. John and Mr. Hamilton took seats on the third and lowest tier, both with microphones accessible to them and all four of us tucked the buds into our ears.

A man with a face resembling a hawk, sharp eyes, and blonde hair, called the meeting to order from the highest seat at the podium above our heads, while his voice came through the buds, and those who weren't already seated made their way to their assigned chairs. When most were in place, he continued with introductory remarks, which seemed procedural, before he finished and Mr. Hamilton spoke. Although I couldn't see his face, his tone was noticeably eager and laced with the proud air of authority. He was clearly enjoying himself. The only part that stood out to me, however, was when he announced this meeting was being held 'off the record'. I bristled while Eran sat emotionless, watching the exits, each of which were now flanked by the same armed, fatigued men who had accompanied us through the halls. When it came time for us to speak, Eran took the helm without hesitation, and I sat back to let the man who had led so many speak for 'our kind'.

"Thank you, Mr. Speaker. Thank you, Mr. Hamilton," Eran replied and then paused to survey the crowd. When he spoke again it was paced, stoic, and articulate. "I hear the words 'type', 'group', 'your kind' and 'species' being applied to us, differentiating us from you. I'm sure that Mr. Hamilton or someone on his team has already briefed you on the finer details of our distinctions." More than a few people nodded in confirmation throughout the audience, but Eran didn't address them. "I'm sure that he has informed you that my youthful appearance and my teenage body is somewhat counterintuitive given my true age." More nods followed. "I'm sure he has recounted that I have been alive to witness what has taken place on this earth spanning the last several centuries, how I've come with appendages attached to my shoulder blades, how I have certain unique abilities. And I'm fairly confident all that must have been relatively disconcerting to hear." He concluded that point with a smile, which surprisingly was met with a few grins. And that was when I saw it. Eran was fearless throughout his speech, devoted to protecting us through diplomacy, and capable of winning hearts and minds of not just our kind but of the humans. They watched him closely, never moving, only slightly breathing, encased in his natural charisma. And I knew Mr. Hamilton was correct. There was no better delegate than Eran. "Now I'd like to describe to you how we are similar," Eran said, his voice a bit louder, firmer. "When you die, as we all do, myself and Magdalene included, you will return home, to your true, original home. You will pass the threshold that separates this realm from the other, be greeted by deceased family and friends, and you will take up residence in the province you created there and left behind when you came here. Magdalene," he said gesturing to me, "and I will do the same, going to the same place you will, taking up the same existence as you will. And when the urge arises, you will return here again, just as we may. When we do, all of us in this room – Magdalene and myself included – will seek the same things … Relations with those who love and support us. A good job to pay the bills. A warm bed at night. Good food on the table. But when you return again, it will be with no memory of your true home or of your experiences before your birth, while Magdalene and I will have the privilege – and oftentimes the burden – to remember all that has taken place."

A beep, crackle, and voice filled the arena then. "I don't understand. Are you saying we are like you in that you think we have wings too?" The senator sounded incredulous as he shook his head in disagreement.

Another cacophony of electronic sounds followed before the man with the hawk face spoke out. "Please hold all questions until the guests have concluded their remarks."

"That's all right, Mr. Speaker," Eran replied. "That is a distinction that Mr. Hamilton was correct in. No, Senator, you do not have wings. You see, you and I have come here with different objectives. For my purposes, and Magdalene's and those like us, we are required to bring certain assets. Memory being one of them. Wings – as you call them – being another. The third and final asset we bring is a unique skill. Why don't you bring these when you return here? Because your purpose in coming here is different. You have come to learn, to perfect yourselves. You have and likely will continue to encounter obstacles that will test you throughout your life. This classroom, this realm, this earth was created and designed for that purpose alone. I should mention that my telling you all this is taboo. My actions here upset the paradigm, but ..." He hesitated, or allowed their minds to clear before announcing an unsettling theory. "Maybe the paradigm is changing. Maybe the classroom is evolving. And there is a purpose as to why Magdalene and I are here, meeting with you, disclosing details of your existence to which no one should be made privy. I am under the belief – and this is the sole reason I came today – that your classroom could be altering and this information I give you here today is a lesson that is now required in the course of your education."

Apparently, that notion was too impactful and wide-reaching for them, because they sat with glazed stares. Then one leaned forward and pressed her button.

"You said Magdalene and you are here for another purpose. What is that?" Her question was so important to the others that the Speaker forgot to be frustrated with her interruption.

Eran paused to sweep his gaze across the room, taking in their faces, their riveted attention and eager expressions. "We are here to help you along the way."

"So you are saying you are not like Marco?" she asked before leaning back to one of her peers to ask if she'd gotten the name correct.

"Marco is the name of the Fallen One, or FO as you call them, now in your custody," Eran confirmed. "And while Marco is here to learn, to perfect himself, and clearly has taken several steps back in his evolution, we are here to help you stay on course, regardless of any hostile interactions you may have with him or his associates."

"Associates meaning other FOs?"

"Correct."

"But those FOs are incapacitated, are they not?"

Eran purposefully waited for Mr. Hamilton to respond. He pressed his button, a little too quickly to pass it off with any confidence, and promised, "Yes, yes, they are, Ms. —"

Another beep, crackle, and impatient sigh. "Then why is this Marco here?" she demanded.

Eran retook the helm and explained, "Well, somewhere along the way, when a misguided soul has committed an egregious act against humanity, they are sent here. Why were they sent here? For the same reason you came yourselves. To learn. So that they may be given a second chance to perfect themselves. The difference between you and them is that they were cast here, you came of your own free will. We had ... incapacitated the other FOs ... while Marco sheltered himself in hiding. We only now learned of his escape."

"Then there could be others you missed, could there not?" the same lawmaker pressed.

A hum of nervous voices rose up before the Speaker cracked a gavel and quieted them with a few choice words. When the room calmed, all those present waited on Eran with breathless suspension.

"Yes, there could be."

Again the room exploded, forcing the Speaker to stand and shout into his microphone, but it wasn't until the audience settled some that he could counter, "There is little chance that any more are in hiding, is that not correct?" He fell silent, apparently waiting on Eran's answer.

"From what I understand, Marco was chosen as the only one to stay behind and remain in hiding while the rest of his brethren were incapacitated on the field of battle."

"All right, why him? Why *only* one?" a senator demanded so enflamed he forgot to use his microphone, his voice carrying forward across the now-rigid audience.

"One was all they needed," I said, and all eyes turned on me. My stomach sank then. I'd never enjoyed the spotlight and hadn't thought of the consequences of blurting out.

"What does that mean?" the same senator asked.

I swallowed back my nerves and announced, "One was all they needed to convince you to lift the rest."

No one spoke. No one breathed. No one moved. They digested the implications of my unveiled accusation in stark, speechless fear. Before panic could set in, the room cracked with a cough and Mr. Hamilton stuttered.

"I'd – I'd like to remind everyone that the rest remain catatonic, oblivious to their surroundings."

That was when the first phone rang.

"Please people," the Speaker sighed, "please turn off all electronic devi–"

Then the second phone rang and then the third. Quickly, like the onset of a downpour, cellphones began ringing. People dug for their devices. As they pinned the phones to their ears, it became evident something wasn't right. Some stood, others moved toward the doors with nervous forcefulness. Then a congresswoman screeched.

John was already on his cellphone, his head ducked against the sounds of the growing alarm surging through the upper and lower houses of Congress. He said one word in reply, dropped his phone to his hip, stood, and motioned to someone across the room. My eyes darted in that direction as an assembly of armed, fatigued men swept toward the podium where we sat.

"Mr. Chairman?" Mr. Hamilton asked, trembling.

John's retort was sharp and pointed, and left no doubt about the urgency of the situation that the others in the room were just now absorbing. "They're awake and have taken over the facility."

"They?"

"The FOs," John snapped.

"I thought you said you wouldn't revive them," I accused, standing, shouting over the chaos as people fled for the exits.

"We didn't," John said, turning to face us. "They did so on their own."

"When?" Eran asked, already on his feet.

"Just now."

"So why didn't they act out earlier?" Eran asked out loud, to himself.

"They were instructed not to," Mr. Hamilton said.

Eran braced himself as he leveled hard eyes on Mr. Hamilton. "By who?"

Mr. Hamilton gasped then as if he'd just deciphered something serious. "Marco wasn't waiting for some*thing*. He was waiting for some*one*."

A wave of fear shot through me, pricking my skin. "Lotharius."

The pressing of Eran's lips into a scowl as he stood rigid next to me told me that I was correct.

Mr. Hamilton's wide eyes met Eran's as he answered, the impact of what they had done hitting him fully now "What do we do?"

I could only think of what Marco had told me in the hallway at school, and then I drew in a sharp breath, registering the deception. "He was waiting," I told Eran. "Lotharius was waiting until the last of his disciples were freed."

Eran nodded, once, firmly. "Yes." And in the same breath, he warned, "Hold on."

"Hold on?" I restated, and then his arm swept around my waist and I was lifted off the ground, the air suddenly brushing past my body with his velocity.

"What — ?" I asked, my head falling with the

momentum.

Meeting in a cluster below us, like ants swarming to a piece of meat, John's men formed a pool of patterned green camouflage and raised their weapons in our direction.

Eran pivoted horizontally, pumped his appendages powerfully and angled us toward a door. Several people screamed below, having caught sight of us. Then we were falling, diagonally, toward the ground.

"Eran?" I asked just before our bodies hit, bounced, and jostled to a rest on a blue carpeted aisle.

"ERAN   ?" I screamed at his lifeless body.

Gripping his shoulder and rolling him face-up, I found his translucent blue-green eyes closed, his mouth ajar, a dart protruding from his neck.

"ERA - !"

His name was choked off as I was hauled violently backwards. Instantly, fatigued men were on Eran, taking hold of his limbs.

I dropped to my knees, throwing the men controlling me off balance, twisted my wrists free and used my fists as anchors as I thrusted my legs backwards. My feet hit armor that gave way and I knew I'd made contact with their torsos. Rotating around, I snapped to my feet and stood, sending a back kick into another fatigued man advancing on me. He stumbled backwards and fell over the edge of a pew. Another two men came at me from both sides, requiring me to release my appendages. They snapped outward, hitting the men in their faces, propelling them backwards. Then a man pointed a modified rifle at me.

John shouted, "Stand down! Not her. Detain her awake."

Taking that opportunity, I lunged into the air, searching for Eran on the ground as I felt the weight of a net land over me. I pumped hard, but my appendages met resistance, the top edges of them feeling as if wet burlap was weighing them down. I tried again as the ground grew closer. On my third attempt, hands grabbed my arms and back, and I was thrown to the ground, where my wrists were bound. As I frantically sought Eran in the crowd, and despite not finding him, the restriction to my arms pinched my appendages and they instinctively withdrew into my body.

"NO!" I screamed, tearing my throat raw. "*NO!*"

Mr. Hamilton appeared to be in a panic, still standing at the podium, his head swiveling from one side to the other, trying to discern what was happening.

"Is this your interpretation of all due respect?" I shouted at John, who approached me.

I was yanked sharply to the left, down the aisle toward the door where we'd entered, falling forward as my feet tangled in the net. When I was lifted onto someone's shoulder, I raised my head to glare at John as he trailed us.

"Your accommodations will be –" John began to assure.

"Shut up!"

To my surprise, he complied, as did the rest of the fatigued men seizing me. As they walked, I took in my surroundings, the number of doors we passed, the exit signs, the number and sequence of turns, in case I saw an opportunity to escape. I didn't. When that became obvious, one long thought ran through my head – one I knew Eran had already taken into account:

They had deluded us perfectly – escorted us away from our friends, surrounded us with adversaries, interrogated us, and then seized us. We were now entirely at their mercy.

10 DESPERATION

I was shoved into a van, my arms were bound behind my back, my head was bagged, and I was driven through the city to an airport. Being able to gauge if it was the same one we'd come through earlier was impossible, but it didn't seem to matter. I lost all sense of bearings the moment the helicopter – which I estimated to be military judging by its sounds – left the ground. My kidnappers, John included, remained in my proximity, and were fed pieces of information throughout the flight; and with the words like 'carnage' and 'havoc' being spoken loud enough to make their way through the fuselage, I didn't interrupt them until we landed.

"If you hurt Eran, you will all go to hell," I informed them flatly.

No one responded.

"I'll make sure of it." That not so veiled threat would mean something to John even if it didn't to anyone else.

Still, the bag and hand restraints remained.

I sighed as they hauled me from the helicopter.

"The only way to help yourselves is to free Eran," I warned as I was led across a landing pad or tarmac; I couldn't determine which.

Our surroundings were silent, other than the steady wind. No birds sang. No traffic droned past. We were somewhere remote, and elevated, judging by the chill in the air. When my foot landed on ground that gave way and crunched below my boot's heel, I knew we were in the snow.

"Either way, keeping me here only harms you. It'll delay Eran helping you – if he still chooses to do so and you better pray that he does – while he finds and frees me, and if he's forced to do *that*, it will piss him off. All while our mutual enemies are pillaging *your* world."

Still, no one answered. Their rubber soles crossing cement and then crunching through the snow were their only sound. There were fifteen, if I assessed them correctly, one heavier set and one light-footed.

A grinding noise broke the monotony and then the chill left the air. Walking became easier on the smooth, dry surface, which I detected was tiled. Our footsteps echoed off the walls, and still no one spoke.

I was turned abruptly, yanked forward, spun around, and slammed into a chair hard enough to make me exhale.

"Is that really necessary?" I said through the bag, before it was yanked off my head.

The idiot lackey kneeling at my side finished securing my wrists to the chair and joined the army of feet marching into the distance.

Blinking against the brightness, I found John at eye-level in front of me, the two of us surrounded by blinding light. When my eyes adjusted, I took in the entirely white room – ten feet by ten feet, devoid of any décor, with only a small grey camera in the corner breaking the swath of monochrome color.

John's arms were laid across the top rail of his silver metal chair, his legs straddled over the sides, as he sat in the chair backwards. The bag dangled from one of his hands. All pretense of administrative flair was gone. He was visibly easing back into rank-and-file demeanor.

"Did you hear me?" I pressed. "Eran –"

"Is in the same situation as you," John replied, controlled. "And, yes, I heard."

"Then you know where you will end up if he's hurt."

"Down in that hole in the London field?"

"Yes."

"I understand," John replied passively, resigned to it.

I shook my head at him, shrugged irritably, and again felt my constraints. "Why, John?"

He drew in a deep breath and sighed. "You two are now prisoners of war.

"Wa-?" I exhaled.

"Devices, resources," John added stoically, "for bartering should it be needed."

My eyebrows snapped skyward in shock. "You mean as in an exchange? Lotharius doesn't want us. We are as much his enemy as you."

"You and Eran still serve a purpose with the FOs."

"A purpose?" I said, more to myself. "We are a *threat* to them." Then I blinked, unable to believe what I was coming to understand. "You mean we are a threat to them and thus we would be of some value in a trade. A trade for your safety."

"If that's what it must come to."

My mouth fell open. "You would sacrifice us, the only ones capable of helping you, for a truce with the FOs?"

John's mouth tightened.

"You don't actually expect that truce to last?" I asked, appalled.

I jerked my head back and stared at the white ceiling for a second before letting it fall back to John. "You've learned nothing by observing us."

"More than you think."

I let that strategy sink in before asking, "So what's the plan, John? Keep Eran and I locked away on a mountain top?" John's eyes betrayed him when he blinked, and I knew I'd been correct. "While the FOs wreak havoc and leave carnage across the earth? Those were the words I heard on the way in. And that's what's happening out there, isn't it?"

"Yes."

"I strongly encourage you to reconsider your actions before it's too late."

John opened his mouth but hesitated, and then spoke. "Eran will be treated better than you. I hope that brings some consolation."

"It doesn't."

John pursed his lips and continued. "We can't let you sleep, Maggie. Doing so brings the added risk that you'll relay to your friends – your guardians – where you can be found."

"We've been through this before. It won't stop –"

John cut me off. "But this time will be a longer stretch. So I must apologize for what you will be put through to keep you awake."

"And what exactly will that be?"

John actually coaxed a sympathetic frown on my behalf and stood. "Please do your best to remain awake and lucid. I don't want to have to hurt you."

He rotated on his heel and marched from the room, closing the door behind him and shutting off the dark, unidentifiable hallway beyond. Once he did, music crackled and smoothed out through speakers in the ceiling – soft rock by a group I actually liked.

"The Creamed Bagel Band?" I said to the camera. "Really?"

Truthfully, I was impressed. The band only played small venues. The fact the DJ on the other end of the speaker heard of them was noteworthy.

Immediately following that song, another came on, this one harder, faster, more pounding. Then came a folk song. Then a tribal song. And as I surveyed my room for weaknesses I began to realize the music wasn't going to end. Eran had asked about torture techniques. This was one of them. Although it was being used on me now.

My heart tightened when the image of Eran's body on the blue carpet, being pulled at by strangers, came back to me. Another image swam into my consciousness: Of Eran bound to a chair in a vacant room in a remote location, vulnerable to the whims of those who wish to hurt him. And I finally understood what Eran had been warning me about as I had tried in vain to convince him that I couldn't be hurt. He knew better than I did what can affect me, and he understood that it wasn't what could be done to *me* that would hurt but what could be done to *those I love*. And now Eran was experiencing the full extent of that fear. A wave of rage coursed through me, blinding me, wiping all thoughts clean but the vision of an imprisoned, exposed Eran.

If they harmed him ... My lip curled against the possibility as I again tried my bound wrists and growled when there was no give. That rumble in my throat built into a scream, and propelled by the burst from my lungs, turned into a roar. My head shook with the ferocity of it, my hair quivering against my head and my mouth stretched painfully wide to emit as much emotion as I could.

Huffing, my head fell and as I closed my eyes against the view of my chest rapidly rising and falling, I called out to Eran.

You heard me once. When we were separated before. I'm sending you another message. Tell me you are okay. Tell me that you aren't hurt. Tell me you are not incapacitated.

With my eyes closed, I focused on connecting to anything beyond my touch, anything beyond the walls of my cell, through that vast void we pay no attention to.

It came several minutes later, like a whisper in the dark, a sensation that was weak but distinct from everything else. Anger. Frustration. Struggle. But it came with passion and that told me that Eran was uninjured. And that was all I needed to know.

I exhaled in sheer relief, my shoulders fell forward, and my head cranked back as a smile glanced across my lips.

I hear you. I feel you... I love you.

Attempting to send a mental image of what I'd felt outside, I explained: *I am on a mountain, snow covered, elevated. No population nearby. In a room. And I am not hurt. Where are you?*

I waited, eyes closed, holding my breath, feeling for his sensation.

Then a blast of shrieks screamed through the room. My head snapped up, eyes opened wide, my arms yanked forward in defense only to reach the ends of their binding.

The music crackled back and continued to play.

Confused, I stared at the speaker and then John's words returned to me. *Please do your best to remain awake and lucid. I don't want to have to hurt you.*

And I understood what he meant.

"I wasn't sleeping!" I shouted at the camera. "Morons!"

And still the music played.

I sighed and adjusted my body on the cold metal chair. "Can you at least unbind me?" I asked the camera.

But the continuous music was my only response.

The minutes stretched into hours and each time my head fell and my eyes closed a blast of sound erupted in the room. Squeals, screeches, and blasts were my only other company.

Eventually, I looked at the camera and called out, "Mental stimulation would be helpful."

The sound immediately lowered and a square panel behind the white wall in front of me came to life. Clearly visible through the translucent plastic was a medium-sized television, playing rock videos, which became the only sound piped into the room.

I cocked my head at the camera and chided, "Really? Did they *tell* you my actual age?"

The television blinked and a program on deep space began, voiced over with the sound of a well-known actor.

"Better," I said to the camera. "Thank you."

That programming ran continuously for the next several hours until the door opened and Paper-Pusher entered carrying a tray. Scowling, he pulled a chair inside with him and let the door shut. Setting the chair before me, he plopped down, positioning the tray between us on one hand.

Pasta with tomato sauce, cut up.

Paper-Pusher picked up a spoon, scooped the food onto it, and brought it to my mouth.

I raised an eyebrow at him and his expression turned to one that made it obvious he abhorred the task too.

"What will you do when I need to use the bath –?"

He shoved the utensil into my mouth, catching my lip, and tipping it. Pasta and sauce tumbled down my chin.

"Eat," he commanded.

I turned my head and spat the food on the floor. "Untie me."

He tipped his head to the side. "You really think we're that stupid, don't you? Releasing your hands will allow your wings their freedom, and what then?"

"I eat."

He snorted. "You attack."

He violently dipped the spoon into the plate and lifted another mound of food.

"Untie me, Benson. Help yourself."

"Sergeant Benson," he corrected.

"Sergeant?" I sat back, tilting my head to observe him better. "You fought hard for that rank, I imagine."

"I did," he said and made another attempt at my mouth. I diverted my head.

"Think that rank will have any meaning to the FOs once they rule your world?"

His lips pressed together harder but there was no further reaction.

"They don't care about you. You are a tool, Sergeant Benson. All of you are. They will –"

He made another attempt to force the food into my mouth but I was quicker and the food ended up rolling off the edge and onto the floor.

He sighed, tossed the fork on the tray, bent down and wiped the floor clean. Without another word, he stood and marched out the door. Before it closed, I shouted out, "Think about what I said. You'll be at the bottom of the barrel, again."

The smell of pasta lingered in the air for the next span of time, of which I estimated to be an hour based on the length of the show's programming playing on the wall. Then time slowed for me and I did grow tired. My body had been given little sleep over the previous days, including at the cabin with Eran, where I had done my best to stay awake, not wanting to miss any of it. Here, there was little to keep my attention and none of it could compete to the smallest measure with what Eran could do to me; so my head began to dip and my eyes blurred until the white expanse of the walls blended together. Each time I did, an ejection of sound exploded in the room. What I assumed to be night was one long attempt to fight off exhaustion, failing, and being punished for it. Once, Paper-Pusher entered, yanked my head back, and sloshed water down my throat. I choked through it until it had cleared my lungs and resumed my attempt to remain awake. As I did, I was almost certain they thought it was my attempt to follow their rules, but it wasn't. I wanted to be alert, rather than dead weight, when Eran arrived.

But that arrival didn't come.

Groggy, in a haze, and still trying to keep my eyes open and head up, Paper-Pusher entered with eggs and toast. This time, I ate, to keep up my strength. Neither of us spoke.

The television was now showing a black and white episode of a late 1960s show in which the world was grand other than the fact that a kitten was lost. After two more episodes, I looked up at the camera and called out, "Bathroom."

The door opened and Paper-Pusher entered, as if he were waiting on the other side.

"Not now," he declared and stepped back to allow someone else to enter the room.

She was mid-forties, with dark brown hair trimmed properly to her shoulder, and swathed in a business suit that identified her immediately as a politician. Crossing the room, she extended a hand. I motioned to my restrictions and she appeared embarrassed before sinking into the chair Paper-Pusher had left in the room.

"I'm the fourth district's –"

"I don't care," I said, and her expression sharpened.

"Why are you here?" I asked, bluntly.

"Well." She attempted to cross her legs and realized there wasn't enough room and abandoned the attempt. "I had a relative in Gettysburg at the time of the civil war, a sheriff there by the name of –"

"Yes, we crossed paths," I confirmed, and her head jerked back in surprise.

"I –" she said, losing her train of thought. After clearing her throat and shifting in her seat to sit straighter, she began again. "He told a story that has been passed down through my family about winged people, one of whom performed the service of relaying messages to and from the dead." She paused, looking as if she still had trouble buying into the theory. "Given that the winged people part was true, I asked around if the part about you and others like you delivering messages was also."

"It is."

"Yes," she said curtly. "I know. That's why I'm here." She frowned. "I – I will have you deliver a message –"

"Will have me?" I rebuked.

"I expect you to –"

"Expect me?" I repeated again, appalled.

"You do understand I can have you held here indefinitely?"

I cocked my mouth in a smile. "You'd be surprised how short that really is."

She sighed and sat back as Paper-Pusher broke the disgruntled air she was emitting into the room.

"You will aid the senator in anything she asks," Paper-Pusher demanded.

"I'd be happy to dedicate myself to it," I promised. "But first, you'll need to free Eran, then me, and then, maybe, after a few hours of recuperation from this torture you've submitted me to, and once I regain the feeling in my legs, I'll be able to sleep and finally deliver this fine woman's message for her."

"I don't like being patronized," she growled.

"I don't like being held prisoner," I countered. "Now what can you do about that?"

237

We narrowed our eyes at one another before I disrupted the silence. "You said you were related to the sheriff in Gettysburg?"

"Yes," she replied.

"He was pathetic," I informed her. "That trait appears to run in the family."

Her nostrils flared and Paper-Pusher stepped forward, a hand on the firearm at his holster.

"Go ahead," I urged and, knowing he couldn't, he leaned forward to speak directly to the senator. "What you all don't seem to understand," I said, interrupting, "is that unless you free Eran and me immediately you will likely be reunited sooner than you would like with whomever you wish for me to deliver a message to."

"Do not threaten the senator," Paper-Pusher snapped.

"That is advice," I said to her.

"I have security," she replied.

"Not for this."

She sat in unnerved silence, observing me, trying to deduce whether I spoke the truth.

I stretched my right arm outward but my restraints noticeably held me back. "You'll learn your own limitations soon enough," I cautioned and sat back.

She stood, frowning, and strolled gracefully to the door. After waiting for Paper-Pusher to open it for her, she left and he followed. And the volume on the television resumed.

"Bathroom?" I said to the camera. When nothing changed in the course of a few seconds, I knew they were withholding it.

The television suggestively changed to a program about the most arid desert on earth, the Atacama. While enlightening, the episode was surprisingly effective and eventually the pain in my bladder ebbed.

Hours passed. No one returned, not even with food

or water. Without indication of the movement of the sun I could only estimate the day was merging into another. The television continued, alongside the explosions of sound, as my solitary source of company. My overseer began to change the channels before the programs were over, leaving me with absolutely no understanding of time. The blasts to keep me awake seemed to come more frequently then. It was on one of these interruptions that my head jerked up and I saw Eran standing in front of me.

"Eran?" I whispered through parched lips, my body weakened, my lungs struggling against the exhaustion of being awake for days.

He smiled and a breathtaking glimmer rose to his translucent eyes, but he didn't move.

"Eran?" I repeated, nervously.

His smile faded but he remained stationary, watching me with feet astride, absorbing me from afar.

"What are... What are you doing?" I asked. "My hands are bound."

His legs, positioned astride, stayed in place, his muscles protruding visibly through the fabric across his thighs. His arms, straight in front of him and interlaced at his waist, remained clasped, the sinewy muscles down them never flexing with movement.

"I don't ... understand," I exhaled, tired, so tired. "I don't ..."

Then I blinked and he was gone.

"No," I breathed and searched the room, my eyelids languishing, my eyeballs dry now and abrasive. "Where are ...? Eran ...?

I blinked several times to clear my sight, desperate for him to return, and when all I saw was white walls I hung my head and cried tearless sobs.

An incalculable amount of time later, a sudden spark ran across the back of my neck and I snapped my head up to glare at the camera. "I'm hallucinating!" I screeched. "Where is your humanity?"

To my shock, the television blinked off, and the wall returned to solid white, just as the speaker cracked and a voice came through it. "They never had any to begin with."

They? I thought through the haze. That pronoun was used to refer to those other than one's self.

My hands began to perspire and the shock to my neck grew steadily more intense. When the door opened and I recognized the face staring back at me, alongside the faces of those behind him, I shook my head, which only slightly disrupted the sharp pain to my neck.

"It's not you," I whispered. "Not you."

"My dear, what have they done to you?"

His foul breath brushed my face as I reopened my eyes and found he'd moved forward quickly. Now sitting in the chair before me, legs dressed in black leather and crossed over the knees, hair wild but still a single stripe of white down the center of his shaved skull.

"Don't worry," he wheedled, "they can't hurt you anymore."

My neck was on fire now and it wasn't diminished by the beads of perspiration running from my scalp.

"No," I moaned, understanding his meaning fully.

"Yes," he assured. "They have been dealt with swiftly and severely."

"No ..."

He laughed with pity at me. "Even still, you care for them."

I tried to raise my fists, to swipe at him, to administer damage, but my arms had gone numb a day earlier and the pathetic attempt looked more like a shrug.

"Do you remember me, Magdalene?" he asked, and I

realized his voice was just as I recalled, patient, cajoling, sympathizing. When I could not answer, he rotated in the chair to Marco who stood behind him.

"Yes, Lotharius," he confirmed, "she remembers."

Appeased, Lotharius shifted back to me.

"Good. It has been some time since we last saw each other."

I shook my head, which again did nothing to stem the pain at my neck.

"No?" Lotharius seemed confused.

"I saw you," I said, barely audible, fighting against my weakness to overcome his presence riveting my body's alarm. For a brief moment, with the speed of a shooting star, I regained control and addressed everyone present. "I saw all of you."

My gaze swept across the others standing behind Lotharius, the ones who followed him here, who were led by him, who had been his soldiers for centuries. Abaddon was unchanged, his skin more translucent than the others, his nose bowed into a beak that nearly dipped past his thin, peeling lips. Sarai, his ever-loyal daughter, stood beside him, her almond-shaped eyes watching me like a spider observing its prey at the end of its web. Her chestnut-colored hair still hung polished and glistening to her waist, and her skin – which had been carved deeply with a scar at one point but was now plump and flawless – reflected the youth of the teenage girl she had become when she fell to earth. Elam stood just behind Abaddon, always, his closest confidante, ready to act on his master's behalf. His youthful, highbrow posture belied the cunning that his sharp, beady eyes confessed. That stare had been pinned on me more than once, and I'd considered whether he harbored more pure hatred for me than the others. Achan appeared the most relaxed among them, his long-fingered, delicate hand resting across a crossbow, his eyes lazily taking in the scene. Sharar was the newest of Abaddon's followers and still didn't appear to have blended with them. Not that it mattered. Sharar seemed comfortable in his place, given that he always appeared ready to disengage and leave their group on a second's notice even while suddenly and ferociously defending his associates when the need arose.

Lotharius regained my attention after a sharp inhale, and I shifted my gaze to him as his mouth cocked into a grin. "You visited us while we were … immobilized." He sounded touched.

"Surveilled," I corrected and his face fell.

"But of course, you did. You being the only one capable of visiting our prison underground and living to tell about it. Which brings me to the reason I am here."

I rolled my neck to pinch back the persisting pain but it did nothing to deter it, and then, despite my exhaustion, I refocused on controlling it. As Lotharius spoke, I retrained my senses to narrow to my environment, essentially cutting out the impact these Fallen Ones had on me. The chill seeping in from the outside found its way down my throat. The smell of blood permeated the room now, although there was no sign of it, drifting in from the bodies the FOs had left in their wake.

"The Chairman's offer to acquire you and Eran was tempting. One that I must say made me salivate slightly. I could not pass up the chance to consider it, and thus requested access to you. I thought they would concede, given the destruction their world is now befalling at the hands of those like me, but they played with me, sending a video as proof of life instead; and, so you see, that is the only reason I killed those guards outside your room. I did not want to, I assure you. Human life is *valuable*, Magdalene, an ideology I am working to instill in my brothers and sisters out there who seem so bent on embracing their new-found freedom. And having no trouble at all showing it. But you mustn't suck the well dry before the next rain. We must conserve what we have. I don't think they've thought it through, but instead are acting on long-suppressed emotion. But who will serve us if the mortals become extinct?" He clucked his tongue at such short-sighted thinking. "The Chairman will return soon and discover that I've located his treasure trove and find his people here in the manner in which we've left them and you … gone. And he'll understand better." Lotharius ended his monologue with a deep, restful breath, his calm expression and the hands folded in his lap projecting perfect ease.

"Gone?" I asked, splitting my focus between his answer and the thump – thump – thump of someone approaching.

"Incoming," Sharar announced, leaning back to peer out the door and down the hallway.

Lotharius's mouth turned downward in disappointment.

"There's no time to take her," Sarai insisted quickly.

"No," Lotharius agreed, "not now."

His hand moved swiftly from his lap to over his shoulder, where Abaddon placed a dagger in his waiting palm before returning his cold stare to me. Lotharius moved even quicker then, the dagger cutting through the air until Lotharius's knuckles were pressed against my belly. I shivered, repulsed by the touch, minding his fingers more than the blade embedded in me. When he pulled away, his hand was already wet with my blood.

"But all we have is time, sweet Sarai. While we leave Magdalene here now, twill not always be so in the future."

With that threat hanging in the air, he stood abruptly, spun, and marched out the door, on the heels of the others just as the pain of his memento seared across my skin.

I groaned and looked down, where blood was already dampening my tee-shirt and the waist of my jeans. Recalling a biology assignment, I assessed its location and determined it had missed all major sites of serious damage. Muscle damage and infection would be my primary concerns. And the pain, I was reminded as it burned across the area where I'd been punctured.

I realized then that the agony and the FOs presence had made me remarkably mindful again. The thump of appendages grew louder and then ceased entirely in my ears. The crunch of snow followed.

"Magdalene."

I opened my eyes to Eran's voice but was not able to locate him. He moved too swiftly, with the speed of an eagle having found its target.

"Eran," I breathed.

Then he was bent before me and his warm, firm hands cupped my face and his sweet exhale coursed over it. His lips came to mine, soft, needing, distressed. Moving far faster than I knew possible, my hands were freed and in one swift motion my body rose through the air and was cradled against Eran's warm, solid torso. His scent, the aroma of earth on a fresh summer day, enveloped me. I wanted to curl into that part of his body and sleep but I thought of who had just been in front of me.

"Lotha..." I moaned, struggling to speak.

"I know. Save your strength. The wound isn't the problem. Your body is depleted."

I tried to nod.

"I'm taking you home."

We had just breached the outside door and Eran's foot had pressed into the snow when the spark returned to my neck.

"My dear, long lost protégé," Lotharius's voice called

244

out. "So good of you to join us, Eran."

Eran had already halted, as I opened my eyes to the bright sunlight. Sergeant Benson laid across the snow, his head twisted at an odd angle, with another three of his men a few feet away with the same lethal injury. Lotharius stood on the opposite side of the peak, facing us, his followers who had been in my small room now standing in a line on either side of him.

"I'm not joining you," Eran called out.

"Not yet," Lotharius teased.

A flap of appendages and clothing disrupted the air and then the ground shook, and after I blinked I found four people standing defensively between us and them, the puffs of snow settling around their feet. The one in the center, dark-skinned with strikingly white hair, turned his head back toward Eran.

"They circled back around," Campion explained.

"I deduced," Eran replied.

"Not that they could hide from us," a smaller boy to Campion's right side declared.

"Ah, yes, I've always admired your ability to find us," Lotharius called out to him. "Gershom."

Gershom bristled, and it was evident that he'd never actually interacted with Lotharius, despite having once been one of Abaddon's followers until rejecting them entirely.

The remaining two arrivals stood quietly, one a woman in a thick, ornate dress long enough to lay in the snow at her ankles and with auburn hair pulled into a bun similar to Ms. Beedinwigg's, the other a teenage boy made of both meat and muscles. While the woman's skills were as yet undetermined, the boy would help our odds significantly when the fight began.

I squirmed to be set down but Eran only tightened his hold on me.

"What do you want, Lotharius?" Eran called out.

Lotharius wrapped his arms around his back and clasped his hands behind him as he stepped into a stroll. Instantly, those on our side withdrew swords, but he didn't seem to mind.

"By now you've learned that this – all of this – has been my plan, and was – with Marco's governance – executed with impeccable precision. The world is being consumed. Eran has done a fine job attempting to preserve it, but fatefully it was not to be so, and now you must consider your options. There is an eternity of bliss awaiting you, one in which your every desire will be fulfilled, your every whim, every impulse … met. You may have all this," he said, holding up an empty palm. "Or you may have …" He held out his other empty palm. "Pain, suffering, war, defeat." He returned to his pacing, traveling a line along the front of his followers, carving a path through the snow. "Think of it, Éléonore," he said and the woman in front of us squared her shoulders. And that was when I recognized her. She wore a similar dress to the one that had been hanging in Mr. Leroux's museum, this one free of dried blood. "You've lost your son once, Éléonore, do you truly wish to go through that devastation again?"

She reached out and stepped in front of the boy at her side, protectively, but to his credit, he sidestepped her and regained an opening in the line.

"And you, Campion, having lost the love of *your* life in the very same fight." Lotharius tipped his head at Éléonore, who seemed surprised by this revelation. "Do you truly wish to spend another century hunting down the person responsible for her death, yet again?"

Éléonore turned inquisitive eyes on Campion, who never took his focus off Lotharius.

"Tell me, Campion, wouldn't you much rather simply avoid the aggravation and live happily into eternity?"

Lotharius strolled a few paces farther and rotated suddenly to a stop in front of the boy, who expanded his chest and raised his chin.

"And what about you, Arnaud?" Lotharius swept a hand back toward Sarai suddenly. "She awaits, and this you know. You had a choice to remain in the afterlife but you chose to return here as an Alterum. Why? Is it not obvious?" He asked the rest of us before returning to Arnaud. "Your time with her so abruptly ended all those years ago. Who can blame you for leaving the afterlife when you discovered she had been resurrected? I cannot. Look at her. She still weeps for you." He motioned to Sarai, who's permanent cold scowl, projecting only anger and rage, had melted away and the beauty of her once serene state glowed through.

Sarai took an eager, desperate step toward Arnaud, a sob escaping her, but when Éléonore moved again to separate Arnaud, she halted. He shifted around his mother in an attempt to meet Sarai, only to find his mother's sword at his throat.

That did not deter Lotharius, however. "Don't you wish to be together?" he incited. "After all this time? Your passion is still there; and it so obviously ... *palpable.*"

Arnaud made a gesture that appeared to defy his mother when the world suddenly exploded in white. I was hurled backwards, Eran's arm tightly wound around me. I sensed we were spinning, which came to a sudden end and was followed by the feeling of weightlessness. As I gained my bearings, I found we were hovering in flight off the side of the cliff where we'd been standing, the rock formation where the building had been turned into nothing but a jagged, charred monument of rock. I didn't see Campion or Gershom or any other bodies.

"Eran!" I screamed, although the compression impact to my chest had been enough to blast the air from my lungs.

Then I saw them, rising above the settling snow and smoke, their appendages lifting them into clear air. Campion was hauling Gershom by the collar and several yards behind them Arnaud and his mother were moving to reunite with Campion.

"They'll be all right," Eran assessed, and I reasoned he had used his ability to survey wounds within others' bodies, as he had done when he first saw me earlier.

My eyes swept from them across the horizon where I noted a line of winged bodies.

"Did they …?" I said, struggling to make sense of it all.

"No, they were hit too. It was the United States Air Force." He tipped his head to the southeast where a fighter jet was circling around for target confirmation.

"Campion, Éléonore," Eran called out and gestured to the aircraft.

Instantly, each of them, Gershom now fully revived, launched into a rapid flight. We met them in the air, all heading for what I assumed to be New Orleans. I remained tucked into Eran's chest, working on keeping my eyes open.

Campion positioned himself beside us, Eran's lengthy appendages keeping him at a distance from us but easily within talking range.

"My apologies, Colonel," Campion shouted, "for not seeing that coming."

"No apologies needed."

"And for not being present to prevent your incarcerations."

"It's not your fault, Campion. I escaped, once I found the kinks in their cells." Eran smiled briefly and acknowledged, "I understood where you'd been when you appeared beside me in flight on the path here."

"Attempting to track down Lotharius," Campion

summed.

"While I was trying to track down Magdalene," Eran revealed. "And if Lotharius hadn't ignited Magdalene's alarm, I would have come to you."

"And we would have guided you to her," Campion assured.

"We?" Eran asked, darting a curious look in his direction.

Campion answered by nodding toward Gershom, Éléonore, and her son.

"You were all in the ambassador's employment?" Eran asked, which Campion confirmed with a nod.

"When Marco appeared and the military began lifting the Fallen Ones, we left and began our surveillance to locate Lotharius," Campion explained.

Eran nodded, letting his head fall briefly to his chest with a satisfied smile crossing it, visibly pleased by his first lieutenant's initiative. That smile fell when we came across the first burning city.

Smoke billowed into the air, smothering the buildings and streets below it. From our elevation we couldn't see or hear the panic on the ground, but we knew it was there. And when we crossed over the next burning city and the next one and the next one, I finally knew what had been taking place while I had been locked inside the building on a remote mountaintop.

Lotharius had done exactly what we had expected. He'd set his kind free.

And instinctively, Eran tightened his hold on me.

11 UNITED

"Felix, what nourishing food do you have in this kitchen?"

Eran barked this question as we came through the backdoor of Ezra's house. It was evening now, and the lights had been turned on, so their beams created strange waves behind my eyelids, which were now too heavy to lift.

Felix sprang to his feet, judging by the sound of the chair he'd been sitting in tipping and dancing until it steadied.

"Left over black beetle stew, snake sassafras soup, ant and honeybee casserole," he rattled off. "Where has she been, Eran? What happened to her?"

Ignoring him, Eran snapped, "Rufus?"

Understanding the urgency, he replied, "Chicken soup. Still warm."

"Get it out."

I was set down, although thankfully not in a chair this time. The hard mounds of Eran's thighs caught me in my descent as his arms wound around me, loosening only to take hold of the spoon.

Someone entered to our left, gasped, and must have retreated. A few minutes later, as Eran gently wedged the edge of a spoon into my mouth, a swab pressed against the inside fold of my left arm, then a prick touched that area and the feeling of something hard slithered under my skin.

"An IV," Ezra's calming voice whispered in my ear. "For potential overdoses, should one of my kids arrive in that state, but it'll work just fine in your case. Then you'll need to rest."

"That," Eran grumbled, "she is fighting."

Felix breathed out loudly. "But she needs it. Look at her."

"Col-lect ..." I whispered.

"Eat, Magdalene," Eran interrupted, and warm, salty liquid slid across my tongue again.

I swallowed. "Col ..."

"What's she saying?" Felix asked, his voice close in the chair next to us.

"Collect," Eran griped. "She wants to gather everyone and mount an offensive strike."

I attempted a weak nod but I was sure it wasn't in any way noticeable.

"She can't fight!" Felix said, horrified. "She can't even stand."

"No," Eran said tightly and then his tone turned soft. "Not yet, but she will. And then she'll be nothing short of unrelenting."

"Yes, I do believe she would be," Éléonore said quietly in observation.

After a brief pause, Campion cleared his throat, stepped forward and made introductions, adding that he and Gershom were already well known to our housemates, given their histories as good friends to Eran and me. But it was Éléonore's name that made them pause in revered silence.

"You — You killed the wife of Abaddon, the disciple to Lotharius?" Ezra asked.

"In an effort to protect my son, yes. And I would do it again," she added, leaving no uncertainty about it.

Gershom gasped then. "So you ... and you ... *do* have past relations with Abaddon and Sarai ..."

Without having to open my eyes, I knew he was pointing to Éléonore and her son, processing that Sarai and Arnaud had once been in love and that Éléonore and Abaddon had kept the two of them apart.

"The daughter of a Fallen One and the son of a messenger ..." Gershom exhaled.

"Yes," Arnaud said, almost impatiently.

Unaffected, Gershom acknowledged, "I understand why Éléonore stepped between them on the mountain now."

And Arnaud exhaled.

An uncomfortable pause followed before Felix questioned, "So is that what happened to Magdalene? Did she get tangled up with them? The messengers have been waiting for her on the other side every night but she never arrived. And you ... we figured you two were together. Do you have any idea what's going on out there?"

That underestimation was met by a cynical chuckle from within the cavern of Eran's chest.

"The fact is, Magdalene is right," he conceded. "We need to gather everyone. Can you do that for me, Felix?"

"We can," Ezra interjected. "Now?"

"Yes," Eran replied. "*Now.*"

Then, finally, I allowed myself to sleep.

* * *

"Paris, London, New York, Beijing."

These cities were being listed when I reached the last step of the stairs still available, stopping at the back of a guardian who knew I was there but didn't bother to turn from the spectacle below. Once again, guardians and messengers, none of whom had been in the afterlife when I'd arrived, had been called to Ezra's greeting room, and were again squeezed together until they stood shoulder-to-shoulder with just the coffee table separating them. And as before, whispered words transmitted the discussion to those down the hallway and spilling into the kitchen.

"Every major city," Felix interrupted Ezra. "In flames, being pillaged. The media is no longer covering it, having left their jobs to be with their families. Government offices are closing. The military is strained. There seems to be more and more of them coming, but from where?"

"There isn't," Eran stated. "They are simply reincarnating, as they do when their lives end here on earth, as they have done since being sent here, a process that has always worked against us."

"So ...," Felix said, deducing, "if they can reincarnate and we can't, how and when will it end?"

"It won't," Eran assured. "This is the first phase. It's designed to put us in our place and instill fear."

Rufus emitted a gruff snicker and adjusted his thick, tattooed arms across his massive chest. "Well, I'll tell ya ... it's workin'."

Ezra sighed and turned to Eran. "What is the next phase?"

"To round up the survivors," Eran said, and allowed that to sink in.

"For what purpose?"

"Ultimately ... bondage and servitude."

Groans and gasps erupted from those within audible distance. A second later, more came from those in the hall and kitchen.

"So we have a choice," Eran stated, shifting his feet further astride while leaving his arms crossed over his chest. "We can let them," he asserted and watched Ms. Beedinwigg's face fall as she stood in the corner listening. "Or we can fight them." When no one spoke, Eran continued. "I've made my decision, and despite the fact that it will be more challenging to execute it without you, I cannot force this on you as a duty. It is not one. Guardians' roles are to protect the messengers. Messengers' roles are to deliver messages for the people. Protection for the humans is in my hands and the hands of my army, many of whom are already working to suppress the violence alongside the country's military where they are positioned ... albeit clandestine and anonymous," he added under his breath.

"But you need help," Ms. Beedinwigg surmised. She stood in the corner, arms folded too, alone. Mr. Hamilton was nowhere in sight.

"A greater force brings greater strength," Eran agreed, and fell silent to await our verdict.

He stood there, shoulders squared, firm in his stance, blue-green eyes shimmering with energy, exuding strength and wisdom, and I knew as I watched him that he was in his element. He hadn't simply become a leader because a role had been assigned to him; he had faced the trials and misfortunes that preordain souls for greatness, and all that he had faced alone had only made him stronger in mind and body. He would, without reluctance, leave this nest of safety, part with friends and confidantes who he had fought beside for centuries, and enter the terror and turmoil willingly, alone, and dedicated to seeing it through. Because he had faced conflict, with others and within himself, and from it he had learned how to overcome his uncertainties and how to act despite them. He was, by all accounts, our leader.

"I'm with you," I stated as loudly as my weak body allowed, and all heads shifted toward me at the top of the stairs.

Eran's face changed from stern determination to warmth at seeing me on my feet, to subtle interest as his eyes dropped down the length of my body, again covered in my black leather suit. They were searching for signs of my recovery but stopped at my hands, where I held each of our swords, which I'd retrieved after waking and dropping from my balcony to carry them back from the shed. I grinned slightly at him.

"We're also with you, Colonel," Campion said, sweeping a hand across the room, gesturing to the guardians.

Several of them joined in with shouts of acceptance, Gillis going so far as to lift his hammer, a weapon of choice.

Eran nodded his head, hiding a pleased grin. "Thank you, Guardian Legion."

"Huff ... Huff ... Huff," they replied in their traditional chant.

"As are we," Hermina announced, the undeclared but de facto overseer of the messengers, while many of them nodded in unison.

Again, Eran tipped his head, a quiet smile thanking them.

"Will that be enough?" Ms. Beedinwigg asked, and raised her eyes to meet mine.

"Because we know where we can find more," I added, concluding her inference.

Suddenly, my left wrist snapped upward and the sword I had gotten for Eran from the shed jerked from my arm. A second later, Joyeuse cut through the air, above the heads of those on the ground floor and snapped into Eran's waiting palm.

"Then let's go get them."

The crowd parted for both of us and we left the house among curious, mumbled discussions.

Ten minutes later, Eran and I were well overhead, the lights from the city of New Orleans glimmering through the vacant streets. There were no fires, no clouds of smoke, no offensive military operations, and in fact it looked like any other night.

A quarter of an hour more and the city's glow was gone almost entirely, the horizon gradually having swallowed it, and we began our descent over a slender, weaving strip of blue-black punctuated on both sides by a small, dull string of hazy yellow smudges. As we grew closer, the familiar sight of the channel through bowing cypress trees and illuminated by lanterns came into focus. Surrounded by houses on stilts set back in the Louisiana bayou, the water that served as a roadway through this village was just as empty as the streets of our city. The only signs of life were the flickering lamps hanging from posts at the end of each short dock lining the waterway.

"Maybe they're in hiding," I suggested as we landed on a wooden pier and retracted our appendages.

"That's what we do best," a voice from the shore called out and a small moss-coated canoe emerged from the inky shadows. "Wouldn't you agree?"

Jameson smiled while drifting out from the gloom, his strip of perfectly white teeth gleaming in the lantern's light. "Good to see you," he said, stepping up to the pier and tying off the boat. Turning to face us, he announced, "We've been expecting you."

Eran attempted a smile.

"Ever since the first city went down, we figured you've been busy," Jameson said, waving us inside the tiny one-room shack.

"Any of your people affected?" Eran asked.

"We tend to keep to the outskirts," he said, nearly

disappearing inside the dark, sparsely-decorated room. He lit another lantern on the wall and glanced over his shoulder at us. "And we can move surreptitiously when needed."

"I remember," Eran said.

"How's Jocelyn?" I asked.

"Fine," she replied, her feet just landing on the pier outside. She strolled inside, pausing for a greeting hug. "Thanks for asking."

She and I exchanged smiles, although they were weak, given the circumstances that had brought us together again.

"So let me guess," Jameson said, folding his arms across his chest and stepping astride, "you're here to see what kind of an investment we can make."

Eran grinned tolerantly. "This wouldn't be like the seven Fallen Ones who controlled your world."

"How would it be different?"

"Our strategy then was to take those Fallen Ones one at a time, quietly, to prevent the remaining Fallen Ones from scattering, which is the sole reason I didn't invite my army to participate –"

"You have an army?" Jameson asked.

"It would have drawn attention," Eran continued. "Stealth assaults were necessary."

"But they aren't now?" Jameson pressed.

"We won't have that luxury."

"Why not?" Jocelyn argued.

"Because this time, they'll be on the offensive, unified, and they'll be ready for us."

"Sounds risky," Jameson pointed out.

"Less so than waiting until they get around to coming after you," I blurted.

Jameson was struck by my sudden departure from an amicable discussion and paused for a moment to assess it. Like Eran, he showed no emotion or detectable thought as he watched me, but eventually, he admitted, "You make a good point, Maggie." He opened his mouth to add to that statement when a motorized roar sucked all other sound from the air and the wood below our feet and surrounding walls trembled so violently that Eran and I raised our weapons and started for the door.

Outside, the tree limbs flapped furiously and the narrow, once-placid waterway was now churning up whitecaps. The lanterns' dull lights swung back and forth as if an invisible hand were placed against them, giving each an aggressive shove. Two fell but their glass breaking was absorbed by the thump-thump-thump above. Eran and I looked up to find the underside of a black helicopter, its rotors pummeling the air, lights from its fuselage reflecting only fragments of the interior and the shoulders and knees of at least four men onboard. Between us and them, descended a pair of flat feet, pressed between a dangling rope. We quickly stepped back and a large man in fatigues hit the pier hard enough to make one board below his feet crack.

"Eran, Maggie," John greeted with a casual shout, unwound his hands, motioned to the helicopter and waited for it to ascend before speaking again. He didn't seem to notice Eran step between us.

"John," Eran greeted, reticent. "Come to apprehend us again?" There was no indignation to his tone, only mild curiosity.

"Let's go inside," he said and gestured to the shack. "I've been waiting for you."

Eran and I exchanged a glance, but followed him nonetheless.

With the helicopter only a steady, quiet rhythm now, their voices lowered.

"Jameson, Jocelyn," John said, extending his hand to each of them as they narrowed their eyes at him. "I'm

John."

"John," Jameson said, taking his hand with less reluctance than Jocelyn. "Who are you, how do you know this place and our names?"

"Well, Jameson, you've been on our radar just about as long as these two," John said and tipped his head at Eran and me. He then went on to answer Jameson's questions without hesitation, blanketed in shadows, but forthright and accurate in his candor. In the end, Jameson seemed duly satisfied, and appropriately inferring the reason for John's intrusion. "Then I'm assuming you're here to ask us for help."

John chuckled to himself, his expression contrite, and said, "You assume correctly."

"After you arrested our friends?" Jocelyn replied curtly, making it clear that she had overheard Eran's reference to it outside and didn't find it defensible.

"Well, Jocelyn, we non-winged humans are a primitive type. We're still learning how to defend ourselves and we have and will make mistakes."

"We don't have wings either," she countered pointedly.

John steadied his gaze at her, temporarily staggered. "Oh, yes, you do."

An awkward silence followed before Eran stepped in. "What exactly do you have in mind?"

"Our strategy is to send out teams to all affected areas, air-lifted from New Orleans, which remains curiously untouched –"

"Because they know we are here," Jameson asserted, and John paused to process that belief before nodding in agreement and continuing his description of the plan.

"And with each team containing my people, your people," he said gesturing to Jameson and Jocelyn, "and a guardian and, of course, a messenger, for obvious reasons. Without the messenger, we cannot eliminate

259

the threat. Something we now understand unequivocally," he added, confirming without further words that he had suffered significant loss reaching that conclusion. "We leave in the morning, at daybreak, from Jackson Square. You can fly alongside or be airlifted with my people. Our air and artillery squads are moving into place now." He paused and looked at the four of us. "We're hoping you'll join us."

Jameson and Jocelyn exchanged glances with us before Eran and Jameson stepped forward together.

"We're in."

"We'll be there."

John shook each of their hands and strode to the door, gave a courteous nod to Jocelyn and me, and stepped outside. Eran followed.

"Your Alterums are about to arrange an assembly –" John began to inform before Eran interrupted.

"I know. It has been called off."

Subdued again by Eran's efficient communication channels, John leaned back, nodded abruptly, and motioned for the helicopter to descend. As it did, John looked at Eran, his face twisted in regret.

"Eran, I …" He began but went no further. That was the extent of John's capability in the area of apologies.

"I understand, John," Eran assured, "but know this … If you touch her again, you will learn the full extent of my capabilities. The solitary reason I am letting you leave here is because her empathy for your kind is greater than my own desires – *at this point in time*. Do *you* understand?"

I could not see Eran's face, with only his rigid back to me, but I could see John's, and for the first time since he had entered our lives, true uneasiness crossed it.

Eran wasn't prone to threats. In fact, I had never seen him make one. Ever. Warnings were common, to allow his opponents the option to avoid a mounting conflict, but never threats. This one was unambiguous in its nature and in his intent, and it stunned me. As a guardian, tasked with protecting his ward, he proactively pursued risks but this time the risk was ahead of us, set in an unforeseeable future, and he wasn't waiting to see if it transpired. He was threatening that risk, informing the menace capable of initiating any endangerment I might face that he would be in jeopardy for doing so. However, unlike a typical guardian, Eran conveyed the chilling resolve of patient execution of harm, a resolve born from an undying love that would move heaven and earth to make it so.

"I do."

Eran stepped back, allowing John to take the rope that had been lowered, and watched him rise to the helicopter. I stepped beside him as John crawled into the fuselage and the craft darted over the trees into obscurity.

Eran spun around, stopped when seeing me in the doorway, my expression locked in awe. In his typical style, he ignored the openly chivalrous act he'd just committed and moved on to a more urgent topic.

"We don't have much time."

"No," I said, finding my voice. Twisting around, I informed Jameson and Jocelyn, who stood beside each other in hushed conversation. "We'll see you in Jackson Square."

They broke their exchange and Jameson nodded.

"Be careful," Jocelyn said.

"You too."

I met Eran at the pier's edge and together we expanded our appendages, and took to the air with new conviction.

Back at Ezra's house, Eran reiterated the plan to the guardians and messengers, with not a single one seemingly obliged or pressed into subjugation. A few of the guardians, all being trained in the craft of war, even turned to each other with bright eyes and launched into eager discussions. The messengers, while capable in conflicts, were saner and therefore less enthusiastic.

After a brief, private conversation with Campion, Eran found me in the crowd and tipped his head toward my bedroom. I agreed with a smile and climbed the remaining stairs from the second step where I had inserted myself in the crowd when he had launched into his speech. I found him in my room, my French doors ajar, as I entered.

"You cheat," I said over the chorus of excited voices below.

"Easier," he explained succinctly, a grim smile stretching his face.

"What's wrong?" I asked, instantly surmising there was a reason for this meeting greater than our need to be together.

We stood on opposite sides of the room, inspiring me to cross it, but he noticed my forward motion and held up a hand to stop me, and despite the festivity below our feet the air around us turned suddenly and almost tangibly tense.

He drew in a heavy breath.

"What?" I urged.

"I've been considering your role in this conflict."

"And?" I said, tenuous now.

"And you won't like the nature of where I'm placing you."

"Placing me? I'll be beside you, in the air."

Eran's mouth pressed into a thin line, as his silence answered my question.

"They can't hurt me, Eran."

"They can," he insisted. "As I've explained, it is far more difficult to watch the demise of your friends than to suffer it yourself."

"I understand that now," I admitted but immediately following my attrition, we fell into opposition, each of us resisting the other with rigid bodies and disapproving stares; and I understood why he had kept me on my side of the room.

"You can't stop me."

"I can," he replied simply.

"I won't let you."

He tilted his head to the side, asserting with his expression how futile my threat was to him.

"I will not stay behind," I said, raising my voice, "when I am needed."

"I know you won't," he said tolerantly, and I blinked.

"Then what are we talking about?"

"There is one role I will allow you to fill."

"Allow?"

"Yes," he replied firmly. "Allow."

He drew in a breath, shook his head at my obstinacy – for which I offered no apology – and said, "I need someone to bring our people back."

"Bring back …? You mean those who end up below ground," I deduced.

"Yes."

"That positions me outside the fight."

Reluctantly, he admitted the obvious truth. "Yes, it does."

My head began to shake in rejection.

"Magdalene, it makes sense. You're the only one who can do it and it's needed," he reasoned.

"You've been strategizing my role since accepting John's plea, haven't you?"

"To keep you safe, yes. And I feel no shame over it."

I huffed and threw my sword on the bed.

"Wait at the hole," I summarized. "That would be my role?"

"No," Eran said. "You'll need to be underground where you can see them arrive upon their death."

And that was when I understood that Eran wasn't expelling me to the sidelines of the fight. The anxiety so evident in him wasn't entirely caused from my quarreling with him, but primarily for two other reasons. First, he was sending me into the only place, alone, where he could not reach me if I were to need him. This went against everything he opposed. Second, he was concerned where my mind might wander when the detail of my exact location was revealed. And he was correct to worry.

"I see," I muttered to myself, my gaze drifting to the walls, away from his nervous eyes. "You're right. It does make sense. I am from the darkness, where souls battle within themselves. I was born within the fight, that's all I've ever known is the fight and now I have brought the fight to the humans."

He was suddenly in front of me and his palms were pressed against my cheeks, hot and urgent, attempting to redirect my attention back to him. But the noise from downstairs had faded away. I no longer felt the floorboards beneath my feet. The air seemed thick around me. And all I heard was the quiet sadness emanating from my heart.

"You're right," he said, his voice hollow, from down a tunnel. "You *were* born within the fight and fighting is all you've ever known."

My lungs felt heavy as I inhaled. "Yes," I whispered.

"You have been fighting since we first saw each other. The first time we met, you were fighting me."

"I was …" I agreed.

"So, yes, Magdalene, you do fight. But look at the purpose of those conflicts. In spite of your background, and very much because of it, you fight not to harm, but *to help*. You pour your soul into those fights." His fingers splayed across my skin, which caught and tugged gently against his calloused hands. "I used to wonder what it was you fight against, as I watched you argue with me, train others, and storm into battle without thought. And it took a while for me to see it, as it surely has with you." He ducked his head to catch my gaze but it had fallen to his collarbone, a spot I often reveled in and now saw nothing at all.

"See?" I exhaled, still suffocating in my dejected surreal world.

"You are a warrior, Magdalene, as sure as I stand in front of you, as sure as the threat we face outside this room. You are a fighter, Magdalene, but what you haven't realized is that you are a warrior for peace. You don't fight for the sake of it. You don't exact harm for sport. You fight with purpose, a deep driven desire, and do you know what that purpose is?"

I didn't move.

He set back and scoffed. "You still don't know why you were given the ability to deliver messages between earth and the afterlife, do you?"

Again, I didn't respond.

"You originated in a terrible darkness, Magdalene, and rather than succumbing to it, instead of embracing it, you chose to fight against it. Your purpose, Magdalene, has been to bring the light against the dark, to balance this world. And *that* takes a fighter, Magdalene. That is why you were given the gift of being a messenger."

"So, do not believe for a moment that you brought this fight to the humans. This fight is theirs, between the humans and the Fallen Ones. We are nothing more than allies, coming to the aide of the humans. We are *not* the ones who initiated this conflict."

I pulled my head back, seeing him for the first time. His blue-green eyes were pinned to me, oblivious to the world now too, desperately seeking me in the abyss that had consumed me.

"You don't think I'm the cause? I put the FOs in the ground, Eran."

"And who raised them?" he persisted.

"But they wouldn't have been in the ground if I hadn't prompted the battle in the London field."

"And who would have stopped and imprisoned them if you hadn't?"

Eran's face fell slightly. "It is my responsibility to protect the humans, Magdalene, and I have done so to the best of my ability. But it has always been you. Without you, I could not have done it. You are the key, Magdalene. You always have been. And that's why I need you there during this fight, where you can do the most good, where you can save the innocent souls who end up there because of this conflict that the humans have started."

Slowly, understanding crept over me, a change that Eran saw.

"Now, you need to draw yourself out of that hole you've put yourself in. It's as black as the one you'll be going into shortly. And I need you to be ready. Because …" He stopped and exhaled in open frustration. "Because unlike here and now, I won't be there to guard you."

I looked up and found his eyes continued to lock onto me, the look of despair and helplessness wrought through them. And that was what pulled me free. Him. Only him. Because I could not bear to see those limitations in Eran, a man invincible until it involved me.

I had to be stronger.

"All right," I whispered.

"All right?"

"Yes."

He drew in a long, lingering breath, held it, and released it, carrying away the nerves that had kept it in.

"Good, because we need to get moving. The sun is almost to the horizon."

Five minutes later, we left the house in single-file, Eran and me leading the way. As we descended the stairs, the crowd of guardians, messengers, and Alterums, with Ms. Beedinwigg as the only human, parted to form a path to the front door. As we left and our toes reached the porch's top step, our appendages expanded, and we lunged into the night. Ms. Beedinwigg slipped into her armored SUV and took off through the empty streets in the direction of Jackson Square.

On breaching the treetops, dawn's strip of cerulean peach hues smudged the skyline, a beautiful sight if it weren't for the reason we were present to witness it. The houses and roadways below us were dark with only intersecting strings of lights linking the way to our destination. As we approached it, the world came alive again – one that had transformed into a drab, colorless place.

On any given day, Jackson Square was an energetic blend of colors, dynamic movement, and pleasures trumpeted through a steady stream of noise. Now, there were no tourists, no dazzling booths of artwork, no color at all. Thick, circular beams of light stretched across the dim sky to connect with the surrounding buildings, splashing them in violent white. The strip of pavement around The Square was a hive of activity again, but now filled with black armored vehicles, helicopters, and communication units with armed men and women in somber camouflage as they strode swiftly into position.

This was the sight of urban warfare. The beginning of it, anyways.

I imagined that Eran had seen enough conflict in his

past that the location didn't affect him. But this was my city. Full of irreplaceable history, captivating people, intriguing places, a center of culture born over hundreds of years. And despite my profound will to protect it and my disappointment at how it had transformed overnight, I was deeply proud that it would be the launching point of a retaliatory assault.

We reached the angle where we needed to return to earth when a new group of bodies appeared over the rooftops, scattered in loose, small clusters of lines dotting the sky, all without appendages, all strategically positioned around those with suspension abilities.

We lowered together on opposite sides of The Square, as all human activity came to a sudden, intoxicated halt. We crossed the pavement to meet our counterparts and extended hands to Jameson and Jocelyn first as the others looked on.

"Excuse me," came a curt voice, loud and clear over the hushed crowd. "Excuse me!"

Those on Jameson and Jocelyn's side parted to reveal a giant moving through them. With muscles nearly ripping the seams of her clothes, I first thought she was a misplaced guardian, having lost her way and was pushy enough to fall into her rightful place. But while she was familiar, she wasn't a guardian. Tipping up her flattened nose and allowing her rough, thick strands of un-brushed blonde hair to fall back, she broke her frown to scowl at us.

"Miss Ingrine," Eran called out.

"Now just a moment," she barked. "You can wait for this."

She turned her massive frame around and beckoned with mammoth-sized hands over her head to someone behind her, and suddenly a beaten, rusting truck emerged, slowly backing up to us.

At an adequate distance from us of only a few feet,

Miss Ingrine snapped, "All right. All right! STOP!" With an exasperated sigh, she turned back toward us. "Some minion at the perimeter insisted he drive my vehicle. After I had to threaten his life to let me in." She rolled her eyes, not caring that he was now stepping out of her driver's seat and easily overhearing her, and released the truck's tailgate. Inside, stacked without category or reason, were swords piled so high they nearly breached the truck's bedrails.

"I didn't have time to organize," she mumbled. "Broke my heart."

Feet scuffing behind me drew my attention and John appeared beside us, marching directly up to Miss Ingrine. Extending a hand, he smiled widely at her.

"Miss Ingrine," he heralded, "I'm a great admirer."

She jerked her head back and hesitantly shook his hand.

"What you've been able to do with metal and the trade of historic iron ..." he said and shook his head in wonder.

She leaned to the side where she could see Eran and me, with a face contorted in bewildered appreciation.

"Your process of casting is remarkable, Miss Ingrine, truly revolutionary. You have one foot planted in historical accuracy while carving a path of inspiration for future innovations."

Her mouth slightly open, she nodded, dumbfounded.

John shifted around her to the truck. "I cannot thank you enough for bringing your supply."

"Well, that's all of it," she was able to mutter.

"It'll be of great benefit," he assured her.

"Yes, well," she replied curtly, as if that notion were a certainty that didn't need voicing. "I heard of your plan, thought you might need some assistance," she added with a shy shrug.

"Indeed, we do. And from you, it is an honor," John

said.

Still stunned and not knowing what do with herself or John, she spun on her heel and marched off through the crowd.

Without a glitch, John bellowed over the rest of us, "All right, everyone without a sword, step up!"

The crowd shifted quickly and Eran and I moved to meet Jameson and Jocelyn by the gate surrounding The Square, not far from my parcel of land where I took messages from clients on more unremarkable days.

"That's not all," Jameson said as we reached them, withdrawing a pliable stack of white fabric from his pocket. "Mr. Leroux brought the armband from his museum to Madame Benoit this morning and asked her to make as many as she could before dawn." Jameson handed the stack to me, over Jocelyn's gleaming face.

On closer inspection, it wasn't simply strips of commonplace, ordinary material. Madame Benoit had sewn armbands with the insignia she had imprinted on my leather combat suit, each with the words 'Defensor Piorum' clearly visible.

My conversation with Eran just minutes earlier came back to me and the meaning of that phrase caused a lump in my throat. Unable to speak, I nodded my gratitude.

Seeing my reaction, Eran took them from me and suggested, "We should start distributing them. Sun's almost up."

The dark was being pressed back with the advancing light, as he had noted, so we parted and began handing armbands to our respective sides. Within minutes, the bands were wrapped around the biceps of each person in The Square, and although we came in a mixture of armor – from fatigues to everyday clothes to black leather combat suits – we were unified by the white strips across our arms.

When the sun's light breached the peak of the rooftops, John moved up the steps of the cathedral and administered instructions over a loud speaker. He gave no lofty, motivational speech, being a man of fewer words, but he did, with great respect, remark that he could ask no finer individuals to accompany him into battle. He then assigned teams before leading the path to the waiting helicopters and armored vehicles. Jameson and Jocelyn's people followed and our kind extended our appendages, ready for flight. The helicopters' thump-thump-thump gradually increased in speed, as if their rotors were the heart of the machine and it were revving up for battle. They, in turn, made my heart accelerate, as Eran reached out and took hold of my hand. With unspoken agreement, we would part ways in the air and I would shift direction toward the outskirts of London. He squeezed my palm tenderly, released me, and looked to the sky, planning the path of his ascent. When he sprang from the ground, I followed. And when we lifted ourselves past the rooftops, I peered through the cluster of helicopters to carve a path to my own destination. That was when I saw them. A thick strip of bodies so dense they blotted out the horizon's light, undulating like a flock of birds, their wings clear even from a distance.

What unnerved me was their speed. They approached us like a squadron of jets, targets locked, ready and intent on conflict.

It became clear then that New Orleans wouldn't be spared after all.

12   INCURSION

I swore I could feel the thrust of the oncoming force, like a train propels a gust of wind ahead of its path, just as Eran's warning to Jameson ran through my mind: *This time, they'll be on the offensive, unified, and they'll be ready for us.*

The concrete reality of that statement should have made me turn and flee, as I saw one helicopter maneuver to do from the corner of my eye, but logic had escaped the confines of my mind, leaving plenty of room for nothing more than uninhibited instinct. It was this that made me pivot horizontally in the air and head for the advancing FOs.

No further thought came to mind as my body became a mixture of reactions. My heart burned with determination, and my lips curled back into a snarl, the speed of my flight drying my teeth as I went. I felt the pain of the air hitting my scalp, like a drill head was making its mark, and yet I didn't care. The pain felt good. Because it meant I was moving fast, with the potential to reach the FOs before they reached the humans.

As I closed the gap between us, their presence took

up residence across my neck, igniting an inferno across the skin. I was acutely aware of it, even as I heard my heart rate increase in my ears and felt the sweat slick my palms, leaving my sword precarious in my grip against the wind's resistance. My alarm had reached maximum amplitude by the time I could hear the sound their appendages made, one that eerily paralleled the intensity of an advancing tornado.

The singular word that commonly came to mind when faced with this kind of circumstance reached me again.

Control...

At this point, I would slow my breathing, my heart rate would follow. Then my fingers would unclench and the perspiration across my hands and forehead would dry.

This time, it didn't happen. My emotions churned through me, uninhibited and unquenchable, making any attempt to quell my detection of the nearby enemies absolutely pointless. The only effect from my radar that remained was my ability to experience a heightened awareness of the FOs.

I could smell them from across the stretch of sky, their odor a strange and pungent mixture of various aromas - spoiled cabbage, soiled clothing, bodies slimy with sweat, hair that had accumulated grease over the course of several unwashed days – like a mound of trash allowed to sit undisturbed in the middle of summer for a week. The air pressure pushing forward before them seemed to press against my skin with evil, unrelenting determination. Their panting breaths, not in harmony, but with a unifying element of pitch were eager and furious and all together excited. It was both terrifying and motivating.

Then arms came around my torso and my wings hit something solid, obstructing their full span, and I was suddenly being hauled backwards.

"What are you thinking?" Eran shouted in my ear, furious.

I wrestled his grip, trying to break free, needing to get to the FOs before they could collide with the humans; but his physical strength was far superior to mine and the distance between me and the FOs grew again.

"Stop!" I screamed. "Stop!"

Eran's arms held firm, pulling me against his ribcage as his appendages dragged us backwards, my hair burying my face and sight. I twisted my head to tamper it but only managed to catch one side against Eran's chest. It was enough though, to see my targets falling away by Eran's impressive pace.

When we passed the first helicopter, which was either at a standstill hover or moving slowly, a blast of heat hit my face and the sky around us lit up, and two fireballs streaked across the morning sky toward the thick black, advancing line. The flames, a mixture of orange, yellow, and bright white, left trails of fire behind them that burned bright and hot as far back as several hundred yards from their source. When the rockets reached the condensed strip of FOs, ready to puncture through, the line parted with amazing fluidity, making them appear more like dashes across the horizon. The rockets passed through the gaps and the FOs returned to form, into what seemed to be an impenetrable mass.

"We need to help!" I cried out. "We need to help!"

"We will! Now stop fighting me!" Eran demanded.

I didn't, of course. Seeing the efficiency of a group of FOs working in unison with a capable leader at the helm for the first time filled me with desperation.

"Stop!" Eran shouted as another round of rockets, smaller but faster, darted past us, this assault being greater in number. I estimated twenty.

By the time we passed the next line of helicopters, which seemed to be the remainder of the squadron, lined in perfect formation, the band of FOs again broke apart and quickly reconstructed after our weapons passed. The image of this could instill fear in anyone because it conveyed two facts. The FOs were coming in relentless in their pursuit and they had been trained on what to expect.

They were close enough now that I could identify them. The Kohler triplets were reunited again, side by side, their heads of blonde hair a strip of color against the blurred swath of black. Fernando Vega flew beside them, handguns in both arms, custom-made for extended magazines and greater rounds of ammunition. Seti flew on his other side, a wide grin below insane eyes.

Then my view was obstructed as bodies leapt from the helicopters, appendages sprouting as they began to fall. The white wings pumped and lifted the bodies next to each aircraft just as I noticed that only two were emerging from inside. Recognizing their great, muscular bodies next to their thinner, more frail counterparts, I knew them immediately as guardians and messengers. Jameson and Jocelyn's people remained in the fuselage.

Then the FOs reached the helicopters, colliding violently with them, and the machines did not win. The closest FOs landed on the fuselage with hands and feet connecting to their prize and their backs arched, like rabid monkeys across a cage. Their weight threw the helicopters off course, tipping them and sending them careening off to the side.

The remaining FOs, the thick black strip that had sped across the horizon broke apart and swallowed the now-exposed messengers and guardians. I screamed but could no longer see them, partly because of the chaos fanning out in front of us, but also from the sun that had pierced the skyline and was now blazing beams of light directly into my eyes. I blinked rapidly, trying to clear the spots from behind my lids as I felt Eran drop hastily. By the time I could see again the fight was above our heads and we were looking up through the throng of clashing bodies and weapons. Swords, hammers, hatchets and miscellaneous weapons swung through the air. The crackle of discharging firearms rose above the shouts and screeches of the clashing bodies. In the midst of it all, fire and ice and earth darted through the fury, signs that all combatants were using their unique gifts any way they could.

From our vantage point, one fact became instantly clear. Our defenses were uncoordinated, and it was exactly what Lotharius had expected. He was relying on a surprise attack, just as we had intended. But he beat us to it.

I realized that Eran had stopped to hover and lean into my ear.

"Can you fight?"

"Yes!"

He released me and the cool morning air surrounded my appendages. I flapped them, hard, to gain elevation and their newly-rewarded litheness gave me hope.

Then the first body fell from the sky.

It was Vasko, one of Eran's guards. He dropped past us, his limbs trailing his body toward the earth. He had given my eulogy at my first death, before Eran had also been killed by the same FO: Abaddon.

Now Abaddon watched Vasko sink through the air, a content grin pulling at his translucent skin.

I aimed myself directly for him, and he saw me coming, but another body intercepted and blocked my approach. Her thick dress did nothing to slow her down, and oddly seemed to allow her great leverage over earth's restrictive atmosphere. Her body, thick around the hips, causing the dress to flare, only served for a more remarkable hit when meeting with Abaddon. He was thrust backwards, into the crowd around him, where he was stopped by another two bodies in the middle of their own assaults. He contorted his body, jerking his black appendages so that he slapped the ones behind him, and aimed for his attacker.

I was almost to them when the woman's sword snapped toward him, causing him to dodge its tip. It was the weapon I recognized before the woman. Owned and moved with demonstrated capability, Éléonore sent her sword at Abaddon again before they suddenly became engulfed in the crowd.

As I reached the conflict, it surged to the side, shoving me several feet before a hand wrapped around my forearm and yanked me farther away. I turned to find Eran gripping me but with his head tipped back to look upward. I followed his line of sight and found a helicopter dropping through the fight, rotors slashing, carving a path through the mass. The ones caught below the fuselage worked to free themselves before the magnetic pull of the earth and the weight of the helicopter's descent became too much. A few sprang off the sides but several went down with it.

Rotating my head halfway, I called out, "Thank you!"

"You're welcome!" Eran said, his voice thick with adrenaline.

The searing pain across the back of my neck became a remote irritation as I tightened my grip on my sword and urged my appendages downward to gain entry into the fight. When I did, it was with Fernando Vega. He had just sliced a wound across Gershom's shoulder as I reached them. He grinned a mouthful of yellow, twisted teeth and raised a firearm at me. My sword was quicker. Swinging hard, my blade cut through his wrist, nearly severing it. It dangled loosely as his fingers released their hold on the weapon and the firearm fell. He was in the midst of lifting his snarling face when I sent my sword's tip across his throat. If he immediately realized what had happened, I don't know. It was a mortal blow, so I turned away to engage another Fallen One.

Being on the outskirts left me at a disadvantage. I could see inside the struggle where guardians and at least two messengers were surrounded by FOs and performing awe-inspiring resistance against the odds.

A body fell close to my right shoulder, his limp fingertips brushing me on his way down. A Fallen One, I noted.

Looking up, I found Eran hacking through the conflict, and more bodies plummeted past me.

In that brief span of time, the length of a blink, I noticed the way his body twisted to accommodate his strikes, bent to the side, head in line, arms extended, muscles strong and flexed. He was formidable, and stunning.

I took on four more Fallen Ones, each easy enough to incapacitate, and dodged the rockets the humans sent into the crowd several times before screams and the roar of an engine disrupted my focus. Looking to my right and slightly overhead, I saw the cause. Another helicopter was sliding to the side, directly into the heart of the battle. People inside scurried to grab hold while Fallen Ones climbed through the open doors. The body of the craft became one dark shadow as the helicopter swung horizontally, freed itself of the conflict, and oscillated back into it again.

Another scream rose above the others and a girl slipped from inside, dropping to the earth, her long black hair snapping wildly around her face. I couldn't recognize her, given this, but I did the boy who leapt out after her.

Jameson, arms straight along his sides, back rigid, his

face of sheer resolve, formed a dart in his descent to reach her. I expected to find his back roll forward and appendages bud outward, but several yards in and this still hadn't happened. Neither had Jocelyn's appendages extended, nor did she use her ability to levitate, made improbable, I guessed, by the velocity of her fall.

Angling myself toward them, I assumed the same posture as Jameson, although I used the advantage of my appendages. Gaining on him, I prepared to grab hold, reaching my left arm out, splaying my fingers for greater certainty over my grasp, when suddenly a flash of white nearly hit me in the face. It moved away and behind it another one appeared a short distance away. Moving in synch, they drew together, shuddered, and widened again, leaving three loosened, white feathers behind.

I hooted in my excitement, which Jameson heard – judging by the sharp turn of his head before thinking better of it – and I pulled back. He caught up to Jocelyn easily, catching her around the waist and drawing her into the safety of his chest. Her eyebrows drew together in confusion and on seeing the appendages working from his back, her mouth fell open.

I was about to turn toward the fight when a swift moving lump of bodies rammed directly into them. The impact and pitch snapped Jameson's head back and it met the head of the Fallen One who had been attempting to retreat from Campion's blade. The Fallen One sank against Jameson's body, leaving Campion with enough certainty that the threat was annulled as he spun around and climbed back to the battle. He never noticed that Jameson had been affected.

Jameson crumpled forward onto Jocelyn's shoulder and his wings retracted into his now bare back, his tattered black shirt the only thing moving there now.

Their bodies picked up speed toward the ground, as

I judged the distance between me and them and they and the earth. They had less space between them and the earth, meaning I had to move fast.

Bending forward again, I renewed my aim for them when suddenly white appendages sprang from Jocelyn's back. Her expression contorted into bewilderment as she messily flexed and then flapped them. They tipped, their drop slowed, she righted them with a flap of her right appendage, and glanced over her shoulder at the new-found attachments. Jameson's eyes fluttered and his head came up, and the two of them hovered in flight, each taking in the awe of what had just been confirmed.

My lips moved into a sideways smile as I lifted my head back to the battle only to be stopped by another sight.

Sarai and Arnaud hung several feet away, her grey wings and his white ones slowly flapping in unison. But rather than fighting, they were clinging to each other, their hands freed of weapons and cradling the other's face as they stared into one another's eyes.

It was clear the world did not exist for them. They had touched one another again, and with it came a desire that had withstood lifetimes apart and opposing family members who were at the moment fighting to take one another's lives. Nothing mattered in the moment. They could have just as easily been embracing during a still, peaceful morning sunrise. It seemed all the same to them.

Strangely, what still raged over our heads was in stark contrast to the passion I saw below it. And I was needed there.

Leaving them to their reunion, I adjusted my posture to take aim at the horde when a screeching whoosh came in from the right and sent the bodies on that side spiraling out of control. Limbs swung wide, bodies were tossed aside, as an explosion in the midst of them vibrated the air.

A military jet curved up over its target and off to the north, its engine rumbling in my chest and its heat blast scorching those near enough to it on the outer rim of the fight. But the humans weren't finished. Another jet soared in, sending more missiles into the center of the contending mob.

"NO!" I screamed, ineffectively, while searching the spinning bodies for Eran.

I couldn't identify a single one, not Eran, not Campion, not Gershom, not one of my housemates. All figures tumbled like ragdolls or fell burning through the air, as more jets sent their arsenal into them.

"ERAN!" I cried out, rotating my torso as a body with grey wings plummeted close by. "ERAN!"

I shifted aside for a view of those remaining in the sky, searching for the love of my life, when a realization hit me with the power of the missiles the humans were using: The human's new strategy is to kill all of us and sort out the living and dead later.

My heart leapt into my throat and my stomach twisted furiously in my gut, and the scorching pain at the back of my neck left my consciousness entirely.

"ERAN!"

My fists were clenched, with one hand gripping my sword handle so tightly I thought it could melt into my skin. I yelled his name again and caught sight of a flash of stark white hair connected to a black-skinned scalp. Campion was battling both a Fallen One and the jet's wash, working to remain steady against both.

More jets made their passes, more bodies were falling now. I had to angle around them as I made my ascent.

Campion got the upper hand and sent the FOs head spinning off into a cluster of remaining fighters.

"Eran!" I shouted when close enough.

Campion turned his head just enough to recognize me before pointing his sword straight down. I followed the motion and found Eran pursuing Achan in flight. They had almost reached the ground and if they kept going, would drop right into Jackson Square.

"Do you need my help?" I shouted to Campion who gave me a look of disgusted offense.

I darted downward, keeping my eyes on Eran. He had almost caught up with Achan and was just now cutting over a corner of The Square to intercept him. I pumped my appendages harder and came close enough to notice a cut in Eran's forearm, when the blast hit overhead.

It was quick and massive enough that I had no time to react before I hit the ground. I did, however, with distinct clarity, see the dirt patch and its jagged boundary of struggling grass blades rapidly approaching before the world went black.

I snapped my eyes open and sat up, drawing a hoarse, wheezing breath.

The noise had silenced suddenly to a peaceful thickness that only a vacant, empty hall can possess. The light surrounding me was bright, but more so than the dawning sun over The Square; it emanated from every pocket, every beam, every scroll.

"What the ...?" Jerod's voice shouted behind me, and I twisted at the waist to find him also sitting up on his stone bench.

"We've been knocked —" I had time to say before he was gone, having been pulled back to earth.

"How's your body on earth?" Hermina asked, her voice coming from in front of me. I snapped my head forward to find her looking over her shoulder at me, her bench located a few ahead.

"I'm not sure. You?"

She opened her mouth to answer and was gone just as fast as Jerod.

As I sat, legs still outstretched, arms propping me up, several more messengers appeared and disappeared, none of them with any time to speak, some in the middle of swinging a fist.

Impatient now, I growled out loud and swung my legs off my bench to bend over and place my face in my hands when the pull began. My torso and all attached to it yanked backwards and I felt the thick heaviness of my earthly body surround me. I was no longer face-down, however. My side lay against something solid and yet forgiving, and I was sitting up, cradled against something warm. Then Eran's distinct scent of earth and sun filled my nose. And I grinned, filling my lungs with him.

"That's it. Wake up, my love," he whispered into my ear, the words edged with his English accent and sending a pleasant vibration through me.

I had anticipated deafening chaos and the need to protect myself on returning. This was the farthest thing from the greeting I expected.

As my eyes fluttered open, I paid more attention to the fingertips tracing a soft, comforting path across my temple and the delicate trail of warm kisses across my forehead than my surroundings; and when I looked into Eran's eyes, I knew there was only one reason for him to be holding me and patiently coaxing me back to life: The conflict had ended, or at the least, lulled.

Finally, when he came into focus, I sighed at the sight of him.

Blood had dried in drops and smudges along his right temple and his skin had been sliced across his left cheek. A drop of blood had caked in one nostril before the phenomenon of rapid healing related almost exclusively to guardians could stop it.

I watched as the injury to his cheek smoothed, faded, and left nothing behind but healthy skin.

"Are you hurt?" I asked, anyway.

He chuckled. "Am I – Am I hurt?" he asked, astonished, eyebrows lifted in exasperation. His reaction lessened leaving behind a softer expression. "I'm glad you're back."

"What happened?"

"They set off a bomb."

By *they*, I knew he meant the humans.

"Damn stupid move," he said under his breath. "Hurt just as many of us as it did the FOs."

"They were aiming for all of us," I said. "Indiscriminately."

Eran didn't respond other than to raise his head, stare across The Square, and tighten his jaw in quiet fury.

He had been preoccupied with the conflict, and ending it, and had no time to observe the humans. I had.

"Where are they now?" I asked, rolling to a sitting position, which unfortunately brought me out of Eran's arms.

The Square was fairly empty, other than the bodies, many charred, and singed pieces of helicopter parts scattering the pavement. Craning my neck up, the sky was blue and vacant. No helicopters hovered, no fight raged. In fact, it was unnervingly quiet.

"Regrouping," Eran replied.

Then sounds ruptured the peace, gradually, metal clashed in the distance and a muffled grunt echoed from inside one of the buildings surrounding The Square.

"The fight hasn't ended," I observed, scanning the area, noting that the eerie stillness stifled any further sounds.

"It won't," Eran asserted. "Until we suppress the

threat."

I searched the ground for my sword and found it protruding in a slant from the grass a few feet to my left. It drew my attention to two bodies beyond it, leaning against the shrubs that lined the fence surrounding Jackson Square. The bright rust-colored hair pressed against a massive chest, naked other than the blanket of tattoos painted across it, was what stopped me. In a much less impassioned embrace, Rufus held Felix.

"Arr," Rufus was growling. "Ya git up now. Git up ya wanka'!"

Rufus shook Felix, more tenderly than I would have expected, and Felix's head lolled lifelessly from side to side.

"Don't ya ..." Rufus said, his voice breaking. He cleared his throat. "Now ya listen to me now and git your damn feeble, weak-kneed, puny physique up onta yer feet. And ya do it now!"

I moved onto my knees, preparing to stand and race to Felix's side, a knot in my stomach at the sight of his limp frame sloping against Rufus.

"YE DO IT NOW!" Rufus roared, his breath stirring the rusty tendrils around Felix's temple. "YE GET UP! YA AIN'T GOIN' TA LEAVE ME HERE BY MESELF, DAMNIT." He stifled a whimper and regained his fervor. "NOW DO AS I SAY, FER ONCE! N' DO IT NOW! OPEN YER DAMN EYES, YA WILTED LITTLE –"

"All right, all right, all right ... Sheesh! Just stop bellowing in my ear!" Felix lifted a palm to rub it against the side of his head. "Your shouting is leaving a louder ringing than the hit to my head!"

Rufus jolted and leaned to the side, making certain Felix had revived.

Felix dared a glance at Rufus, and hunkered between his thin shoulders, he ventured, "I thought you ... I thought you said if my life were at risk I was as good as dead."

Rufus's face went berry-red and he flustered, preoccupying himself with standing. "Aye, well if you die there'll be no one around ta make me look good."

Felix's face rose into a mild grin. "You're welcome," he said, barely above a whisper.

Rufus jerked his head down at Felix, who was still sitting upright on the ground. "*You're* welcome," he barked, insulted. "I'm goin' ta find Ezra," he muttered, and stomped toward the park's gate before realizing he had appendages to lift him over.

Felix stood, brushed off his clothes, smiled to himself, released his appendages, and followed in Rufus's wake, neither of them ever noticing Eran and I just a few yards away. We watched them leave when a movement caught my eye at the corner of an adjacent street.

The tweak to the back of my neck, spurring my innate radar, came at the same time as I saw him, the streak of white hair down the center of an otherwise shaved head being the only indicator I actually needed. I had to clench my teeth before asking, "What did you say? About how to end the conflict?"

"By suppressing the threat," Eran remarked.

He couldn't feel Lotharius and a shrub prevented Eran from seeing him, but he knew I meant Lotharius without any further words needed. Without hesitation, directly from a seated position, Eran's great body bolted into the sky, his appendages opening wide before his feet ever left the dirt patch where he'd been sitting. I stood, ran for my sword and kept my pace, extracting my own appendages, and soared over the edge of the park into the streets after Eran.

On the first avenue we reached, a guardian and Fallen One were so committed to their opponent they didn't know we'd passed. The same happened on the next street, as we continued our search. And I learned that what had been one massive brawl in the sky had evolved to individual skirmishes on the ground. There was only one FO we needed to apprehend though, and he was elusive. We tracked him through the barren city, onto Bourbon Street, through the small side streets that lead back to Jackson Square and ended where we'd started. At the corner to St. Louis Cathedral, Eran and I came to a sudden stop and he placed a comforting hand on my shoulder. I swallowed and knelt beside the body, a jagged piece of glass protruding from her neck.

"Hermina ..." I exhaled and shook my head.

This wasn't the first time I'd seen her lifeless, but it was the first instance when I hadn't been with her when she passed.

"I'll come for you," I promised, and then I sensed him. Not on the cobblestone streets or debris-riddled pavement before us, but overhead.

Standing, I stepped out from beneath the cathedral's shadow, far enough that I could see the roof, and there Lotharius − his arms stretched wide, back erect, feet together − had camouflaged himself against the cross built into the center spire of St. Louis Cathedral.

His head dipped in my direction and then his body followed, plummeting downward toward us, his dark grey appendages streaked with black expanded wide. Eran and I met him airborne, my fist connecting with his face as Eran's fists slammed into his chest. Lotharius wrapped his arms around us, drawing us in, his strength greater than I'd anticipated. Quickly, my face was shoved into his chest, my mouth buried there in the sickening slick of sweaty fabric, unable to take a breath. I heard Lotharius grunt and knew Eran had made a successful strike, but the grip on me never loosened. The pressure in my head formed and I grew dizzy, as my concentration was entirely on the hand that was suffocating me. Then the force against the back of my head weakened and even as the hand continued to grip my skull my head was freed. Only when I pulled my head back and the hand slid down to my neck, brushing at the painful sting of my radar, and fell away completely did I realize what had happened.

Lotharius's stump was now clutched to his chest, where my head had once been, his eyes wide over the stems of his white hair wildly snapping in the wind. Eran's fist entered my view, and the glint of metal he held flashed in the sun. It was gone a second later, when the long, narrow piece disappeared into Lotharius's shoulder. I glanced to the side and found Eran's firm grip on the stem of my sword, bleeding as his fingers gave way to the blade's edges.

Lotharius screamed, his head falling back, his mouth spread in pain and distress. It was more satisfying than I imagined it could be.

We slammed then into an unforgiving wall and Eran's arm, which I learned was wrapped around my waist to keep me aloft, pulled me back and away. Lotharius, however, didn't move, one appendage angled awkwardly askew where my sword had pierced through his shoulder and into his wing's leading edge, pinning him to the building.

As Eran's deep breath raged in my ear, we floated backwards, his arm secure beneath my ribs, Lotharius's writhing body and his one-handed attempts to pull the sword free becoming less the attraction than the location. Looking up at the three spires again, I knew he discovered he was adhered now to St. Louis Cathedral. He screamed nonsensically, his legs pounding the building's exterior as if he were attempting to climb it, his crimson blood leaving a streaking mess against the whitewashed exterior.

"Threat," I said, drawing my first deep breath, "suppressed ..."

Eran's shoulders trembled and he released a loud laugh. "Yes, it is, Magdalene. With the help of your trusty sword."

Noises that revealed others' fights had not finished began to reach our ears then.

"Can you fly?" Eran asked.

I nodded, and he let me go.

I dropped a foot before my appendages sprang out and pumped once, bringing me level with Eran again. However, he was no longer in place. He moved forward, took my sword's handle, snapped it downward and freed its tip from the cathedral wall. Lotharius remained impaled, his hand and stump attempting to expel the sword from his shoulder without any measure of success.

Eran's appendages pumped several times, carrying them both above the rooftops, Lotharius looking like a stuck scarecrow and entirely nullified. Eran flew over the city, low enough to be seen, high enough that he could foresee any threat coming, as I trailed behind. Several fighter jets made fly-bys for closer observation but left us alone, opting to loop several hundred feet above us and observe.

At first, I didn't understand, and then the first FO took to the air, rapidly, and in the opposite direction of us, away from the heart of the city and the conflict itself. Then another emerged. And another. Marco's distinct profile crawled out from a bed of smoldering rubble and disappeared to the east; and a few blocks farther Abaddon took to the air, with Elam and Achan close behind. A few minutes later, a boy and a girl with the unmistakable shape of Sarai and Arnaud discreetly left hand-in-hand toward the north, over Lake Pontchartrain. None remained after seeing Lotharius, their industrious leader, spiked, bleeding, and nearly lifeless. After several slow circles, and it was clear all living FOs were gone, Eran settled down in Jackson Square, directly next to John and a handful of soldiers.

Lotharius crumpled to the ground, causing John to ask curiously, "He still alive?"

"He wishes he wasn't, but yes," Eran said, standing beside the limp leader without concern.

"Men," John said and motioned toward Lotharius.

They jerked into movement, hauling Lotharius to his unstable feet, and dragging him toward a black armored vehicle. Eran's hand on my sword kept the blade from going with him and it slid from Lotharius like a hot knife through butter, causing a fresh spring of blood down Lotharius's back.

"Cauterize the wounds. He dies and you'll answer for it," John called out before turning back to us and opening his mouth to speak. He was interrupted when Lotharius shoved one of the men in the side and was working to free himself from the other.

Calmly, John's hand went to his waist, un-holstered the firearm there, twisted his torso for the shot, and sent an anesthesia dart into Lotharius's back. Sure of its impact and resulting effect, John turned again to us as Lotharius's body slumped and the men dragged him the rest of the way.

"We've learned a thing or two about our cells," John commented offhandedly as he re-holstered his weapon. "From you, Eran. And you can rest assured Lotharius will remain there."

Eran smiled coolly. "That's good to know."

John chuckled and then said through a sigh, "So, a drink? In celebration?"

Eran's grin fell away. "Another time. Our work isn't done."

John tilted his head at him, curiously, when a fresh-eyed private stopped just outside our huddle.

"Sir, your …" the man said, hesitantly while handing Joyeuse to Eran.

"Thank you," Eran said, but the private's handover slowed as he recognized it.

As an afterthought, the man mumbled, "Sword …"

As Eran took hold of it and it sank to his side, the private's eyes followed it.

"Is that …?"

"Yes," Eran replied flatly. "It is."

The man raised his stunned face to Eran, chuckled from the side of his mouth in open respect, snapped a salute to both him and John, and left.

"Well, *I'm* going for a drink," John announced. "Been a long day and it isn't even seven o'clock in the morning. I'll be seein' ya."

"Soon," Eran said, watching him leave.

Eran then glanced at me. "Ready?"

"I'm sure they are," I said, cryptically while knowing Eran understood.

We didn't take our time rising to the clouds, but went hastily, despite John's point that it had been a long morning. Others we knew and loved were waiting for us. Once aloft, we headed to the east.

A few jets passed us but there were no commercial airliners in the sky as we crossed the eastern seaboard, angled toward the United Kingdom and descended on the spot that had caused so much alarm and destruction.

The hole in the field on the outskirts of London was not immediately visible from the air. The temporary buildings that SIEF had put in place were disheveled, caved in, and askew, concealing it. So we lowered ourselves to the dirt churned up on the FOs successful takeover of the site and walked through the wreckage. Computer hard drives were toppled, some exposed to the elements as they lay on their sides outside the walls that once held them. Those walls were collapsed, torn, burned, and gaping, and inside the furniture was in pieces. The only piece of property SIEF had placed here that had been left unmarked was the crane. It remained erect but hanging over a building.

It took us a few minutes but we did find the hole, partially covered by the edge of a shifted building, neglected and seemingly unimportant.

As we stood over it, staring into the darkest hole on earth, Eran mumbled something to himself.

"Hmm?" I nudged.

"Oh, I ..." he mused. "I was thinking they got a small taste of what they brought unto themselves by raising the Fallen Ones, they have no idea how destructive those who they left behind could be."

"They're catatonic," I reminded him, trying to absolve him of any guilt for having me enter the place below, on my own.

Eran nodded, again deep in thought, somehow broke free from it, grabbed hold of both my forearms and pulled me to him. His kiss was firm, urgent, and almost angry. When he pulled away, his head was shaking at the idea of me dropping into the darkness.

I brought my hands to his forearms and leaned into him until our foreheads met, until all I could see of him were the tranquilizing blue-green of his eyes.

"I'll be fast."

"Promise me," he demanded.

"I promise."

"I know what's down there," he said, his voice catching.

"So do I," I replied firmly.

"I created it," he emphasized.

"And from it, I was born."

He pulled back, frightened and in wonder all at once, coming to realize this for the first time. Relief washed through him, weakening his grip; and I took that opportunity to step outside his control and drop into the hole.

Instantly, I was consumed by the dark, with not even a beam of sunlight from the world above to cut through it. Suppressing sadness swallowed me whole, whittling its way through my chest and into my heart before expanding through my limbs. The misery that consumed me was embedded in this place, or maybe this place came to be through that misery. Maybe it had been just a hole in the earth before, void of any emotion or existence at all. When Eran and his guardians had found it, they had done something to it, something I had not ever asked for clarification on because I did not want to dwell on the past or the darkness I'd left behind. Now, as I plunged through the terror and sadness that filled me inside and pressed against my flesh from the outside, I wondered.

When my feet touched down in the dull, compact sand, the cavern around me came into view. Much like our prison in the Alps, it was made of jagged rock walls, sprouting corridors, and held no discernable features. But unlike there, here were bodies of the damned, curled into themselves, huddling against their own knees, in continuous desperate and senseless mumbling. Some I knew, others were covered in black feathers, as if they had been charred to living death.

I stared up at the grey rock above and to my sides, not really seeing it but instead sensing it. If this place were alive, with emotion and powers to embed those emotions, I wanted it to hear me, to know that I was alive and full of emotion.

"You do not own me," I called out, my voice echoing off the walls and returning faintly to me from the adjacent chambers. "I may be from this place, but I am not *of* this place. I am free of you. Do you hear me?

I am free to come and go, and I will do so as I wish."

A surge of resilience ran through me, a power that came from within, shoving back and out the depression this place thrived on. I could have stood there and waited for it to press its claws back in, but I knew it wouldn't. I knew without reason or proof, but I knew, it had heard me.

I crouched down, placing my hand under the arm of the one closest to me, her pale face tucked into her thin, folded arms, rocking back and forth.

"Battle's over. Time to go, Hermina," I said, not minding the rise in my voice as I said it.

And then I lifted her to the surface, my appendages pumping hard to bring us both up and through the hole. She was awake by then, struggling to free herself from my grasp, not yet understanding, but Eran caught her as I let go and sank downward again. And that began my morning, a well-spent morning, carrying the messengers – my friends and family – back to life.

13 CONCESSIONS

Two Weeks Later

Eran leaned over the paperwork, inspecting it closely, as I stood beside him. Across the small, round table used for family meals in Ezra's kitchen, John sat stoic but attentive to Eran's slightest reactions. The word at the top of the document holding Eran's focus was clearly visible to us all. Treaty. Below it, in thin paragraphs, dotted with the acronym 'SIEF', was a contract between the humans and us.

"This makes no sense at all," Felix griped from the corner of the kitchen, between the counter and refrigerator, arms folded in repudiation.

"Shhh!" Rufus balked from his spot leaning against the kitchen sink.

"But we're all the same," Felix argued. "Humans. Alterums."

"SHHH!"

"Felix?" Eran asked, still bowed, eyes still zigzagging across the papers.

"Yes?"

"Have I ever steered you wrong?"

Felix tilted his head back in contemplation and his jaw jutted out in curious thought. "No."

Eran sat back, finally, and raised his head. "And I don't intend to now. Pen?"

"Pen?" John said reticently.

Ezra stepped forward from her place in the kitchen door and delivered it before swiftly stepping back to the archway, her size belying her ability to move swiftly both in battle and in service.

John bent over the table to squint his eyes at Eran's handwriting in the document's margins. "Aberdeen and Mount Weather?" he said and paused before humiliation flickered across his expression. "How did you –"

"Know?" Eran pressed. "Your secrets are not as well kept as you might think."

And John's lips pinched into disgruntled disappointment.

"What's Aberdeen and Mount Weather?" I asked, peering over Eran's shoulder.

Eran replied evenly. "The two additional locations holding both the anesthesia drugs used in the darts to incapacitate us and the research used to develop them. The contract agrees to relinquish all vials and notes from all government and private facilities, but withheld those final two sites. I've added them in." Eran eyed John steadily. "An oversight, I'm sure."

"An oversight," John agreed, although his cool expression told otherwise.

Eran signed the document then and handed it to Mr. Hamilton, who hesitated.

"I wasn't privy to –" he began to explain, still working to regain our trust.

"I know, Mr. Hamilton. I don't hold you accountable."

Mr. Hamilton stepped away again, as if he were eager to leave Ms. Beedinwigg's unforgiving eyes staring him down next to Ezra, but he stopped and nodded awkwardly, almost graciously.

"I'll get a copy for you right away."

"Thank you, Mr. Hamilton."

He moved to the back door, took hold of the handle and paused again.

"I'll be right back," he assured, attention pinned on Ms. Beedinwigg. "My primary responsibilities will conclude then and you may do with me as you wish."

The rest of our faces shifted inquisitively, but Ms. Beedinwigg's glare never lessened at him. Drawing in a deep breath and rolling her eyes, she conceded, "I've decided – against my better judgment – to give you a reprieve." Mr. Hamilton's eyes widened, spurring her to clarify, "This is a postponement, not an annulment."

His excitement settled, he appeared humbled, and nodded civilly again before quickly exiting through the door.

Once he was out of earshot, I asked, "A reprieve?"

"On his execution," she stated.

"You were serious when you threatened him with that?" Felix asked, warily.

"Yes," she replied flatly, barely giving him a fleeting glance.

Silence filled the room as nearly everyone held back grins. When the door reopened and Mr. Hamilton walked in with his promised duplicate, no one spoke and he left as rigidly silent as he had entered.

"Well," John said, standing so that his chair scraped across the floor. "I have to be in Washington by one. Eran?" He extended a hand and Eran took it. "This alliance is a good step."

"Yes, it is," he agreed.

John tipped his head to me, grinned almost undetectably at Ms. Beedinwigg, and strolled out the back door, in Mr. Hamilton's wake.

"Ms. Beedinwigg?" Eran said, almost immediately. "Will you take the responsibility of overseeing the safety of this document?"

"With all the resolve as the Book of Dossiers," she declared, stepping forward and taking the paperwork from Eran's fingers. "I'll be seeing you two at school," she added, before turning to Jameson and Jocelyn, who were leaning together at the kitchen counter. "You two as well."

Jameson tipped his head at her, affirming.

She then looked to Ezra.

"Bronte," Ezra replied, "Lunch on Friday?"

Ms. Beedinwigg nodded again, briskly, and left the house through the front door.

Ezra shifted to the counter where she topped-off her mug of coffee. Over her shoulder she gave us a quirky smile. "What exactly *are* the final terms of that treaty?"

"It's a solid compromise, with both parties given equal weight –"

"Eran," she interrupted, impatient with his attempt to get around a true answer.

Having been caught, he grinned to himself and conceded. "In short, Ezra, it protects all Alterums from harassment, oppression, or pursuit, among other finer details."

"So they can't hurt us?" she concluded.

"That's the idea."

"And you think they'll uphold their part of the agreement?"

Eran shrugged. "We will see."

Rufus, who narrowed his eyes in suspicion, groaned dubiously from the counter. "And what do the blimey snouts get in return?"

"They get their world cleansed again," Eran replied simply.

"From the FOs," Felix concluded.

Eran nodded, reaching to the floor and grabbing his bookbag.

"And who exactly will be doing the cleansing?" Ezra asked, uncertainly. "The guardians and messengers have all returned to their regular lives. What team do you have that will do the work?"

"You're looking at them," Eran replied, and a stunned silence fell over the kitchen.

"Them?" I said, breaking the serenity.

Eran smiled mischievously. "I figure it is about time your training in the art of Fallen One warfare was taken to the next level."

I blinked, working to hold back a smile until I understood exactly what I was hearing. "I'm hesitant to remind you that you're my guardian."

"And I always will be," he asserted, picking up my bookbag.

"And I'm your ward," I stressed.

"And you always will be."

"But you're agreeing to let me fight?" I didn't like the way that sounded and corrected, "Conceding that I have the right to fight?"

Eran caught the clarification and smiled patiently. "Yes."

I looked in amazement to my housemates, who had witnessed my ongoing battle with Eran over this topic, and saw congratulatory grins beaming back.

"It's what you were born for," Eran said, a reminder that hit home.

He was correct. I was created to fight; I had fought my way free of my origins, fought for my independence over being a ward, fought to eradicate Fallen Ones. I had always fought. It was engrained in me, as much as it was for a human being to breath.

"Yes," I exhaled, thoughtfully, "it was."

Eran began walking toward the door, even as I

remained planted.

"When do we begin?" I asked the rugged outline of his back.

He stopped and his shoulders trembled from a silent chuckle before he shook his head. "In due time. Right now, we have school."

I frowned but Ezra's approving grin made me concede.

"All right," I said, walking past Eran. "We begin tonight."

He laughed audibly then. "As you wish."

We left the house, noted our swords stowed again within the cobwebs of the cluttered workbench in the shed, and rode my bike down the driveway. I drove it directly to Mr. Lefrau's bakery, where his staff was gradually returning to service the growing line of customers. He remarked that things were returning to normal as he handed us our sandwiches, and we smiled politely at him without mentioning that he was more correct than he could possibly know. Eran and I had lived in the world imbrued with Fallen Ones for much of the time we'd been on earth, with only a few brief months of peaceful respite. Now they walked the earth once more, and we would again be the authority over their demise. I relished the thought.

We made it to school just before the warning bell and parked in a spot near Ms. Beedinwigg's black armored SUV, a location noticeable to Paul Davies. He strolled to us, a cocked smile on his face, and I sensed Eran immediately on the defensive.

"So, uh, where were you guys during that whole thing?" Paul asked suspiciously, stopping beside my bike.

"Whole thing?" Eran asked off-handedly, stowing our helmets. "You mean the military maneuvers with the proprietary winged apparatus that went awry?"

"Yeah, the maneuvers," Paul said mockingly. "Which weren't really maneuvers, and the winged apparatuses, which weren't really winged apparatuses. Unless you believe the story that they're putting out through the media, which I don't."

"They who?" Eran countered as he took our bookbags in one hand and my palm with his other before beginning a swift walk toward the main entrance.

"*They*," Paul replied amazed. "They. The ones who run the show."

Eran laughed casually.

"Oh, come on," Paul sighed. "I know you were involved. You were in that video."

"What video?" Eran replied calmly, even as a flash of nerves shot through me.

"The video! The one with you two and the guy with the wings in Congo Square. The video plastered across the media. You were right there. Next to him."

Eran stared blankly, causing Paul to sigh and draw out his tablet. From there, he tapped the screen with growing irritation.

"We talked about this," Paul mumbled, his finger punching the screen harder. "All the sites say the video has been removed."

Eran and I exchanged a glance and I knew what he was thinking. A name, of whom I was silently thanking.

John.

"It was here. But it's, they're all ... gone."

"Well, let us know when you find it again," Eran suggested and clapped Paul on the back.

Not to be deterred, Paul launched into his speculations. "Listen, you two are always going missing whenever something breaks out around here. Then you come back and act like nothing's happened. Ms. Beedinwigg's office window is broken through by armed military troops, and you go missing. Mr. Task is tied up and left in the janitor's closet, and you go missing. The head of the military comes to escort you out of school right before winged beasts appear to ravage the world, and you go missing. So, where were you this time?" He quickened his pace to get in front of Eran. "You were involved, weren't you? Working with the military?"

"Not exactly," Eran replied, avoiding Paul's eyes, and those of the rest of the student body collected on the lawns. There were more coming out of hiding each day making the grass barely visible through the number of bodies.

Paul gasped and skipped with excitement at having gotten some kind of response from Eran. "Okay, okay, what does that mean? Working with the government overall?"

"Not exactly."

Paul's eyebrows dipped, then Eran used the tactic on him that hadn't worked on Ezra.

"Magdalene and I have a cabin in Pennsylvania," he said, opening the door to the main hall for both Paul and me.

"A cabin?" Paul said, repulsed, staggered enough that he stopped in the doorway. "You hid out in a *cabin*?"

At Eran's shrug, Paul scoffed in disgust, strode through the doors and headed toward the science classrooms, apparently toward his first class.

"I think he left unsatisfied," Eran remarked.

"I believe you are right," I said, grinning.

Eran released his hold on the glass door to step inside and wrap his arms around my waist, pulling me close to him. His warm embrace permeated my tee-shirt and encircled me in his delicious, seductive scent as the students entering swept around us carrying in the cool morning air. A band of sun ran across Eran's face, catching the glint in one of his translucent eyes, and I knew he was no longer paying attention to any of the students at the Academy of the Immaculate Heart, except for one.

"I have to admit," he said, staring into my eyes. "The cabin *does* sound like a good idea."

"Yes, it does." My imagination began to run freely, bringing my lips into a smile, one that Eran matched.

"What do you think about delaying your training for a day or two."

My arms, which had instinctively curled around his solid waist, tightened as I leaned into him. He felt safe and teasingly seductive. "You're intentionally trying to test my resolve."

"Yes," he replied, his mouth rising into the smirk I loved, setting my skin on fire.

Unable to hold it back, I smiled at the way he held my emotions, while knowing he had not captured my will. "What do you think about training at the cabin and then spending the remainder of the time recuperating together?"

He tipped his head back and laughed, tinged with a blend of amusement and admiration.

"Your tenacity ..." he muttered, but the rest of his observation was cut short by the first bell, which pinched my heart in disappointment. Only when he leaned down and kissed my lips with sultry tenderness did the pinch ebb; and when he spoke again in a gentle whisper it brought the fire from my skin into the heart of my belly.

"Oh, I do believe that can be arranged, my beautiful warrior wife."

Laury Falter is currently at work on the next book in the Guardian Saga. In the meantime, experience the perils and suspense of Eran and Magdalene's spellbinding, star-crossed romance from the very beginning. Here's a sneak peek at the first book in the bestselling Guardian Saga, *Fallen*...

PREFACE

Abaddon's eyes met mine, and I turned to head down the dark street toward a quieter spot, a less public place. I wasn't sure what Abaddon had in mind, but I knew it wasn't going to be pleasant. I didn't want anyone to accidentally find us or to valiantly step in, trying to be a hero.

As I headed farther away from the commotion of Bourbon Street, into the darkness, I didn't need to turn to make sure they were following me.

I could feel them.

As we got farther from safety, my radar grew more and more intense, as if it was sensing their anticipation of what was to come.

I approached a dark alleyway and figured this would be as good a place as any to do it. Only the hazy illumination of a streetlight reached here, and no doors or windows could be seen, just the back sides of two buildings.

An efficient place to die.

It was here and now. I turned to face Abaddon, startled to find him leaning down, merely an inch away.

1 ENCOUNTER

I was picked up my last day of school, in a U-Haul truck. Aunt Teresa was sitting in the driver's seat with map in hand and piles of boxes stacked, haphazardly, across the back seat. She was smiling and waving at me through the window. I didn't feel much like smiling back.

"Can we have another expression?" she called out.

I shrugged, as I slipped into the passenger's seat. "What would you prefer?"

"Boy, anything at this point. Your face has been frozen in a frown for the last week," she complained, turning the key in the ignition. The truck shuddered violently and then rumbled to life.

I glanced out at the sprawling Las Vegas desert, my face stiff and unaccommodating. No, there was no chance of anything other than a frown.

"Think of this as an adventure," she urged. "New Orleans is a fantastic city with lore, jazz, Creole and Cajun food, alligators, ghosts…"

I rolled my eyes. "Right. I'm sure it'll be great."

"It will be," she insisted.

Aunt Teresa is a traveling photographer who would be spending less than an hour in New Orleans before leaving me and flying to Paris for a year-long, nomadic shoot. Because of Aunt Teresa's opportunity, I was being banished to a city completely unknown to me and without a single familiar face.

Aunt Teresa had pointed out, more times than I cared to count, that I shouldn't be so uncomfortable with the idea, and to be truthful, she was right. She and I had changed addresses every three months since as far back as I could remember, so one more address change really shouldn't make a difference.

What didn't thrill me was the realization that I'd be forced to live under one roof for the next twelve months. I was going to miss my wild, unpredictable, roaming lifestyle.

Living in one place for an extended period of

time…I couldn't imagine a more dull existence.

Worse, being eighteen and apparently incapable of taking care of myself, I was being forced to stay with her friend, Ezra Wood.

The fact was, I really enjoyed living with Aunt Teresa. There were no annoying rules, no enforced bedtimes, no lights out and no antiquated…traditional…status quo…culturally-enforced family traditions.

Unfortunately, I had the distinct feeling that Ezra Wood would not be so lenient.

It took us a full day, plus five hours, to reach New Orleans proper. Thirty minutes later, we arrived downtown. Aunt Teresa turned onto Magazine Street and stopped in front of a purple and pink Victorian-style house.

We found the ad together which boasted "charming, quaint, and under-valued." That couldn't have been further from the truth. The house had shingles torn from the roof, a yard full of weeds, and a porch which, judging by the number of broken branches and piles of leaves collected in the corners, hadn't been swept in months, if not years.

"I had a different image of it in my mind," Aunt Teresa spoke my thoughts, as she peered warily at the neglected dwelling from under the truck visor.

"I'll be fine. I'm hardier than this."

Aunt Teresa tapped my knee excitedly. "That's the spirit. It's an adventure, remember?"

"Right," I mumbled.

A beefy man, wearing a pink shirt and green plaid slacks, stepped out of a beaten up Chevy and shuffled toward us.

"Ezra Wood, I presume?" I said, keeping my voice low since the truck windows were rolled down.

"Not funny." Aunt Teresa glowered back at me as

she heaved open the truck door, ignoring its groaning hinges.

I followed, reluctantly.

"Mr. Wilkes, this is Maggie. She'll be one of the tenants," said Aunt Teresa, noticeably yanking me closer.

He started to openly assess me.

I'm what you would call a slim girl, standing no more than five feet tall, with wavy chocolate hair dangling to my waist. My face alone, with my tiny, narrow nose and overly wide, brown eyes, which I always thought could rival the size of tea saucers, probably gave the impression I was innocent. I was once told I looked like a pixie only several times larger.

Mr. Wilkes must not have found any glaring concerns, because he turned without any verbal acknowledgment and waddled toward the house. He stepped over a long-dead bush that covered half of the front steps, muttering in a thick, southern accent, "Nah, ya ain't goin' ta find a betta place than this."

"Okay," Aunt Teresa's voice sang out eagerly, and I knew immediately that she was ditching me. "I have to get to the airport," she confirmed, already pulling out her cellphone to call a cab.

"Aunt Teresa…already?" I sighed.

"You'll be fine. You've done this enough times. You don't need my help."

That much was true.

"Yes, I need a cab…," she said, into the phone.

I glanced back at Mr. Wilkes, standing on the porch now, frowning. Apparently, he didn't like to be delayed. I ignored him.

Aunt Teresa closed her phone and loped toward me, beaming. "You'll take care of the truck, right?"

"Yes," I replied, though not at all happy about it. "I always do."

"I know. You're so good about it." She gave me a firm hug and pulled away, still holding my shoulders. "You're going to like it here. I can feel it in my bones."

I felt my face settle back into a frown, which she paid no attention to.

"Now go see your new home." She said this with far more enthusiasm than I felt.

Grudgingly, I went to meet Mr. Wilkes at the front door where he was already slipping the key into the rusted lock. He had to shake the lock, jarringly, and rattle the door, harshly, against its hinges, not seeming to care in the least that his potential client was watching from behind him.

I looked back over my shoulder where Aunt Teresa stood, grinning. She gave me an animated wave. I gave her a lackluster one back.

"Yeah...," Mr. Wilkes mumbled, drawing my attention as he swung open the door. "Best place ya kin' find."

Inside was dank and musty. Clearly the house hadn't been walked through in a very long time.

"Watch ya step. Floorboards slope."

I nodded, realizing the one I was currently standing on didn't slope but sagged.

A small room off to the left, which I guess acted as the parlor, was mostly empty with the exception of a cobweb-encased poker next to the fireplace. The remaining rooms were much the same. No furniture, but lots of remnants of the other animals and insects who will be sharing my new home with me.

Great.

Throughout the tour, while I tested lights and turned on faucets, occasionally finding a short or a bad line that would sputter at me, Mr. Wilkes occasionally repeated the same phrase, nodding to himself, "Yea, best place 'round hea."

Then, we reached the first bedroom, and I was sold. The room was fine enough. It was spacious with a walk-in closet, which I really had no use for, because clothes were the last thing on my mind. What caught my attention was that it boasted a full-sized balcony overlooking Magazine Street. Stepping through the doors, I stared off each side. Aunt Teresa was gone now, but oddly, the disenchanted, lost feeling I thought would wash over me never came. Instead, I stood on the balcony watching the street below, and for the first time in my life, I felt like I was home.

A single plastic chair had been tossed, possibly by the wind, up against the railing. Instantly, I wished I could upright the seat, settle in, and wait for the sunset – allowing myself to forget Mr. Wilkes' tour and just hand him the first month's rent right then. Prudence and logic fought my need for spontaneity and eventually won. However, I did linger on the balcony, as Mr. Wilkes disappeared inside.

From somewhere in the distance I could hear Cajun music twanging and then the sudden burst of a foghorn. Across the street was another small house with a building in the back, both appearing vacant. From the remaining houses, down each side of the street, I could see residents sitting on their lawns, returning with groceries, or taking their dog for a walk.

It was perfect.

"Ya comin?" Mr. Wilkes called out from inside the darkness of the house. "Need ta show ya the back."

It took a lot of self-control, but I finally coaxed my body to move and met Mr. Wilkes downstairs.

I followed him to the kitchen where it was obvious from the number of paint peels that it, too, had been neglected. Yet, someone had taken the time to adhere a single strip of wallpaper as a border to the ceiling. It was yellow with tiny, white flowers, and I thought it looked very appropriate in the small room.

"Appliances are a bit old," admitted Mr. Wilkes. For proof he turned the knob to ignite one of the stove's burners and a flame shot a foot above his head. Shocked, he stepped back, laughed to himself, and turned the knob off without another word about it.

He opened a small door from the kitchen leading to the back where we found the yard overgrown but large, with a small, wooden shed in the corner. I immediately approached it and grasped the lock.

Mr. Wilkes stepped up behind me, grunting, as he dug in his pockets for the key. He handed it to me, and I inserted it. Unlike anything else in the house, this lock worked fluidly. I swiftly opened the door and found a surprisingly spacious area inside. Good enough for a motorcycle at least.

"I'll take it," I said instantly.

Mr. Wilkes nodded once, self-assured. "Knew ya would." He then handed the rest of the house keys to me while quoting a price for the rent.

It was slightly higher than what the ad had listed, but I didn't mention it. Mr. Wilkes didn't strike me as a man who would negotiate. I could walk away from the property, having plenty of money stuffed in the backpack slung over my shoulder, and find a far more luxurious house.

But this place had already settled in me. I was home.

I dug through my backpack and gave Mr. Wilkes the amount he quoted. He gazed seriously at me as he took it. "Same amount...every first of the month...no exceptions."

"That won't be a problem."

"Hope not. Kin rent this place any time. Best place 'round hea."

I had trouble keeping myself from laughing. I wasn't sure if he seriously believed what he said or not and didn't want to offend him either way. "I understand, sir."

He gave me one final, long stare, spun on his heel and marched back toward the street. At least he was gracious enough to help me unload the bed frame and move it into the upstairs bedroom...for fifty bucks. It was the only piece of furniture I owned as my frequent moves inhibited me from ever buying more. I had learned to live on very little.

A few minutes later, Mr. Wilkes left. I heard his engine rev and saw his car pass by a few seconds later from where I stood on the balcony.

I pulled a piece of paper from my back pocket and looked at the directions. There was one stop I needed to make before returning the U-Haul truck.

It took me an hour to get there since the house was on the outskirts of the city. I knew I'd reached it when I saw the broken, wooden sign hanging across the gate entrance that read Hicker Ranch. The property was thick with overgrown trees and boasted several decrepit buildings, but the main house wasn't hard to find. Still, it was a challenge to reach, surrounded by weeds that reached my knees. I learned this after I jumped down from the cab. Watching my step as I walked closer to the house hidden in old oak trees, a frail woman in her seventies crossed the wide, sagging porch and stopped at the steps. In a scratchy voice, tarnished by years of liquor and cigarettes, she greeted me. "It's around back in the barn."

With that, I made a sharp right and walked through the dead weeds of her property to find a dilapidated barn. The barn doors were unlocked but it took me a good amount of muscle to push them open.

There, in the dusty shadows, I could see it.

My Harley Davidson 883 Sportster. It was a beautiful mesh of silver chrome and black metal that could take me just about anywhere I wanted at speeds of up to 120 miles per hour if I chose. It didn't look like much on the eBay ad and I didn't know a lot about motorcycles to begin with even if it had. But, it took my breath away when I first saw it. Even though it was not the wisest purchase for someone who had never owned any mode of transportation before, that didn't matter. It would be all mine.

"You have the money?" The woman's scraggy voice came up behind me.

I nodded, without looking at her. Instead, I reached down into my backpack and pulled out four bills, one thousand dollars each.

She gawked at me before I had a chance to explain, "You said over the phone you didn't mind large bills."

"Huh," was all she replied, mouth still agape, taking the money. I turned away and swung a leg over the bike, settling into the seat; I felt like a queen on her throne. The woman dangled the keys toward me, though her expression appeared uncertain. "You sure you can handle this thing?"

"My aunt's ex-boyfriend taught me to ride," I asserted. For proof, I took the keys and inserted them into the ignition with great confidence.

"Hmmm." She scratched her nose and leaned her head to one side. Her eyes narrowed at me and she said, "Not that I'm accusin' you of anything but…where'd you get this kind of money?"

I paused and it occurred to me that I would eventually need to have an explanation for how I made my income. It wasn't as if an elderly woman selling me a bike through eBay would be the only one to ever ask the question. I needed to have a story; one simple enough to prevent further questions but that adhered to my belief system of telling the truth. I certainly couldn't tell the whole truth so I settled for telling just half my story.

"I'm a messenger."

The woman snorted and chuckled under her breath. "Well...now you'll have a faster bike."

I grinned back, even while knowing that no bike could get me where I went to deliver messages.

"Ya wanna take it for a test ride?" she offered.

I turned the key and listened to the engine rumble to life – a heavy thud, thud, thud, thud.

I felt exhilarated, a grin drawing up my cheeks.

She handed me a black, shiny, perfectly new helmet which I strapped securely to my head.

I circled her property a few times, getting a feel for how it handled before stopping outside the barn doors.

Her eyebrows rose, questioning.

Then, with a deep breath, I waved goodbye, shifted into gear and pulled out onto the dirt road, heading back to load it on the U-Haul truck.

The bike was mine.

After returning the truck, I drove my motorcycle until just after sunset, unable to stop smiling for most of that time. I decided to find the house I'd rented, and after locking my bike in the shed, I headed upstairs and swung open the French doors leading to the balcony. I took a seat at the edge in the plastic chair and propped my feet up on the rail, dozing as I listened to the Cajun music filtering up from the bars.

I had learned to sleep pretty much anywhere, but it surprised me when I woke up the next morning still in the chair. Lifting my head, I felt the kink in my neck, but the pain ebbed when I remembered I had a new motorcycle to ride.

I hurried to take a shower, using a towel I carried in my backpack to dry off, and headed downstairs. Standing in the kitchen, the house was empty, silent and still retained that musky scent, but I smiled my way out the door anyways.

I rolled my bike from the shed and started it, enjoying its rumble even more today. After a quick stop at a local coffee shop, for a shot of espresso and a croissant, I took a tour of the French Quarter.

The roads were narrow and most were cobblestoned or had broken pavement that made it challenging to ride, but that didn't bother me much. The city was captivating.

The streets were lined with aged, bowing trees that shaded weathered, brick buildings and intricately designed iron balustrades. Small shops opened to colorful art galleries. Restaurant's propped doors and window shutters opened to allow the teasing aroma of spicy southern food to waft out. There was a certain peacefulness to the city, even between the bursts of thrumming jazz music, with everyone moving slowly about their business. Their leisurely pace may also have been because of the soaring temperatures and ridiculous humidity that fell over the city like a stifling blanket. The air was the only thing I would have trouble adjusting to.

After my brief tour of the French Quarter, I arrived at Jackson Square.

It was a raised park of green grass and shrubbery set in a square shape; an enormous iron statue of Andrew Jackson on horseback standing in the center. Jackson Square is historic because slaves were often sold here during the 18th and 19th centuries. Now though, along the outskirts of the park, it clearly had become a place for artists to sell their wares and for tourists to have their palms or tarot cards read. The traditional other name for the park is Place d'Armes, but I naturally decided to call it "The Square".

I parked my bike and walked through the tarot card and palm readers, caricature artists, and local craftsmen. I stopped a few minutes later at a woman's table, scanning the hemp products crowding her space.

"Looking for anything in particular," she asked, pleasantly.

"No." I shook my head. "Actually, I was wondering something…"

"Uh huh," she encouraged me to go on.

"How do you set up a table here…as a vendor?" I asked, even while still wondering if I was going to pursue it.

She explained the lengthy, bureaucratic process and then wiggled her finger at me, beckoning me closer. When I leaned in, she added, "But don't waste your time. Just grease the security guards with a hundred dollars and they won't say a word."

I was surprised at her frankness but appreciated it. "Okay, I will."

"What is it you sell anyways?" she asked, only seeming remotely intrigued.

I opened my mouth to draw in a breath but stopped. I realized that if I told her, she wouldn't believe me anyways. Instead, I decided to respond cautiously. "I'll show you tomorrow."

The woman smiled, now curious. "I'll be waiting."

I strolled The Square a while longer and was about ready to leave when something happened. The hairs on the back of my neck stood up – and they had no business standing up on such a hot, humid day. Suddenly my hands began to shake and my stomach went queasy.

Something was very wrong.

With all the noise and movement, you'd think I could easily have missed him, but as it turned out, I didn't. In fact, I knew he was there before I saw him.

My eyes scanned the crowd with some faint notion that I was looking for whatever was causing this reaction in me. A large man chewing on a sausage, his chin smothered with grease, passed by. Next was a pair of thin women in business suits leaning together and gossiping. Either of these scenes would have been enough to make me nauseous, but I instinctively knew they weren't the cause of my sudden inability to control my body's reactions.

All of a sudden, there he was…leaning against the wall of the St. Louis Cathedral, hidden in the shade, hands in his pockets, despite the day's heat, and his eyes positioned directly on me. There was no doubt in my mind that he was staring at me because he didn't bother to look away when our eyes met.

As I stood in the sun, a chill ran through me.

My first instinct was to run. This stunned me since I never ran from anything…ever, but I couldn't shake the feeling that I needed to leave immediately, as if something deep in my core were screaming at me to escape. This made no sense to me, so I ignored it completely and turned my attention back to the creepy guy.

He was still staring at me.

I noticed that his mouth was turned down now and his nostrils flared out. Clearly he was furious about something.

I wondered if he was an official thinking I was about to shoplift. Wearing a dress shirt and slacks, his professional appearance definitely sent that message. But in a brief moment when our eyes locked, I noticed something different about him. He wasn't old enough to be in a position of authority – even if he came across as holding it. His outward appearance made him look young enough to be my age, yet something in his demeanor, his stance, told me that he was much older.

No matter what his issue was, I was about to leave. It was getting dark and my balcony was calling to me. I slid up on my bike and headed back to the house.

I was conscious of him as I left The Square, feeling

him following me without having to look to confirm it. As I moved through the intersection, I turned to find him sitting behind the wheel of a blue Ford Mustang. Once more, his eyes were fixed on me with that same fierce glare.

My skin broke out in a cold sweat and my hands started to shake. I never had this happen before – but then I'd never been afraid before either. It took a moment to realize that this was what I was experiencing…actual fear. It was new to me, completely. But I couldn't deny it. I was trying to gain control of my nerves that were now shooting panic to every inch of my body.

It took me an entire street block before I started to get my breathing under control and that was only after I glanced over my shoulder at the stop sign to make sure the guy wasn't following me. I didn't see him, but the hair on the back of my neck was still standing up, which didn't calm me at all.

I turned down my street and focused on the third streetlight that was lighting the pavement in a dim orange circle. This was the entrance to my driveway on the side of the house, and I was only a few feet from it when something entirely unexpected and unforeseeable happened.

Just outside the hazy glow of the streetlight stood someone who I was absolutely certain had not been there a moment ago. He appeared without warning and from nowhere, suddenly standing directly in front of me, as if he had intentionally put himself in my path.

This last thought occurred to me as being ridiculous, but it was the way it seemed nonetheless.

Despite the swiftness at which the event happened, I saw something with absolute clarity. He was handsome, so much so that he would look more appropriate on a runway than standing on my street. I knew instantly that he was around my age. But unlike other teenagers, he stood tall and assured, towering over me, even from my height on the bike. What he wore did not reflect the most recent fashion either. His clothes had an age to them, still clean and well-kept but traditional. His hair was dark brown — as best I could judge in the dim streetlight — and cut to be shaggy yet just short enough to keep it tidy.

I instantly felt guilty for being in the motion of running him down — which would certainly result in injury at this speed.

What I also recognized in that brief moment was his expression. It was not filled with terror as would be expected when a five-hundred pound motorcycle is bearing down on you. He was not spastic, looking for a way to escape or even frightened at all.

He was frustrated.

I, on the other hand, was frantic. My bike was about to pummel a complete stranger, and I didn't seem to have any way of avoiding it. I had felt in control of my bike from the moment I first took a seat on it. Yet, in that moment, I had as much control over it as I did over directing a planetary alignment.

"Right!" he yelled in an English accent, pointing in that direction with a long, toned arm.

But I was already going left — completely by chance. Realizing that it was now or never, I gained control of myself. At least now, with the ability to function physically, I turned the handlebars to the right, but it was too late.

My front tire was less than a foot from him now. We were going to collide.

Suddenly my bike took on a life of its own. It trembled slightly and the handlebars jerked to the right, nearly throwing me off, and just as abruptly, it righted itself as it turned into my driveway. Again, I was almost launched off when my wheels hit the gutter's dip but it caught me at just the right angle. I only vaguely registered somewhere deep in my subconscious that I was not controlling my bike but it was controlling me. It caught me from falling off with each jarring move and each forceful bump. This made no sense to me, so I quickly disregarded it.

I focused instead on the fact that I should have been sprawled on the pavement with my giant five-hundred pound bike on top of me – I was definitely leaning far enough over that it should have happened. But the bike swerved its way down my neighbor's driveway, plowing me into the hedge that separated our properties. The bike ended up leaning against the hedge and the motor cut off a moment later.

Jostled and completely confused about what had just transpired, I took a moment to inhale deeply. It was alarming to realize how ragged my breathing had become. This was the first time I'd ever felt my breath that way. I instead chose to focus on freeing my leg from the overgrown shrubbery.

I wiggled it up and over my bike, falling to the gravel driveway in my effort. I immediately picked myself up, brushed off tiny stones engrained in my palms, and unfastened my helmet.

Already, the fear I'd felt a few seconds ago had disappeared. It was completely gone and in its place was fury.

I pulled my helmet off, craning my neck painfully in the process and not caring.

All of a sudden he was right there, standing directly in front of me.

"Are you all right?" he asked, although his mouth was slightly puckered and he sounded more aggravated than concerned.

Despite my anger brewing, it dawned on me that this

boy was even more attractive up close. I was angry and wanted to stay that way. I definitely did not want to be intrigued; yet, that was how I felt. In the intensity of the moment as I stared at him, I noticed that he had a certain kind of smoothness to his skin that seemed untouched by time. He carried himself with assurance and grace; if it weren't for his size, I would have thought I was looking at someone several years younger. But, this wasn't what stunned me. His eyes, which locked with mine and refused to free me, were the blue-green color I'd only seen in the waters off the coast of Florida. Translucent, warm, and welcoming. I had leapt off piers into that water uninhibited, free – but I was feeling neither of those emotions in my current state.

No, I felt angry.

"Am I all right?" I scoffed. "I almost ran you over. What were you doing just standing in the street? Did you want to be hit?"

He squinted his eyes, weakening the intoxicating effect of their beautiful blue-green color, and I was thankful. It allowed me to regain a bit of clear thought.

He stared back at me as if he were trying to answer a very challenging question. "You're angry with me?" He sounded confused and a bit appalled.

I threw my hands up in the air. *That wasn't clear?*

"You were standing in the middle of the street! I had to avoid hitting you! I ended up in a bug-infested hedge!" I crossed my arms, waiting for an apology.

He leaned back and folded his own arms across his chest in a seemingly unspoken challenge. "So I assume you didn't notice the Ford Mustang barreling down the street behind you? The one that was about to run you over?"

Stumped, I turned back toward the opening of the street. "Mustang? What Ford Mustang?" I asked, thinking in the back of my mind, *Wasn't the creepy guy from earlier today driving a Ford Mustang?*

"It's gone now," he replied, frowning. "You didn't think it was going to stick around after nearly running you down, did you?"

He was mocking me, which infuriated me even more.

"You realize I could have easily killed you?" I demanded.

"I doubt that," he replied, a hint of a smile resting just beneath the surface.

I couldn't comprehend why he thought this was funny. Did he have no sense of self-preservation?

"My bike is a heavy piece of machinery," I stated to emphasize my point.

He nodded casually, still retaining that subtle grin. He had no rational fear about what had just happened. That much was clear to me.

I laughed at the idiocy of the situation, which made one of his eyebrows lift skeptically.

Finally, he responded. "That doesn't apply to me."

"What doesn't?" I asked, now thoroughly confused.

"Your bike and its dangers."

"How is that? Are you a stunt person?" I asked, coming up with the only logical explanation I could think of on the spot.

He appeared to find my assumption humorous, tilting his chin up and releasing a deep chuckle. When he was through, he brought his head back down and looked me deep in the eyes.

"You really have no idea, do you?"

"About what?" I nearly screamed, thoroughly perturbed at this point.

Then his expression changed from smug humor to stunned surprise. He stood this way for some time, staring at me, with his mouth slightly ajar and his eyebrows creased. "No idea at all…," he muttered then.

"I don't understand what you're talking about," I replied.

"No, you wouldn't," he said, with sincerity, apparently now having overcome his shock at whatever unknown realization he'd arrived at a moment ago.

"Where did you come from anyways? One second you were not there and the next..." I recognized my voice was calming now along with my emotional state.

He seemed to have difficulty answering, opening and closing his mouth several times. Finally, he responded, his voice almost teasing and that slim smirk returning to lurk beneath the surface. "It looked like you needed my help."

"I didn't," I replied, putting my hands on my hips in protest.

"How did I know you were going to say that?" he teased, allowing that smile to breach the surface, lighting his face with such beauty it caught my breath.

Something happened in him then. It was subtle but I noticed it. He relaxed. His muscles eased up and his expression loosened. It was as if he'd just now encountered a very old friend and fell into the same welcomed, tolerant pace at which that friendship had existed.

"You didn't answer my question. Where did you come from?"

He considered how to answer for a moment and then replied coyly, "That doesn't matter. What does, is that you are safe...Right?"

I rolled my eyes. "Look," I said, clenching my teeth against my irritation. "I don't need your help. Okay?"

His eyebrow rose even more as he peered at me in disagreement. "Well...I would say that everything points to the contrary."

As I considered his bold understatement, I felt my lips purse in aggravation. To avoid showing that he'd made an observation far too close to the truth, I turned my attention to my bike. It was still leaning against the hedge, making a clear indentation in the once solid wall of green foliage. I reached down and took hold of the handlebars and then leaned back using the weight of my body to try and lift the enormous machine back up. It was heavy, despite the adrenaline still pumping through me, and even after several struggling heaves it hadn't moved at all. I could sense he was still behind me, watching.

Catching my breath, I warned, "If you laugh, I am going to..." He cleared his throat and I stopped myself. I couldn't be sure but I think he was trying to cover his chuckle.

I could feel him beside me then. The skin on my arm closest to him tingled – not like with creepy guy earlier today – but in a nice way. I had to fight the unexplainable force inside me that wanted to lean toward him, and knowing it just made me angrier. Never in my life had I felt this way about anyone – much less a stranger. Typically, I tried to avoid boys, always knowing that I would be moving on soon and starting anything would be ridiculous and futile. But, here I was drawn to this stranger. It made no sense.

"Still don't need my help, eh?" he muttered, glancing at me with a playful grin.

"No, I do not," I replied resolutely, despite the obvious contradiction of my statement. As he moved my bike to stand right-side up for me, it occurred to me that he was not drawing in any heavy breaths at the exertion of what he had just done. Not a single grunt, or even a minor muscle tremor, was released. His body didn't seem opposed to lifting a weight far more than his own. In fact, he did it effortlessly, as if he were merely pulling out a chair.

When he turned to face me, he must have caught

sight of my shock. "Something on your mind?" he asked casually, smirking once again.

"That bike is over five hundred pounds," I pointed out, insinuating.

"And?"

"And you had no trouble moving it."

He chuckled lightly, still easily holding my bike upright for me by the handlebars. "Just be thankful you have me here to help you."

I laughed sarcastically. "I wouldn't be in this situation if it weren't for you."

This time it was *his* lips that pinched in protest, and for a moment, I wondered what response he was holding back.

I slid into the seat and refocused my glare on my bike, thankful there was no body damage. Then I turned the key. It spurted, hiccupped, and, after a few seconds of honest effort, died.

I looked up at him in frustration and motioned toward it. "Great…"

He had the audacity to sneer at me as he reached across, grazing my arm - simultaneously sending a shock wave through my body - and swiftly turned the key. The engine rumbled to life.

I glanced up at him, appreciative and amazed. Those feelings were immediately subdued when I heard his English accent shout over the rumble.

"Maybe it was reacting to your attitude."

Appalled at his nerve, I felt my jaw hit the inside of my helmet as it fell open. Before I could even draw a breath, he spoke again. "Looks like my work here is done. Good night and be safe." He then added an afterthought – something I am sure was meant to irk me. "I don't want to have to save you again before daybreak."

With that, he turned and strolled casually toward the

street, rounding the hedge's corner and disappearing from sight.

I frowned at him even though I knew he couldn't see it. I rode down to the edge of the property and paused, glancing in the direction he'd gone.

I expected to see him sauntering in all his conceit toward the street corner, but I was stumped.

There was no sign of him.

I stared blankly at the empty sidewalk, a single thought frozen in my mind.

The irritating, attractive boy who had saved my life had just completely vanished.

ABOUT THE AUTHOR

Laury Falter is a bestselling author of young adult romantic suspense and urban fantasy. She conjures worlds in which love is born and tested against seemingly insurmountable events. She has three series out: the Guardian Saga, the Residue Series, and the Apocalypse Chronicles.

Find out more about Laury and her novels on her website at www.lauryfalter.com.